FROM ONE MAN
TO ANOTHER

John spoke slowly. "The minute I saw you, I wanted you. Edith and I have a comfortable life, so I've never approached you. I really don't have anything to offer you, Kathy. We couldn't be seen together, go out, do all the things people do when they're in love. And I am in love with you, Kathy. You said you've been through all this before with a married man, and I can't ask you to do it again. I do want you, but the decision must be yours."

Kathy sat quietly, thinking. Then she started talking, almost like thinking aloud. "Of course, if I say no, I'll have to quit — it would be too hard working together after tonight. And then there's the fact that you're married — I rather like Edith. But if I said yes, it probably wouldn't hurt her if we can keep things in the proper perspective. I'd have to continue on with Dwight for a while — you said you weren't jealous of him, and I do need some social life. I don't know if I'm in love with you or not, John, but I do know I'm sexually attracted to you." She looked down at her watch. "It's 3:30, much too late to try to sleep, and we don't have to be at the hospital until 7:00. Do you want to make love now?"

He had been listening to her, scarcely believing his ears. She sounded so clinical about the whole thing. "Kathy, sometimes you amaze me. I don't know about you, but I need a drink to relax."

She smiled at him uncertainly, suddenly nervous. "I'll have one with you — and then no more talk tonight. I don't want to think, I just want to feel."

Bitter Dreams

Dolores Hughes

LEISURE BOOKS ❧ NEW YORK CITY

A LEISURE BOOK

Published by

Dorchester Publishing Co., Inc.
6 East 39th Street
New York, NY 10016
Copyright © 1984 by Dolores Hughes

Printed in the United States of America

Chapter 1

The young woman drove along the freeway at a steady clip, checking the speedometer frequently, careful not to exceed the speed limit. Her hands were sweaty, twisting constantly on the steering wheel, and her green-flecked eyes kept shifting nervously to the rearview mirror. It was ridiculous, she knew; no one was following her. He couldn't possibly know she had even left yet—unless he came back from New York unexpectedly, and Maude told him. But not even Maude knew where she was going.

Suddenly, she slowed the car, and pulled off on a shoulder. Maybe she should go back, maybe this wasn't such a great idea after all. She turned off the ignition and wiped the perspiration from her forehead and the back of her neck, thinking, until she felt Topsy's soft tongue licking her other hand. She looked down at the dog, and petted her automatically. No, she couldn't go back now, or ever. She switched on the ignition, and cautiously edged back into the late Sunday afternoon traffic, heading further away from Hollywood.

She got as far as the San Gabriel Valley before she heard

the slight clunking sound in the rear. Damn, she'd just had the car checked, and intended to drive late into the night, and now this.

She pulled off the freeway at the next small town, looking for a gas station. She passed three, but they were all closed, and she was beginning to worry. She doubled back, driving slowly, looking for a motel that was close to one of the stations. The car would have to wait until morning.

The small motel room was typical, with the standard plaid bedspread and curtains. She brought in Topsy's food and her overnight case, and tested the bed. She was more tired than she had thought. The hot shower took some of the tension from her, and she began to relax. Maybe there was nothing seriously wrong with the car; but she had expected to put in a good hundred and fifty miles tonight, and she was less than thirty miles out of town. There was nothing she could do about it tonight, so she might as well make the best of it.

The heat was still oppressive when she got out of the shower, and she turned on the fan. Topsy was already on the bed, exploring her new surroundings. Kathy pulled back the spread, then the blankets, and went to bed.

She slept badly, and woke with a start; she looked around slowly, wondering where she was. She had been dreaming—something about being in a huge empty building—but the dream faded quickly as she recognized the room. It was still dark, and very humid, and she thought of her own light and airy bedroom high in the Hollywood Hills with longing. But it wasn't her bedroom anymore, it wasn't her apartment, and she suddenly felt very sad and lonely. Muggy as it was, she shivered, drew up the blankets, and lit a cigarette. She inhaled deeply several times, and felt a little better. It had been her decision, and hers alone. She had been on a dead-end road leading nowhere, and she wasn't going back. She crushed out the cigarette, turned on her side, and almost at once was asleep again.

She left Topsy at the motel, and was at the gas station when it opened in the morning. The mechanic had three cars ahead of her, so she went back to the motel and took Topsy for a walk, had breakfast, then walked back to the station. It was worse than she thought.

"It's your rear wheel bearing, your universal joints. . ." he went on talking, but she was completely lost. She knew next to nothing about cars. He could have been talking in Greek, and she wouldn't have known the difference.

"How long will all that take?"

"Better part of a week, at least. Next Monday or Tuesday, for sure, it'll be ready."

"But I just had the car checked!"

"Well, whoever did it, lady, sure didn't know his business. The points and plugs are okay, and your battery, but as for the rest—look, if you don't believe me, take it to another station."

She started to protest, then remembered; her regular mechanic had been on vacation when she'd had her car checked; dammit, thirty bucks down the drain, and for nothing. She took the car back to the motel, unpacked, and brought it back to the station, then walked back to the motel, sat down on the bed and tried to think. Monrovia; she had never even heard of it, and now she was stuck here for a week or more. Well, she couldn't sit here in this room all that time, so she inquired at the desk for a Rent-A-Car Agency.

She picked out a small Dodge, and started driving around. The small towns all seemed to blend into each other, but there were distinctions; Arcadia was nice, El Monte grubby, Azusa so-so, Covina building up. She went as far as Riverside, then drove slowly back. Funny, that a little thing like your regular mechanic being on vacation could change your plans. Nobody would think of looking for her in the San Gabriel Valley. Chicago, maybe, or Dallas, but not here. On impulse, she stopped and got the local paper, a mapbook, and a bunch of nickels on her way to the motel.

She decided to find an apartment first; finding a job could come later. She was lucky; the third place she looked at was a small bungalow in the rear of a larger one. The elderly couple that owned it assured her that Topsy wouldn't bother them at all, and the rent was reasonable. Then she went back to the motel, called Maude and told her what happened.

Maude couldn't stop laughing, and finally Kathy got irritated. "Listen, if *your* car went out on you and you were stuck, what would you do? And who would look for me here? Will you please stop laughing and listen?"

Maude choked, but tried to control herself. "Okay, I'm listening."

"What did Pete say when you told him?" Her voice was low.

Maude's mirth immediately disappeared. "I don't think I can repeat that kind of language. He took it very hard."

"Does Bruce know yet?"

"Not unless Pete called him. I don't think he did."

Kathy breathed a sigh of relief, and changed the subject. "I rented a bungalow today. It's furnished, but it's a little bare. I'll send you a list of the things I can use, then maybe you can rent a garage to store the rest, instead of the storage company."

"No problem. As soon as you know what you want, I'll send it out. Monrovia, you said?" She tried to muffle her laughter, and said goodbye.

Kathy stared at the phone, frowning. Maude was the closest thing to a mother she had ever known, but she could be very irritating at times. Then she started writing a list of things she wanted for the bungalow.

Kathy picked up her car the following Monday, and drove to the first employment agency on her agenda. She tried to ignore the weather—worst July heat wave on record for ten years, the radio had said. Instead, she concentrated on what she'd write on her application form. She had thought a lot about that. Being under contract to Universal Studios for a year certainly wouldn't help her, and she couldn't tell them where she'd really worked. Instead, she had decided to say she had been a secretary for one of the accounts the Ad Agency handled. She knew they couldn't check, as the account had gone out of business.

The man at the agency, Mr. Terrell, was a middle-aged, slightly balding, paunchy individual, whose forehead glistened with perspiration. He gave her a long, slow, appraising look, and went through the card file on his desk. He pulled out one and made a phone call. The job was filled. On the second call, he made an appointment for her for 2:30. He glanced at her and picked up the phone again. Kathy was beginning to feel uneasy. He made another appointment for her at 4:00, extolling her qualifications.

Then he filled out two cards and handed them to her. "Well, Miss Foster, you should like one of these jobs. They're two of our best openings. This here one is at Keith Oil Company—secretary to the head of the export division. Salary's open, you might talk them into paying the fee. This other one is for a psychiatrist, should be interesting. Those two cards, they'll introduce you. Then you let me know how you make out." He spoke with a slight twang, all the while giving her that same slow look.

Kathy thanked him, and started to leave.

"Tell you what," he stopped her. "Better yet, stop by here when you're through. Might have a new job to celebrate. There's a nice little bar around the corner, and seein' you're new in town and all. . ." he waited.

"That's very kind of you, Mr. Terrell," she said, ignoring his implication, "but I have another engagement. I'll call you, though."

9

Kathy walked to her car, glad to breathe fresh air again. She had seen that look often enough to last her a lifetime. Oh well, she shrugged mentally; men were men, whether they lived in Hollywood or Cucumonga.

The slight depression left her as she drove to her first appointment. The waiting room at Keith Oil Company was cool and spacious, with a friendly receptionist at the switchboard. Kathy filled out her application with growing apprehension—she had the feeling she was leaping from one world to another. Resolutely, she concentrated, and completed the application. She hesitated when it came to next of kin, then listed Maude Cunningham.

She waited for a short time, then was shown into a large modern room that passed as an office; completely glassed on one side, with large rubber plants and leafy ferns artistically placed, a long low couch, blond satin desk, and two straight-back armless chairs. There was no other furniture in the room. A blonde, rather attractive looking woman was seated behind the desk. At first glance, she appeared to be about thirty-eight or forty, until Kathy noticed the small fine wrinkles around her eyes, the faintly sagging chin. She was dressed in a deceptively simple dark blue linen, with large, rather ornate earrings. Her pale blonde hair was pulled back tightly and done in an intricate chignon. Kathy wondered irrelevantly if she'd had her face lifted.

She smiled pleasantly enough. "Please sit down, Miss Foster." She spoke in a low, studiedly cultured voice. "I'm Mrs. Keith."

Kathy didn't pay too close attention to what she was saying as she told her about the job. The woman's voice and manner fascinated her. She could spot a phony a mile away, as long as it was a woman, and this one seemed to be trying to give the impression that she was a brisk, successful career woman, and at the same time, a poised, gracious lady. She didn't come off well as either one. Kathy disliked Mrs. Keith instinctively, but tried to concentrate on what she was saying.

"So you see, Miss Foster, the position would entail your taking over the export division when Mr. Keith is out of town. We really want someone who speaks Spanish, though." She spoke regretfully. "Well, suppose I give you a letter, then I'll have a typewriter brought in for you."

Mrs. Keith dictated a letter, which Kathy took down without enthusiasm, as she'd already decided she didn't want the job. But she couldn't very well say she'd changed her mind without making a fool of herself.

Mrs. Keith finished dictating and rang on the intercom for a typewriter. "It's too bad Mr. Keith couldn't meet you today. He's in a meeting and he'll be tied up for hours." She glanced at her watch. "As a matter of fact, I'm late for a meeting myself." A dark-haired girl came in, pushing a stand and typewriter. "Thank you, Phyllis . . . So if you'll type that up and leave it at the reception desk, we'll call you in a day or so, after we've seen the other applicants and made a decision." She stood up, smiled graciously, and walked out.

Kathy sat there glumly, staring at the typewriter. She knew damn well Mrs. Keith didn't want to hire her, anymore than she wanted the job. Well, there wasn't much she could do except get the letter typed, then go see the psychiatrist. She put a fresh sheet of paper in the machine, and started typing.

She was almost through with the letter when a young man poked his head in the door. "Oh, has Viv left already?"

She could have made book that he'd never studied acting, if his pretense at surprise was any example.

"If you mean Mrs. Keith, she left about five minutes ago." She smiled at him and he grinned back, walked in and sat down on the couch facing her. Kathy was startled by the change in his features when he smiled. In repose, his face was

11

serious, even somber; a young-old face with deep creases around the corners of his eyes, and a downcast slant around his mouth. When he grinned, his face broke into a myriad of laugh wrinkles, and she was reminded of an impish little boy caught with his hand in the jam pot.

"Did Viv tell you about the job?"

Kathy nodded, and finished the letter automatically.

"It's really not too difficult. After you learn the routine, you'll be pretty much on your own, and I'm sure you'll like it here."

"Wait a minute!" She couldn't help laughing at his enthusiasm, "I'm not hired yet." She pulled the letter out of the typewriter, not bothering to look for errors.

"You're not?" He sounded disappointed. "By the way, I'm Dwight Keith."

Kathy was curious. He couldn't possibly be Mrs. Keith's husband; or son, for that matter. "How many Keiths are there?"

"There's my father, Duncan Keith—he started the company. Then there's my older brother, Scott, and me. You'll be working with me." He smiled at her. "Then there's Viv, of course. She's my father's second wife," he added offhandedly. Then he changed the subject. "You new around here?"

"Yes." She figured he'd read her application, and changed the subject. "Aren't you supposed to be in a meeting?"

"Meeting?" He looked puzzled. "I don't have a meeting today."

"I must have been mistaken." Kathy smiled at him. That bitch, she thought.

Dwight started telling her about the export division, and how much he liked travelling, especially in South America and Mexico.

Kathy interrupted him. "How does your wife like your

being gone so much—or do you take her with you?" She tried to keep an innocent expression on her face.

"Wife? I don't have a wife." His expression changed, and she thought he was going to say something else, but he was deep in thought.

"I really must go." She got up to leave. "Nice meeting you, Mr. Keith."

The grin was back again. "Please call me Dwight," he said, then blurted out in a rush, "Can I call you sometime? Maybe we could have dinner." He actually blushed.

"I think that would be nice." She was amused and touched by his boyishness.

"How about Saturday night?" He pressed his advantage. "Where would you like to go?"

"You decide. Call me Saturday afternoon. Now I really have to go, I'm late already."

Dwight walked her out to the reception desk. "See you Saturday night." He said it loudly enough for the receptionist to hear, looking like an impish little boy again.

Well, she didn't have a job yet, but she *did* have a date. She thought about him as she drove to the doctor's office. He was probably a couple of years older than she, in years but not in mileage; she was used to men at least ten years older. Well, anyway, his father owned an oil company, so he must be pretty stable.

She arrived at the doctor's office a few minutes early. It was in a long low medical building with offices facing inward on three sides to a huge tropical garden. The psychiatrist's office was air-conditioned to the point of being almost uncomfortable. She wondered idly if mental patients were subject to hot flashes. To amuse herself while waiting, she tried to conjure up a mental picture of the doctor, which was based mainly on what she had seen in films.

When he appeared in the doorway, his general appearance was all wrong; in fact, for a moment she thought she was in

13

the wrong office. He was the typical ex-collegiate; tall, broad-shouldered, slim-hipped. He wore a casual sports outfit, which was also unexpected. Kathy had always held the opinion that most psychiatrists almost always were in need of psychiatry themselves, and his first words strengthened that impression.

"Miss Foster?" He walked toward her, and crushed her hand in his. "I'm John Carter, I understand you want to work for me. Can you start right away?"

Just like that. No preliminaries or polite chit-chat, no questions. She must have looked as dumbfounded as she felt, as he laughed suddenly.

"Come on into my office, and we'll talk."

"But," she hesitated, "don't you still have a client—I mean patient—in there?"

"No, he went out the back door," he explained. "You see, he's a doctor too, and he doesn't want any of his patients to see him coming or leaving. Come on in and sit down, it's more comfortable."

His office was small, uncluttered, done in tones of beige and grey. She sat down in the large leather armchair in front of his desk, feeling relaxed and completely at ease. She suddenly decided she liked this man. "Aren't you going to ask me any questions?"

"No." he said, and smiled. "You'll tell me what you want to, or you'll make something up, which I'll find out about eventually."

She looked at him, wondering if he could read her mind. "Well, that's honest enough. Do you mind telling me something about the job?"

He offered her a cigarette, lit another one for himself and leaned back. "About half the patients are regulars; that is, they come in once or twice a week at the same time. Some of the others come just for one visit, for an evaluation. They're sent by the welfare agencies, some by parole officers, and

14

some by their families." He inhaled deeply, and continued, "I handle court cases, too, and I'm usually at County Jail Monday mornings. You'll have some five- to ten-page reports to type up, but not too often, besides the regular office routine. The hours are nine to five, hour for lunch, and nine to twelve on Saturday. Think you can start tomorrow? I'm jammed up on paper work."

Kathy hesitated for about fifteen seconds—she liked him, the salary was good, and the work sounded interesting. "All right." Then (she didn't know what made her ask this), "What happened to your last secretary?"

An almost imperceptible change came over his face. "I had to let her go." His voice was flat. "She was identifying with the patients."

"She was *what* with the patients?"

"That means that in recording a case history, she'd see something in it that would remind her of herself," he explained patiently. "It's a common occurrence among psychiatrists' assistants. Do you think you can handle it?" He was looking at her very seriously.

She looked at him closely; then she couldn't help it, she burst out laughing. "Oh really, Dr. Carter, I don't think I'm off my rocker. I've seen plenty of psychos without, as you call it, 'identifying' with them. Believe me, that doesn't bother me one bit. Besides, I think the field is interesting. I've fiddled around with it a little; in fact, I even went in for hypnosis. Although, I suppose you're opposed to that?" God, she hoped not; she didn't want to lose the job before she'd even started.

"No, I sometimes use it myself. Just remember, a little knowledge can be a dangerous thing." He was very grave. "Don't get too interested in any of the case histories, and don't try to figure out how you'd handle them. Just type them up and forget them. This isn't a difficult job, but there are four basic rules, and I expect you to follow them: be in the office when the patients come in and leave; don't discuss the patient's case with him, or get into any unnecessary conversation; don't read any of the patients' folders, no matter how curious you are. And most important, don't go out with any of the patients."

Her eyebrows shot up, but she made no comment.

His mood lightened. "And, I like coffee almost cold at three, so if you go down to the coffee shop about a quarter of, it'll be just about right. You can wear a nurse's uniform if you like, but it isn't really necessary. Any questions?"

"No, that sounds simple enough. If you don't mind, I'd like to start at noon tomorrow. I think I'd rather wear a uniform, and it's too late to go shopping today."

He smiled at her. "Fine. Meet me in the coffee shop a little after twelve and we'll have lunch. I don't have a one o'clock tomorrow, so we can go over the office routine." He walked her to the door.

There was a dried-up, wizened little baldheaded man sitting in the reception room, obviously irritated at being kept waiting. He looked more like another psychiatrist than a patient. Kathy found out later that he was a homosexual with uncontrollable urges to write dirty words and draw obscene pictures on walls and fences.

She drove home, thinking about the doctor's rules. Certainly it would be no problem to be in the office when the patients came and went. She might be tempted to read a folder now and then, but surely he couldn't think she would deliberately go out with someone who was unbalanced. Yet the doctor had been so serious . . . She heard a clap of thunder in the distance, and looked up to see storm clouds gathering. She increased her speed, before she was caught in the summer storm.

The first few days at the office went by quickly for Kathy; she caught up on the paper work by Friday afternoon, and was relaxing with a cigarette when a slim little dark-haired nurse popped her head in the door. "Hi," she whispered, "been on your coffee break yet?"

Kathy wasn't completely at ease with the "instant friendship" routine. "Well, no," she managed, "I usually don't go until two-thirty."

"Fine, I can go any time. I noticed you were new, and wanted to give you a few days to get settled in. I work for Dr. Sturgess down the hall, so come on down when you're ready for coffee." She started to leave, "Oh, by the way, I'm Pam Sterling."

"I'm Kathy. . ." she started to say, but the girl had gone. Kathy had seen her several times in the coffee shop; it would have been hard not to notice her. She had coal-black hair, deep-set green eyes, and a tan that was emphasized by her white uniform.

Why does she want to have coffee with me? Kathy wondered, then caught herself. Stop it—you're so used to the phony bastards in Hollywood that you can't recognize an open act of friendship when you see it. "I must be getting neurotic," she murmured aloud.

"What, already?" Dr. Carter had come out of his office and was lighting a cigarette. "You haven't been here a full four days yet."

"Oh, I didn't hear you come in. I don't generally talk to myself. It's just that most people I've known have an ulterior motive, and I guess I'm too skeptical. Stupid, isn't it? One of the nurses asked me to have coffee with her."

"No, it's not stupid," he said casually, leaning against the door jamb. "With your equipment, I imagine you've had quite a few ulterior motives thrown at you."

Kathy grinned at him. "Doctor, I never thought you'd notice; these nurses' uniforms leave a lot to be desired."

"Oh, I've noticed," he reached down and squeezed her shoulder gently. His hand was warm and firm, and gave her a tingling sensation. "Well, go get your coffee," he smiled at her, "and bring me back a cup." He turned back to his office, then stopped. "By the way, are you having coffee with Pam Sterling?"

"I think that was her name. How did you know?"

"Oh, just a hunch." He crushed out his cigarette. "I understand she has *her* uniforms made to order, but don't tell her I told you." He went back to his office and closed the door.

Kathy reached for her compact automatically and checked her lipstick. Her cheeks were flushed, and she could still feel the warm pressure of his hand on her shoulder. Resolutely, she put it out of her mind, and went to have coffee with Pam.

They settled in a booth and ordered; Kathy, black coffee, and Pam, hot chocolate and two sweet rolls. She wondered how Pam could eat like that, and still keep her figure.

"Oh, it's easy," Pam smiled, flashing a set of blindingly white teeth, startling against her tanned skin. "As a matter of fact, I used to eat a lot more. But then, I exercise a lot; you know, swimming, tennis, golf. Do you play golf?" she asked, "I'll take you to the Club with me tomorrow."

"No," Kathy stammered, "no, I don't. As far as tennis goes, I haven't played in years, and I never learned to swim." Good God Almighty, was *that* all people did out here?

Pam looked mildly surprised. "What are your hobbies?" she asked, biting into her second sweet roll.

Men, Kathy felt like saying, but resisted the impulse. She searched her mind, but could come up with nothing that would match this superwoman's athletic feats. She considered saying "skiing" for a few seconds, then was certain Pam did that in the winter. "Well, I read a lot," she said weakly.

Pam looked at her oddly. "Well, come to the Club with me, anyway," she said. "We can lie around the pool."

"I'd really like to, Pam, but I have to work tomorrow

morning, then I have a dinner date. With Dwight Keith," she volunteered, wondering why she did.

Pam looked surprised again. "You mean the one whose father owns Keith Oil Company?"

"Yes," Kathy said. "Is there something wrong?"

"Oh no, not really." Pam sipped her chocolate. "It just seems kind of odd, asking you out on a Saturday night. You knew he was married, of course."

Kathy almost choked on her coffee; My God, this couldn't be happening again—she might as well be back in Hollywood. "Oh, no! He can't be! As a matter of fact, I *asked* him, and he said. . . Oh God, I can't remember just what he did say now."

"Well, I wouldn't worry about it. I understand there's been some trouble there, anyway. How'd you meet him?"

Kathy started to tell her about her interview at Keith Oil, trying to remember her conversation with Dwight. She talked too much, and when she glanced at the clock on the wall, it was almost three. "Pam, I'm late, and I haven't ordered the doctor's coffee yet." She signalled the waitress.

Pam scribbled something on a piece of paper. "Here's my phone number and address. Come over for cocktails Sunday, if you have nothing better to do. Bring Dwight along, if things work out. A few other people will probably be dropping in. About five-ish."

Kathy thanked her and said she'd let her know. It was funny; she knew practically nothing about Pam except that she played golf and tennis, and she seemed content to let other people do the talking. Oh well, it was probably that low curve about Dwight's being married that had made her run off at the mouth. But he *couldn't* be—he'd been much too open about asking her out.

The doctor was in the little cubicle that served as her office when she returned with the coffee. "Sorry I'm late."

"That's all right," he assured her easily, "Ebenstein just

19

left, and the next patient's Jack Wentworth. He's always late, if he shows up at all. Tony Rodriguez just called and cancelled his eleven o'clock tomorrow, so I crossed it off in your book. See if you can't get hold of Mrs. Enwright for that time, she's called a few times this week for an appointment.''

"I know,'' Kathy said. "She's been almost rude, when I couldn't put her through to you.''

"*Almost* rude? That's an understatement—wait until you meet her.'' He reached in his pocket. "I almost forgot. Dave Ebenstein left his lighter in my office, and he may be back for it.''

He put it on her desk as the next patient walked in.

"Not too late this time, am I, Doc?''

Kathy called Mrs. Enwright, confirmed the appointment for Saturday, and posted the entry. She noticed the ashtrays in the reception room were filled, the magazines disarranged, and decided to tidy up. While she was dusting, wondering about Dwight, and if she should ask him point blank about his marital status, the door opened and Dave Ebenstein walked in. He seemed very nervous. "Is the doctor in?''

"Well, you just. . . .oh, your lighter.'' She smiled, and walked through the short hall to her office. "Here it is,'' she handed it to him through the small round opening in the window.

He looked at her blankly, picked it up and put it in his pocket. "I'd forgotten. Is the doctor still in? I've got to see him.'' His agitation increased. "There's something I forgot to tell him.''

"He is, but he's with a patient. Do you want to make another appointment?'' She picked up her pen and looked at him. His head was stuck almost through the opening in the glass window, his eyes glaring at her darkly. Oh God, she hadn't even closed the door to the reception room, and the doctor had told her to keep it locked at all times. She mustn't panic. "I'll try to get a note in to him.''

"Call him on that thing," Ebenstein gestured towards the intercom.

"Oh, I can't," she said, "he never wants to be interrupted when he's with a patient."

"Why not?" He glared at her again. "He's been called in there plenty of times when I've been with him."

Kathy had a stroke of inspiration. "Well, that's because with the patients who aren't very sick, I *can* call him, but with the really sick ones, I've had strict orders not to disturb him."

He thought this over, then his face brightened. "Then that means I'm not one of the really sick ones, doesn't it?"

"Suppose you go sit down and read a magazine, and I'll try to get a note in to him." She smiled nervously.

He complied docilely enough, and she pretended to write on a slip of paper. She walked down the longer end of the hall slowly, waited a few minutes, then quietly walked back and closed and locked the door. She leaned against it for a short while, trying to regain her composure, then walked briskly back to her cubicle. Ebenstein was still sitting where she left him, turning the pages of a magazine. She tried to look busy.

Suddenly, he was back at the window again, grinning widely. "Say, you know, maybe you better not interrupt the doctor after all. It's not really something I forgot, but I didn't know whether or not to tell him. So I'll tell *you*, and you can tell him."

She tried to stop him, but he paid no attention. "It's this thing that happened the other night, see. I was sitting up in bed, reading *True* magazine, and all of a sudden these giant pink crabs started crawling across my bed. Oh, I knew they really wasn't there, 'cause I could see through them, but you know, I could see the dents they were making in the blanket. Sounds kind of queer, don't it? But since you said I wasn't as nutty as those other freaks. . ."

Kathy interrupted him nervously, "Now wait a minute, I

21

said nothing of the kind. I am *not* the doctor. I'll make a note of it, and tell him when he's free."

He looked as though he hadn't heard her, and went on conversationally, "You know, when I was a kid, I used to have all these wild ideas, like grabbing a girl, taking her up to the mountains and raping her, then cutting her up and throwing her in a ravine; used to make me feel good all over, know what I mean? But then, everyone has those normal childhood thoughts, don't they?" He looked at her for confirmation.

"I wouldn't know, Mr. Ebenstein," she said weakly, thankful the door was locked. "Like I said, I'm not the doctor, but I'll be sure to tell him. Now, I've got to get some work done."

After he left, she leaned her head wearily on the desk. Then she looked at her watch; ten minutes of four. God, Ebenstein hadn't been there more than twenty minutes, and it seemed like hours. She noticed his case history on the edge of her desk where Dr. Carter had left it. Idly, she started to open it, then closed it firmly and slammed it in the filing cabinet. She'd had enough of Dave Ebenstein for one day.

The doctor should be finished shortly; she walked quickly to the bathroom, splashed cold water on the back of her neck, put on fresh lipstick, and ran a comb hastily through her hair. She had just gotten back to her desk when he came out with Jack Wentworth and walked him to the door, chatting amiably. He came back, put the case history on her desk, and leaned against the door.

"Did you call Mrs. Enwright?"

"Yes, she'll be here at eleven." Her voice sounded funny, even to herself.

"Is something the matter?"

"Ebenstein came back, and he acted sort of odd."

He was instantly concerned. "What do you mean, odd?"

She took a deep breath, and chose her words carefully. "I

22

was cleaning up the reception when he came in and I gave him his lighter, but I forgot to lock the door. He told me he saw crabs crawling on his bed, but he knew there weren't really there."

"Why didn't you call me on the intercom?" he asked gently.

"He wanted me to, but I didn't want you to think I couldn't handle it. I managed to get the door locked, and after a while, he left."

He cupped her chin and lifted her face slowly until her eyes met his. "Kathy, now do you see why it's so important to keep that door locked at all times? There are other reasons besides disturbed patients, but we don't have to go into them right now."

"What other reasons? I think I should know what I'm up against."

He looked at her gravely. "You're right. I don't want to alarm you, but we've had a few narcotic thefts in the building." He saw her stiffen slightly, and hastened to reassure her. "There haven't been many, and it's not likely to happen again. I'm just warning you to be careful. A few months ago, there were some drugs missing, and at first, they thought it was a careless drug count. But it was happening in too many offices."

"But why in here? Why rob a psychiatrist?"

"Why not?" he shrugged, "Whoever's been doing this can't tell from the M.D. after my name on the door what kind of a doctor I am, and I do keep a certain amount of drugs here. On the other hand, if it's someone who works in the building, he, or she, would probably attempt a robbery in here to throw the police off the track. Anyway, that's their theory. They haven't come up with anything definite, and the thefts stopped about four or five months ago. Incidentally, this is highly confidential, and the police are still working on the case. Only the doctors and nurses actually involved in the robberies know about this, so don't discuss it with anyone, all right?''

"I won't say anything." He started to go back to his office, but she decided she had better tell him everything Ebenstein had said. When she finished, his face was grim.

"It would seem he's been telling you more than he tells me." He went to the filing cabinet, pulled out Ebenstein's file and scribbled something in it. "By the way, did you read his file?" he threw the question to her over his shoulder.

"No, I didn't. I started to open it, then I remembered what you said, so I just put it back in the cabinet."

He looked at her steadily for a long moment, trying to make up his mind. "I think it's time we both had a short brandy, don't you?" He took her by the hand and led her into his office. Then he opened one of his desk drawers, pulled out a bottle and two shot glasses. He poured the drinks and handed her one, waiting until she drank it. "Feel better?" he asked, refilling her glass.

"I feel fine—now."

"Well, drink up, then I'll walk you to your car. I'd suggest you go home, take a hot bath and go to bed; you've had quite a day."

Kathy drove home slowly, stopping for a hamburger on the way, then put the car in the garage. Topsy started barking as she put the key in the lock. She petted her, let her outside and headed for the bathroom. She started the bathwater, threw in a large handful of bath salts, then went out to the kitchen and made herself a stiff bourbon on the rocks. She stood there for some time, thinking back over the events of the day. Topsy's scratching and barking at the door brought her back to the present. She let her in, petted her again, and opened a can of dog food. She picked up her drink and downed half of it in one gulp. Why is it people keep talking about leading a dog's life? she wondered idly. It seemed to her that dogs had it made; they were fed, bathed, cared for

24

and loved, and in return, all they had to do was lick their owner's hand. She ruffled Topsy's neck affectionately.

She finished her drink, went in and turned off the water, then undressed, and sank into the hot scented water gratefully, and relaxed. She didn't think about anything in particular, until the water started getting cool . . . she sighed, wriggled her toes, got up and patted herself dry. She was considering having another drink, when she suddenly remembered . . . she hadn't thought about the past all day.

As though she were sending out thought waves, the phone rang suddenly, breaking the silence in the cozy bungalow. She let it ring several times, considering not answering at all. Almost against her will, she moved towards it, and picked up the receiver slowly. "Yes?"

"Kathy?" Maude's voice was on the other end, brisk and to the point. "I thought you ought to know. Bruce got back to town today."

Chapter 2

Irene Enwright drove down the highway, cutting deftly in and out of traffic, thankful that Dr. Carter had a cancellation this morning. She thought about last night's dinner party, and savagely crushed out her cigarette. Ted was late, as usual, although she had purposely called his secretary to remind him to be home early. Ann was already serving the canapes when he arrived. Irene had greeted him with a smile, a light kiss, and an "if looks could kill" glance that only pass between a husband and wife of long standing. He had sat through dinner, looking bored and disinterested, then excused himself early, pleading an early morning golf game.

She wondered if her friends found him as dull as she did; even worse, if they pitied her. They had slept in separate bedrooms for three years now, and on the rare occasions when he had come to her bed, it had been disastrous—almost worse than no sex at all. Their love-making had deteriorated gradually into a sort of perfunctory ritual; he would kiss her, play with her breasts briefly to assure himself that her nipples were hard, poke his finger inside her to satisfy himself she was lubricated enough, and commence with the "Act of Love."

Lately, he'd had to use the vaginal jelly more and more frequently. She sighed, and lit another cigarette. It was always the same; same position, same heavy breathing—she could almost count the number of strokes before he'd reach a climax. The few times she had become aroused, he'd had an orgasm long before she was ready, then rolled over and went to sleep.

Irene would lie there for hours, listening to his deep, even breathing, feeling frustrated and cheated. At times she had the horrible idea that he thought of sex as some sort of health protection, like brushing your teeth, taking a shower, or Blue Cross. At others, she had a sneaking suspicion that he could feel her beginning to respond, and came as quickly as possible just to spite her.

It hadn't always been that way; in the beginning he had been tender and romantic, imaginative and inventive; damn, was he inventive! Several months after their marriage, Ted had come home with a book—God only knows where he got it—called "99 Different Ways To Have Sexual Intercourse." Irene had been visibly shocked, but Ted had laughed and teased her. "Well, honey, it's not so bad. After all, we've tried most of them." The next day, after he had gone to work she had leafed through the book, guiltily at first, then with avid interest. Well, they hadn't *really* tried most of them, she had thought, although they had tried quite a few. They eventually got around to almost all of them, though.

The trouble started, she supposed, after April was born. It hadn't been an easy pregnancy; Ted had been delighted at the prospect of a child, and was terrified when she almost miscarried in her third month. The doctor had ordered her to bed for six weeks, so they got a housekeeper. The expense didn't bother her, as Ted's real estate and construction business was building rapidly, but the abrupt lack of sex did. Ted was sleeping in the den now, explaining that it would be easier for both of them.

In her fifth month, the doctor pronounced her hale and hearty, and said she could resume her normal activities. Somewhat shamefaced, she had mumbled something about sex, at which he laughed. "Well, that's a normal activity, isn't it?" She had waited for Ted to come home eagerly that night, but he seemed embarrassed when she told him what the doctor had said.

"We've waited this long, honey," he said. "I don't want to jeopardize your health, or the baby's. Let's wait until after he's born."

She was hurt, of course; but after a while she started thinking how thoughtful and considerate he was, and tried to concentrate on the baby. But try as she might, all she could think about was after the baby was born, and they could resume their normal sex life. Several weeks later, she had walked in the bathroom and found Ted masturbating. They had both stood there frozen for a moment, then she had walked out quickly and closed the door. Looking back, it seemed like some sort of comic, grotesque tableau. At the time, she tried to console herself that he was doing it for her, for the baby, that at least he wasn't playing around with other women. The incident was never discussed, but it was then she began to hate the unborn child in her belly.

April was a breech birth, and perfectly beautiful, Irene had to admit. She had none of the wrinkled redness that most babies have, but Irene didn't love her. She bathed, changed and fed her perfunctorily, while Ted simpered and beamed with proud fatherhood. He had insisted the baby be breast fed, and watched the somewhat Pagan ritual (she thought) at every opportunity. He was deeply disappointed when her milk dried up so fast; secretly, she was delighted, as the pulling and tugging irritated her.

April was exactly six weeks old when Ted finally went to bed with her, the standard time prescribed by the doctor. It had been over seven months, and Irene had tried every way possible to seduce and coerce him before the time was up, but on this point, he held firm. She had put the baby to bed early, and was in a feverish state of excitement when he came home. She ran and clung to him, kissing him deeply. "Wait a minute," he said, "don't you have to feed the baby first?"

"She's been fed, and she's asleep. Ted, please!" She looked at him pleadingly, and some of her desire seemed to spill over into him.

"All right, now," he said roughly, picked her up and carried her to the bedroom. He shed his clothes quickly and got into bed next to her, spreading her thighs apart with easy assurance. She had come almost as soon as he touched her.

"God, you're hot!" His voice was hoarse. He kept playing with her, using his fingers, teasing her, but each time she was about to reach a climax again, he'd stop. Finally, she could stand it no longer. She reached down and grasped him, and he was hard and erect.

"Oh Ted, please put it in," she moaned, and instantly he was on top of her. She was wet with desire, and he slid in easily, despite the stitches and the long months of abstinence. He pulled her legs up around his neck and pushed in even deeper. "Don't hold your climaxes," he murmured.

She couldn't, even if she tried. She wondered why it was taking him so long to come, but pushed the thought to the back of her mind. Finally he said, "Now, honey, now!" and she felt the burst of hot fluid deep inside her. He rolled her on her side, still inside her, and started playing with her breasts. "God, you were hot," he said again, and then, "I wonder if this will bring your milk back?"

Tears came to her eyes, and she had hated the baby more than ever.

Oh well, that was a long time ago; thank God, April was safely ensconced in school in Switzerland and didn't need her father anymore, not really. Irene had thought about divorce briefly at times, and as quickly discarded the idea. She had no rapport with her daughter, and little or none with her husband, but the thought of being divorced rather frightened her. She had plenty of money; God knows, that's all Ted did any more, was make it. Almost all their fights were about money; it would usually start out with her saying, "All you do is think about making money!" ending up with his inevitable standard reply, "Yes, and all you do is spend it."

Well, that was true enough, she thought bitterly; what else did she have to do? Good God, she was only forty-four, and Ted was only forty-six. Was life supposed to end then? At times, she had thought of taking a more or less permanent lover, but she was too well known, and might get caught. When her sexual urges became almost impossible to control, she would drive to San Diego or Long Beach, sit at some dark, sleazy bar, and wait to be picked up. These excursions were always one-night stands, and sometimes she even paid for the motel. Her sexual relief was always short-lived; on the long drive home she started feeling slightly soiled. Each time she thought, never again, but deep down, she knew she would. Oddly enough, she never had any guilt feelings about these interludes, but blamed Ted for his inadequacy.

Irene had started seeing Dr. Carter as more or less of a lark, a whim, because it was the "in" thing to do, to see a psychiatrist. Then she started opening up to him, and it was a tremendous relief to be able to talk to someone frankly and honestly. At first, she had talked about him constantly to her friends, thinking it added to her social status, but lately she hadn't mentioned him at all. She had started thinking of him as a kind of father-confessor figure, as he acted neither shocked or surprised at anything she told him. Also, there was far less stress on her libido and pocketbook than the San Diego or Long Beach trips. She came away after an hour with him feeling calm and relaxed, although it didn't last very long. At times, she wondered if he thought of her as one of those rich society matrons, with nothing better to do than have a sneaky little bed encounter with a stranger, or visit a psychiatrist? "Oh God, what in the hell am I going to do?" She tossed her cigarette carelessly out the window and drove into the parking lot.

Kathy looked up as the door opened. Irene Enwright didn't just come into a room, she made an *entrance*. "I'm Mrs. Enwright. The doctor's expecting me," she said crisply.

"Yes, I know," Kathy said coolly, deliberately dawdling at her desk. "He'll be with you in a moment." The woman's rudeness on the phone still rankled.

Instead of sitting down, Irene stood outside of Kathy's window, tapping her long fingernails nervously on the counter. She was a tall, broad-shouldered, big-boned woman, impeccably dressed in a champagne beige pants outfit that matched her carefully tossed champagne beige hair.

"You're new here, aren't you?" she asked.

"Yes," Kathy answered briefly, and got Mrs. Enwright's folder out of the filing cabinet.

"I'm glad you could fit me in." Mrs. Enwright smiled slightly, "I've a tendency to get somewhat obnoxious if I don't get my own way. Sorry if I was rude."

"Oh no, that's all right." Kathy was surprised, and taken off guard. "We all have our days." Oh Christ, she thought, that was certainly a diplomatic remark. The slight smile froze on Mrs. Enwright's face, but luckily the doctor came out then, so there was no need for any further conversation.

Kathy had debated with herself all morning; she had opened the mail, sent out the statements, and started the bank deposit for Monday morning. Mrs. Enwright would be with the doctor for one solid hour, and there was nothing else for her to do. Resolutely, she went to the file cabinet, pulled out Dave Ebenstein's folder and stood there reading it, ready to shove it back in quickly in case the doctor came out unexpectedly.

She sat down at her desk again, the words imprinted on her brain; four arrests for indecent exposure, insufficient evidence; a fifth arrest for child molestation, with a conviction that had stuck. Sentenced for five years, with parole after three for good behavior. She shuddered slightly and tried to think of something else, like what she was going to wear for dinner tonight with Dwight. It was a toss-up between the blue chiffon or the black taffeta. Idly, she wondered whether or not she'd go to bed with him, and just what social protocol was all about in such matters in San Gabriel. Fleetingly, she thought of asking Pam, then giggled aloud at the prospect.

"Pamela, my dear, since this is my first date with Dwight, should I have sexual intercourse with him, or wait until he asks me out again before we cohabitate?" She could almost see Pam's look of shocked surprise, and grinned wickedly. She decided on the blue chiffon.

Dr. Carter came out of his office with Mrs. Enwright and introduced them; "Irene, this is my new assistant. Miss Foster, Mrs. Enwright." Mrs. Enwright's smile was rather glacial; "We've met," she acknowledged the introduction briefly, and left.

"What's her hangup?" Kathy asked.

"Oh, too much money, too much time on her hands; her husband loused up her dinner party last night." He put her folder away, lit two cigarettes and handed one to Kathy.

"Some problems," she said, inhaling deeply, "I wonder how we poor slobs manage to survive without too much money and no ruined dinner parties?"

He shrugged slightly. "Some things that don't seem to matter to most people can become painfully important to others, and blown up all out of proportion." He didn't seem

32

too anxious to leave. "Look, if you don't have anything planned—that is, Edith's out shopping today, and I hate to eat lunch alone—what I mean is, will you have lunch with me? We could go to the Zanzibar."

She hesitated for a moment; Dwight was due to pick her up at 7:30, and she had planned a leisurely afternoon, giving herself a facial, doing her nails . . . all the things a girl does when she's going out with a man for the first time. On the other hand, the Zanzibar was supposed to be one of the nicest places out here. "All right, I'd love to, but can I go in my uniform?"

"Why not? People wear just about anything out here. You lock up while I get the car."

The Zanzibar was cool, spacious and dimly lit, not unlike the better restaurants on La Cienega or in Beverly Hills. The maitre de greeted the doctor by name, and showed them to a small table in the cocktail lounge. It was still early, and very few people were there.

He ordered two vodka martinis, very dry, without asking her, then offered her a cigarette. "How did you know I drank martinis?" she asked.

"You look like the type. Champagne cocktails are a little too obvious for you, and scotch and water or bourbon and soda are a little too simple."

Kathy didn't answer for a moment, as she wasn't quite sure she liked his remark. It was hard to tell with the doctor what was intended as a compliment or a direct insult. The drinks arrived, and she sipped her martini. "Is that supposed to mean I'm as complicated as a mixed drink, and simple ordinary things bore me?"

He settled back in his chair comfortably. "Not necessarily. Everyone is complex to a certain degree, but some much more so than others. And some people seem to attract the complex, the off-beat. Ordinary, everyday living palls after a while,

33

and though they may not consciously seek the unusual, their subconscious craves it; needs it, in fact, in order to exist."

"Well, that's certainly not true about me," Kathy said rather heatedly. "The main reason I moved out here was to get away from what you term the 'complex.' As far as seeking out the unusual, that's just plain nonsense. All I want to do is meet some nice normal people and lead an ordinary existence."

"So you go to work for a psychiatrist," he interrupted. "Why?"

The question stopped her for a moment. "Well, where I work has nothing to do with my private life," she said. "Besides, it's interesting," and immediately felt like a fool.

He smiled. "Interesting—and you know *why* it's interesting? Because right at this present moment you have nothing odd or unusual in your life. You're determined, consciously, to subjugate your life to the mundane, the ordinary, but your subconscious rebels."

She thought this over slowly. There was a definite possibility that he was right, but that didn't make her like it any better. "Supposing you were right—mind you, I'm not saying you are—which side would win out?"

He turned his empty martini glass idly, making wet circles on the shiny black table. "That's hard to say at the moment. I don't know enough about you; or for that matter, which side *should* win out." He signalled the waiter for another round. "Why did you really move out here?"

"Why did you decide to open your practice out here? You could be making a lot more money in a big city."

He looked at her quizzically. "You know, that habit of yours of parrying a direct question with another has probably helped you a great deal; but don't forget, I'm a psychiatrist."

"Well, you were a man long before you were a psychiatrist," Kathy said shortly, and started on her second martini. She wasn't quite sure she liked the turn this conversation was taking, and tried to change the subject. "Anyway, I don't think I want to be psychoanalized over martinis."

He laughed at her outright. "My dear girl, I'm not psychoanalizing you, although I probably should. Everyone has a few mental kinks that need to be ironed out."

"And just what kinks do you think I have?" she said evenly, and had an insane desire to kick him, viciously.

As though reading her mind, he crossed his legs casually, and continued, "As I told you, I don't know enough about you yet. I can tell you one thing, though—you seriously believe you moved out here to get away from Hollywood and the frenetic sort of life you were living. Yet you'd lived that kind of life for years and never pulled up stakes, so something pretty drastic must have happened to make you take the plunge. You don't strike me as the kind of person who moves around aimlessly, without any definite reason. Was it a man?"

The question hit her suddenly, without warning, and she finished her drink quickly to cover her confusion. "Yes, there was a man—isn't there usually? Just what kind of a loaded question is that?"

He signalled the waiter again, ordered another round and lunch—lobster newburg for Kathy and a steak sandwich for himself, again without asking. The martinis were beginning to make her feel slightly dizzy, however, so she didn't press the point.

"You want to tell me about it? I promise I won't psychoanalyze you." The doctor's voice was kind, gentle, the tone she had already come to recognize as his doctor-to-patient, the oh, so understanding, you-can-confide-in-me voice.

"My dear Dr. Carter, you can save the dulcet tonal quality for your patients," she smiled. "No, I don't want to talk about him, it's all been much too recent and much too painful to ruin a perfectly good lunch." She sat quietly sipping her drink while the waiter served them. "You know," she mused, "I think I would have been a good psychiatrist. I never have been much of a person to discuss my own personal problems, yet it seems like all my life I've been listening to other people's troubles. Frankly, I've got to admit that most of the time I've enjoyed it—listening to someone else's problems seem to minimize your own, or put them in the proper prospective. At the very least, you forget yourself for the time being. Then other times, I think there just aren't any happy people left in the world. Oh, you think they are for a while; married couples, that is, until you get to know them better. Secretly, I've always thought of most marriages as a boiling cauldron of seething emotions, with a glacial layer of social behavior on top—I hope that doesn't sound too dramatic. I don't think I've ever met a completely happy person in my entire life; have you?"

"Of course not," he said definitely, and signalled the waiter. "Can you stand another one?"

She counted swiftly, and nodded. "But that's my limit."

"Happiness is a matter of degree, Kathy," he continued. "I suppose the closest you can come to it are the incurably insane, whose brain cells have been damaged to the extent that they live as vegetables. But even these people are neither happy or unhappy as they live in a vacuum, as far as medical science can determine. Suppose you, for instance, were completely happy; how would you know, if you'd never had unhappiness to compare it with?" He paused reflectively. "I don't think I'd want to be a completely happy person—happiness is a very precious commodity, Kathy, and even more precious when it comes in small doses."

She picked at her lobster for a while, then looked at him deeply. "You know, my ex-husband said something like that to me once, not quite in the same words. I was too young at the time to understand, but now I really think I do. You know, you're very easy to talk to.''

He burst out laughing. ''Good God, I hope so! I'd be a pretty lousy psychiatrist if I weren't.''

''Are you analyzing me now?'' she asked suspiciously.

''Definitely not. Now finish your lunch—do you want coffee?''

She looked at her watch. The time had flown, and it was almost four o'clock. ''No thanks, I have a million things to do.''

He drove her back to her car, telling her to come in late Monday if she wanted to, that he would be at the jail until one o'clock. ''Just be sure to call the exchange to get the messages.'' He looked at her and smiled. ''You're a very unusual girl, Kathy.''

''Now just what did he mean by that?'' she wondered as she drove away. Then she thought of that tired old psychiatrist's joke, and laughed.

At six o'clock exactly, Kathy was just dipping her right foot in the hot steamy bubble bath, when the doorbell rang. Thinking it was the landlord or an Avon lady, she threw on a robe and opened the door.

''Dwight, what are you doing here now? You weren't supposed to pick me up until seven thirty.'' She tried to pull the robe around her more tightly.

''Now don't be mad,'' he looked at her anxiously. ''I got through playing golf early, and I was going to wait in the bar, but then I thought, why not pick up some stuff and make you a martini while you're getting ready?'' He held up a paper bag. ''What a cute dog.'' Topsy was jumping up and down insanely, barking and lurching at the screen door.

''Well, come on in. There's nothing like being informal,'' she said, unlatching the screen. ''You make yourself one, and fix me a bourbon and soda, light; you'll find everything in the kitchen. I was just about to take a bath.''

"You're not mad?"

"No, just a little surprised." Not much she wasn't mad; she was furious, and painfully aware of the torn pocket on her robe and cold cream on her face.

She had barely gotten in the tub and was wiping the cold cream off her face when he knocked. "Here's your drink." She got out of tub, slopped water all over the floor, opened the door and stuck her hand out. "Thank you." A few minutes later he knocked again. *God, is there no privacy?* This time she got out of the tub for good, and wrapped a towel around her. "What now?"

"Do you have some iodine, or something? Your dog bit me."

Good! she thought. She rummaged around in the medicine cabinet, and came up with some. "Sorry. I'll bandage it when I come out." She dropped the towel and began applying her makeup. Well, the evening was off to a grand start. She wondered briefly if he'd still be in the apartment when she finished dressing, but at this point, she really didn't give much of a damn.

Dwight took her to the Rainbow Angling Club, a huge rambling building with a large man-made lake, plentifully stocked with trout. Everyone seemed to know him, and they were seated immediately at a table overlooking the lake, although the club was almost filled. The owner came over and greeted Dwight effusively, and complimented him on his choice of dinner companions. Kathy was beginning to relax and enjoy herself.

"The club used to be private," Dwight explained after the owner left. "Then it was either raise the dues or open it to the public."

"It really is very beautiful," she admitted, gazing out over the water. Revolving lanterns were placed strategically among

38

the tall pine trees, making shifting patterns on the lake.

"Would you like to walk around? We could take our drinks with us." His enthusiasm was catching.

The lake was a good mile around, and she had on a brand new pair of shoes that weren't broken in yet, but she could always take them off. "Why not?" she agreed amiably.

Dwight carried the conversation as they walked, telling her the history of the club, then about his job with the export division, while she listened with half a mind. It was really lovely and peaceful, with the pungent aroma of the pines, the silvery blue fish darting gracefully, the occasional splash of water as they leaped in the air. "Lovely," she murmured. Dwight was shaking her arm. "What?" Kathy said.

"Hey, where've you been? I said, how'd you like to catch your own trout for dinner?" He beamed at her, pleased with his inspiration.

She stared at him in amazement, certain he was some kind of nut. Did he honestly think she wanted to go trout fishing in a cocktail dress? Suddenly, the clean aroma of the pines disappeared; in its place was the smell of fish, and her new shoes were beginning to pinch her feet. "Oh, I don't think so, Dwight," she managed. "I've never acquired a taste for trout."

Conversation during dinner was extremely dull, to say the least. She couldn't help comparing him with the doctor, and Dwight came off a very poor second. The more he drank, the more often he asked her if she was absolutely certain her dog's rabies vaccination hadn't expired. God knows, he had made a big enough fuss about it at the apartment. Topsy's small teeth marks hadn't even broken the skin, but Kathy had obligingly applied some more iodine and slapped on a bandaid, assuring him that the rabies certificate was packed away in one of the boxes in the garage.

He wasn't only a nut, he was a hypochondriac as well, she decided. By the time she finished her shrimp cocktail, she was absolutely certain she wasn't going to bed with him, and by the time she was halfway through her steak, she wasn't even sure she'd let him kiss her goodnight.

Dwight had just ordered coffee when Irene Enwright walked in with a tall, distinguished-looking man. Her glance swept the room, and she spotted their table almost immediately. She said something to the man, and they started toward them. Kathy wondered what protocol was about acknowledging acquaintance with a patient outside of the office, but she needn't have worried.

"Well hello, Dwight, my dear," Irene said, kissing him lightly on the cheek, "How's your dear mother? You know, we haven't seen nearly enough of you lately." Turning to Kathy, she said, "It's Miss Frazier, isn't it?"

"Foster."

"Oh, you two know each other?" Dwight sounded surprised.

"We've met, briefly. Well, do give my love to your mother, and I'll tell her how well you're looking when we play bridge Thursday. Come along, Ted."

Kathy sipped her coffee, thinking. Sure, Irene was going to wait until Thursday to talk to Dwight's stepmother. No way. Instead she'd be on the phone in the morning as soon as it was decently possible to tell her—casually, of course—that she'd spoken to them. Irene had seemed surprised to see them together, and Kathy wondered why.

She had decided earlier not to say anything to Dwight about her conversation with Pam, as she had decided not to go out with him again, but now she changed her mind.

"I had coffee with a nurse in the building yesterday," she said mildly. "She seemed rather surprised when I told her I was going out with you tonight."

"Surprised? Why?"

"Well, she seemed to think you were still married."

Dwight looked astonished. "Still married! Who would tell

40

you a thing like that? Well, technically, I'm not divorced yet, but the only thing holding it up is the property settlement. I haven't lived at home for over three months. Who told you that?'' he repeated, the picture of outraged innocence.

"Pamela Sterling."

"Pam?" he looked more outraged than ever. "Why, I've known Pam for years, and she knows perfectly well that I'm not married any more! I ran into her a few weeks ago, and she told me how sorry she was about the breakup.''

"Well, maybe I misunderstood her."

"Listen, I'm taking the children fishing in the mountains tomorrow. Why don't you come along and see for yourself?''

"Oh no, Dwight, I don't think that would look quite right, with the children and all," she said. "Not until after your interlocutory." Kathy listened to her own words with amazement. Could this be her, sounding so proper and righteous, when she didn't particularly give a damn if a man was married or not? However, she did think it slightly premature for a family outing on the second date. "Tell you what. Pam asked me over for cocktails tomorrow; why don't you come along with me after you've taken the children home? She told me to ask you."

"Well, I certainly will. There are a few things I want to straighten out with her."

"Oh, I wouldn't do that," she said hastily. "I probably got it mixed up, but it's straightened out now. So why not just drop it?" She smiled, coaxingly. "There's no sense in stirring up trouble."

He agreed grudgingly, but on the drive home she could tell it still rankled. She listened to him with half a mind, but her thoughts were on Pam. Why had the girl lied? She must have known Kathy would find out the truth. And why hadn't she told her she knew him? She hadn't said she didn't, but it was a pretty glaring ommission. For the life of her, Kathy couldn't figure it out. She was extremely curious, but decided against asking Pam outright; she usually found out things in her own good time.

She was beginning to think, however, that people out here weren't going to turn out to be quite as simple and uncomplicated as she thought.

Chapter 3

After Dwight left, Kathy closed the door with a sigh; she was tired, but not so tired that she wanted to go to bed right away. She washed and creamed her face, fixed herself a stiff drink, and curled up on the couch with a cigarette. She had let Dwight kiss her a couple of times, but when he wanted to come in, she had begged off, pleading a slight headache. His last words had been to be sure and get the rabies certificate out of the garage.

She had changed her mind about going out with Dwight again for three reasons; first, she knew Vivian Keith wouldn't like the idea, and she got a sort of vicious pleasure from the thought. Second, and worse, if she only went out with him once, Mrs. Keith might think he had dropped her, and she couldn't stand that. Third, he knew all the right people, and she didn't know anyone out here yet; it logically followed she would meet others through him. She had no intention of going to bed with him, but she was sure he could be easily handled. This settled and neatly decided, she put him out of her mind.

Her thoughts wandered back to lunch with the doctor.

Here was a man who really stimulated her, and that hadn't happened since she had left Bruce. What was it the doctor had said about happiness? "Happiness is a very precious commodity, and even more precious when it comes in small doses."

Well, that was certainly true, she thought, fixing herself another drink. Fred had put it in different words, but the thought was essentially the same: "If you had your choice, would you rather be deliriously happy one day out of seven and sort of down the other six, or just go along on an even keel?" he had asked her. Naturally, she had said one day out of seven; what girl of eighteen wants to go along on an even keel? Certainly not one with as little sense as she had at the time.

She curled up on the couch again; Topsy turned over, snuggled closer to her, and started snoring.

She was still a virgin when she met Fred, which was unusual in Hollywood; come to think of it, it was unusual anywhere in this day and age. He took her out almost every night for two weeks, and they always ended up necking and petting in his car. She knew her resistance was gradually weakening, as his hands became more and more familiar with her body. She finally fell for the old chestnut about "Do you want me to get all hot and bothered, and then have to go to bed with another girl?" Kathy very definitely did not, so this time they got in the back seat of the car. It was cramped and uncomfortable, and it hurt; it was also very messy.

Looking back, she wondered why she had held her virginity in such esteem. Fred had been surprised, but he had been neither pleased or displeased. They had found better places after that, usually his apartment when his roommate was out. Fred made good money when he worked, but acting in Grade B movies wasn't the steadiest profession in the world. He'd finish a picture with a bundle, they'd have a ball for a while, and a few weeks later, he'd be broke. With typical young girl illogic, she thought she could change him, and two months later they eloped to Las Vegas.

She sighed, took a sip of her drink, and picked up her hairbrush. Ten days after they were married, he had burst into their bedroom drunk, and awakened her from a sound sleep. "You know, I never should have married you, you're a lousy lay." His voice was slurred and nasty.

Bewildered, she had looked up at him. "Well, what are you bringing it up now for? You told me that before we were married."

"Yeah, I know. I thought you'd get better, but you've just gotten worse." Then he fell on the bed in a drunken stupor and started snoring.

She had lain awake for hours, troubled and confused; just why had he married her in the first place? After that incident, their arguments became more and more bitter; if it wasn't about her inability in the sex department, it was about money matters. Looking back, she wondered about that one day out of seven when she was supposed to be "deliriously happy," and couldn't even remember very many happy hours. In desperation, she had gotten a job modelling, and it wasn't long before she got a small part in a movie, then a six-month stock contract. Oh God, if only she had left him then! She realized it was a dangerous game, playing "if only I had" but she was slightly drunk now, and continued thinking of the past.

At the studio, she was considered a young sex symbol, but Fred kept harassing her, and she began to develop a deep inferiority complex. Finally, she went to a gynecologist.

Two hours later, she walked out of his office feeling greatly relieved, and hating Fred. After a complete examination, he had told her that her pelvic bones were slightly narrow, and her vaginal area smaller than most, although she was in all ways entirely normal. After looking at a lot of graphs and charts, he had suggested that her husband come in for consultation. If her description of his genitalia was correct, he was extremely underdeveloped.

Instead, since Fred was on location for a few days, she had taken the opportunity to move quietly out of their apartment and file for divorce.

Fred had been furious when the papers were served, and threatened to contest the divorce. Finally, she told him that if he wanted to fight dirty, she could too, and mentioned the gynecologist—he had to back down.

She had almost finished another picture, but now she couldn't concentrate, and her work suffered. She blew her lines, and her acting was wooden. It was too late to replace her and she got through it somehow, but at the end of six months, the studio dropped her option.

When word got around that she and Fred had split, men flocked around her as if she were a bitch in heat. They all had the same tired line: "Well, honey, you've had it regularly now, it's not good for you to go without it," as though they'd be bestowing some special favor by giving her stud service.

She was hesitant about going to bed with anyone for a while, as Fred's constant harping on her lack of expertise in sex had left its mark. The gynecologist's reassurance had done little or nothing to undo her deep-seated inferiority complex. After a few too many one night, she finally did, with a friend of Fred's. She was nervous at first, but when the initial embarrassment wore off, she began to enjoy it, and he thought she was just great. After that, there were a succession of men, but nothing very serious. With some she liked it, with others she didn't. Sometimes she would get aroused to the point where she was sure she'd reach a climax, but she never did; it was always over too fast.

She got a job with an advertisting agency in Beverly Hills,

and it was much better than working at the studio. There were a lot of out-of-town clients from New York, Chicago and Miami who were certainly a cut above the Hollywood crowd she'd been running with . . . at least, they all had money, and weren't broke half the time. Occasionally, her boss would ask her to have dinner with a client and show him the town. He always slipped her a fifty-dollar bill and told her to come in late the next day. Sometimes she would go to bed with the client, and she would find another fifty or hundred-dollar bill stuffed in her purse. She hadn't felt there was anything particularly wrong about this at the time. There was never any discussion about money at all, except for an occasional, "Here, Kathy, go buy yourself a present."

She wondered what Dwight would think about all this, and fixed herself another drink. Looking back, she realized she was nothing better than a high-class call girl, with a legitimate job on the side. It hadn't bothered her for the simple reason that she hadn't thought about it at all.

She had worked for the agency over two years and had just passed her twenty-second birthday, when she began to feel a little uneasy. She was neither happy or unhappy, but the days and weeks had begun to take on a certain sameness. She made good money, but it was hard to save, as she had to have an extensive wardrobe, and her apartment was expensive. The feeling grew gradually, but she was beginning to get bored, and wondering just where she was headed.

It was a day just like any other when she met Bruce . . . She glanced at the windows and dawn was breaking. Oh Kathy, she thought, don't start thinking about him now! She finished her drink quickly, crushed out her cigarette, and went to bed.

"Yes, goodbye, dear, and thanks for calling," she said sweetly. Vivian Keith waited until she heard the click before she slammed the phone down viciously, then got out of bed and started pacing her bedroom. Trust Irene to bring her bad news before she was hardly awake!

She started to ring for the maid, then remembered it was Sunday, and looked in the adjoining bedroom at Duncan. He was still sound asleep, so she went downstairs silently. She very rarely drank, but this morning she fixed herself a Bloody Mary—she needed something to calm down, and time to think. The Foster girl—from Irene's description she was certain it was the same one, but how had they met? She had known at the time she interviewed her that she wanted to keep her away from Dwight, and thought she had handled it very well. Evidently, she'd gone wrong someplace. Well, she hadn't worked and maneuvered this long to have some clever little redheaded bitch outsmart her. She had approved of Dwight's choice of a wife, as she was dumb, docile, but socially acceptable, and completely disinterested in the company business. She didn't consider Dwight too much smarter, and had relegated him to the export division which kept him out of the country most of the time.

Vivian was thirty-two when she went to work for Keith Oil, widowed by a tragic auto accident, and with absolutely no skills. She started as a file clerk. Duncan had taken a fatherly interest in her, and she was grateful for the opportunity to make a living. She went to night school, learned typing and shorthand, and moved up to a secretarial position. When Duncan's wife died suddenly, she used this as a common bond of interest, and started a course in business management.

She also took the time to discreetly find out all she could about Duncan's family. Duncan and Jeanne had married young, and started Keith Oil Company on a shoestring. They had worked together for years, building up the business. Both of them had wanted a family, but it didn't seem to be in the cards. They had given up all hope, but after a brief vacation in Mexico, Jeanne had gone to see Dr. Sturgess, thinking she was having an early change of life. When they found out she was pregnant, it almost seemed like a miracle. Duncan was forty-two, and Jeanne thirty-five. They named their first son Scott, after Jeanne's father, and two years later, Dwight was born. Jan had been a complete surprise when Duncan was fifty-four, and a hard pregnancy for Jeanne, who was forty-seven, but they were both delighted that their last child turned out to be a girl.

Duncan had taken his wife's death very badly, and Vivian used every opportunity she could find to sympathize with him. There was almost thirty years difference in their ages, but she had ingratiated herself into his life, and that of his poor motherless children. She became his private secretary, then his public relations representative, then his wife. She had been thirty-seven and Duncan was sixty-four.

She walked down the steps into the sunken living room and looked around her; Louis XVI furniture; some Chippendale; a pigeon blood urn from the Ming Dynasty; a Renoir and a Degas on the walls. She hadn't done too badly in the past eleven years, but she had worked hard, and earned every penny of it.

Her first husband had been a fly-by-night car salesman who couldn't hold a job for very long, and half the time there wasn't any food in the house, but there was always enough money for liquor for him. Ironically, a life insurance salesman had come to their tiny apartment just two weeks before his accident. He had laughed and said, "Oh, Viv, why do you want to worry your head about things like that? Insurance is for old folks."

Duncan had taken her to Europe for their honeymoon, and it had been her first real taste of luxury. He had been gentle and sweet to her, indulging her every whim. She bought Dior and Chanel originals, and went wild over Yves St. Laurent. He was still potent then, and she submitted to his embraces gracefully, with pretended enthusiasm. She respected his intelligence, and was even fond of him in a way.

She wandered out on the large flagstone terrace overlooking the swimming pool, sipping her drink. Duncan had been astonished when she mentioned something about getting back to work; he had just assumed she would want to stay home. It had taken a good deal of adroit talking on her part; she had told him it would just be temporary, until they could find someone suitable to replace her, that she'd just work part-time, and he had been lulled into agreement. Oh, at first she had interviewed some applicants, even hired a few that she was sure wouldn't work out, but that had stopped a long time ago. She had admired Duncan's brain and she picked it gently but thoroughly; it wasn't too long before she knew every facet of the company as well as he did.

She shopped around quietly on her own for a good business and tax consultant, and it took her six months before she found Alex Dunbar. He was slightly on the seedy side, but that was exactly what she wanted. She started siphoning off stock dividends, in a small way at first, and setting up dummy corporations. The oil fields in Mexico and South America were also juggled, and some of them were making enormous profits that didn't show up on the tax reports or corporation statements. She was careful to send Dwight to check on only the oil fields that were still being run legitimately. Everything looked legal and aboveboard on the surface, as long as there wasn't a thorough examination.

But why should there be? Keith Oil Company had been in business almost fifty years, with a reputation of absolute honesty and integrity. She had a finger on every pulse-beat of every phase of the operation, and it had been running like well-greased machinery since she had started manipulating.

Duncan was seventy-five now, and not quite as sharp as he used to be. It was easy for her to make suggestions, even convincing him that they were his own ideas. He was the titular head of the company, but she made all the decisions. At the board meetings, it was Duncan's voice the stockholders heard, but the words were Vivian's.

She had hoped that Dwight and Nancy would reconcile, but this Foster girl seemed to have thrown a monkey-wrench into her plans. Well, she had worked too long and too hard for anyone to upset the applecart now; not Dwight, not Scott, and not Jan. They were all just sitting around waiting for their father to die so they could divide up the loot, no matter how much they pretended they loved him—well, not Dwight, maybe, but the other two. By God, they were going to have one hell of a fight on their hands; she'd give them a modest block of stock each, and that was it.

She heard Duncan stirring in the house, and decided to have one more Bloody Mary before she started preparations for the inevitable Family Sunday Dinner.

Pam finished the dips, put them in the refrigerator, and checked the kitchen. Satisfied it was spotless, she went in the living room and filled the huge brandy snifter on the coffee table with several different brands of cigarettes. She checked her watch, and saw that she had a good hour to get dressed.

Kathy had called early this afternoon, saying she was bringing Dwight. Pam sat down at her dressing table and turned the switch on the large makeup mirror, studying herself. Her eyes were a little too small, the nose a little too aquiline, the upper lip not quite full enough, but her overall coloring minimized these defects. She worked on her tan constantly, since without it she considered herself rather pasty and uninteresting. In ten years' time, her skin would probably look like leather—but in ten years' time she could be dead, too.

Her body was flawless, though; high, firm, globular breasts, a tiny waist gently swelling out to small rounded hips. She would never run to fat, she observed with satisfaction. Her legs were especially good, she thought, and showed them off at every opportunity. She wore shorts as often as possible, and decided to wear them today. Finished with this clinically detached appraisal of herself, she began the long, tedious job of applying makeup so it would appear she wasn't wearing any.

She'd been right about Kathy, she thought, massaging the turtle oil gently into her skin. The girl could be a definite threat to her. She was not only beautiful—creamy magnolia skin, a magnificent mane of auburn hair and a perfect figure, although a bit over-abundant, to Pam's taste—she was also smart. She hadn't made one remark about Dwight's marital status, and Pam couldn't figure it out.

She had told Kathy that Dwight was married to find out if she was the kind of girl who would date married men, and she had seemed genuinely shocked at the news. Pam had been curious about her reaction when she found out the truth, but she had gotten none. Kathy was a cool customer, all right, she thought, starting with the translucent eye shadow. Only in town a couple of weeks, and she'd snagged Dwight. It wouldn't be too long before she latched on to Jack Wentworth, if she hadn't already. Not that Pam wanted either one of them, really, although she felt possessive about Jack. She just didn't want anyone else to have two of the most eligible men in town.

She had decided when she first saw Kathy that they'd either have to be friends or enemies, as Kathy's flamboyant beauty wasn't something one could just ignore. She wondered how she'd fit in at the Country Club; actually, it had been an impulsive act on her part to ask her on such short acquaintance. She weighed the pros and cons; Kathy was older than she, which was definitely to Pam's advantage. She was sexier looking, possibly, to a certain type of man; but then she knew absolutely nothing about sports, which Pam considered a plus on her side. She peered at herself critically, considered the odds, and was sure they were in her favor. She decided to make Kathy her friend.

If anyone had told her she was an out-and-out snob, she would have reacted with honest astonishment. She lived by her own code of standards; certain people were acceptable and others were not; certain people you associated with, and others you did not.

She started applying her pale, almost colorless lipgloss, and wondered whether Vivian knew about Dwight and Kathy. On impulse, she reached for the phone, about to ask the Keiths over for a drink, then checked herself. No, that would be too obvious; better wait and see what developed. She finished her makeup, and decided to take another pep pill; she had taken one when she first got up, but she wanted to be at her best today.

She got up and rummaged around in her dresser until she found the aspirin bottle. She giggled slightly; it would be awful if she got drunk sometime, and got the real aspirin bottle in the bathroom cabinet mixed up with this one. Suppose someone really wanted an aspirin? They'd sure be in for a surprise. But she'd never be so careless. She opened the bottle, shook the pills out in her hand—and could scarcely believe her eyes. Could her supply have gotten so low this fast? This morning, she'd been so groggy, she hadn't noticed. She popped a pill in her mouth, and counted what was left. She really must cut down, she thought. In the meantime, though, she'd have to get to work early tomorrow, in order to stock up. Monday morning was the day the salesmen came around with their pitches for orders. They almost always left her a few extra samples. . . .

Kathy staggered into the apartment with the last of the unpacked cardboard boxes in her arms. She had awakened late, gulped down two glasses of tomato juice, then remembered about the rabies certificate. Trying to rummage around in those boxes in the garage was next to impossible; old love letters, birthday cards, travel posters, worn-out ball point pens, out-of-date calendars; you name it, she had it.

She dumped the first box out on the living room floor, sat down cross-legged, and started tossing junk in the empty box. God, she was a lousy packer; pictures taken in night-clubs with men she didn't even remember, recipes she'd clipped out of the Sunday *Times*, newspaper clippings about her when she was a starlet. She envied people who packed and moved neatly—she always started out all right, labelling boxes of linen, dishes, silverware, pots and pans; but there was always a hopeless hodgepodge of leftover miscellaneous which the movers had to pack. She worked methodically, making small piles of clippings and pictures on the couch; she decided against saving the recipes, some of which were ten years old, yellowed and frayed around the edges.

She had called Pam earlier to get her address.

"Oh fine, I'm so glad you're coming over!" Pam sounded pleased, "Is Dwight coming with you?"

"Yes, he said he'd love to." She waited for a response, but evidently Pam was waiting for more information.

"Great. Around five okay with you?" She sounded slightly less enthusiastic.

"I'm not sure, exactly. Dwight had something to do today. I'll call you as soon as he gets here, though."

"What did he have to do? Did he. . . ."Pam cut herself off abruptly.

"He told me, but it slipped my mind. Did he what, Pam?" Kathy said sweetly, knowing perfectly well what she had started to say.

"I meant, did you and he have a good time last night?" she answered hastily.

"Oh sure. We went to the Rainbow Angling Club and walked around the lake before dinner. Pam, I really have to go now, there's someone at the door. See you later." She hung up quickly. The "someone" was Topsy scratching to get in, but she didn't intend to get into a long discussion about Dwight. She was satisfied that Pam's curiosity was aroused, and intended to keep it that way. If she wanted to play cat-and-mouse, Kathy was no novice in that field; she'd had a long apprenticeship in Hollywood.

She finished the first box and dumped out the second. Topsy watched her for a while, her head cocked to one side, then decided this was some new kind of game, and started jumping around playfully among the debris. Kathy slapped her little bottom, which she seldom did, and was rewarded with a hurt, indignant snort, after which the dog went in the bedroom and sulked.

Kathy rummaged through the things on the floor, and couldn't find the thick blue envelope with Topsy's papers and rabies certificate. Undoubtedly it would be in the last box she went through, which was usually the way.

She picked up another night club photo in its heavy white folder embossed with gold, and flipped it open casually. It was a picture of Bruce and herself taken at Scandia's that she'd almost forgotten about, it seemed so long ago. She sat there staring at it for a long time, the tears welling up in her eyes, remembering. He was the most incredibly handsome man she had ever seen in her life, with thick black wavy hair, a touch of gray at the temples, heavy long lashes that were almost indecent for a man, startling blue eyes, a sensuous mouth.

The first time he walked in the agency, her first reaction was, "This can't be for real" then, "He's got to be an actor from New York, and terribly conceited." Even his name sounded actorish; Bruce Kennedy.

"Hello," he said in a deep masculine voice. "I'm Bruce Kennedy, I have an appointment with Mr. Logan."

"Oh," she said, or something equally inane, and rang Pete Logan on the intercom.

Logan came bursting out of his office with enthusiasm, and slapped Bruce on the back with affection. "My God, am I glad you're here! Look, it's almost lunchtime and I'm starving; why don't we go to Frascati's and discuss the details there? Want to go with us, Kathy?" Both men stood there looking at her.

For some unaccountable reason, she felt nervous. "I'd like to, but I can't. I already have a luncheon date."

She swore at herself silently after they left. Why had she said that? She didn't have a luncheon date. She knew she didn't want to get tangled up with any more actors; but then she wasn't absolutely sure he was an actor. She walked down the hall to Logan's secretary's office. Maude had been with him for over fifteen years, and if anyone could tell her who Bruce Kennedy was, she could. "You want to have lunch with me?" she asked.

Maude looked up at her in surprise. "Kathy, you know perfectly well I never go out to lunch when Mr. Logan's out." She pulled a paper bag out of her desk drawer, and grinned. "Oh, I get it. You want the lowdown on Kennedy. Tell me, is he still as beautiful as ever?"

"Am I really as transparent as all that?" Kathy asked ruefully.

Maude didn't say anything for a moment as she took the sandwich out of the bag, and busied herself unwrapping it. "Okay, Kathy, I'm going to give it to you straight. I met Bruce Kennedy about three years ago when we tried to steal him from another agency, but it didn't take. This time it did. If the deal gels, and I'm sure it will, he'll be working out of the New York office, but he'll spend about half his time out here. He is very much married, very much Catholic, and has three children." She got up, poured herself a cup of coffee from the percolator she kept constantly going on top of the filing cabinet. "Want some?" she said, turning to Kathy.

She shook her head. "No, thanks."

Maude sat down again, started to take a bite of her sandwich, then decided against it. She put it down, looked at Kathy, and took a deep breath. "Now I'm going to give you some advice which I'm sure you'll resent. You can take it or leave it, and I'm pretty sure you'll leave it. Oh, I know you think I'm a middle-aged old maid who doesn't know anything, but I've seen the way you're heading, Kathy, and it isn't good. I'm the one who has to transform those fifty-dollar handouts from Mr. Logan into a couple of twenty-five-dollar customer lunch vouchers for the books. Maybe it hasn't gotten through to you yet—you're only twenty-two and a nice kid—but you're not *always* going to be twenty-two. You've got everything going for you, but you just don't realize it. I know you're not going to take my advice, but at least think about it. One night stands are bad enough, but you get mixed up with Bruce Kennedy, and you've had it. Now, I've said all I'm going to, so I'll get off my soapbox." Maude picked up her sandwich and took a bite. "Go on out to lunch, kid. Try to remember what I said, and good luck."

Kathy thought about Maude with affection, although at the time, she had deeply resented her. She had taken it for granted that any financial transactions were strictly between Logan and herself, and could still remember her cheeks burning with embarrassment and humiliation as Maude told her otherwise. For the first time in her life, she began to feel slightly cheap, and she didn't like it.

That night she stayed home, and decided to evaluate what Maude had said. She glanced around the large, expensively furnished gold and white living room, walked over and pulled the drapes that opened onto the small terrace overlooking the glittering lights of the city. True, she wouldn't stay twenty-two forever, but she had a long way to go before she hit thirty, and forty she couldn't possibly imagine. Granted, her life hadn't turned out exactly as she imagined it would, but she really wasn't dissatisfied, particularly in comparison to most of the girls she had gone to school with.

She ran into some of her old friends at times, and occasionally had lunch with them. It was always a mistake. My God, they were the same age as she was, but they seemed more like settled-down matrons! Their conversation was completely alien to her; the sale on pork chops at Von's, the new furniture polish that was the "best ever," the relative merits of different brands of disposable diapers. After a while, the lunches stopped—they really had nothing in common any more.

Kathy had wanted a child desperately when she first married Fred, but now she was awfully glad she hadn't. "Ties you down too much," he had said. No matter how drunk he was, or how passionate, he always made sure her diaphragm was in before making love to her.

No, having a baby by Fred would have been a terrible mistake; he would have been a rotten father. Her period had been almost a week late once. He had been furious when she told him about it, and stormed out of the apartment. When he came back a few hours later, he forced her to drink quantities of gin and tonic until she was dizzy and nauseated. He made her sit in a hot bath for what seemed like an eternity, as the sweat poured down her face and stung her eyes. Her heart pounded heavily and slowly from the gin and the heat; she watched her skin turn the color of a well-cooked lobster as Fred leaned against the basin, hurling scathing insults at her.

"You're nothing but a two-bit whore, you bitch, and don't think you're going to foist some other guy's bastard brat on me! You've been flipping your ass all over the studio, and don't tell me any different. I won't ask you who the father is, you probably don't even know. No, stay in there, bitch!" He reached over and shoved her back down as she struggled weakly to get out of the tub, and turned on more hot water. "You'll get out when I say you can." His mood changed suddenly, and his voice became icy cold and calm. Almost conversationally, he asked her, "Tell me, Kathy, how many men have you been screwing around with while I've been on location? Five? Ten? Fifty? Or maybe you've lost count. I hope you picked a few who could help you, like a casting director or two, and a couple of good cameramen; you know, your left profile isn't nearly as good as your right. Or did you just settle for grips and extras?"

She had bitten her lip and kept silent; in spite of her dizziness and the steaming hot water, a chilling fear shot through her.

"I asked you a question, bitch; answer me!" His voice continued to drone in her ears, but it seemed to be coming from a distance now. "How many? Were they any good? *How many?* You must have some idea. Answer me!" He reached down and slapped her viciously, and her cheek stung with the pain.

"None," she whispered. "Fred, please let me get out, I think I'm going to faint. . ." The next thing she knew she was in bed, with Fred putting cold washcloths on her forehead.

"Well, that was a dumb trick," he muttered angrily, seeing her eyelids flutter open. He picked up a small box from the bedside table. "Lift your ass." She did as she was told, terrified, and he shoved two pillows under her hips. "Now spread your legs."

Her eyes widened in alarm. "My God, Fred, not now, please!" she moaned.

He looked at her with disgust, opened the box and took out a small pellet. "Don't worry—right now you're about as appealing as a dead mackerel. Now relax, I have to shove this all the way in."

"What is it?" she managed to ask. She was completely exhausted, but the terror returned. What further torture did he intend to put her through?

"It's something to make you start your period, and I had one hell of a time getting it without a prescription, so do what you're told."

"But what is it?" she asked again. "Please, Fred, don't hurt me any more."

"You should have thought of that before you went and got yourself pregnant," he sneered, and glanced at the box. "It's called 'Amniotin Pessarys.'" He spread the lips of her vagina and pushed it in as far as he could with his fingers, then flipped the box over, reading. "It's made out of pregnant mares' urine, and a bunch of other stuff."

Kathy shuddered, but was too tired to protest.

He stood up and looked at her critically, then put another pillow under her. "Put your knees up. There." He pressed down hard on her stomach with the palm of his left hand and put his middle finger inside her again, shoving the pellet in even deeper. Satisfied at last, he straightened up again. "You've got to stay in that position all night. Turn over on your side and the stuff'll run out before it has a chance to work." He went in the living room, came back with two large sofa pillows and propped them up on both sides of her. "Now go to sleep." He went out to the kitchen and she could hear him fixing a drink.

She lay there uncomfortably, acutely aware of the ludicrous posture she was in, wondering just how long before this magic pellet would start working.

Fred came back in shortly, wheeling the portable TV, his drink balanced on top. "Want to watch television for a while?" he said magnanimously. She barely had the strength to shake her head in reply.

She woke sometime towards dawn with a dull throbbing ache deep in her abdomen. There was snow on the television screen, and Fred was passed out in the chair, snoring, a half-empty glass on the table. Her legs felt cramped and uncomfortable, and she tried to shift them slightly. The sharp pain hit her suddenly, and she bit her lip to keep from crying out. She lay there as long as possible until the agony became almost unbearable, then quietly eased herself out of bed. She could feel the slime from the melted pessary begin to ooze down her legs as she stood up. She was doubled over with cramps, but she forced herself to walk slowly to the bathroom, careful not to awaken Fred. She eased the door shut and sat down on the toilet, arms tightly clasped around her knees as she urinated profusely. She sat there for some time, waiting until the pain eased slightly. When she saw the first faint trace of blood on the toilet paper, her feeling was of overwhelming relief that she wouldn't be forced to go through another night like this.

Fred was delighted, of course. He had rushed out and bought her the biggest box of Kotex he could find, two boxes of Midol and a five-pound box of candy. Then he went off for the weekend on a fishing trip, leaving her with her cramps and her thoughts. She should have left him then, of course. But, young and foolish as she was, she kept trying, and it wasn't until two months later that she finally saw the gynecologist.

She shivered slightly; the terrace was chilly. She wandered back in the living room and lit a cigarette. No, having a baby would have been a bad mistake. What would she have done with it? Nursery school while she was at work, baby sitter while she was out with clients? That was no life for a child. Later on, if she remarried, would be time enough to think about having children.

Her life was happy enough right now; she had a lovely apartment, an interesting job, lots of dates. If she got "little gifts" now and then, that was just so much icing on the cake. Other girls were doing the same thing she was doing, and if it paid off better for her, it just meant she was that much smarter. If a vague feeling of emptiness and drifting occurred to her occasionally, so what? Nobody could be happy all the time. No, Maude meant well, but she was just old fashioned. Thus rationalizing, she had gone to bed and slept soundly.

Bruce had been with the agency for several weeks, and Kathy had made absolutely no progress. She kicked herself mentally every day for not accepting that first luncheon invitation, even though it had come from Logan; no more had been forthcoming from Bruce. He had asked her to have coffee with him several times, but then he had asked every other girl in the agency, too, including Maude. Especially Maude, when you came right down to it, but they had business to discuss.

Kathy had always prided herself on being glib, witty, quick on the uptake. When she was around Bruce, however, her mind became a blank, and she answered him in mono-syllables. She felt like a complete and utter fool, and was sure he thought she was mentally deficient. She thought of all kinds of bright and clever things to say to him when she was alone, but they whirled away somewhere the moment he spoke to her.

Occasionally he dictated a memo to her, sitting casually on the edge of her desk. All the other men in the agency dictated memos to her, too, but they generally stood behind her and found some opportunity to touch her. Bruce was neither a toucher, a feeler nor a pincher, and this indifference made her feel more unsure of herself than ever.

When he finally did ask her out, it happened so spon-taneously that she didn't have time to get flustered or nervous. She had literally bumped into him coming out of Logan's office late one afternoon, and he had grabbed her arms to steady her.

"Hey, slow down. You want to get where you're going in one piece, don't you?" he grinned down at her. "Look, I'm bushed; how about having a drink with me after work?"

She smiled back. "I thought you'd never ask." Well, that was certainly a glib, witty acceptance. At least she didn't say she had a date but she'd break it. That would have been too corny. She did, though, with a feature writer from the *Hollywood Reporter*, for dinner and an opening he had to cover; but she'd worry about that tomorrow. She freshened her makeup carefully in the ladies' room, and brushed her hair until it shone. Satisfied at last, she went to meet Bruce in the lobby.

They settled in a dark corner of Frascati's and ordered cocktails. Kathy was definitely more at ease in a cocktail lounge as they exchanged light conversation; then he started in on a long dissertation about last night's Dodgers' game, and she realized she wasn't getting any farther with him than she had in the coffee shop. Bruce was pleasant, courteous and casual, and that was all. She didn't know what she had expected, exactly; certainly not playing "kneezies" under the table, but definitely not a lecture on baseball.

He broke off what he was saying. "You don't talk much, do you?"

She looked at him uncomfortably, then smiled. "Most men I go out with say I talk *too* much. I'm also supposed to be a pretty good listener, even if what I'm listening to isn't very interesting." Oh, good God, why had she said that? Well, she had, and there was no way to wriggle out of it now. "I didn't mean you, of course," she said lamely.

"Are you bored?"

"No."

"Is something the matter?"

"Do you really want to know?"

"I really want to know."

"I don't understand you. Most men fall into one category or another, but I can't figure you out, and it makes me nervous. And I hate baseball."

"Why didn't you tell me you hate baseball?"

"You didn't ask me."

"Why do you hate baseball?"

"Because when I was in high school I went with the captain of the baseball team. Every afternoon I had to watch the team practice. I read the sports section of the paper, *Sports Illustrated*, and learned all about the famous players just to impress him. One day I decided it wasn't worth it, and just stopped cluttering up my mind with a bunch of useless trivia that I wasn't interested in, anyway. To me, a bunch of men dressed up in knickers who hit a ball with a club, then run around in a square. . ."

"Diamond," he corrected her.

"Diamond, just to get back where they started from, is perfectly ridiculous. I don't understand it."

"Well, listen to that, the girl can talk," Bruce said, and leaned over to kiss her cheek.

"That, I understand."

"I don't suppose you like football either."

"It's worse."

"Why is it worse?"

"Because it's more bloodthirsty, and they get hurt a lot more. Bruce, please don't look at me like I'm some kind of a nut, everybody's entitled to their own opinion. I know a lot of people say that watching violence gets rid of tension and hostility, but I don't believe that. Besides, I don't happen to have any hostility. And even if I did, I'm sure that watching a bunch of grown-up sweaty men tackling each other wouldn't do a thing for me. I think that women who get up and yell and scream at games are disgusting and unfeminine. I also think they're slightly unbalanced and sadistic. Don't even ask me about prizefights—they make me sick."

He looked at her with amusement, his deep blue eyes twinkling. "You must be awfully popular with athletes," he said teasingly.

"Would it surprise you if I said I was?"

"Definitely."

"Well, I am; after all, they're human beings. Oh sure,

they like the adulation and the women fawning all over them sometimes, but it wears pretty thin after a while. Some of my best friends are ball players, but we very seldom discuss sports. I kind of think they like to get away from it for a while. A few of them, of course, are conceited as hell, but there are always a couple of bad apples in every barrel. I don't like to see anyone making a fuss over a celebrity—it offends me for some reason. It usually seems so insincere. Did you say I didn't talk much?''

''I've changed my mind.''

''Is that good or bad?''

''I'll let you know.''

''I still don't understand you.''

''What don't you understand?''

''I thought you'd be terribly egotistical, but you're not. You let me go on and on, and you actually looked like you were interested in what I was saying. I mean, really interested in *me*, not just what I looked like. And you haven't tried to hand me a line; like, 'my wife doesn't understand me,' or 'she understands me too well,' or any of the other variations. You should hear some of them.''

''You can see through a line?''

''I think so.''

''And you don't think I've been handing you a line?''

''Not unless it's some new kind I've never heard of. You confuse me.''

''Is that good or bad?''

''I'll let you know.''

He signalled the waiter for the bill. Kathy looked at her watch; it was 8:15. She hated the evening to end, but there wasn't much she could do about it.

He swung the car into the traffic on Sunset and headed back toward the office where she'd left her car. She was quiet as he drove, wondering if he'd kiss her goodnight. ''Bruce, you passed the office.''

He looked at her, surprised. "You don't want to go home now, do you? I thought we'd have dinner at Santa Ynez. It's nice at the beach this time of year." Without waiting for an answer, he turned on the radio, reached over and pulled her closer to him. He draped his arm casually around her shoulder and brushed his lips against her hair. It felt right, and good; she snuggled against him, completely relaxed and content.

The note was slid halfway under the door as she fumbled for her keys. Picking it up carelessly, she stuffed it in her purse, slammed the door after her and walked to the mirror. Kathy studied herself ruthlessly; was she losing her looks, or appeal, or what? The skin was glowing and flushed, the eyes clear and sparkling with anger. There wasn't a hint of a wrinkle, and the little pinched white lines around the corners of her mouth would disappear by morning.

Dinner had been relaxed and easy; for the first time in her life she had actually looked forward eagerly to going to bed with a man, but all that happened was that he drove her back to her car, kissed her casually, and told her to drive home carefully. She burned with frustration and resentment as she fished the note out of her purse; it was from the *Hollywood Reporter* man:

"Kathy, my sweet; Kept calling you until ten, then I thought I'd drop you a note. Needless to say, I didn't ring the bell, as I didn't want to interrupt anything important, and I'm *sure* it must have been important for you to miss a Terrence Harvey opening. A phone call from you would have been appreciated so I could have made other plans. Incidentally, don't call me, I'll call you."

She crumpled the note into a ball and threw it on the floor; that fat, pompous, pot-bellied son of a bitch, who did he think he was, writing to her like that? The phone rang shrilly;

probably the ass-bastard checking to see if she was home yet. "Yes?" she said icily.

"Just wanted to know if you got home all right." Bruce's voice was warm and deep. "And since it's Saturday, how about the races today?"

When she hung up, she hugged herself with delight and looked in the mirror again. She felt like a teenager, completely young and completely vulnerable. . . .

Several weeks went by, and although they were together almost every night, Bruce hadn't made the slightest attempt to go to bed with her. He took her to small, charming, off-beat restaurants, and apparently didn't have any concern about being seen in the right places by the right people. Kathy knew he wanted her, and she knew his reputation with other women; but for some reason unknown to her, he held back.

Curiously enough, although she wanted him more than she had ever wanted any man in her life, she was content to wait. Deep down, she knew that eventually going to bed with him was inevitable; but for the present, just being with him was enough.

He stimulated her mind, and it wasn't long before she realized that with infinite patience he was guiding her, leading her into forming and expressing opinions of her own. She began to think of the person she was before she met Bruce—a sort of stereotype "yes" girl, who said what men wanted her to say, thought what men wanted her to think, a glorified caterer to that superior being, MAN.

She still felt extremely inferior to Bruce mentally, and probably always would, but his genuine interest in her thoughts and ideas exhilarated her. Before she met him, her opinions had usually seemed to her too inconsequential to inject into a conversation, but he coaxed her into laying them out for discussion, expounding, enlarging, and following them through to their logical conclusion. Sometimes he played the devil's advocate; he began to teach her the value of taking a subject and examining all its sides and slants and points of view, and her mind reacted eagerly to this mental stimulus.

Bruce had been unusually quiet this evening, and Kathy had fallen in with his mood. It was a hot sultry August night, and they were sipping brandy on the terrace when he told her, "I'm leaving for New York on Tuesday." His voice was deliberately light, and there was a peculiar expression in his eyes.

She felt her stomach lurch, but she looked at him unblinkingly. The silence was heavy between them until slowly, against her will, the tears welled up in her eyes and spilled down her cheeks.

"How long will you be gone?" She tried to match his tone, but her voice sounded strange.

"Four months, maybe a little longer—I'm not sure."

Four months! She looked at him, shocked, not trusting herself to speak. Time had stretched out endlessly before them, and now it was almost gone! Her mind spun crazily. Oh God, he must have known about it before now—there were arrangements to be made, plane tickets to be taken care of. Why had he waited until now to tell her? Tuesday, he was leaving *Tuesday*, and it was Friday now. All the contentment, the willingness to wait was gone now, and the violence of her longing frightened her. "Bruce, sleep with me tonight," she whispered, almost humbly.

He was silent for a long time before answering. "You know there's no future in it, Kitten."

Her eyes widened, stunned. Here she was, Kathy Foster, who had never asked a man for anything in her life, begging him to go to bed with her, and he might as well have slapped her in the face. All of a sudden something clicked in her mind and she was angry, more angry than she had ever been in her life, and she wanted to hurt him as much as he had hurt her.

"For God's sake, who's asking you for any future?" She spit the words out at him, her voice loaded with venom. "Just what is this pious, sanctimonious attitude, anyway? I'm not asking you for any gilt-edged certificate that guarantees you'll service me whenever you're in town. I know you're married and you're Catholic, and I also know that you've fucked around plenty. Those girls in the office don't just talk about planting petunias, you know, and they've certainly had a lot to say about you! So just what in the hell is it? I've been laid before, by more men than I care to remember; in fact, I think I've even lost count. So what's one hump in the hay, more or less?" Her voice resounded in her ears, shrill and harsh, her words coarse and vulgar, and her anger dissipated as quickly as it came. She leaned back, exhausted and spent, disgusted and ashamed at her outburst.

Bruce's face was hidden by the shadows on the terrace, and her hands were shaking as she lit a cigarette.

"Are you quite through?" he asked quietly. She nodded her head, unable to speak. "All right, then listen to me, and listen carefully, because I don't want to have to say this twice. Sure, I've played around, certainly a helluva lot more than you've heard about. I'm away from home a good deal of the time, and the opportunity is always there. It's in every bar, every office, any streetcorner; I don't even have to look for it. I have normal sexual needs and I take care of them; but that has nothing to do with you and is no concern of yours. As far as office gossip is concerned, you don't have any corner on the market. Men talk just as much, if not more than women, so I guess you and I have pretty much the same reputation in the 'round heels' department. Are you honestly so naive that you don't know everybody in the agency is sure we're sleeping together?"

Kathy felt the blood coursing to her cheeks and was thankful for the darkness.

"But what you've done has nothing to do with me and is none of my business," he continued. "At the risk of sounding trite, if you and I went to bed, it wouldn't be just a one-night stand, or another 'hump in the hay,' as you so colorfully put it; you know it and I know it. I'm not saying I'm in love with you; I've been with prettier women and smarter women, and certainly more sophisticated women. I've used them and enjoyed them, gotten bored with them and gotten rid of them. But you've got something for me that none of the rest of them had. I can't see myself getting bored with you, but I can easily see myself getting possessive; and I haven't the right to do that. I wouldn't want you sleeping around with anyone else, for instance, yet I don't have the right to ask you not to. You know I'll never get a divorce, so any way you look at it, you'd be getting the dirty end of the stick."

"Bruce," she said wearily, "do you have to talk so much? I appreciate what you're trying to say, I really do. But you're leaving Tuesday, and right now that's all I can think about. And I don't *want* to think about it, I don't want to think at all, I just want to *feel*. So please, darling, don't sit there being analytical, dissecting the pros and cons of whether we should or whether we shouldn't. We have so little time."

"I guess I really can't argue with that." He stood up and took her gently in his arms.

He held her for a long time, until Kathy began to tremble slightly. He cupped her face in his hand, looking down at her in the dim light. "You're sure?" Not trusting her voice, instead of answering, she buried her head against his chest, clinging to him. He released her slowly, still holding her hand, and led her to the bedroom. She followed meekly, slightly dazed that it was finally happening. He switched on the amber bedside lamp and turned as she started taking off her earrings. "No," he said softly, "let me do it." He came to her quickly and held her, his mouth inches from hers as his hands slid slowly down and pulled her tight against him. Her lips were moist and quivering as his mouth closed on hers, lightly at first, his tongue gently exploring and caressing. She felt weak and giddy, barely aware of him taking off her earrings, ruffling her long auburn hair until it fell around her shoulders. He reached for her zipper and pulled it down slowly, expertly, his mouth still glued to hers.

She stepped out of her dress and he led her to the bed. He was in no hurry, and she felt a delicious awareness of her body, an awakened sensuality in every part of her his hands touched. He undid her bra and let it fall to the floor, cupping her breasts as he buried his face in the hollow between them. Her nostrils breathed in the clean warm male smell of his body, her senses roused to fever pitch. He pulled down her panties inch by inch, his hands caressing the silky softness of her thighs.

She was trembling now, barely able to stand, and the slow warm pulsing between her legs grew into a hot throbbing living thing, the very core of her being an aching center of quivering, sensitive flesh. As if sensing her need, his lips pressed against her breasts, his tongue darting hotly and inquisitively. A low moan escaped her, and he stood up quickly and stripped off his clothes.

Gently, as though she were a child, he picked her up and laid her on the bed. He tilted the lamp shade so the soft light played across the entire length of her body. "Oh Bruce, I love you so much," her voice was barely above a whisper. He kissed her softly, leaning on one elbow as his hand caressed her slowly, sensually. He traced his fingers lightly up and down the inside of her thighs, scarcely touching the heated furnace between her legs, and her body responded, reaching up to him spasmodically. Finally, she couldn't stand it any longer. "Bruce, please . . . I want you so much."

The corners of his mouth quirked upward in a slight smile.

"Take it easy, Kitten, we've got all night. I'll fuck you, don't worry." His thumb pressed gently on her clitoris as his fingers played with her soft tender flesh, gradually spreading her legs apart. She was hot and moist as his fingers slowly and expertly worked their way deep inside her, caressing and exploring. With the shock of the first slight spasm, her muscles closed around him tightly; his thumb pressed harder and his fingers probed deeper as she writhed on the bed. She tried to pull away, but he held her tightly. "Go ahead and come," his voice was deeper now, "I want to feel you come this way."

The complete spasm of climax rushed upon her like a tidal wave crashing against the rocks, as she moaned and thrashed wildly. Bruce held her until the waves gradually subsided and the shuddering tremors left her body.

"You know, I never really had an orgasm before," Kathy finally said in a small voice, almost primly.

"So I gathered." His voice sounded amused.

"But you didn't."

"Don't worry, I will. You will again, too." He kissed her on the tip of her nose, and sprang out of bed lightly.

She lay there, feeling relaxed and fulfilled, as she listened to the sounds coming from the kitchen. He came back with two snifters of brandy, handed her one, and stretched out on the bed again. "Happy?" he asked, lighting a cigarette and handing it to her.

"You know I am." She smiled at him and sat up to sip her brandy. "You know, I've never heard you use that word before."

"What word? Oh, you mean 'fuck'? Come to think of it, I've never heard you throw around the language you used tonight, either. Tell me, Kitten, just how many longshoremen have there been in your deep, dark past?" He grinned up at her, and she stuck her tongue out at him. "Seriously though, it all depends on how you look at it and how you use it. I don't toss it around in public like Logan does, for instance, and I certainly don't think it has any place in polite social chit-chat; I prefer to think my vocabulary isn't quite that limited. Besides, it loses its punch when you use it all the time. It can be a very dirty word or a very, very nice word. There's a helluva lot of difference between someone saying 'fuck you' in anger, and you looking down at me, smiling sweetly and saying 'fuck me,' which I'm hoping you'll do as soon as you finish your cigarette."

In answer, she crushed out her cigarette and lay down beside him again, whispering the words. He made love to her again, slowly and rhythmically at first, then savagely ripping into her as her nails raked his back and her legs tightened around him. They came together with an explosive orgasm that left them both exhausted and spent. She fell asleep in his arms almost immediately. . . .

The shrill jangling of the phone brought her back to reality, and she looked around at the boxes of litter on the floor.

"Hi!" The boyish voice was filled with enthusiasm, "I just dropped the kids off. You about ready to go over to Pam's?"

"Give me a half-hour, Dwight. I'll hurry."

"You find the rabies certificate?"

She answered, hung up the phone and stared at it distastefully. Oh God, from the sublime to the ridiculous! She looked at Bruce's picture for a long time, then got up slowly and put it in her bedside table drawer. She hurried back to the living room, rummaged around until she found the rabies certificate, threw everything else back in the boxes and stuffed them in the closet.

Chapter 4

"She's a dyke," Pam said casually, returning the wave of the tall, angular blonde walking toward the cocktail lounge.

"She's a *what*?" Kathy took off her sunglasses and looked at Pam, surprised.

Pam peered at her critically. "Better turn over on your stomach or leave those glasses off, you're getting a white line around your eyes." She grinned at her. "Don't look so shocked; I know lesbians aren't exactly a novelty in Hollywood, but we have a few around here, too."

"How do you know she's one?" Kathy watched the blonde disappear inside, mildly curious.

"Oh, you know, there are ways," she said vaguely. "Little mannerisms, things she says. She's not at all interested in clothes or new hair styles, but she'll talk your head off about ERA. She never dates anyone more than a couple of times, although now her mother's trying like mad to marry her off to Carl Meeker."

"To each his own." Kathy shrugged, turning over on her stomach. "But I wouldn't go around badmouthing anyone like that, even if I were sure." She pulled down the shoulder straps on her swim suit and shut her eyes.

It was a hot, lazy Labor Day weekend, and poolside at the Country Club was practically deserted this late in the afternoon. She had seen a lot of Pam in the past few weeks and was grateful to her in many ways. She had introduced her to all the "right" people, was sponsoring her membership in the Club, and had taken her over to the "little dressmaker" who made her uniforms. There were things about Pam that irritated her, though; she couldn't say anything about anyone without knocking them. "Vivian Keith has the most beautiful home I've ever seen, BUT. . .," or "Dr. Sturgess is the greatest doctor in the world, BUT. . .," or "Liz Taylor is still the most gorgeous woman in the world, BUT. . ."

Kathy had called her on it once, laughing to take the sting out of her words. "Pam, can't you ever say anything nice about someone without knocking them in the same breath?"

Pam had looked at her with honest surprise, and she hadn't brought it up again. After all, there must be things *she* did that were just as irritating. Pam never talked about herself, but what the hell—there were a lot of things in her own past that she wasn't particularly anxious to discuss, either.

She had found out a few sketchy facts, though, from Dwight and some of Pam's friends. Her mother had died in childbirth, leaving Pam with her father and eight-year old brother. Pam had been sixteen when her brother had died in some sort of an accident on a hunting trip, and her father had a light stroke soon after, followed by a massive one a few years later. He was in a rest home somewhere in Riverside. Pam had never mentioned any of this, and Kathy had never told her she knew.

Actually, they had very little in common except they both mistrusted most women, were allergic to strawberries, and were exceptionally attractive. We make a good contrast, Kathy thought, dozing, the sun beating warmly against her back.

"Well, did you?" Pam was nudging her leg with her toe.

"Did I what?" Kathy answered, still half-asleep.

"Did you know any lesbians?"

"A few."

"How well?"

Kathy rolled over and lit a cigarette. "If you mean, did I ever sleep with one, no."

"Oh, of course not, that wasn't what I meant at all! Sometimes you say the most outlandish things, Kathy." Pam was sipping a martini.

"Sometimes *you* ask the most outlandish questions. Lord, I must have slept; I didn't even hear you go get a drink."

"I brought one for you, too. No, what I meant was if any of them ever told you why they were so—abnormal."

Kathy looked at her quizzically; this conversation was certainly taking an odd turn. "No, not really. A psychologist I knew tried to explain it to me once, in simple terms; he said it had a lot to do with genes and hormones. If a girl has too many female genes, a man is just too masculine for her, but a masculine woman isn't—and if she has too many male genes, a man is too much like herself. Anyway, that's the general idea I got out of what he told me. I wasn't all that interested in the subject."

"I wonder if they're all born that way."

"Most of them, I guess." Kathy shrugged. "Although I suppose some of them just do it for kicks; I hadn't really thought about it that much. Why all this sudden interest in lesbians?"

"When I was a child I wanted to be a boy," Pam said unexpectedly. "Daddy loved my brother so much, and I wanted to be just like him." She stared at her empty drink, frowning slightly.

Kathy tried to hide her surprise. This was the first time Pam had mentioned her family, and she felt uncomfortable, as though she was intruding on private memories. She had a presentiment that Pam was about to tell her something she'd regret later, and tried to lighten her mood. "Lots of little girls feel like that. I remember once when I was very little, I thought there was something wrong with me because I wasn't a boy. The neighbor kid—Johnny, I think his name was—we were playing in our back yard and he had to go to the bathroom. He pulled his pants down and urinated, then he said, 'Now you do it.' I ran in the house crying; my mother had been watching from the window and she thought I was crying because the little boy exposed himself, but it wasn't that at all. I thought I was deformed because I didn't have a penis. For a long time, every morning I'd run in the bathroom to see if one had started to grow." Kathy shook her head, smiling. "I can laugh about it now, but it was damn serious to me then. Kids get some screwy ideas."

Pam looked at her, but she wasn't laughing; her eyes were troubled. "I did everything I could, Kathy, after Jimmy died, but it just wasn't enough. My mother died when I was born, you know; I never knew her. Daddy and Jimmy and I used to have so much fun together; when I was old enough they used to take me on camping trips with them, and they never let on that I was only a girl, that I was in the way. I always knew Daddy loved Jimmy the best, and I wanted to be just like him. It hit Daddy pretty hard when Jimmy died. Sometimes, I. . ." She stopped abruptly.

"Sometimes what, honey?" Kathy asked gently.

Pam shook her head. "No, forget it. Someday, maybe, I'll tell you all about it. I really don't know what made me start thinking about it at all." She gestured towards her empty glass, smiling slightly. "Martinis in the sun, I guess. Let's go in the bar and have another one."

They gathered up the suntan lotion and towels. Lots of girls worshipped their older brother or their father, or both, Kathy thought; it wasn't so much what Pam said, it was *how* she said it, her tone of voice—something was terribly wrong.

The cool darkness was an abrupt contrast to the glaring sunlight, and it took Kathy several minutes to accustom herself to the change. The bar was almost empty; the club members that weren't out of town for the long hot weekend were home preparing for the night's activities. Saturday night was a big deal in the San Gabriel Valley. In Hollywood it was considered almost gauche to plan a big night on the town—Saturday was for the squares and out-of-towners. Out here, it was "The Night," and given a great deal of careful thought and planning.

Tonight, for instance, there was the outdoor barbecue at the Enwrights'. She was on fairly good terms with Irene now, although they had gotten off on the wrong foot. She had coffee with her occasionally after Irene's appointment with the doctor, and of course, she saw her at the Club. She knew the doctor disapproved of any social contacts with the patients, but after all, what was she supposed to do? She couldn't very well say, "Sorry, Irene, but you're seeing the shrink, so I can't come to your party." Anyway, so far Irene hadn't tried to pump Kathy about how much she knew regarding her case; not that it would have done any good if she had. Her case history had been typed up by some receptionist long since gone, and the notations in her folder were done in the doctor's "squiggles." He had his own peculiar hieroglyphics and try as she might, Kathy could never decipher them.

She knew that Irene had invited her because she'd been going out with Dwight, but this didn't bother her. What did bother her was she knew Irene's express purpose in throwing this party was to show off the new additions to her collection of modern and pop art, and Kathy dreaded this. Her idea of art was Gainsborough, Degas, Cezanne, Matisse; Picasso was way too far out for her, and she wondered how she could possibly manage to fake enthusiasm for a painting of a blown-up beer can or a dish of beef goulash. At least, she could recognize these; the abstracts were completely impossible.

Bruce had taken her to Mexico City once, and they had gone through the Museum of Modern Arts. The main floor was given over almost completely to primitives, which she thought were perfectly awful. He had tried to explain to her the imaginative use of color, the boldness of line, but they still looked like the finger-paintings of a bunch of four-year-olds. The abstracts were on another level, and looked like nothing more than a mess of paint thrown haphazardly at a canvas, then accidentally stepped on or deliberately smeared.

She had reacted violently when Bruce had paused to admire a particularly nauseating mish-mash of color, predominately in shades of orange and purple. "Oh Bruce, how can you call that art? I wouldn't have that thing hanging in my bathroom—*especially* not in my bathroom. It's enough to make you throw up."

He had grinned at her. "Kathy, I'm afraid you'll never be a connoisseur. But at least it got a rise out of you, stirred your emotions; perhaps that's what the artist meant."

"Well, my emotions get stirred when I see a bloody accident on the freeway, but I certainly wouldn't want a reminder of it hanging around," she had retorted.

Oh well, tonight she'd be two-faced and hypocritical; but at least Irene would be happy. She glanced at her watch; there was plenty of time before Dwight picked her up.

She thought about Dwight with mixed emotions. There was something quite touching about his obvious devotion to her. He was thirty-one years old, but he still seemed like a boy. So far, she'd been able to keep him out of her bed, but that couldn't last indefinitely. On the other hand, all these other men she'd thought she'd meet—oh, she met them, all right, but Dwight was always there, constantly at her elbow. Kathy despised an open display of affection, but he was forever pecking her on the cheek, hugging her, holding her hand. No wonder everyone considered her "his girl," even Pam.

Pam came back from the powder room, makeup freshened, eyes bright, her mood considerably lighter. "We'd better leave after this one; I need a nap."

Odd, Kathy thought; Pam could be so down at times, almost sluggish, then a few minutes later she'd be full of vitality again, almost as if she'd been recharged. She shrugged. "I'm in no hurry; to tell you the truth, I'm not exactly looking forward to the Enwrights' party tonight."

"Neither am I." A man's arm dropped casually around Kathy's shoulder. "Buy you two girls a drink? Move over, Pam." Ted Enwright slid down on the stool between them.

"Oh God, Ted," Kathy stammered, "I didn't mean that the way it sounded. You see, I. . ."

"Don't apologize." He grinned at her, white teeth flashing against his deep tan. "I hate pop art, too. This is your first initiation, isn't it? Believe me, Irene'll give you the cook's tour. Another round, Sam."

"Ted, shame on you!" Pam smiled at him coquettishly, "You should be home helping your wife."

"No way!" he stated emphatically. "I'd only be under foot; besides, Irene's a bitch on wheels when she's organizing a party. However, by the time you arrive she'll be calm, cool and collected, the epitome of the perfect hostess, and you'll never know that only an hour before she was a raving, raging maniac."

"Oh Ted, you're always kidding," Pam gushed at him. "Irene's a darling."

Kathy sat quietly sipping her drink, listening while they started discussing his tennis game; she was beginning to feel annoyed. Every time Pam got around a man, her voice changed drastically; her "man bait" voice, Kathy called it. It became girlish and flirtatious, and after a few drinks, almost babyish. Right now, it was downright simpering.

She wondered if Pam could possibly be unaware of this, but it hardly seemed possible. The cloying Southern Belle act irritated her, it was so obvious; yet men didn't see through it, or if they did, it didn't seem to bother them. It wasn't as though she were after any one man in particular—she acted that way with all of them. Yet Kathy was sure she wasn't promiscuous; in fact, she didn't even think she was particularly interested in sex. Bruce would have seen through her immediately, she thought; she could just hear him summing her up: "The personification of a prick-teaser."

The bartender interrupted her train of thought. "Phone call for you, Mr. Enwright."

Ted shook his head and put his finger to his lips. The bartender hung up the phone and came back. "That's the third call, Mr. Enwright."

"Now, you see?" Pam said triumphantly. "Irene does want you home."

"Wrong again. If I showed up on time for one of her parties, she'd drop dead of shock. This way, it gives her a legitimate excuse to bitch and nag me; besides, it really isn't such a bad fault. Irene has everything she wants; a beautiful home that she's filled up with that garbage she calls art, her own bank account, her clubs and her charities—and she has me. And I have my business, my tennis, and my boat. Actually, I'm practically the ideal husband." He leered at Kathy wickedly.

"If you were brave, clean and thrifty, and walked little old ladies across the street," she looked at him candidly, "you'd almost qualify for the Boy Scouts."

"Ouch!" He grinned wryly. "You really know how to hurt a guy, don't you?"

"Not at all," she replied. "I have a very healthy respect for 'forthrightness' and 'honesty'." She emphasized the words. "I'm sure your wife just doesn't understand you."

"Good God, I hope not!" he laughed, "Do this again,

Sam.'' He indicated the three empty glasses.

"Not for me, Ted, thanks,'' she said quickly. "It's going to be a long evening. Coming, Pam?''

"Not right now, honey. I'll keep Ted company for a while.''

The phone rang again, and the bartender looked at Ted inquiringly before answering. Ted shook his head, then changed his mind. "Tell her I came in for a quick one and just left.''

Kathy turned to wave at Ted and Pam from the door, but they were deep in conversation. Pam's nap was evidently forgotten. She thought about Ted as she drove home—he was attractive in a big, craggy sort of way, and likeable enough. She disapproved of the casual way he spoke of Irene, but then, it seemed to be the fashionable thing to do. Lord knows Irene complained about him enough. She wondered what their relationship really was. It was hard to associate Ted in connection with big business; his relaxed and easy manner seemed much more typical of a tennis bum. Yet she knew he was one of the biggest land developers in the Valley. He had made some shrewd investments, and had plunged heavily when others were afraid to take the chance. "The man with the Midas touch,'' Dwight had referred to him. Well, that was a side of him she had yet to see.

Irene hung up the phone, fuming. In the past seven (or was it eight?) years since he'd started this, she should have gotten used to it, but she never had. She was sure he did it deliberately, but it never failed to exasperate her. He seemed to take some sort of peculiar delight in goading her to the point of distraction every time she gave a party. Of course he had been at the Club when she called, but what could she do? Make a fool of herself by arguing with the bartender? Unthinkable. She smoothed her hair, sipped her scotch, and tried to compose herself.

Every time she tried to discuss the matter with him calmly,

they always ended up in a fight. Well, that wasn't quite true; *she* ended up doing the yelling and screaming, while *he* remained calm and relaxed, which infuriated her all the more. When he did show up, always late, his only excuse was, "Don't give so damn many parties."

The slight twinge in her side that had been bothering her for weeks hit her with a suddenness that doubled her over with agony. "Nerves, just nerves," she groaned aloud. She struggled upright, took a deep breath, and downed the rest of her scotch. The pain subsided slowly, but she felt clammy and sticky. She brushed more powder on her face and dusted her cheeks with blusher.

She peered at herself in the mirror—she still looked a little pale, but that wasn't what bothered her; maybe it was something more than just nerves. The past few times she'd picked up men down at the beach had been more painful than pleasurable.

The last one, for instance; he couldn't have been more than twenty-two—tall, blonde, healthy, vigorous. The minute he walked in the Pico Club and sat down a few stools away, she had felt the familiar tingle of anticipation. She had ordered another drink and walked down to the cigarette machine, casually brushing against him on the way. She liked the Pico Club—it was small, dark and dingy, with sawdust on the floor and incredibly bad records on the juke box. It smelled like a mixture of garlic, stale perspiration and rotten fish, but then, it was on the Pike, and everything smelled like that on the Pike. She felt absolutely safe here; she was a different person in a different world.

It had been easy for her to pick him up, but then it usually was for her. The motel had been slightly more complicated; she hadn't minded paying for his drinks in the bar, but paying for the motel room depressed her slightly. His manner in the Pico Club had been eager and attentive; lighting her cigarettes, standing up when she had to go to the john, shyly squeezing her hand. He had actually seemed to enjoy her company, but as soon as they got in her car his attitude changed abruptly. His hand slid up between her legs with practiced assurance as he gave her directions to the motel.

Once inside the room, there had been no preliminaries, no kissing, no tender lovemaking. He had stripped off his clothes quickly, and looked at her, surprised to see that she was still dressed. "Well?"

She stood there awkwardly, then kicked off her shoes and started unbuttoning her blouse. "Here, I'll help you." He undressed her swiftly and threw her on the bed. She hadn't had enough to drink to feel relaxed, and the sharp pain when he plunged inside made her moan and gasp for relief. She tried to twist away from him, but he mistook her actions for passion and redoubled his efforts. She lay there tensely, biting her lip, her mind whirling from one thing to another; the barbecue Saturday night, her last fight with Ted, her next appointment with the doctor. God, would he never finish? There was no pleasure in this for her, only pain, and she hated him for it, and hated herself even more for submitting.

Finally, after what seemed like an eternity, he muttered in her ear, "Get ready, baby, I'm coming." She moved her hips slightly and dug her fingernails into his back mechanically, while his sweat dripped down on her face and between her breasts. The relief when he finished left her weak. She watched him as he got up to light a cigarette.

"You're pretty good, baby. You get down this way often?" he asked her casually, pulling on his Levi's.

"How do you know I don't live around here?" She pulled the sheet over her, feeling tired and soiled. God, what made her do this?

"Oh, come off it, baby. The clothes, the fancy car, sitting in the Pico Club? I know you society broads—always looking for a new thrill." He pulled his T-shirt on. "Look, next time you're down this way, just stop in the Pico Club and ask for Johnny—they'll know where to find me."

"Sure."

They looked at each other for a long moment, and finally she turned her head away. They both knew they'd never see each other again.

After he left, she lay there smoking, as the old familiar feelings came over her. It was almost dark, but there was no hurry. Ted had a meeting and wasn't expected home until all hours. The boy's perspiration had dried upon her body, leaving her salty and sticky. She felt cheap and degraded, but in her own mind, she didn't associate this with guilt. The guilt was Ted's, and only Ted's. Oh God, if only he were some sort of a husband to her—how had they drifted apart, what had happened to them?

The doctor; he was the only one she could really talk to. She wondered if she could get an earlier appointment than her regular time. But then, Kathy might think it odd if she called up, and she was coming to the barbecue Saturday. My God, there had been no way to avoid asking her; the girl had wheedled her way into the middle of their social life—going with Dwight, and joining the Club. She wondered if the doctor confided in her about his patients. Several times she had been on the verge of asking her, but had checked herself, afraid of the answer. All of a sudden, she hated Dr. Carter—after all, all he did was listen to her, he never gave her any advice. Sudden tears came to her eyes and she revelled in self-pity.

She cried steadily, and the tears seemed to give her some relief. She tossed and turned on the bed, smelling the odor of stale sweat and sex, trying not to think of anything, but thoughts kept crowding in on her. They spun in and out of her mind so fast that she could hardly grasp hold of them—Ted, his smiling superiority; Dr. Carter, his smiling indifference; Kathy, her smiling self-assurance; Vivian, her smiling self-satisfaction. Vivian—her mind clung on to her and held; the dirty bitch, she had nothing to be so smug about! Kathy had Dwight under her thumb; Vivian knew it and everybody else knew it. Her thoughts shifted to the barbecue—they would all be there, and she, Irene, would be captain of the boat.

She turned over and lit another cigarette. The pain her her side had eased considerably, but the stench of the bed was unbearable, so she got up quickly and showered. She washed the boy out of her mind as easily as she washed her body. (Johnny? Was that his name?) Except she scrubbed her body harder. She smiled to herself as the hot water rained down on her, thinking about the barbecue again. . . .

The doorbell rang, bringing her back to reality. She looked at the scotch decanter, then decided against it. After all, it was going to be a long evening.

Dwight and Kathy arrived around seven thirty. It had been one of those long, slow, September days, and dusk was still flirting with the lazy sunlight that seemed reluctant to leave. The house looked deceptively small on the outside; set on the side of a hill, the pale yellow accented by the black lacquered door and shutters, the well-manicured lawn, riotous colors of red and yellow hibiscus amidst large feathery green ferns, the aroma of nightblooming jasmine in the air—yes, this house was definitely Irene.

Irene opened the door herself, and greeted them both effusively, with affectionate hugs and light kisses on their cheeks. "Come on in, you two, you're late, practically everyone's here already."

Kathy looked around the living room and was pleasantly surprised; it was tastefully done in shades of avocado, lemon and beige, contemporary furniture, a few conventional paintings on the wall. All in all, it was a comfortable room, not at all what she had expected. The only people there were two men standing by the fireplace in deep conversation.

She looked at Irene dubiously. "Practically everyone's here?"

Irene laughed, "Oh, they're all down on the lower level. Go on down, Dwight, you know everybody. Kathy's never been here before, and I want to show her this level. We'll be down shortly."

Kathy smiled to herself; how like Irene—not "floor," but "level." Then she stopped smiling; Oh God, I guess this is when I get to see her art collection. She suddenly wanted a drink very badly.

Irene showed her the kitchen first; it was large, gleaming and immaculate, with all the newest appliances. Suddenly Kathy felt a twinge of envy when she thought of her small apartment in Monrovia. Then another thought occurred to her—it was immaculate, all right, but where was the food? She had murmured it out loud.

Irene laughed again. "Don't worry, there's a kitchen exactly like this one right under it. See?" She pulled open a small door in the wall. "This is a dumb waiter, but we're doing everything downstairs tonight. Ted thought it was awfully extravagant of me to want to build a house with two kitchens, but he finally went along with it. This way, if we're on one level, we don't have to go all the way to the other one to get something. You want a drink?" She looked at her inquiringly.

"Thanks, I'd love one." Kathy watched her as she opened the liquor cabinet. She was exquisitely groomed, and really looked quite lovely tonight, but underneath her makeup there was a slight pallor, and her movements were nervous and quick. Kathy had noticed this in Irene, sometimes before, sometimes after her sessions with Dr. Carter, but never quite so pronounced as now.

Irene handed her the drink. "Come on, I'll show you the

rest of this level." Kathy took a deep swallow and followed her.

"You like modern art? Some people don't understand it, but then some people don't have good taste. Ted, for instance; he can't stand it—he absolutely forbid me to put any in the living room or his study." She opened a door briefly. Kathy caught a glimpse of dark panelled walls, a mahogany desk, and deep red leather chairs, then the door was closed. She suddenly understood the living room.

Irene chatted incessantly, as they walked down the long hallway lined with pop art, each one worse than the last. She showed Kathy several guest rooms, again with unbelievably ugly paintings on the walls, *objects d'art* that were undescribable, and asked Kathy's opinion on each one. Kathy tried to respond with tact, but Irene didn't seem to be listening, anyway. "This is my bedroom," she said abruptly, and opened another door.

Kathy almost gasped in surprise. The room was something out of the Arabian Nights, or an early Maria Montez movie, with a huge bed raised on a dais, a tufted satin canopy of lavender, with soft, turquoise chiffon drapes. The whole room was done in turquoise and lavender, with gold-leaf furniture, huge gold-leaf mirrors, and large tufted satin cushions. There was a pirate's chest, very old, at the foot of the bed, and Venetian crystal on the dressing table. Kathy knew very little about modern art, but she knew there was none in this room.

"Do you like it?" Irene looked at her, an odd expression in her eyes. "Come," she took her hand and led her in. "Very few people have seen my bedroom. I had it redone three years ago; Ted doesn't like it, of course. But then he was hardly ever in it before, so why should he object?"

"Irene," Kathy stammered, "do you think you should be telling me all these things? I think it's beautiful, I think it's something out of a fairytale, but on the other hand, I can understand why a man might think it's too fancy to sleep in, unless he were a Sultan. Irene, for God's sakes, we shouldn't even be discussing personal things. You know I work for your doctor. . ." She was beginning to get very uncomfortable. "Don't you think we should join the party?"

"In a moment." Irene walked over to the low dressing table and fingered the cut glass crystal perfume bottles. "Do you really like it?" she repeated. "You know, Kathy, sometimes I walk in here late at night and feel as if I'm in a different world, a different century, and all my problems seem to melt away. It's almost as if I'm a different person." All of a sudden she leaned over and grabbed the edge of the dressing table, her knuckles turning white as she gasped for breath.

Kathy hurried to her. "Irene, what is it?" she said anxiously.

"It's nothing, just a catch in my side." She straightened up slowly, then sat down at the dressing table and opened one of the drawers. She took out a pint of scotch and a shot glass and downed two swift drinks. "Join me?" She waved the bottle at Kathy.

Kathy shook her head; the shot glass and the scotch seemed incongruous in this room, but Irene appeared to be back to normal. "Are you sure you're all right?" she asked, still uncertain.

"Of course I am," Irene said lightly, "Honestly, Kathy, I feel just fine—don't worry about it."

"Well, if you're sure," she said, still not quite believing her. "Don't you think we ought to join the party?"

"In a moment." Irene looked at her, then seemed to make up her mind about something. "To tell you the truth, I'm expecting two more guests, and I thought it might be kind of fun if we answered the door together."

"Who?" Kathy was curious.

"Vivian and Duncan." Irene said with a sly smile.

Kathy looked at her steadily, and hoped her reactions weren't showing. She hadn't seen Vivian since the interview at Keith Oil, but by way of gossip she was well aware that the woman was violently opposed to her, especially to her seeing Dwight. Dwight himself had told her that she had been pretty heavy-handed in trying to get him to reconcile with Nancy, and if Dwight could see through it, she must have been very obvious. Suddenly the corny small town drama struck her as rather amusing, and as if on cue, the doorbell rang. "You know, Irene, you're somewhat of a bitch, but I like your style." She smiled at her. "Shall we?" she reached out her hand, and they walked arm in arm to answer the door.

Vivian hugged her mink stole tightly around herself and shivered. It was really quite nippy for the beginning of September, and she hoped they wouldn't have to eat outdoors tonight. Irene was only four years younger than she, but she had this absolute phobia about being a fresh air fiend. She rang the bell again, and looked at Duncan. He really looked quite handsome and distinguished for his age, and she felt a sudden surge of pride and accomplishment. One thing about Duncan, he was always well turned out. It might take him a little longer to dress now, and his hands might shake a little while he was shaving, but these were minor things. She reached over and squeezed his hand affectionately. "Don't eat too many ribs tonight, dear. I know you adore them, but *you* know they give you gas."

Kathy reached the upper "level" unobstrusively, and breathed a sigh of relief. The noise and the smoke downstairs had given her a slight headache, and she longed for an Alka-Seltzer. For once, Dwight wasn't glued to her side, but was over in the corner in deep discussion with a group of men. She was hungry, and the tantalizing aroma of the smoking meat from the barbecue didn't help any. From the way the party was going, it didn't look like Irene would get around to serving for a couple of hours, by which time everybody would be bombed and wouldn't know what they were eating anyway.

God, she hated parties like this! She'd been to so many of them in Hollywood, and this one seemed to be turning out pretty much the same. She usually didn't have a very big appetite, and had purposely eaten only half a chicken salad sandwich at the Club all day, but now she was starved.

She wandered down the hallway, looking at each painting again with distaste and mistrust. They were all expensively framed, each of them lighted to show off their relative merits. She paused before one and shook her head in wonder. Now really, how could anyone, much less someone with Irene's obvious intelligence, put out good money for a painting of a roast turkey with flies all over it lying in the dirt outside the door of a shack? The sight of it momentarily quelled her appetite. She came to the door of Ted's study and decided to rest for a while.

It was a peaceful room, quiet, and completely shut off from the rest of the house. One wall was entirely lined with bookshelves, and she took a book out, idly. It was a copy of Thomas Costain's "The Tontine," and it evidently had been well read and well used, as had all the other books on the shelves. She looked at some of the others; he had all the classics, a great number of biographies and autobiographies, as well a complete shelf devoted to political and scientific studies, and several shelves filled with real estate and land development books.

She put the book back, sat down in one of the large red leather chairs, and leaned her head back. You could learn a lot about a man from the books he read, a lot more than the impressions he'd like to convey. This bookcase showed a man of learning, intelligence, and a deep interest in the world around him, and had nothing to do with the big, easy-going, tennis-playing, golf-playing yachtsman that she knew.

Take some of the bookcases in Hollywood, for instance. She had actually known some people in the industry who had ordered complete libraries filled with books bound in certain colors to fit their color scheme. Invariably, "War and Peace" and Darwin's "Origin of the Species" were predominently displayed. Some actors were particularly fond of this sort of vanity, while the executives were usually too intelligent for this kind of foolishness.

Her husband was a prime example—he never got beyond the Sunday comic section, or, if he was working, the next day's shooting schedule. Pete Logan, when she worked at the advertising agency, was constantly reading pornographic paperbacks. She had glanced through several of them, and found them obscene and revolting. Come to think of it, she'd never been much of a reader herself, until she met Bruce. History had been her worst subject in school, as she'd considered it dull and stale. Bruce had made it come alive for her, the color and the drama, to the point that she was avidly pouring over books while he was out of town. From history, she had branched out to other subjects, eager and anxious to discuss them with Bruce when he returned. She remembered a particular conversation over Wylie's "Generation of Vipers" when the interpretation of the book had caused a heated and vigorous argument between them. "Oh Bruce," she murmured softly, "will I ever forget you?"

She turned her head slowly as the door to the study opened, and Ted Enwright stood there.

"I figured you'd be up here." He smiled at her, "Away from the maddening throng." He sat down opposite her and lit a cigarette. "Actually, I saw you sneaking up the stairs. Pretty noisy down there, isn't it?"

"Ted, I'm sorry if I've been rude. It's just that I expected something a little different from the parties in Hollywood, and this seems to be the same scene. Are your parties always like this?''

"*My* parties?'' he snorted, "These are *Irene's* parties, and they always have been. I told you at the Club, that's why I stay out of the way until the very last minute, or if possible, avoid them altogether. Don't misunderstand me—about half of those people downstairs are very nice people, who will get slightly bombed, eat, maybe have a few more drinks and go home early. The other half will get completely smashed, won't eat, throw up or pass out, or both, then I get the wonderful privilege of driving them home, because they're too drunk to drive. Then the next day, everybody calls Irene and tells her what a marvelous time they had, and she immediately gets busy planning her next one.'' He shook his head disgustedly, and crushed out his cigarette. "Excuse me, I'm not being a very good host, would you like a drink?''

Kathy shook her head. "No thanks, but I would like a bromo, if you've got one handy.''

"That, I always have on hand,'' he said, walking to the liquor cabinet. He came back with a foaming glass and she gulped it down gratefully, then waited for the fizzing seltzer that was rolling around in her stomach to subside. Ted watched her steadily, an unfathomable expression in his eyes.

"Thanks, that helped.'' She smiled at him. "Now may I have a cigarette?''

He handed her one, lit it, turned away, picked a book out of the bookcase, then put it back—somehow, he didn't seem quite so self-assured as he turned back to her. "Kathy, what's the matter with Irene? You must know, you work for the doctor.'' His eyes were pleading.

Kathy looked at him, hesitating. He was very obviously sincere, but just how far could she go, and what right did she have to interfere? "Ted, I honestly can't tell you. Dr. Carter doesn't discuss his patients with me, and what little he does let drop would be violating professional ethics if I told you.''

She put up her hand as he started to say something. "Wait. . ." he continued to look at her silently, as her mind raced. The doctor had said, "Don't get involved with any of the patients," but good God, she was already involved; what was she supposed to do, leave everything hanging in mid-air?

She took a deep breath and continued. "Okay—what I'm going to say now may be completely out of line, but I'll tell you anyway. I'm no doctor, but Irene doesn't look at all well to me. Maybe you haven't noticed, but she's awfully pale tonight under her makeup, and when we were in her bedroom tonight I was afraid she was going to faint. I don't mean to alarm you, but I think she needs a physical checkup."

Ted looked puzzled. "She looked all right to me. I was asking about her mental condition. Are you sure you're not exaggerating? She has regular checkups," he said, but his voice was concerned, "at least, she says she does."

"Ted, all I know is she was gasping for breath, turned white as a sheet, and had to hold on to the dressing table to keep from falling. Then after she had a couple of straight shots, she was just fine again. Have you taken a good look at her lately? I know I shouldn't have said that, and it's none of my business, but I really think you should look into it—and please, don't say I said anything to you." She sincerely hoped he wouldn't. Why in the world was she interfering in these people's lives, when she had promised herself she wouldn't, and had been sure the old habit was broken? Bruce had said to her more than once, "You might call it having an alert, inquisitive, caring mind, but other people might call it being a busybody."

"No, of course I won't," he hastened to reassure her. "So you were in her bedroom tonight? That's strange . . . she doesn't usually allow that; calls it her 'private domain.' But then, you never know what she'll do, lately," he mused. "What did you talk about?"

"Oh, nothing much, just the usual girl-talk." Kathy felt

as though she was skating on thin ice, uncomfortably aware that he was trying to pump her. "Well, hadn't we better get back to the party?"

He looked at her with a tired smile. "No, you go on down, I'll stay here for a while. And thanks, Kathy."

"*Por nada*." She smiled at him, and shut the door gently behind her.

He sighed, and sank down in the large leather chair she had just vacated. Her flowery scent hung lightly in the air and he breathed it in gratefully. The brunette he had been with last night had worn a heavy, cloying perfume. It hadn't seemed so noticeable when he had picked her up in a bar in Riverside, but when he got her in the motel room, the perfume mixed with stale perspiration had stung his nostrils and almost made him gag. Also, the lights in the dimly lit bar had been kind to her, but in the room, under the bright overhead unmerciful glare, she had looked a good ten years older. The heavy makeup she wore in a pitiful attempt to hide her age had caked, making the wrinkles around her eyes and mouth even more predominant, her bright blue eye-shadow was smudged, and one of her false eyelashes was slightly askew.

He considered calling the whole thing off, but what the hell, his nuts were aching, it was late, and he didn't particularly feel like going to the trouble of calling anyone else. "Go in in and take a shower and wash off that perfume. While you're at it, wash your face, too."

"Don't you like it? It's called '*Nuit d'amour*'."

She looked so hurt and woebegone that he almost felt ashamed of speaking to her so harshly—almost, but not quite. "No, it's my wife," he said in a more kindly tone. "I don't want her to smell it on me."

She smiled at him uncertainly, with pathetic acceptance of his explanation.

"And be sure you wash it *all* off, real well," he called after her. 'My wife has a very sharp sense of smell.''

As soon as he heard the water running, he opened the door and the windows wide, in an attempt to air out the room, then sat down in the lumpy chair by the door.

He hadn't intended to pick up a broad tonight, but it had been a very trying, irritating evening, and that was putting it mildly. Ben Cameron was a big, dumb, arrogant, conceited son of a bitch, who always had some hare-brained, get-rich-quick scheme, and had loused up more construction jobs than Ted could remember. But he was also Vivian and Duncan's son-in-law, and it was a very tricky situation.

Ben liked to refer to himself as a Concrete Mason, but Ted thought of him as a dim-witted cement mixer. He had only two subjects of conversation; how vastly superior he was to anyone else in his trade, and how great he was when he'd played Major League football. Actually, he had played only one season with the Minors before he was dumped.

But Jan adored him, and after they were married, Duncan had made him an assistant foreman. He couldn't make too many serious errors in that capacity, although they were bad enough, but he complained bitterly to Jan about not being given a freer hand. Jan, in turn, had complained to her father, who couldn't deny her anything. Finally, in desperation, Duncan had put him in complete charge of laying the foundation for a small new station near Baker. Vivian had stood by quietly, not saying anything, although Ted suspected she knew what the results would be. (Smart cookie, that one, he thought.)

Ted, out of curiosity, had driven out to look at the site after the foundation had been laid. It had looked all right on the surface, but as soon as building began, great huge cracks began to appear, and the whole job had to be redone.

Ben had tried to bluff his way out of it by saying he'd been given inferior workmen and when that didn't work, by saying he'd been deliberately sabotaged.

This error in judgment and ability had cost the company a sizeable sum, and he had been quietly shifted to sales, on salary plus commission, to one of the smaller, less lucrative territories where he couldn't do the company much harm. Ted doubted his commission checks amounted to much, if he had any at all.

Ben had called him several times in the past week, and Ted had finally agreed to see him that night for two reasons; first, he wanted to get him off his back, and second, Ben was coming to the barbecue and Ted wanted to get any unpleasantness out of the way. He realized Ben wanted something, but he wasn't quite prepared for the audacity of the man.

When he entered the restaurant, Ben was always at the bar, and it was obvious that he'd been drinking heavily.

Ben waved to him. "Hi, ol' buddy," he said in a loud voice. "Want 'ja to meet a friend of mine." He put his arm around the blonde girl sitting next to him and leaned on her heavily. "There here's Ted Enwright, the salt of the earth."

The girl pulled away and looked at him coldly. "Look, I don't know you from Adam, and I told you I'm waiting for somebody. Now if you don't quite pawing me I'm going to call the bartender."

Ted was exasperated; the stupid idiot either wanted a favor or to talk business and here he was, soused to the eyeballs. He nodded to the girl briefly. "Look, Ben, if you want to talk about something, let's find a table; I don't have much time. Sorry if he's been bothering you, miss."

Ben lurched slightly on the way to the table, glared at the girl, then turned to Ted and winked owlishly. "You know," he slurred confidentially, "that broad's just playing hard to get, but I can tell she really digs me. 'Nother half-hour, I'd of had it made. 'Nother hour, I'd of had her in the sack," he snapped his fingers, "just like that. Yeah," he repeated, "she's just playing hard to get. Waitress!"

Ted was more than exasperated now, he was downright angry. "Ben, forget the girl. And lay off the liquor if you want to talk, I'm pressed for time," he said curtly, and glanced at his watch.

"Don't worry about me, ol' buddy, if there's one thing about ol' Ben, he can hold his booze." He tried to put his arm around Ted's shoulder, but Ted pushed him away. "Bring me the same, and give my pal here whatever he wants."

"All right, Ben, get to the point. What do you want?"

Ben looked at him, trying to get his eyes in focus, and sat up straighter. "Okay, ol' pal, I'll give it to you straight. Lay it right on the line. Those dudes at work aren't giving me no cooperation at all, know what I mean? That Baker job wasn't no fault of mine. I laid out direct orders and the crew done it wrong. Not my fault," he mumbled, and downed half of his drink in one gulp. "Now this selling job isn't working out either. I come around to pitch to them dudes and they act like I'm some sort of a leper, if I get to see them at all. And you know why? I'll tell you why," he said, without waiting for an answer. "Because I'm the boss's son-in-law, that's why. They're all jealous of me, and you know why? Because I'm the boss's son-in-law, that's why," he repeated, and looked at Ted triumphantly.

"Well, what do you want from me?" Ted was bored, but slightly amused at Ben's gross misinterpretation of the facts. The men at Keith Oil may have felt sorry for pretty little Jan, and irritated at Ben's bungling ineptness, but they certainly weren't jealous.

"Well, this is it, Ted." Ben looked at him earnestly. "I want to get out of sales, it's just not my meat. I want to get back into masonry. You're starting a new subdivision in a couple of months, so how about making me foreman of the concrete work?"

Ted almost choked on his drink. "Ben, you've got to be kidding. You know Greer's been with me for twelve years."

Ben waved Greer aside as if he were a fly. "Hell, he's an old man. I could do a better job than that dude with one hand tied behind my back and blindfolded."

"It's out of the question," Ted said flatly.

"How about assistant, then?" He was pleading now.

"Forget it, Ben. I've got an assistant and a full crew. Look around for something else if you're dissatisfied, but working for me is out of the question." He finished his drink and stood up.

"Well, just think about it," he begged. "We'll talk about it some more at the party tomorrow night."

"I never discuss business at home, or at parties," he said firmly, "and you better have something to eat before you drive home."

Something brought Ted out of his reverie, and he realized the water in the bathroom had stopped. He got up quickly and closed the door and windows.

He was sitting in the chair again when the woman came out of the bathroom. She looked a little better now that she was scrubbed and clean, but not much.

"Aren't you going to take your clothes off?" she asked hesitantly.

"No, it's too late for that, and I had something else in mind," he said, unbuckling his belt and pulling down his zipper. "Come over here."

He sighed, and lit a cigarette. She'd given pretty good head, a lot better than some of these kids, but damn, he was tired. Eighteen holes of golf this morning, then two sets of tennis, and he was off his game on both. The steam bath had helped a little, but he hoped that once, just for once, this party would break up early. He decided he'd better go down-stairs before they started looking for him. He reminded himself to ask Irene later when she'd had her last physical.

Chapter 5

When Kathy got back downstairs, the noise was a little louder and the smoke a little thicker. She looked around for Dwight, but he was nowhere to be seen. She wondered where Pam was, and glanced at her watch; nine-thirty already and she was starving. She was just about to wander outside when a big hulk of a man appeared at her side.

"Hi ya, beautiful, where've you been all my life?"

"My, what an original approach." She couldn't help smiling at his gaucherie. He was a big, broad-shouldered man, with the remnants of a good physique that was rapidly running to fat. His face wasn't unattractive, with the exception of his nose; it was bulbous and porous, the trademark of a heavy drinker of long standing.

"Get you a drink?"

"Not right now—I was just about to go outside."

"How come I haven't seen you around before, beautiful?"

"Well, I'm new in town. I've only been here about a month." She smiled at him; for all she knew, he might be a good friend of Irene's.

"Only a month? And you're invited to one of Irene's

shindigs? Say, you gotta be one fast worker." He looked at her with open admiration.

Kathy had an impulse to slap his face. Friend or no friend, she had no intention of putting up with such rudeness. She started to walk away, but she saw Vivian approaching, a forced smile on her face.

"Kathy my dear," she tried to sound warmly sincere, "I see you've met my son-in-law."

"Not officially, Mrs. Keith; we were just talking." Kathy felt like bursting into laughter, but controlled herself. So this was the big dumb boob Dwight had told her about, the bungler that was the thorn in the side of Keith Oil, the conceited skirt-chaser who thought every woman he met was fair game. She glanced at him again. He was wearing a brightly flowered Hawaiian sports shirt, lemon yellow slacks, and open toed sandals. Definitely not her cup of tea. Kathy had thought Dwight was exaggerating, that no one could be that much of a character. She'd have to apologize to him.

"Well, then; Kathy, this is Ben Cameron." Vivian smiled. "Ben, Kathy Foster."

"Oh, so *you're* the one Dwight's been raving about. No wonder that dude's been keeping you under wraps."

"I was looking for Dwight, Mrs. Keith; have you seen him?" Kathy asked sweetly.

"Oh my dear, he's talking over some last minute business details for the board meeting Monday with his brother. Just some things I wanted to be sure they had straight, but it may take a little while."

Score one for you, Vivian, Kathy thought, and I'll bet they're some "little details" you just thought up right after Irene and I answered the door together. You really are one hell of a bitch. "But Mrs. Keith," she said evenly, "they'll both be at your home tomorrow for dinner. Couldn't they discuss business then?"

"Oh hardly, Kathy, that's a *family* dinner," she

emphasized the word slightly, "and we make it a point never to discuss business at family dinners."

"But Vivian. . ." Ben started to say.

"Ben," she interrupted him with a level look, "why don't you show Kathy around and get to know each other better?"

"Oh sure," he agreed amiably, "after all, she may be my sister-in-law one of these days."

Vivian's eyes flashed pure hatred for a split second before the smiling mask settled back in place. But Kathy caught it, and Vivian knew she did. Score one for me, Kathy thought, thanks to Ben.

"Come on, let's go get a drink," he said as they walked away. "What was all that about?" he asked when Vivian was out of hearing range.

"All what about?" she asked innocently.

"About her telling you we never discuss business at those shit-kicking family dinners. Oh, excuse me," he apologized, "I didn't mean to use that kind of language." He got them a couple of drinks and they walked outside.

The fresh air smelled good after the smoke-filled room. Kathy was curious. "What are they like, those family dinners?"

Ben snorted. "A damn pain in the ass, if you ask me. Thank God they only come once a month, and at that, it's too damn often. Excuse me again for swearing, but that old biddy gets to me sometimes."

"What are they like?" she asked again.

"They're a damn bore. Everybody brings something and it's supposed to be real folksy, know what I mean? Like somebody'll bring a salad, somebody else a casserole, and someone else a dessert. All Vivian does is make some fancy hors d'oeuvres and has some bakery rolls. Me, I'm a meat-and-potato man, myself. And if you have more than two drinks before dinner, you get that look of hers. I always carry a half pint in each hip pocket to be able to stand it. And no matter

103

what she told you, that's all they do, just talk shop, know what I mean?''

"Don't you talk shop, too?"

"Me? Nah. I'm only an in-law, an outsider." He grabbed her arm and spoke to her earnestly. "Listen, before I married Jan, I was doing just fine, had a great future and a big potential in front of me, know what I mean? But the old man begged and pleaded with me to go to work for him, said he could do a lot better for me, and he finally talked me into it. Shit, that's a big laugh!'' He looked around to see if anyone was watching, then pulled a half pint out of his hip pocket and filled his almost empty glass. "Listen, you want me to sweeten yours?''

She shook her head. "I'm fine." That was a far cry from the story she'd gotten from Dwight, but she let it pass.

"I just don't like to let Vivian see me getting too many drinks at the bar," he apologized. "The old war horse has it in for me enough as it is. She runs the whole show, you know. The old man may think he does, but I'm smart enough to know different. Fact is, I'm smarter than all them dudes. But that's all right with me, I got a deal cooking, a big deal. . ." he broke off. "Listen, you seen Ted around?''

"Well, I. . ." she was about to say he was in the den, but something warned her against it. "He must be around here someplace." She changed the subject. "Will Nancy be there tomorrow?''

"I don't know. She was last month, with the kids, but I guess that was before Dwight met you—oh, I get it. Listen, you don't have a damn thing to worry about, you got her beat hands down." He grinned, pleased at his astuteness, then his mood changed. "But Jan and I will. The kid had a little bit of the sniffles tonight, but do you think she'd get a baby sitter and come with me? Shit, no. But come hell or high water, she'll be at her Daddy's tomorrow. Shit," he said again, pulled out the bottle and refilled his glass. "You sure you don't want any?"

"No, I'll get one at the bar. Listen, Ben, do you know Pam Sterling?"

"Pam? Sure, everybody knows Pam. Great legs, that one." His voice was beginning to be markedly slurred now. "But not nearly as great as yours," he hastened to assure her. "You know, I could really dig you if Dwight didn't have you all tied up. He *does* have you all tied up, doesn't he?"

She started to say "no," and caught herself just in time. "Yes. Ben, have you seen Pam tonight?"

"No, I don't think so," he mumbled.

"Well, I think I'll go look for her and get another drink."

"I'll go with you." He drained his glass and laughed slyly, "Boy, that old bitch will sure think I've been nursing this one."

Just as they entered the playroom, Pam was coming down the stairs. She looked fresh and sparkling, and especially pretty in a lime green sheath that showed every curve of her body. The man with her looked vaguely familiar, but at first Kathy couldn't place him. Irene swooped down on them out of nowhere and greeted him like a long-lost brother.

"Who's that with Pam?" she asked Ben casually.

Ben's voice was derisive. "Him? That's Jack Wentworth, the rich man's son, the debutante's darling," he emphasized the words sarcastically. "I'll bet you that dude's never done an honest day's work in his life. Just look at Irene buttering him up, like he was royalty, or something. Oh excuse me, there's Ted," he said, and ambled off across the room.

Jack Wentworth—she tumbled the name around in her brain until it clicked and fell into place. Of course! He had been in Dr. Carter's office her first week at work when she'd had that frightening experience with Dave Ebenstein. She searched her mind again; he was supposed to come in three times a week but he had called and cancelled, and she hadn't seen him since. By this time she had read all the case histories thoroughly, but there couldn't have been anything very spectacular about his. For the life of her, she couldn't remember a single detail in his file.

She looked at him and speculated—could he be one of *the* Wentworths? Back in Hollywood, she had heard of the fabulous B.J. Wentworth millions, the land holdings, the towering Wentworth building on Wilshire Boulevard, the hotel chain, and God knows what else. He didn't look like anything out of the ordinary—medium build, sandy hair, thin aquiline nose, smallish eyes; neither attractive nor un-attractive, but then most millionaires didn't walk around with a sign pinned to their chests. From what Ben had said, it seemed very possible that he could be B.J. Wentworth's son. If that were true, she thought, there were certainly a lot of healthy, impressive fortunes represented under this roof tonight.

She glanced at her watch again; dammit, this was getting annoying. For once she was sorry that Dwight wasn't glued to her side, and had started for the bar when he suddenly appeared.

"Hi honey, I've been looking all over for you. Where've you been?" Dwight looked at her apprehensively.

Liar, she thought. "Dwight, you know perfectly well you were off somewhere with Scott discussing 'business.' Oh, don't look so surprised," she said, as his eyebrows shot up. "Vivian just couldn't wait to tell me. Why didn't you stand up to her? You know you'll be talking business all day tomorrow."

"Just how do you know that?"

"I met your brother-in-law," she shook her head slightly, "and I must say you didn't exaggerate. He comes on pretty strong."

"Well, you seem to have been pretty busy yourself—I

hope Ben didn't give you a bad time. Let's get a drink." He took her arm accompanied her to the bar. "God, I'm starved!"

After they had gotten their drinks, they went outside and found a couple of chairs in a secluded corner. "Dwight, I want to talk this out," Kathy said seriously. "Why does your stepmother hate me? Oh, it's not just tonight," she waved him to silence when he started to protest. "When I first met her, when she interviewed me, she told me you were in an all-day meeting, which you obviously weren't. Why? And then she's said some pretty disparaging things about me at the club. She's really not as subtle as she thinks she is, you know. It can't be the doting mother routine—she's not the type, and besides, she's only your stepmother. The only thing I can think of is that she wants you and Nancy to get back together."

"Kathy, I honestly don't know," Dwight answered her just as seriously. "It could be Nancy, but for the life of me, I can't see why. When I was living with Nancy, Viv wasn't particularly fond of her. Oh, she tolerated her, but that's about all. Then when we started making noises like divorce, she did a complete about-face. Nancy was the greatest wife and mother in the world, and I'd be a fool to let her get away, things like that. And you're right, she's not very subtle, not any more. But there's a lot more to it than that."

"Something more than just plain bitchiness? Like what?"

He nodded absently, thinking, then seemed to make up his mind. "I probably shouldn't tell you this, but maybe you can give me a woman's opinion. Scott noticed it long before I did. Actually, he wanted to talk to me about it tonight, before the dinner tomorrow, and without Viv around." He handed her a cigarette, lit one himself, and continued. "But I'm getting ahead of myself—to go back a ways, when Mother died, it tore Dad apart. It wasn't as though she'd been ill; I don't remember her ever having a sick day in her life. One day she was there, and the next day she was gone; Dad just didn't know how to cope, it was all so sudden. But then Vivian entered the picture, and gradually Dad started to perk up. She was gay and charming, and she'd take us to ballgames or the mountains, sometimes with Dad, or just herself if he was busy. We'd ask her advice about different things, and it was kind of like having an older sister around. I don't think any of us resented her, or thought she was trying to take the place of our mother; we were just glad Dad had a new lease on life. And we genuinely liked her; at least, I did.''

"That certainly doesn't sound like the Vivian I know.'' Kathy shook her head in disbelief. "What in the world happened to her?''

"It didn't happen overnight,'' Dwight said with a wry smile. "In fact, the change was so gradual that you could barely see it, until lately. When they got back from their honeymoon, I was kind of surprised that she wanted to keep on working, but after all, that was between her and Dad, although he didn't seem to like the idea too much. But things went along fine for the next few years; Dad got used to it, and so did Scott and I. Then things began to happen; like I said, gradually at first, but they were definitely not Dad's doing.''

"Like what?'' Kathy's mind was keenly alert now, and for the time being she forgot how hungry she was.

"Well, looking back, I think the first change was in the advertising department. We've always been a conservative company, then all of a sudden Dad comes up with an Operation Saturation campaign. I don't know whether she persuaded him into it, or actually convinced him the idea was his. Whichever way it was, the idea was sound, and made the company money. Then she started messing around with personnel policies, and changed some of the jobs around. At first, a lot of the employees squawked, but it turned out she was right there, too. Everywhere you turned, every department, there was Vivian's fine hand, and always with an improvement. She knows our business from the ground up.''

''But,'' Kathy interrupted, ''if all she's done is make improvements, what's there to worry about?''

''That's just it,'' Dwight said somberly. ''According to Scott's and my calculations, we should be making a much larger profit, and we're not. Another thing—before, she always stayed in the background and let Dad present her ideas as his. Lately, though. . .'' he hesitated, ''well, just a couple of weeks ago, she openly opposed him at a Board Meeting, in front of Scott and me and all the members. That's not good, Kathy; it presents a very shaky front to the stockholders and it isn't good for company morale. When I was fighting it out with Nancy,'' he continued, ''I admit I wasn't paying as much attention to the business as I should have. But as soon as I moved out for good, I threw myself back into it, to make up for lost time. Viv evidently didn't like this at all, and tried to ship me off to our Bolivia fields, which was completely unnecessary at the time. It's pretty obvious she's up to something.''

''But,'' Kathy spoke slowly, choosing her words carefully, ''from what you've told me, I gather you think she's been tampering with company assets. Couldn't you demand a complete audit by an outside accounting firm?''

Dwight shook his head. ''No good. Scott and I discussed that possibility, but we just don't have enough to go on. Suppose we were wrong? We're a relatively small company, Kathy, but we've got a firm foundation and a reputation for honesty and integrity. You've got to understand, honey, that we're a family business, and any outside audit would cause a big rumble, maybe big enough to knock us down altogether. At the very least, it would leave us in a very shaky position.

And then there's Dad to consider—he thinks the sun rises and sets in Vivian, and either way, whether we're right or wrong, it would just about kill him.''

''Couldn't you just come right out and tell her you suspect her? It might frighten her enough into stopping whatever it is she's doing.''

He raised his eyebrows. ''Honey, for a smart girl, that was a pretty dumb idea. The one thing Scott and I have going for us is that she doesn't think we suspect a thing, and we want to keep it that way. In fact, I don't think she thinks we're too smart, and that's all right, too, for the time being. Kathy, no one else knows about any of this, not even Jan or Scott's wife—until now.''

''I'm flattered. You know,'' she mused, ''I was just wondering what would have happened if you'd interviewed me that day and if I'd gone to work for you, if I could have helped any.''

He laughed, and kissed her lightly on the cheek. ''I'll tell you one thing, I wouldn't have gotten much work done. No, Kathy, for the time being, we're just going to have to keep our eyes and ears open, and our mouths shut. She's already beginning to get careless, and sooner or later she's bound to make a mistake. We've just got to play it by ear. Come on,'' he said, as a couple walked by with plates of steaming ribs, ''I've been so busy talking, I didn't notice they'd started serving!''

Kathy let the dog out, then went into the bathroom and brushed her teeth vigorously. The dinner had been delicious, and well worth waiting for; large succulent ribs with meat so tender it almost fell off the bones, homemade baked beans swimming in honey and molasses, crusty French bread, crisp Caesar salad. But even skipping dessert, she had eaten too much and too late, and now her stomach felt like a lump of lead. She wasn't really sure the food actually had been all that great; the fact that she'd been hungry as a horse might have had something to do with it. She'd used that trick herself when she'd given parties; give your guests plenty of booze, feed them as late as possible, and you have a successful formula.

The seating arrangements were deliberately casual; about half the tables were set up for four or six in the playroom, the other half outside. Dwight and Kathy found an empty table at the far end of the pool. "I'd better go find you a glass of milk." He squeezed her shoulder lightly. "Be right back."

She smiled after him fondly, and sneaked a bite of beans. God, they tasted good! Dwight really was very thoughtful and sweet; he knew she always drank milk with dinner, and hadn't waited to be asked. She could do worse—he obviously loved her, or thought he did, and she had seen a side of him tonight when he was discussing Vivian that had certainly raised him in her esteem. He just might possibly be a match for his stepmother if it came right down to the line. There had been a firmness, a certain steely quality, and for the first time she hadn't thought of him as a boy, but a man. But dammit, why couldn't she *feel* anything for him? The men she'd gone to bed with before Bruce hadn't meant anything to her and had left her emotionally untouched, so why this sudden attack of chastity? It wasn't that he repulsed her; actually, she enjoyed kissing him, but he just didn't arouse her. She sighed, and tried to think of something more cheerful. He was coming back with her milk.

He sat down and handed her the glass. "Just saw Scott and Fran. I asked them to join us."

Kathy looked up and saw them approaching the table. She had met Scott several times before; a slightly taller, older edition of Dwight, with the same warm friendly brown eyes, laugh wrinkles, tanned skin. "Kathy, I'd like you to meet my wife, Fran. Honey, this is Kathy Foster.''

"How do you do, Miss Foster?" She smiled glacially. "I've heard *so* much about you."

"Oh, don't be so formal, call me Kathy, please." She paused. "We're among friends—I hope." She speared a bite of salad and considered this new opponent. Fran was a tall woman, almost as tall as Scott, firmly and compactly built. She looked older than her husband, but this could have been caused by the unbecoming hairstyle that emphasized her rather large, flat features, her heavy eyebrows, and the downward pull of her mouth. "Try the salad, Fran, it's delicious." Kathy smiled at her, determined to be pleasant.

"I'm sure it is," she said briefly, dismissing her, and turned to her husband. "Scott, I just don't know what to do. You know I've been simmering a bean casserole all afternoon for tomorrow's dinner, but nobody will want the same thing two days in a row. Oh well," she sighed, maybe I can whip something else up in the morning."

"You already told me that, Fran," Scott answered her in a warning tone.

She stared at him, then turned to Dwight. "What time are you going over to the folks? Are you picking up Nancy and the children?"

Dwight looked uncomfortable, and temporarily at a loss for words.

Kathy could feel anger bubbling up inside herself—Fran's unmitigated rudeness was unbelievable, and she answered before he could speak. "You know, Fran, these beans are really better than the salad. I hope you don't mind my changing the subject for a moment, but if your beans are one-tenth as good, they should get by." She paused and ate a forkful, as all their eyes were riveted on her. "You know, there's a definite art in making baked beans, just as there is in making conversation." Her voice was calm, masking her anger. "Some cooks simmer it slowly, with just the right touch of tartness and sweetness, a wisp of herbs and spices that don't offend. On the other hand, there are some slobs at the stove that throw in some beans, too much spice and too much garlic, and you just can't swallow it. In fact, it usually makes you sick at your stomach.'' She turned to Dwight, ''Don't you agree, dear?''

His eyes twinkled at her, as he grinned. ''I'm not exactly a connoisseur of beans, but I agree with you completely. Want some more?''

''Definitely. And some more ribs, too, as soon as I've finished these.'' She sneaked a sidelong glance at Fran; her face was white and splotched with anger—Kathy had made her point. She felt a certain cold satisfaction that Dwight had confided in her about the situation at the company, and decided to let well enough alone. She was damned if that bitch was going to spoil her appetite, although the atmosphere at the table now left much to be desired. It was with a definite feeling of relief that she saw Pam and Jack Wentworth bearing down on them, and waved them over.

Jack Wentworth had been brusque, almost taciturn during the introductions that followed, and for once, Kathy was glad for Pam's gay, bubbling personality, her take-over-any-situation attitude. The conversation had taken on a light, impersonal touch, and was further improved when Fran and Scott made their excuses early and left.

Kathy leaned over and whispered to Dwight, ''Thank God they've gone! I thought for a while we were in for an evening of your sister-in-law playing kick-the-can-with-Kathy.'' Then in a more normal tone, as she held out her plate to him, ''Now, would you please get me another helping of beans and three or four more ribs?''

Pam jumped up, empty plate in hand. ''I'll come with you. Jack?'' she looked at him inquiringly.

''I'm fine.'' He picked at his half empty plate listlessly. He made no attempt at conversation after they left, and Kathy began to feel uncomfortable. She was trying to think of something to say, when he suddenly shifted his small blue piercing eyes directly at her. "I know I've met you somewhere before, but I can't remember. Where was it?" he asked abruptly.

His direct approach flustered her. "I—I'm Dr. Carter's receptionist," she stammered.

His face relaxed slightly. "Of course. It always bothers me when I can't remember something or someone, doesn't it you? Tell me, what does the doctor say about me, anyway?"

"That's the second time someone's asked me that question tonight," she replied, feeling easier, "and all I can do is give you the same answer. Dr. Carter doesn't discuss his patients with me, and even if he did, I couldn't discuss it with you." In a sudden burst of confidence, she added, "To tell you the truth, I don't even remember what's in your original case history."

He stared at her, unconvinced, then turned his attention back to Pam, as she and Dwight returned. To hell with him, Kathy thought, although it piqued her that he showed so little interest in her. . . .

Kathy finished brushing her teeth, washed her face, let Topsy back in, and went to bed. Her stomach was still churning, and she tossed and turned before falling into a fitful sleep. . .

She was in a huge, vast loft of a building, overcrowded with desks and chairs, but there seemed to be no pattern in their arrangement. There were a great many oddly assorted people sitting at the desks, some old and gnarled, some young, two or three beautiful girls in gorgeous outfits. She didn't remember how she got there, or why she was there in the first place. She knew she had to change the bandage on her ankle, and she found a desk with bandages, salve and tape, but her hands were dirty. She wandered through the enormous room for what seemed like a long time and finally

114

found a washbasin, but by the time she got back to the desk with the bandages, her hands were dirty again. Back and forth she went, endlessly, from the basin to the desk, but her hands were always dirty, and she couldn't change the bandage with dirty hands. Nobody paid any attention to her as they sat at their desks, although they chattered constantly among themselves.

All of a sudden a loud buzzer rang, and they all got up and started running insanely. She panicked, and started running after them. They ran, one right after the other, dodging in and out between the desks with an agility that only comes from long practice. On some of the desks there were large, glowing balls, and they hit each one, making them ring. Kathy limped along after them, but she was far behind because her ankle was throbbing with every step. She hoped she wouldn't miss hitting one of the balls, and wondered what the penalty would be if she did. On and on they ran, in a haphazard sort of obstacle course, until they finally circled back and sat down at their own desks.

Kathy had no place to sit, so she stood there helplessly by the desk with the bandages, and stared at her hands—they were still dirty. She looked around her, defeated by her hands. "What's the penalty?" she asked, and finally they all turned their attention to her. "I mean, if you miss hitting one of the balls?"

They all chattered among themselves again, and finally one nondescript man spoke to her. "Penalty? We don't know. We *always* hit *all* the balls."

"Then what's the point?" she asked. They all looked at her again briefly, then chose to ignore her and returned to their senseless chatter. She felt outside and alone, and looked down at her ankle. The bandage was soaked through now, and slimy with pus and blood. She was about to change the bandage, dirty hands and all, when the buzzer rang again, and the insane running marathon started all over. She ran after them, feeling as though she were at some crazy Mad Hatter's tea party. "What's the point, what's the point?" she screamed, as she hobbled after them painfully. Someone finally turned around and yelled back at her, "You won't know, until you've been outside."

The insanity ended abruptly, and they were all back at their desks again. Tears coursed down her cheeks, and the pain in her leg was unbearable. A shrill buzzer sounded, louder and different than the signal for the running marathon, and everyone leaped up. "Hurry," they shouted, "outside, before the flood starts!"

"But I can't swim," she shrieked.

An old man swept her along with him. "Hurry," he said urgently, "there's a chance, upstairs on the other building."

She followed the old man outside. The rain had started coming down in sharp, stinging pellets that lashed at her face and cut her hands. The others were already there, standing or clinging to ledges on the side of the loft. They hung at odd angles from the delapidated old building, laughing and swaying. "She can't swim, she can't swim," they chanted.

The old man pushed her into the gulley that was rapidly filling with the icy downpour. "Upstairs, on the other building," he repeated, then turned away from her and suwng up on one of the ledges of the loft. In desperation, she forded the narrow gulley, slipping and falling, but the icy water and her fear momentarily dulled the pain in her leg. She reached the bottom step of the crumbling, rotting, concrete structure, and slowly, painfully, began to drag herself up, while the relentless rain came down with increasing intensity, threatening to engulf her at any moment.

When she reached the top, she expected to feel some degree of security, but there was none. She looked across at the people clinging to the ledges of the loft, still chattering and laughing insanely, then down at the dark, churning water below. The building shook ominously beneath her, and she lay on the rotting concrete and clutched at it hopelessly. Finally, she forced herself to raise her head and look around. Her building was higher than the loft; there were no other buildings. All around her, as far as her eyes could see, there were only large granite mountains; no trees, no foliage, no sign of life.

Then it came to her; she had been here before—no, not on top of this building, which every fresh deluge of rain threatened to demolish at any moment. But she had been in the loft before, many times; and each time she had left before the rains came. Tears filled her eyes again, and she felt like pounding her fists, but was afraid the rotting building would crumble beneath her. Why had she come back? Why? She raised her head and screamed to the people on the loft. *"Why am I here?"*

They fell silent suddenly, and their silence increased her fear. Slowly at first, they began to chant at her, "Look behind you, then you'll know—look behind you, then you'll know." Over and over again, louder and louder, until the sound of their voices became deafening.

Kathy was terrified—she tried to turn her head, but it wouldn't move. She didn't want to know, but she *had* to know. She felt weak, and clung to the shaky building for support. Then gradually, the building began to change; the concrete became soft, like putty—her hands sunk in, then her body, and she was falling gently, softly, into a sea of nothingness. . . .

Kathy awoke with a start. She was clammy with sweat and her heart was pounding heavily. She switched on the bedside lamp, pulled back the covers, and looked at her ankles.

The faint but unmistakeable scar on her left leg was visible, but she didn't dare think about either that or the dream, so she reached over and lit a cigarette. Topsy turned over, snorted her annoyance at the disturbance, then settled down comfortably again at her feet. Kathy lay silently and finished

117

her cigarette. She knew she had to get up for a while—past experience had taught her that if she had a pleasant dream and woke up in the middle, then merely rolled over and went back to sleep again, she usually picked up where the dream left off. But a particularly traumatic dream, such as she had just had, must not be finished under any circumstances. Reluctantly, she got up and wandered out to the living room.

She wondered suddenly if other people dreamed the way she did—in motion pictures, dreams always started off with a wavy, unearthly quality, while hers were always sharp and clear, down to the last detail. Other people, if the few reports on the subject she had read were correct, seldom remembered their dreams; or if they did, it was only for a short time. Hers always stayed with her with crystal clarity; there was always enough of her present-day waking existence interspersed with fantasy to make them seem all too real.

She had bought several books about the meaning of dreams years ago, but they hadn't given her much satisfaction. Some authorities held the opinion that although most people didn't remember their dreams, nevertheless, they dreamed every night. It was very seldom that a night passed when Kathy didn't dream, and she had a deep suspicion of anyone who swore they never did.

When she was a child, she had taken to water like a duck; then one day she had a severe cramp and nearly drowned. She had been badly frightened; shortly after the incident she had dreamed she was in a long, narrow tunnel, lying on her back. She tried to twist her neck to look for the way out, but the tunnel was so long she couldn't see light at either end. Then the tunnel slowly started filling with water, and she tried to turn over on her stomach so she could crawl, but the tunnel was too small. She was terrified and tried to cry out as the water grew higher, but no sound came. Higher and higher it rose, until it was up to her chin . . . then she woke up.

She had the same dream repeatedly for a long time; she

had always feared that if the water came up any higher she would never waken, but she always woke up just in time.

She had never been able to swim since. Oh, she could dog-paddle across a pool, but she could never make the length of one, nor could she bear to put her head under water. Curiously, she loved the water and was a good sailor; there was nothing she enjoyed more than deep-sea fishing and speedboat racing, even in choppy waters.

She knew enough about psychology to realize that although consciously she had no fear of water, it was there. All her really bad dreams seemed to be tied in with water and death. She used to tell her friends about her dreams occasionally, but they had looked at her oddly. Even Bruce had begun to think she dreamed about some very peculiar things, so she had stopped discussing them altogether. Some-day, maybe she'd ask Dr. Carter about her dreams—but not yet.

Thinking about the doctor brought her mind back to Jack Wentworth. In her entire life, she had never had such a negative response from a man. Although she, Dwight, Jack and Pam had spent the rest of the evening together, he devoted almost all his attention to Pam. Instead of the kittenish attitude she assumed around other men, she seemed almost natural, the way she was when she and Kathy were alone. While the other women at the party fawned over Wentworth, Pam paid no attention and seemed to take him for granted.

It had been as Kathy expected—during the course of con-versation it turned out he was the son of B.J. Wentworth, and she marvelled at Pam's indifference. He was really rather attractive when he smiled, and as the evening progressed his personality became more affable.

She wondered what Pam and Jack's relationship actually was—it was obvious they had known each other for a long time, but there was something missing. On the surface, their conversation was normal enough, but there was neither the easy camaraderie of long friendship, nor the casual intimacy of a long affair. Kathy had sensed an undercurrent of some kind; an armed truce, perhaps, or a secret between them that had absolutely nothing to do with friendship or sex.

She shrugged mentally; perhaps the doctor was right; all that talk about identifying with patients when he had first interviewed her was probably sensible. She was probably just imagining things, and the late dinner and nightmare hadn't helped any. She yawned, crushed out her cigarette and went back to bed.

Kathy wasn't the only one who was having trouble sleeping that night. Dawn was slowly spreading across the sky before Ted and Irene, Pam, and Jack, respectively, had closed their eyes—and the Keith family didn't get any sleep at all. . . .

Vivian and Duncan left the party early. He had seemed rather tired and drawn, but she hadn't paid too much attention as her mind was riveted on Dwight and Kathy. She had borne the shock when Irene and Kathy had greeted them together at the door with a great deal of restraint and dignity, she thought, although she had considered the act a deliberate affront on Irene's part. But as the evening progressed, she had become more and more nervous. It had been too easy to spirit Dwight and Scott off to a private conference prior to tomorrow's dinner, especially since her explanation for doing so had sounded weak, even to her own ears. Too easy, and for the first time she had the feeling that possibly she had over-played her hand.

Vivian creamed her face heavily with firm upward strokes, listening with half an ear to the familiar sounds of Duncan brushing his teeth in the adjoining bathroom. She had meant to rattle Kathy, to make her feel ill at ease in an unfamiliar setting and situation; instead, she had been outmanuevered and she herself had become unsettled and unnerved. Kathy had been in complete control of the situation, and Ben's uncalled-for remarks had only served to strenghten her position. Even Fran, as formidable as she could be at times, seemed upset by this newcomer in their midst. It was a condition Vivian had never before found herself in, and she was badly shaken. She continued to cream her face, going well past the nightly fifty strokes as she lost count, her mind shifting swiftly from Dwight, to Scott, to Jan, to Duncan. She tried desperately to list her allies in the family, but thoughts of Kathy kept interfering.

The water in the bathroom droned faintly in her ears as she tried to clear her mind; Jan was tractable, and could be counted on—Ben, the absurd fool, she dismissed without a second thought. Up to now she had discounted Scott and Dwight as being easily managed, but after tonight, she wasn't too certain.

For the first time in her life—or at least, since she had married Duncan—she was unsure of herself, and the feeling was overwhelming. She tissued the cream off automatically as her fears kept crowding in. She stared at her naked, defenseless face in the unkind mirror, the greasy tissues still clenched in her hand. A vague feeling of uneasiness tugged at her subconscious, and the sound of running water gradually became an irritant. Duncan should have finished brushing his teeth long ago.

Her uneasiness increased as she stared at the closed bathroom door, and she experienced the slightest feeling of fear. She sat motionless for a while, as the sound of running water became steadily louder, until it was pounding in her ears. After what seemed like an eternity, she got up and moved slowly, as if in a dream, to the bathroom door.

She stood there, unable to move, staring at it, afraid to raise her hand and turn the knob. Oh God, not now, not when everything was so close! She wasn't ready yet, nothing could have happened to Duncan now, not yet! She stood there in suspended animation, the water sounding louder, louder, bursting in her eardrums, until with a tremendous effort she jerked herself out of her lethargy and wrenched open the bathroom door.

Duncan was crumpled on the floor, his face the cold grey and white mottled texture of marble, his right hand clutched tightly around his toothbrush.

Vivian stood quite still in the doorway, staring at her husband, but she felt nothing. It was amazing, she thought, that she felt no sense of grief or loss, but she supposed that would come later. Mixed feelings of calm, duty and responsibility seemed to emcompass her, as thoughts went through her mind meticulously in the order of their importance. The doctor would have to be called immediately, the family notified, Sunday dinner cancelled. A sense of inner strength seemed to well up inside of her from resources she hadn't known she possessed.

Resolutely, she moved towards Duncan and knelt down, feeling for a pulse in his waxy rigid wrist, then pressing her ear to his chest to listen for a heartbeat. She neither felt nor heard anything, but then a faint bubbling sound coming from his mouth moved her to action. "Thank God he's alive," she murmured aloud.

Scrambling to her feet, she rushed to the phone and dialled the operator. The ringing sound droned monotonously; God, would she never answer? Finally, "Operator, this is an emergency; send an ambulance to 111 Post Road, I think my husband has had a stroke. And please, hurry!"

Chapter 6

Jan waited for Ben to come home from the party much as a bride would wait on her wedding night; eager, excited, fluttery, and at the same time somewhat fearful. She hoped he wouldn't be too drunk tonight; the baby's fever had broken, he was sleeping peacefully, and she meant to keep him that way. Even if Ben was drunk, it wouldn't matter too much, except for the fact that he usually started yelling and swearing and complaining bitterly about his lot in life. She was used to that, but she didn't want him to wake up the baby; tonight, especially.

Usually they spent the better part of every Saturday afternoon in bed while the baby slept, but today his crying had become intolerable. She had tried to ignore it, but in the middle of their lovemaking, Ben had abruptly pulled away from her and demanded she tend to their son. She got out of bed hastily and stood looking down at him; his penis was stiff and erect. She knew he didn't love the child the way he should, that his only motivation for the interruption of sex was irritation. She sighed once and bent down to kiss his closed eyelids, assuring him she'd be right back.

She rushed to little Ben, picked him up and rocked him back to sleep, her body still pulsing with heat and passion. She felt no rancor or animosity toward Ben because of his indifference to the child. After all, it wasn't his fault; nothing was ever Ben's fault. She was oblivious to his shortcomings. It wasn't that she closed her mind to them; for her, they just didn't exist.

Every day, she marvelled at her good luck, and couldn't understand why he had ever married her. She wasn't particularly attractive, and certainly too small and skinny, she thought. But to Jan, Ben was the biggest, handsomest, most virile looking man in the world, and she had fallen in love with him almost the first instant she met him. The thought never crossed her mind that he might be an opportunist who had married her for her money; or at the very least, because the power of her father could advance his position in life. She did not see the bloated, loutish, dull and stupid braggard that he actually was. She would not have tolerated any such references or innuendos had they been made in her presence, but they never were.

In the beginning, her father had occasionally been roused to a burst of anger at some unbelievably bad judgment or outrageously stupid blunder on Ben's part, and had said so in no uncertain terms to Jan. But all she had to do was draw her tiny stature up to its fullest height, stare her father straight in the eye as though he couldn't possibly be talking about the man she'd married, and he was instantly subdued.

Jan wasn't nearly as unattractive as she thought. True, her features by no stretch of the imagination could be called pretty, but they were small and even, she had an abundance of glossy brown hair, and her skin in Victorian days would have been described as porcelain. She was very small, under five feet, and very slender. The tiny bones in her wrists and ankles could almost be seen through the translucency of her delicate skin, and it seemed incredible that she had carried a healthy seven-pound baby boy throughout the full term of pregnancy. Her petiteness and delicacy instinctively aroused a sense of protectiveness in those around her, as though she were some fragile flower that would blow away unless constantly guarded. On seeing Jan and Ben together, it was difficult to imagine their personal and sexual relationship. Had their friends and relatives known the truth, they would have been surprised, startled, certainly shocked, and totally disbelieving.

For ironically, as fragile as Jan looked, she was tremendously oversexed. Ben had been astonished and delighted in the beginning, of course, and especially relieved that there was no false girlish modesty to contend with. Naturally, being Ben, he had bragged about his bride's agility and prowess in the bedroom to his buddies, and was met with raised eyebrows and complete disgust at his outrageous lying. This angered him at first, and more than once he had muttered such things to himself as "sore loser," "just plain jealous," or "too bad you've got a deadass at home yourself."

But as time wore on, he began to feel disturbed. He had considered her eagerness and ready response to his advances due to her being a new bride, and expected that her appetite would lessen and abate in a few months. But her enthusiasm and capacity seemed boundless; if anything, her needs appeared to increase. She was insatiable; if he was tired and just wanted a good night's sleep, she was always there, exploring his body, blowing in his ear, running her tongue lightly around his balls, gently kissing his nipples, softly sucking his armpits.

Oh Jesus! The first time she had done that, he'd almost gone out of his mind. He was dead beat, and nothing had been further from his mind than sex, but her gently licking tongue roused him to a frenzy. He had plunged inside of her with no concern for her delicacy or fragility, but only a desire to hurt; to dig himself in as deep as possible, thrusting first to the left then to the right, and her soft little cries of pain seemed to swell the bulk of his manhood. When he finally burst inside her with the full eruption of his passion, it was hard to tell whether her scream was one of agony or ecstasy.

He had rolled off her, completely drained, gasping for breath. At first, he had felt remorse as he looked at the slight, slender, perspiring creature beside him; as though he were an animal that had raped, ravaged, plundered, and ripped into the soul of her very being. And then, a strange thing began to happen as he looked at Jan. He watched her as she stretched slowly, then curled up into a little ball, her features relaxing into a soft smile of satisfaction, resembling a kitten who had just sucked the last of her mother's milk. It was at that very moment that he began to hate her.

Ben swung into the driveway and switched off the engine and lights carefully, hoping she was asleep. But even as he performed these actions in his more than half drunken state, he knew differently. Jan was always awake when he came home, waiting, eager and lustful. She drained him dry, so that any extramarital activities were not only impossible, but ridiculous to even contemplate. He lit a cigarette, stretched, and considered sleeping in the car. Tomorrow he'd have to face another of those goddamn family dinners, and he certainly didn't feel up to sex, especially after tonight.

Ted Enwright was a dumb, conceited ass, he decided. Ben had counted heavily on his help getting back into masonry, and was completely bewildered by Ted's flat refusal. Oh sure, the night before he'd had a few too many, but for God's sake, everybody did once in a while; and after all, wasn't he the best in the business? He had made sure not to drink too much before the barbecue, but every time he tried to talk to Ted during the evening he came up against a blank wall. And the people there stank; all uppity and snooty, acting like they were better than he was, except maybe for Kathy. Boy, that one was a looker, he thought, and wondered how often Dwight was making it with her. It never occurred to Ben that the people at the party actually *were* better than he was; it wasn't his lack of education or bad English, but his general coarseness and grossness that offended their sensibilities. He would never realize that the only reason they put up with him at all was out of pity for Jan; that he was out of his place and out of his element.

The cigarette started burning his fingers, so he crushed it out and slumped back in the seat, sulking. As he started to drift off, his thoughts meshed in kaleidoscope fashion . . . that Kathy, boy, would he like to get a piece of her, but Jan was fucking him to death . . . and Ted, he was a first class prick, and Ben would rot in hell before he ever asked him for anything again . . . then, in a sudden burst of clarity, Maybe he wasn't the best concrete mason in the world after all; but it was all Jan's fault, she wouldn't leave him alone . . . he could almost taste the hatred for her in his mouth as he went to sleep . . . .

"Ben, Ben!" Jan was shaking him furiously. "It's Daddy!"

He struggled up slowly from the murky depths of unconsciousness, through the muddled sludge of half-awareness, until he finally emerged into the painful state of hangover. He groaned with an effort, and tried to turn away, but Jan was still tugging at him.

With a superhuman effort, Ben forced himself to blink a few times, then looked at her. She wasn't kidding; her eyes were swollen and her face blotched with tears. In spite of his splitting head, he felt a certain sense of pleasure; at least he wouldn't have to lay her tonight, and the old man might kick off and leave Jan and him sitting on Easy Street.

He looked up at her and smiled warmly and sincerely. "I'm awful sorry, honey. You just wait one minute while I take a leak, then we'll go straight to the hospital."

Irene woke up early Sunday morning, with a rotten hang-over, a nauseated feeling in the pit of her stomach, and a throbbing headache. She lay in bed for a few minutes, trying to decide whether to take a Bromo and make herself vomit, or wait until it happened naturally, before she faced the problems of the day. And today, she had a real dilly of a problem facing her, just as soon as Ted got back from his tennis game.

She tried to console herself with the fact that the party had been a smashing success, the food had been excellent, there had been very few people who had too much to drink (with the exception of Ben, but that was par for the course), and the sound of Anne vacuuming downstairs assured her that the house would be spic and span by the time she descended. She decided on the Bromo and headed for the bathroom; but then she didn't need it after all, and barely made it to the toilet. She vomited profusely, followed by dry convulsions that subsided gradually.

She knelt by the bowl of the toilet for a long time, her body weak and trembling, soaked in sweat, pressing her head against the coolness of the porcelain until the shuddering spasms stopped. Wearily, she stood up on trembling legs and splashed cold water on her feverish face. Then she brushed her teeth thoroughly, and decided on a Bromo anyway, hoping to God it would stay down.

She called down to Anne for some black coffee and got back into bed again. Perhaps Ted was right, after all. After the last guest had left last night, she had heaved a sigh of relief, more tired than she cared to admit, kissed Ted lightly, and gone to her bedroom. She had just slipped into bed and was about to switch off the light when he suddenly appeared in the doorway. Ye Gods, not sex tonight! she thought.

"Oh Ted, I'm much too tired to even talk; and you've got

to be at the Club at the crack of dawn—it's almost that now."

He came over and sat down on the edge of the bed. "I know you're tired, Irene; I just want to talk to you for a minute." His voice was very kind, but he was looking at her speculatively. She had caught that same peculiar expression several times during the evening when their eyes had met. "Are you feeling all right?"

She smiled up at him drowsily. "I feel fine." And at that point, she did. "I'm tired, of course, and a little light-headed, maybe, but you know I'm always that way after a party." She yawned. "It did go off rather well tonight, don't you think?"

"Yes, yes, of course," he brushed the party aside as unimportant. "But I didn't come in here to talk about that. Irene, how long has it been since you've had a check-up?"

"Oh, I don't know; eight, ten months, maybe—I don't remember," she mumbled, stretching. "Ted, can't this wait until tomorrow? It's after three, and I'm bushed."

"No, it can't wait," he said emphatically. "I was watching you tonight, and you looked awfully pale. Now you've got dark circles under your eyes." He peered at her more closely. "Have you been having trouble with your periods lately?"

She propped herself up on one elbow and looked at him curiously. "No, I haven't, and if you're hinting that I'm starting the change, I don't think I'm quite ready for that yet. As far as the circles, that's hardly unusual at this hour of the morning. In case you hadn't noticed, I worked pretty damn hard on this party—with no help from you, I might add. Now, doctor, just what is all this extraordinary concern about the state of my health?"

He got up and started pacing the room, avoiding her eyes. "It isn't all that sudden—I've noticed you haven't looked well lately; and then sometimes you get dizzy and white as a sheet and I'm afraid you're going to faint. . . .'' he stopped abruptly, realizing he was parroting Kathy's words, and stood with his back towards her.

She lay in the bed, propped on her elbow, somewhat touched by his concern. It reminded her of the first years of their marriage, when if she had burned her finger on the stove, his consternation had been overwhelming. Then a slight nagging doubt began to tug at her; after so many years of polite reservations and hardly any communication between them, it was out of character that his attitude had changed so suddenly. And besides, when had he ever seen her get "dizzy and white as a sheet and look like she was going to faint?" No, someone must have been talking to Ted.

Suddenly, Kathy popped into her head. She remembered that Ted had been absent from the party for some time, and Kathy had been gone, too. Uncontrollable anger against the girl gripped her, but she tried to control herself. Kathy must have told him about her attack in the bedroom. She tried to keep her voice casual. "I don't remember ever getting dizzy, or for that matter, having any fainting spells. By the way, when Dwight and Kathy left tonight, she couldn't find her lighter; she thought she might have dropped it while you two were talking—I told her I'd ask you.''

"In the den, you mean? No, I didn't see it. I'll look around, but I'm sure it isn't there.'' As he looked at her, her lips curved slightly, and he realized she had trapped him into a disclosure that she had only suspected; suddenly he felt very stupid and slightly guilty. "Well, you're tired and it's late; get some sleep and we'll talk about your check-up when I get home tomorrow.'' He leaned over, kissed her hastily on the cheek, and beat a fast retreat to his own room.

Irene switched off the light, stretched again, and settled down to sleep, feeling smug in her feminine superiority. How could a man so successful and brilliant in the business world be caught by such a simple ruse? But then, by and large, women were much smarter than men; or maybe trickier was a better word. She drifted off to sleep. . . .

Anne came in with a large pot of black coffee and a glass of tomato juice on a tray. She was about to leave when Irene stopped her.

"Anne, do I look all right to you?" she asked abruptly.

"Why, just fine, Mrs. Enwright." Anne sounded surprised. "A little tired, maybe, but that was a big party last night. No, you look just fine," she repeated.

"Did Mr. Enwright say anything to you this morning? I mean, did he ask you about my health, or if you'd noticed anything wrong?"

"Why, no, ma'am, nothing. He just had his coffee and said he'd have breakfast at the Club, and to tell you he'd be home about three. Would you like me to get you anything else?"

Irene shook her head and dismissed her. She suspected the information had come from Kathy, but she had to make sure. It had been foolish to question Anne, though; now she'd start wondering. She sipped the tomato juice cautiously, which felt cool and smooth against her raw throat, then poured herself some coffee. Her anger against Kathy had dissipated during the night; perhaps both Kathy and Ted were genuinely concerned about her health.

She shoved the tray aside, went to the mirror and looked at herself closely. God, she looked awful! There weren't just dark circles under her eyes, but small pouches that looked like bags of soft dough. And the whites of her eyes didn't have the bloodshot appearance of a hangover or too little sleep; they were dull, lifeless, with a definite yellowish tinge. Her skin was sallow, too; crepey, dry, and slack. Fear began to creep over her, and the pain in her side started throbbing slowly but steadily.

Irene rummaged through her dressing table until she

found her old appointment book, flipped through it until she found her last appointment with the doctor; God, it had been thirteen months! How could she possibly have let it go so long? Impulsively, she picked up the phone and dialed him at home, trusting to fate to determine whether he would or wouldn't be there. The phone rang and rang, and she was about to hang up when the exchange answered. No, Dr. Sturgess wasn't home, he had an emergency at the hospital, the cool, impersonal voice at the other end told her; and yes, she was sure he could work her in, to be at his office ten o'clock Tuesday morning. The voice clicked off, and she sat there listening to the steady hum, before she gently cradled the phone back into the receiver. She sat there staring at it, instantly regretting the call; but it was done now, and she had committed herself. At least Ted would be pleased, and she could avoid a scene this afternoon.

God, she hated the thought of Tuesday morning, all that poking and probing; resolutely, she put it out of her mind. There were still Sunday and Monday to contend with, and she was damned if she was going to let worrying about whatever was wrong with her spoil a perfectly good two days. Fatalistically and practically, there was nothing she could do about it anyway.

She called down to Anne for some more coffee and the Sunday paper, then went back in the bathroom and turned on the shower. The stinging needles of hot then cold water seemed to refresh and revive her. Irene went back to the mirror and examined herself again. Not quite so bad now, she thought; the hot water had brought a healthier glow to her skin, the icy water a certain firmness. And she really felt fine, she tried to convince herself.

She drank the coffee Anne had brought her while she thumbed through the Sunday paper, looking for an art exhibition anywhere at the beach; she finally found one in Laguna. Then she expertly applied a heavy layer of makeup, wrote a hasty note to Ted, explaining that she had forgotten to tell him about the art exhibit in Laguna, and adding that she had made an appointment with Dr. Sturgess for Tuesday morning. She dressed quickly, left instructions with Anne, and headed down the highway into the steady stream of traffic.

After all, if the doctor did find something really, radically, wrong with her, she might just as well have one last little fling—and who knows? She might even find a painting that was really worth while. . . .

The air was still crisp and cool as Pam swung onto the Riverside freeway, but the sky overhead promised a muggy and humid Sunday. She was long overdue visiting her father and not particularly looking forward to the meeting; in fact, she was dreading it.

But Jack had asked her last night how long it had been since she had seen her father, and she had been instantly ashamed at the length of time that had elapsed. She had promised him immediately that she would go out there in the morning, without fail. Jack had always had that effect on her; when he asked her to do something, she did it, even though she did it grudgingly.

She swerved as the wind from a passing Mack truck swung her little Rambler, and swore profusely at the driver, which she never did in public. She laughed suddenly, a little nervous giggle, and stepped on the accelerator. The car spurted forward at breakneck speed, passing the truck. Her mind was still on Jack, but she tried to block him out and concentrate on her father. She hoped today would go well; Oh God, she hoped it would! It had all been so long ago, the hunting trip, and it really *had* been an accident. But every time she saw her father, lying there so helpless, staring at her with those hopeless, reproachful eyes, she saw her brother Jimmy again and again and again, and the visits never went well and it hadn't been her fault so why did she have to be reminded and suffer and feel guilty and Oh My God, why didn't her father just die peacefully and let her forget?

She sighed and shook her head; maybe today would be better. Maybe today she could talk about Jimmy and the good times the three of them had together in the past. But it was always so hard; his last stroke had left him completely paralyzed, and she could never really tell if he was listening, hearing, or even caring about what she said. And sanitary as the nursing home was, there was always the smell of sickness and death, that choked up in her throat until she had to swallow her nausea. Tears welled up in her eyes as she thought about him; God, he must hate it, just lying there, with nothing to look forward to other than death. He had been so healthy, so active, so very much a man. God would have been much kinder to have taken him swiftly, instead of letting him linger on in this living death.

Pam swung off the freeway and tried to collect her thoughts; another five minutes and she'd be at Riverview. About the only thing she could talk to her father about was Jimmy. When she spoke of her present life, her job, her friends, what she was doing, there was no response. But when she mentioned Jimmy, a certain warmth seemed to come into her father's eyes. She certainly couldn't talk about her mother; she had never even known her. When she was old enough to realize that her mother had died giving birth to her, she had tried to make up to her father for that. She had adored her father, although with the keen perception of childhood and innocence, she realized he loved Jimmy more. She had loved Jimmy, too, she hastened to assure herself.

Pam frowned suddenly, remembering Kathy and the Club yesterday; she had started to talk about Jimmy and had almost made a slip. A slip about what, she wondered vaguely? Funny; she never mentioned her brother at all, except to her father. And he couldn't even answer her.

But Dr. Carter; now that was a different matter. She had gone to see him about headaches and insomnia, and the first thing she knew, she was talking about Jimmy and her father. He hadn't said much in the few sessions they had together; nevertheless, he had made her feel uneasy. Somehow, she got the impression that the doctor thought there was something unhealthy in her attachment to her father. But that was ridiculous; her mother had died in childbirth, so naturally there was a close bond between them, and her father had never blamed her, she was certain of that. And if he favored Jimmy, that was also natural, he was his first-born; and if there was a certain amount of jealousy on her part, didn't that always happen between brothers and sisters, so wasn't that also normal?

No, she shook her head slightly, to clear her mind. The doctor had just been trying to stir up a hornet's nest where none existed. There had been nothing unhealthy, abnormal or unnatural about her relationship with her father.

Actually, Dr. Carter hadn't really helped her at all; on the contrary, her headaches increased severely, and her insomnia was no better—when she finally did go to sleep, she starting having nightmares. They were strange, terrifying dreams, almost nebulous, but she was always running in slow motion in some unknown place, down and down, with great globs of something falling after her, and she knew if she stopped running she would be buried alive. Somehow, she couldn't bring herself to tell Dr. Carter about her nightmares; but the more she saw him, the worse they became. That was when she began taking tranquilizers. It was also when she stopped seeing Dr. Carter professionally.

It was so easy; Dr. Sturgess had a large supply of all kinds of tranquilizers in his office. A few wouldn't be missed, she had thought. And blessed relief, she could sleep through the night. But after a while, the tranquilizers made her groggy in the morning, so she started taking uppers, which then required more tranquilizers. Of course, there had been that nasty scare when the police had been called in, but luckily she'd just laid in a large supply. Pretty soon, she'd stop all this; lately she'd noticed her tennis game was off, and one round of golf was plenty; yes, she'd stop soon. Maybe on her next vacation. She'd take a trip somewhere, get plenty of rest—she certainly didn't want to get hooked on pills. Not that she ever would, she told herself firmly; she could stop any time she wanted.

Her thoughts turned to last night; it had been a nice party, and she had really enjoyed herself. But then she generally did enjoy herself at Irene's parties, or Vivian's, or the Club. They were almost always the same closely-knit congenial set of people, which made her feel so comfortable and secure, although at Irene's parties there was usually some oddball sculptor or gay artist added to the group.

On the other hand, she enjoyed going to night clubs, too, but in a different way. There were usually a lot of single men around, and even though she always had a date, it gave her a delicious feeling to know that they were eyeing her, mentally undressing her. Actually, she supposed it was a sensual sensation, although for the life of her, she didn't really know what that meant. Sex was just something you had to do after a certain amount of dates, or stop seeing the man; or he'd stop seeing you. The few times she had allowed it to happen, it had been very distasteful. All that panting and sweating, and for what? She supposed she was frigid, but it didn't bother her too much. Certainly no one suspected, she was sure.

Jack Wentworth was about the only man she'd ever dated who never tried to make her. Oh, they did a lot of necking and petting, but that's as far as it ever went. Maybe he thought she was still a virgin; in a way, she was.

The sanitarium loomed up in front of her, abruptly bringing her thoughts back to her father. It was going to be a short visit today, she decided. Then she'd call Jack and maybe he'd meet her for a game of tennis at the Club.

Dr. John Carter had slept late this Sunday morning, awakening to the rich aroma of coffee wafting in from the kitchen. Edith was already up; her soft quiet movements were not disturbing. He glanced at his watch; ten o'clock. It was unusual for him to sleep so late. Normally he was on about the third hole at the public golf course by now, but Norman had sprained his ankle, and he didn't particularly relish the idea of playing with strangers. He wasn't a member of the Country Club; not because he couldn't afford it, although God knows psychiatrists didn't make as much money as people thought they did. But some of his patients were members of the Club, and hobnobbing with them on a social basis was not his idea of being a good psychiatrist.

It wasn't the free advice they asked him for that bothered him so much; all doctors were used to that. But being a psychiatrist was different than being a general practitioner or a surgeon. Somehow, people didn't seem to mind that a doctor was intimately acquainted with their bodies and malfunctions; but being intimately acquainted with their minds was an entirely different matter.

When he had first begun his practice, John had tried to socialize in a limited manner with some of his patients, but soon found this to be a bad mistake. They were uneasy around him; worse, they began to see him as a human being with all his faults and drawbacks, rather than as a father figure, a priest, or an all-supreme being who could cure their mental ills, real or imaginary.

On the other hand, most non-patients who knew he was a psychiatrist tried desperately (although at the same time trying to appear casual) to prove how completely normal they were. Consequently, he had very few close friends.

While he was working for his degree, John Carter had been

young and eager, ready to storm forth and save mankind from the ravages of the sick mind; or conversely, to save the sick mind from the ravages of mankind. He had seriously thought of working in a large metropolitan free clinic, but by the time he graduated, he had met Edith, and the Utopian idea became impractical. Instead, having been raised in a small town, he settled on a small-town practice in Monrovia. Over the years, his eagerness and enthusiasm had gradually been crusted over with a thin veneer of cynicism, although he still clung fiercely to his County Jail and Welfare patients, more as a memory—or, if you would, a tribute to his lost idealism—than anything else.

Edith tiptoed quietly to the door to see if her husband was awake, and he closed his eyes to feign sleep. After she left, he smiled slightly, Edith was a good wife. Over the years, she had softened and spread, but she tried to make him comfortable, and there wasn't a time he could remember, when he was called out on an emergency, that she hadn't had a hot meal waiting for him when he finally came home.

Comfortable; that was the word for their marriage. After the first heat of passion, which he found strangely unrewarding, they had settled into a life pattern of sameness which soothed, calmed and eased him at night, after a day that was often filled with sexual, violent, and sometimes perverted disclosures by his patients.

Edith was a simple, uncomplicated person, and he was very fond of her. If the words "dull . . . prosaic . . . stultifying" loomed up in his mind, he quickly nullified them by shifting his mind to his work, and the raw passions that he dealt with daily. If Edith had been a more complex, demanding sort of woman, his professional life would have suffered. He would mentally have been constantly analyzing, studying, and dissecting her. As it was, the sameness of her attitudes, the sameness of her responses, the very sameness of her being had, until now, acted as a counteractive balm to the tensions of his work. He was content. His life was wrapped up in his work, and, weighing his failures and successes, he had achieved a degree of satisfaction.

Through the years, his faith in himself had been shaken at times; the Calvados boy, for example. John had thought he was getting along quite well in their weekly sessions, and the boy's suicide had been a complete and total shock to him. So much so, that after the funeral and condolences to the bereaved family, he had gone off to a Catholic retreat for two weeks, to Edith's complete and utter bewilderment.

There had been a tacit understanding between them since their marriage that there would be no discussion of his patients, and this had been the first time that he had wanted very badly to discuss a case with her. But the habit of years was hard to break; instead, he had gone into retreat. He had done a considerable amount of soul-searching, and had come back with renewed strength and faith in himself. Since that time, he had returned to retreat at least once a year, while Edith visited her parents in Canada.

He stretched, yawned, lit a cigarette, and rearranged his thoughts. They really had a very adequate sex life, considering. That is, considering the length of time they'd been married; every Saturday night, and at least once during the week, or *almost* every week. Last night, Saturday, had been just the same . . . SAME! There was that damn word again!

Kathy popped into his mind without warning. An enigma, that one. A mixture of naïveté, sophistication, sweetness, hardness, caution, and a certain innocence that was very touching and very vulnerable. She was a difficult person to fathom, much less unscramble. In the few weeks she had been working for him, she had occupied his thoughts more and more. Occasionally, absentmindedly, he had called Edith "Kathy;" on the other hand, he had called Kathy "Edith"—they had both looked at him with the same enigmatic expression.

After their initial lunch at the Zanzibar, he had refrained from asking Kathy to join him again. It had been a foolish, impulsive act on his part, and he had no intention of making the same mistake. In the entire sixteen years of his marriage, he had never been unfaithful to his wife, and he had no intention of doing so now. It wasn't so much out of moralistic conviction on his part; rather, that the introduction of any extracurricular activity into his lifestyle would interfere with his concentration on the problems of his patients.

Not, of course, that John hadn't had many opportunities. Quite a number of his female patients, over the years, had convinced themselves they were in love with him. He was neither flattered nor dismayed; in some cases he considered this a healthy condition, in others, not so healthy, depending on the mental stability of the patient. A great majority of them, fortunately, got over this fixation as their treatment progressed. However, some of them with a deep-seated psychosis or neurosis, he felt he could no longer treat with any degree of satisfaction; and for their own good, he had turned them over to a colleague.

But Kathy intrigued him; on occasions when he had a free hour, or when a patient cancelled at the last minute, which was not infrequent, he would send her out for coffee for both of them, then ask her to join him in his office.

He had hoped to find out more about her past, but in that respect, he was disappointed. He knew she was seeing Dwight Keith, and that Pam had sponsored Kathy's membership in the Country Club. Pam; he shuddered when he thought of that friendship. They were the last two people in the world he had thought would become close friends, but he had been wrong.

Pam had started seeing him professionally almost a year ago, casually telling him she was having headaches and a sleeping problem, and she didn't like the idea of taking pills as a solution. It wasn't long before he was convinced she had a deep-seated emotional problem; he was equally convinced he was getting nowhere with her treatment. After a few sessions, he had suggested hypnosis; although she was reluctant at first, she had finally agreed. She was one of his few patients who were totally unresponsive to hypnosis, and after a few attempts, she had abruptly ceased treatment, with the excuse that her headaches and insomnia had cleared up considerably.

He wondered if she had confided to Kathy that she had been a patient of his, but seriously doubted it. All her appointments had been after regular hours, and she had always come in the back door. In any event, to probe in that direction, however indirectly, would be a serious violation of professional ethics, so he put it out of his mind.

Kathy; it was very strange. Although she was open and forthright about her present activities, she had not said another word about her past life since that day at the Zanzibar. It wasn't so much as if she was trying to hide anything, but more like a conscious effort to put the past where it belonged and get on with the business of living, and the future.

And then a curious thing began to happen. As they sat in his office talking and drinking coffee—gradually at first, so that it was scarcely noticeable—he found her talking less and less, and himself more and more. He told her of his childhood in the Midwest, the hardships he'd endured going through medical school; his hopes, beliefs and disillusionments at times throughout his life. In some inexplicable way, the pendulum seemed to have swung, and in these hourly discussions it was almost as though *she* were the doctor and *he* the patient.

Then in the midst of some revelation about his past, the buzzer in the reception room would sound, abruptly bringing him out of his reverie and back to the present, feeling somewhat foolish. He would promise himself over and over again that this would have to stop, yet every morning when he checked his appointments, there was an undeniable feeling of relief when there was a cancellation and therefore a free hour, and a feeling of disappointment when he was booked solid.

The hospital was a scene of bustling activity and the tension in the small waiting room could be cut with a knife. Dwight had arrived soon after the ambulance, Scott and Fran a little later, Fran's hair still in rollers, which she seemed to have forgotten about. After Vivian's explanations, which she had to repeat twice, once to Dwight, and again when Scott and Fran got there, the room settled into a dead silence.

Vivian had ridden in the ambulance with Duncan, murmuring over and over again, "Oh God, he can't die yet, he can't die yet." She caught herself by the time they reached the hospital—the family might think the word "yet" a little strange.

Each were deep in their own thoughts. Dwight caught Scott's eye, and knew their anxieties were the same. If their father died, there would be no question of an audit, and what would happen to the company then? There were also guilt feelings; they could have been kinder to the old man, spent more time with him, paid more attention to his feelings.

Fran was crying softly, out of fear and nervousness; she had never been this close to death before. To just sit there, not being able to do anything, just waiting . . . then she remembered her hair, and started to take the rollers out with trembling hands.

Vivian sat by herself, hands clasped tensely, like a graven image, although her mind was going a mile a minute. It seemed as though the ambulance had taken forever to get there, and all she could do was sit and wait. She left Duncan long enough to call Dwight and told him to call the others, then sat down on the bathroom floor again. Somewhere she remembered that you were supposed to keep the patient warm, so she took the bathroom rug and wrapped it around him, then sat down again. God, would the ambulance ever get here? It seemed like an eternity before she faintly heard the siren in the distance, and rushed to the front door.

The flurry of the ambulance ride, the explanations, had taken up some time, but now she was waiting again. Duncan was alive, but for how long? She considered calling Alex, but it would look conspicuous to leave the waiting room now, and would have to wait until later. Besides, what could she tell him now? Hurry up, take chances, get out all the money you can? Duncan might recover, and she hoped to God he would. She knew as well as his sons that his death would mean an audit, and she just wasn't ready. And where the hell were Jan and Ben? She caught herself just in time to hide a sarcastic smile. Ben was probably in a dead stupor, and Jan was having a devil of a time with him.

Just then, Jan rushed in, carrying little Ben, tears pouring down her face; Ben dragged groggily behind her. "How's Daddy? He's still alive, isn't he? Oh please, tell me he's alive." She stood there trembling, pleading, looking from one to another for reassurance.

Vivian got to her before Dwight or Scott could. "He's alive, darling. He's in Intensive Care now, but you know we have all the faith in the world in Dr. Sturgess. No, dear," she anticipated her next question, "you can't see him now, the doctor's with him. But it shouldn't be too long before we hear something."

The tension in the room seemed to have broken with Jan's arrival, and she continued crying quietly, rocking the baby. Every ten minutes or so, either Dwight or Scott would go out and inquire if there was any news, but it was almost noon before Dr. Sturgess came into the room, looking pale and wan.

All eyes were riveted on him, all with different thoughts, as he finally spoke. "Well, he made it." He spoke gravely. A general sigh of relief filled the room; again, each for different reasons. "But it wasn't a stroke, Viv," he continued, turning to her, "it was a coronary, and he almost didn't make it. I'm afraid things will be very different from now on, but we can go into that later."

Inwardly, Vivian felt as though a great load had been lifted; he would live, then there was still time—but a coronary, how much time? She covered her face with her hands as Dwight helped her sit down. "When can I see him?" she asked in a muffled voice.

"He's in intensive care, Viv, and very groggy. I'm afraid there won't be any visitors for a while yet." He turned to Jan. "He kept asking for you, my dear. I don't think it would hurt if you just went in for a minute; but don't let him talk, and keep a grip on yourself. Your father's been through quite an ordeal, so don't act surprised when you see him."

Jan, although she was crying tears of relief now, crumpled in Ben's arms, and drew away from him. She handed the baby to Ben, dried her eyes, and tried to pull herself together. She looked out the window briefly, and when she turned back to the doctor, her eyes were dry, her voice steady. "Alright, let's go."

Jan walked to her father's bedside, and although she was prepared for the worst, she was glad his eyes were closed. His face was gray, and his head seemed to have shrunk. All she could think of was a death mask. She put her small hand on his, and his eyes opened groggily; the same blue as hers, but duller now, and filled with pain. He started to say something, but she stopped him quickly. "Daddy, the doctor says you're not to talk—that's the only reason he let me in here."

"Jan, there's something I have to say, and there might not be too much time." He spoke with difficulty, "Always remember, my dear, no matter what happens to me, or to the company, you'll be provided for." His voice was thick and slow, fuzzy from the medication they had given him. "Don't say a word about this to Vivian, or the boys, promise me. My attorney is the only one who knows."

"Daddy, please don't talk anymore, you don't know what you're saying, and the doctor will make me leave. Nothing's going to happen to you, you're going to be just fine. Just let me sit here by you, quietly. . ." she pleaded.

"Promise me, Jan," his tone was more urgent now. "Please."

"Alright, I promise. Now rest, Daddy, you need all the rest you can get. Just close your eyes, and I'll stay here with you until they make me leave."

Satisfied, he sighed, and shut his eyes dutifully, still clinging to her hand. When the nurse came in a few minutes later, she had to very carefully disengage his fingers from Jan's.

Jan stood outside the door of Intensive Care, puzzled, and trying to think. What could her father have meant? Nothing was going to happen to the company. She'd have to ask Dwight or Scott; then she stopped herself. She wasn't to say a word to anybody, but why especially Vivian? Then she took hold of herself. Nothing was going to happen to her father. Lots of people had heart attacks and they lived for years, if they took care of themselves properly. And she, for one, would make sure that her father did.

Dr. Sturgess had wanted to start his morning rounds, then go home and fall into bed, but Vivian had been insistent on details. Wearily, he resigned himself. Duncan had had a coronary, and it had been nip and tuck for several hours. If all went well, he'd be out of Intensive Care in the next few days, but he really didn't know how long he'd have to be in the hospital. He would have special nurses around the clock, of course. When he did come home, he'd have to have complete bed rest for a time. Vivian would have to make one of the downstairs rooms into a bedroom. Above all: NO WORK,

NO TENSION. The special diets and private nurses would come home with him. Then he waited for questions, but none were forthcoming.

Vivian, Dwight and Scott all looked at each other. Vivian spoke first. "Well, I guess we all know this means a special Board Meeting as soon as possible. A week, at the outside, don't you think?" Dwight and Scott, relieved that the decision had been hers, had agreed immediately. "I think, in the meantime, I can take over for Duncan," then she added hastily, "with your help, of course."

Dr. Sturgess looked at the three of them sardonically. Ben didn't count, he was curled up on one of the couches, asleep and snoring. These three people, who just a short while ago were weeping and worrying about Duncan's death, were now discussing board meetings! They could just as well be making funeral arrangements. He shook his head, and left the room. As long as he had been a doctor, he was still not inured to the foibles of human nature. He met Jan outside, and felt a sudden rush of sympathy for her. She was the only one, he decided, who was genuinely concerned about her father. Very gently, he explained the situation to her. She looked drawn and spent as she listened to him gravely.

"Will he live, Doctor?" she tried to keep her voice from trembling.

"With proper care, he could live for years, Jan, but the next few weeks will still be crucial. And even after he's been home for a couple of months, and begins to think he's feeling better, there will be no more going to the office. Above all, he's to have no worries, especially business worries, and that's going to have to be up to the rest of the family. As for you, my dear," he continued, "you can be a big help to him. Spend more time with him alone; I wouldn't bring little Ben too often. Children can be much too taxing for a man in your father's condition."

She gazed at him calmly enough, although she knew what

he was thinking. Don't bring Ben, either, he meant. Well, she didn't intend to. Last night, for the first time, Ben hadn't quite measured up to her expectations of him. The talk on the way to the hospital, for instance. Of course, she realized he was still drunk, but it hadn't been concern for her father's life that he'd talked about, as much as the money she'd inherit. She looked through the glass door of the waiting room and saw that he had passed out again. Slowly, the first tiny feeling of—what, disgust?—crept over her.

And she had been so happy earlier tonight, even though she hadn't been able to go to the party. Her period was four days overdue, which wasn't too unusual, but the thought of having a little brother or sister for little Ben had excited her. Should she tell the doctor? No, it was too soon for that, and she wouldn't tell Ben either; her father was her first consideration now. "May I come back later, in case my father asks for me again?" she asked. "I think I'd better drive Ben home now."

"Of course, Jan," he replied, "but get some rest yourself first, you're going to need all your strength in the next few months." He glanced at his watch, "Now, I've really got to make rounds."

He walked off down the corridor. Jan watched him until he disappeared around a corner, then braced herself to go back in and collect her baby and Ben, who was still snoring noisily.

They all looked up when she came back in, and Dwight and Scott started asking questions. She mumbled something about her father wanting her to reassure everyone that he'd be alright, then had drifted off again. Vivian was looking at her pointedly, but she tried to ignore it.

Vivian was looking at her for a reason—her explanation didn't ring true, and why had he wanted to see her instead of his own wife? Granted, she was his favorite offspring, he had never made any bones about that. But it couldn't have anything to do with the company, she was sure. If that had been the case, he would have asked for Dwight or Keith. Still, there was something Duncan had found important enough to tell his daughter, and Jan wasn't talking. Vivian was determined to find out just what that something was.

Chapter 7

Irene lay on the doctor's table, her feet in the stirrups, waiting for the doctor. She gazed steadily at the frosted glass ceiling and the number of dead flies lying on it. They really ought to hose off the roof more often. She got tired of counting dead flies, and sat up. Dr. Sturgess would be late, she knew. She hated waiting like this, but the doctor was still at the hospital. Terrible thing about Duncan; when Vivian had called her late Sunday night, she'd been shocked, then guilty at the stunt she'd pulled on her the night before. She rummaged around in her purse for a cigarette, then remembered—God, no ashtrays. Larry Sturgess was dead set against smoking, so she had a peppermint instead, and lay down again.

Why did they have to make these tables so damned uncomfortable? She glanced at her watch, then put it to her ear; was time going that slowly?

Sunday had been a complete waste—the art exhibit had been tacky, and most of the artists had been old. The few young ones had looked so grubby, she hadn't been interested at all. And all the time, the thought of Tuesday morning was lurking in the back of her mind.

She tried to keep her mind off the examination, but it was no use. She'd already had the blood test and EKG, and she'd brought in a urine sample, but now came the hard part. All that poking and probing, then sticking that thing inside her while he looked at her insides with a mirror on his forehead. All in all, it was very undignified. And it *hurt* so damned much. She wondered why, since it was a skinny little instrument, and sex, even if the man was large, didn't hurt at all. Until lately, that is. Oh God, she hoped it wasn't anything very serious. What if it was a venereal disease? She'd always worn her diaphragm, and douched afterward, but there was always that chance. Now how would she explain that to Ted? She shuddered at the thought. Oh, come on, Larry, this place is driving me stir crazy.

When he finally did arrive, her nervousness increased. The first thing she did was ask him about Duncan, who was still in Intensive Care, but coming along nicely, he said. All doctors said that, she thought, *Coming along nicely*, and you could be dead the next day.

"Well, Irene, it's been a long time," he said briskly, slipping on his rubber gloves. "You're running a slight temperature." He put her feet back in the stirrups and lifted the sheet.

"Damn," she groaned.

"Irene, I barely touched you. Now, take deep breaths and try to relax, you're just making it harder on yourself."

The poking and probing began, and it was pure agony. She bit her lip, and wished she'd had a few drinks this morning, although she knew Larry didn't approve of that, either. His fingers stopped at one point and pressed harder. She couldn't stop from screaming out in pain. He took his fingers out instantly, and the relief was immediate. He started putting the mirror on his forehead. "Irene, how long have you been having these pains?"

"Not until you started doing this," she lied.

He didn't answer her directly, but got out the long silver instrument. "This is going to hurt, but it won't take long, and I'll be as careful as I can." She tensed immediately. "I told you to relax," he told her sternly. As the long silver tube slid in, the pain was unbearable, but she bit her lips again, unwilling to give him the satisfaction of knowing what she was going through. He peered inside her for what seemed like a very long time before removing the object. The nurse pulled the sheet back down, and she lay there, bathed in perspiration.

"What is is, Larry? Please don't pull any punches."

He didn't answer her right away; instead, he started putting his instruments away, and motioned the nurse to leave the room. She was scared now, really scared. The pains during sex lately had been bad enough, even though they'd been dulled by alcohol, but this had been terrible.

"I can't tell yet, Irene. You have a cyst on your left ovary, that much I can tell you for sure, and you'll probably have to have a hysterectomy. I want to get some X-rays and run some other tests; we'll know more then."

She breathed a sigh of relief. A hysterectomy wasn't so bad, not any more, with the hormones and the other things they gave you. Besides, when it was over, she wouldn't have to worry about that damn diaphram.

On the way home, she started thinking. She had stopped at the desk to make an appointment for the X-rays and tests, but she hadn't bothered to ask Larry any more questions, she was so anxious to get out of there. His tone of voice, though. Now that she started thinking about it, it didn't have his usual cheerful quality. But it couldn't be anything else, she'd asked him to give it to her straight. A sudden thought flashed through her mind, and she almost swerved off the road. *Could it be cancer?* Oh no, that was something that happened to other people, not to you, and it usually ran in families, there was no cancer in her family. Then she remembered great aunt Mavis on her mother's side; but they had put that down as old age, not cancer. Even so, she was always complaining about having pains "down there," as they called it in those days, and she did have fainting spells.

Well, there was no sense in worrying about it now. The tests were set for Thursday, and she couldn't possibly get the results until Monday. She decided not to tell Ted anything; after all, what consolation was he? And April—she hardly ever wrote any more, although to be fair, she didn't write her daughter much either. It was strange, she thought, jealous of her own child, and now she had a sudden desire to see her. After all, it had been two years. Before that, she always came home for summer vacations and Christmas, but for the past two years there had been excuses; staying with friends from school, touring Europe, skiing trips. At first, she'd hoped that April's staying in Europe would bring Ted and her closer together, but it hadn't. If anything, they were driven farther apart, as though it was *her* fault that April preferred living abroad.

She had been glad to see her when she came home, but was relieved to see her leave. Ted and April were so close they made her feel left out, and seeing April's fresh youthfulness didn't improve her spirits, either. Each time she came home, she thought it would be different, but it never was.

Well, there was nothing to do but wait now. Suddenly, tears came to her eyes. Sure, she gave the best parties in town, and she knew everyone worth knowing, and got asked everywhere, but she didn't have any friends; that is, any *real* friends. Certainly not anyone she could confide in. She couldn't blame it all on Ted; after all, it took two to make a marriage disintegrate. And the church she belonged to, she only went spasmodically. Most of the members were hypocrites, she thought. All the women looked around to see what everyone else was wearing, and for the life of her, she couldn't concentrate on the sermons.

She got home around one o'clock, told Anne she was going to bed and didn't want to be disturbed until she called, then she wanted a light supper. She stopped by Ted's library on the way up to her room, and found the book she wanted. She picked up the book, and for the first time since she was very young, started reading the New Testament.

Kathy arrived at the office intentionally early Tuesday morning, checked to see if the doctor had come in the back way, then got out Jack Wentworth's file. What had the doctor said? "Be in the office when the patients change." (Well, that rule she'd broken.) "Don't discuss the patient's history." (Strike two—at least with Irene's husband.) What else? Oh yes, "don't go out with any of the patients." Well, she hadn't done that, not yet.

She sat down, flipped open the file and started reading avidly. Usual background material, no siblings, served in the United States Navy as a medical orderly, history of masturbation in childhood and early teens, married in his late twenties, divorced three years later, extreme resentment of his father, dating back to childhood. Drinking habits; "says normal, but some doubt."

At that point, the typewritten report ended, and the other entries in the file were in Dr. Carter's own scribbling. Damn the doctor, she thought, and just when it was getting interesting.

She heard the key in the back door, and hastily slipped the folder back in the file. "Good morning, Kathy," Dr. Carter stuck his head in the door. "Have a nice weekend?"

"Oh yes, but rather quiet," she answered, hoping she didn't sound guilty. "Here's a list of today's patients."

He looked at the list and grimaced. "I'm going to be taping for a while. Bring us both some coffee in about a half hour, will you?"

The weekend actually had ended up pretty quiet, after

Saturday night. Dwight had called her Sunday morning with the disturbing news that his father was in the hospital, in Intensive Care, and she had considered herself quite sympathetic, since it was six-thirty in the morning. When he called her back twenty minutes later to say there had been no change, she had again assured him she was very sorry; after that, she had taken the phone off the hook.

She flipped through the doctor's appointment book idly, waiting until it was time to get the coffee. She had been here seven weeks now, and knew all the patients by name, and most of their problems. Jack Wentworth's name appeared regularly, every Monday, Wednesday and Friday, with most of the appointments marked through in red. All of them, in fact, except the one time he'd come in since she'd worked here, and that time she had barely noticed him. She went back farther in the book to the first of the year, looking for his name. January and February he'd come in fairly regularly, March and April spasmodically, and May only twice. She looked at the clock, and there was still ten minutes to go until she went after the coffee. She started back through the book again, reading more slowly, then suddenly she stopped. January 28, 1946, 5:15; Pamela Sterling. The name had been scratched through, but in a different color ink, and she could still read through the scratches. She looked further through the book, but there were no more entries. And she knew there was no file on her, unless it was under a different name. Odd; Pam and she had become pretty close now, still she hadn't said a thing about seeing the doctor. She looked at the clock again, called the answering service, and went to get the coffee.

The rest of the day had flown by, and she was about to close the office when the phone rang. "Kathy?" The man's voice was slurred, but it sounded slightly familiar.

"I'm sorry, but the doctor's left for the day. May I take a message?"

"I didn't want to talk to him, I want to talk to you," he said fuzzily, "and don't you tell him I called, y'hear?"

"I just told you, he's not here. Who is this, anyway?" She had a pretty good idea who she was talking to now, but she had no idea why he was calling her.

"It's Jack—don't you remember me? We met at the party the other night."

She sat down at her desk again. Jack Wentworth; well, he was certainly loaded for this early in the day, but if that was what it took to get him to call her, it was worth it. She smiled slightly, and decided to play around a little. "Jack who?" she asked, "what party and what night? I go to a lot of parties."

"Jack Wentworth," he sounded almost outraged. "Last night, or the night before, I guess, at Irene's and Ted's," he sighed, and his voice was thicker than before. "Don't you remember me? What day is it, anyway?"

She began to be concerned. This was Tuesday, and that meant he'd been on a three-day drunk. "Jack, have you been drinking?" she asked, although the answer was obvious.

"Yeah, a little; can you tell? But don't you tell the doctor." He seemed to have forgotten she'd told him the doctor was gone. "Just between you and me," he whispered confidentially, "I took some pills, too."

"Pills! On top of liquor? What kind of pills, how many pills?" She was really concerned now. My God, she had wanted him to notice her, but not this way.

"Oh, I dunno," he slurred vaguely. "Four, maybe five. I forget. Little white ones. Can you come over? I need someone to talk to."

Seconals; oh God, she hoped not. "Where are you, and what's the quickest way to get there?"

"I'm in bed, of course, where else would I be? I'm all alone in my big lonely bed, just lying here waiting for you. But now I'm gonna get up and put on my brand new pajamas. Oh dammit, there goes that cuckoo clock again, the people next door just bought one, and it goes off every fifteen minutes. I think I'll go over and break that sonofabitching thing, then I'm gonna punch the bastard in the nose.''

''Never mind, I'll find the place myself. Now you just put on your pajamas and heat some water for coffee, and keep walking 'til I get there. You do have some coffee, don't you?''

She checked his address from the files, swept the papers on her desk in her drawer, and was out of there in record time, running to her car. She swerved in and out of traffic, ran two red lights, and pulled up in front of an expensive looking apartment building near the racetrack. His apartment was towards the rear, and she had to walk the entire length of the pool to get to it. Several of the tenants were still lounging by the pool, and they looked at her rather strangely.

She suddenly realized what a sight she must be, her long hair tousled by the wind racing down the freeway, obviously in new surroundings, and in a nurses' uniform, yet. Well, at least they couldn't think she was a hooker.

Each apartment had its own little outdoor patio, separated from the pool and barbecue by high redwood fences. She finally found Jack's, opened the latch, and went in the small enclosure. The front door was slightly ajar and she hesitated, not knowing what to expect. Then she pushed open the door and called to him. The living room was large and modern, surprisingly neat for a bachelor. ''I'm in here,'' he called from the bedroom. She walked down the short hallway, running her fingers nervously through her hair, and stopped in the doorway, shocked.

He was sprawled across the kingsize bed in striped pajamas, freshly shaved, and freshly showered; the steam was still coming from the bathroom. There was also a faint aroma of aftershave lotion in the room, and a fresh drink on his bedside table. He may have been drinking, but he was nowhere near the condition she'd expected to find him in. She picked up the small bottle beside the drink and looked at it. Valium.

"Jack, I could gladly kill you. If you knew what you put me through; I nearly broke my neck to get here, thinking I might be too late, that you could be dead, and here you are, ready to start in all over again. Either you have amazing recuperative powers, or you put on the best damned act I've ever seen. I'm leaving."

As she turned to leave, he grabbed her quickly and pulled her down on the bed with him, laughing. She tried to get up, but he was much stronger than she, and they rolled and tussled until he had her shoulders pinned down. "I'm sorry," he grinned down at her, "but would you have come over otherwise?"

She stopped struggling, and glared up at him. "Now, that's something you'll never really know, will you?"

Instead of answering, he leaned down slowly and started to kiss her. She tried to fight him again, but the long months of abstinence were too much for her. She began to relax, and the pressure of his mouth increased until her lips parted. She returned his kisses just as deeply, and as his hands roamed and explored her body with easy assurance, she felt the familiar burning sensation welling up inside her. Suddenly, the cuckoo clock started, and they broke away from each other, laughing.

"This is one of the long ones," he said, glancing at his watch, "and you should hear it at midnight. So help me, one of these days, I'll kill that son of a bitch. Want a drink?"

"No, thank you," she said politely. What she really wanted to do was take her clothes off. "Jack, if it bothers you so much, why don't you just go over there and ask them to move it to another wall? After that, if they don't do anything, tell the building owner."

"I *am* the owner." He looked at her peculiarly. "You must know I'm in real estate." He finished his drink and listened. "Well, the clock's stopped; shall we get back to

157

what we were doing before we were so rudely interrupted?"

In answer, she stood up, slipped out of her dress, shoes and pantyhose. He pulled her down to him again roughly, ripping her slip in the process. His lovemaking was almost savage in its intensity, and her body responded eagerly. He felt her response, and his actions became more violent, more basic, as they rolled and thrashed, bodies locked together, mouths glued together. She was caught up in the turbulence, the world locked out, and her nails raked his back as he gripped her tighter, tighter, until the final eruption of primal unadulterated sex.

When their passion subsided, they rolled away from each other, sweating, satisfied and spent. He lit cigarettes for both of them, and they lay there smoking quietly. Kathy came back to reality slowly. She had never known sex like this before; there had been nothing civilized about it, no love, no tenderness. Animals mated this way—and she had loved every minute. She wondered what he thought of her, and couldn't look at him. God, she must have seemed easy; she cringed at the thought. In her wildest dreams, she never would have imagined Jack could have made love that way; correction, have sex that way. Suddenly, the doctor popped into her head: *don't go out with the patients*. Well, she hadn't gone out with one of the patients, she'd topped that one; so much for Rule #3!

"I think I'd like to take a shower," she said finally.

"Oh no, not yet, let's talk for a while. We'll have a couple of drinks here, then we'll go out to diner. I want you to meet some of my friends." He rolled out of bed and walked over to the dresser, which was neatly lined with liquor bottles. Evidentally, he used the bedroom for his bar, which partially explained the neatness of the living room. "What can I get you?"

"Bourbon on the rocks, please." She figured she had a lot of catching up to do, and she might as well get started. She was also slightly miffed; he was certainly acting very casual about everything. Then again, maybe this was an everyday occurrence with him. He handed her the drink, fluffed up the oversized pillows behind them, and got back into bed.

"Tell me, honey," he asked offhandedly, "what's the doc say about me?"

Here we go again, she thought. "I told you the other night, Jack," she chose her words carefully, "the doctor doesn't discuss any of his patients with me, and I *don't* read his files," she lied. "If you don't believe me, and think a little sex and a few drinks are going to start me talking, we might as well forget about dinner. I think I'll just put my clothes on and go home."

"A *little* sex!" he exploded indignantly. "Well, I'll try and do better next time; that is, if there is a next time." He squinted at her quizzically. "Please don't go home, I was just asking. It's only normal, you know. Doesn't that sound funny, coming from me?" He took a sip of his drink, and lay back against the pillows, reaching for her hand. "You know, when I go see the doc, which isn't too often lately, I'm sure you know, I have all kinds of things to tell him. Then I lean back in that lousy chair of his, and my mind goes completely blank for a while. Either that, or I can't think of what to start with first, so we just sit there, sometimes for half or more of the session. That's an awful lot of money, don't you think, fifty bucks an hour, for just sitting?" He didn't wait for an answer. "Then when I finally do start talking, he just leans back in his chair, closes his eyes, and if he didn't say something once in a while, I'd think he was asleep. Come to think of it, sometimes he *doesn't* say anything. Do you think he really goes to sleep?"

She laughed at the thought, because she'd wondered herself. Several times when she'd brought him his coffee, she'd found him in the same position. "Of course not, Jack, what a question," she felt a little guilty at the half-truth. "He's just letting you talk out your hostilities, letting you arrive at your own conclusions. If he did all the talking, then he'd be imposing his thoughts and conclusions on yours, and that's not the point of psychiatry at all. He might throw in an idea or two once in a while, but that's just when you get off in the wrong direction. Of course he doesn't sleep."

"Well, I hope you're right." He didn't seem entirely convinced. "If he did, I'd be just as well off with a tape recorder. Well, I guess I'll start seeing him again. Can I get in at two tomorrow?"

Kathy looked at him, surprised. "Jack, is that why you've cancelled so often? Of course you can see him, we've never stopped making your regular appointments, even though you didn't show up—much less call," she said pointedly. She shook her head in wonderment. Of all the crazy things to do. If he thought the doctor was sleeping, why didn't he just cancel out altogether, and see another psychiatrist? Then she remembered he was a nut, or he wouldn't be seeing the doctor in the first place, although his case history didn't seem too much out of the ordinary. "Fix me another drink, would you please?" Obligingly, he went to the dresser, while she stared at his lean tanned back intently. I wonder, she thought, just exactly what *is* wrong with him? He appeared normal enough, although his scheme to get her over here was certainly elaborate, especially after practically ignoring her at Irene's. Then too, he seemed to overreact to the cuckoo clock, particularly since he owned the building. She decided to turn the tables on him. "Tell me, Jack," she asked, "just what *do* you talk about with the doctor?"

He turned to her as swiftly as a cat, outraged, and his face was like a thundercloud. "Now what in the hell kind of a question is that?"

Just then the cuckoo went off again, and he ran to the living room, and started banging on the wall so hard she thought his fist would go through, yelling, "Turn that damn thing off!'' He kept on banging and yelling until she heard something fall, but the clock kept right on chirping until it had run its course. There was dead silence for a few minutes, and it was awful. She didn't know what to expect next.

He walked back to the bedroom, grinning. ''They must have been out.'' He finished mixing their drinks, and she took a big gulp of hers. ''Tell you what; let's trade. You tell me what the doc says about me, and I'll tell you what we talk about.''

She wasn't exactly sure she wanted to know anymore, but she didn't want to get him stirred up again. She had never in her whole life seem such a mercurial change come over a person, and just as quickly disappear.

''I really don't know, Jack, and that's the truth. I *did* read your file, but all it said was that you were divorced, didn't like your father very much, and you were in the medical corps . . . wait a minute, you knew just how many pills you could mix with booze and still be safe, didn't you?'' She was so angry, mostly at herself that she'd been taken in, that she forgot to be afraid of him.

''Sure,'' he admitted slyly, ''I was wondering how long it'd take you to figure that one out. What else did it say?''

''That's all. All the rest is written in the doctor's notes, and I can't read his writing.''

''That's all?'' He sounded disappointed. ''Come on, honey, there must be something else. Doesn't he ever talk about me?''

''No, he doesn't, and that's all there is.'' She leaned back, smiling smugly. ''And now, it's your turn.''

As though on cue, the phone rang. He grinned at her wickedly. ''Saved by the bell.'' He let it ring a few times before answering it.

''Hello?'', he said pleasantly. Then his voice changed, ''Oh, it's you.'' She could hear a man's voice speaking rapidly, but not loudly enough for her to tell what he was saying. Jack said nothing, but his face was sullen, and began to turn beet red. The voice at the other end of the line grew louder, and she caught something about a dinner and the guests were still waiting—the rest she couldn't make out. "Are you just about through?" he said in a chilling tone. "Listen, you bastard, I told you last week I had no intention of coming, and you can tell that motherfucking wife of yours that I'll never set foot in that house again, not until she's six foot under."

Kathy gasped; she knew he was wealthy, but no matter how much money he had, he had no right to speak to anyone that way. She assumed it was a business acquaintance, or a friend he'd had a falling out with, but surely that was no way to make friends and influence people. And what if his father heard about it?

"Besides that," he continued, "I don't want you calling me at home any more. If we ever have anything to discuss, although at the moment I can't possibly think what it could be, you can call me at the office and make an appointment." (She was right, it did have something to do with business.) "Now," he said firmly, "since I have company, and she's a very beautiful girl, I am going to hang up on you and take the phone off the hook. You can tell Betsy to go to hell for me, too," he added as an afterthought. He pressed the button down firmly for a few seconds, listened for the dial tone, then put the phone under the bed. He laid back against the pillows and stared off into space, while the red slowly receded from his face.

"Well," she said weakly, not quite knowing what to say, "I guess you don't like that man very much."

"Not much," his voice was noncommittal.

"But, Jack," she protested, "you just can't go around calling people names like that, not in a small town like this. Word gets around; suppose your father heard about it?"

He turned towards her then, his mood completely changed. He had an amused smile on his face, as though he had some private joke. "Kathy, honey, you don't understand. That *was* my father." Then he pulled her to him, and they made love again, with the same intensity as before.

This time, when it was over, she lay in his arms, wanting to feel the closeness of him. She was terribly curious about his father, but had no idea how to broach the subject without upsetting him again. She'd had just about enough scenes for one night. But then, she didn't have to question him because once his sex needs were fulfilled for the time being, his mind went back to his father.

"That lousy bastard," he said grimly, as though he was talking to himself. "All that fucking money, and he made me pick cotton."

"Cotton?" she said weakly. That just didn't make any sense. Why would his father make him pick cotton? Besides, there wasn't any cotton around here, not that she knew of. All this was becoming very strange.

"Yeah, cotton," he said defiantly. "He sent me to the best private schools he could find, then in the summer, when all my friends were having a good time, he sent me down to Louisiana to pick cotton. Said it would make a man out of me. I broke my ass down there, fourteen hours a day, with nobody to talk to, and for what? A lousy twelve cents an hour, can you believe that? All I did from sunup to sundown was work—the food was slop, and we were lucky if we got meat twice a week. Practically all the other guys were black, and some of them tried to help me with my work sometimes, but we didn't have anything in common. What could we talk about, anyway? They were poor blacks, and I was rich white. "Redneck," they used to call me. That first summer was sheer torture, believe me, but I stuck it out. Mainly, I guess, because I didn't think my father thought I had the guts to take it. And I was only sixteen.''

He took her empty glass and got up to make them drinks, while Kathy waited for him to continue.

''My mother was dead set against the idea from the beginning, of course, but the old man ruled the house with an iron fist, so there really wasn't much she could do about it. I never blamed her; she just couldn't stand up to him. And she was a lovely, lovely lady,'' he said softly, remembering.

''When I came back,'' he continued, ''I was bitter at first, hating him, but the old man was just busting with pride, telling all his friends what I'd done, while all the other kids were swimming and having fun; I kind of forgave him. Next summer, I thought, I'd really make up for it, for all the time I'd lost. But then next summer came, and he wanted me to do the same thing again. I couldn't believe him, at first.''

''Hell, Kathy, you know how much money he's worth? I don't even think he knows himself. When the depression hit, when I was a kid, we still weren't hurting any. But for appearances sake, he shut down the main house, and we moved into the servants' quarters. Even the servants quarters had a swimming pool. He made a killing on the crash, even though he did go around crying 'poor mouth.' ''

''But to get back to this cotton business. When I got home from school next summer, I flatly refused to go, but he said he could force me, that I was still underage. We argued constantly for three weeks, and my mother couldn't do anything about it. Everytime she'd try to interfere, he'd shout her down, and her health wasn't any too good at the time, anyway. Just how bad it was, I didn't find out until later. She never complained, though. If she had, things might have been different.''

''Then it hit me—I'd be eighteen in a few months, and I'd join the Navy. It wasn't exactly the ideal solution, but what a jolt for old B.J.! He'd had me enrolled in Harvard for years, and I could just hear him trying to explain that! I was bursting to tell somebody, but there was nobody I could trust, not even my own mother. I pretended to give in, and packed to go back to the Delta. I had plenty of money socked away, enough to last me until I was eighteen, anyway, but I'll never forget saying goodbye to my mother—I'll never forget that day as long as I live. . . .''

Kathy listened quietly, afraid to break the spell. Jack was different now, and she realized he was scarcely aware of her presence; he was thinking out loud, reliving old memories, painful memories, and she felt his pain; it was as though she had been there herself as he continued:

"She was lying on the pink chaise in her bedroom, reading a copy of *Madame Bovary*. I don't know why she liked that book so much, she must have read it a hundred times—maybe something about the misery of Emma reminded her of herself; I don't know. There was a faint scent of lavender in the room, and she looked very pale, but very pretty. I told her that I'd come to say goodbye, and then I just stood there in the doorway.

"She sighed a little, put down her book, and stretched out her arms to me. 'Come here, son,' she said quietly. 'You mustn't be too hard on your father,' her voice was very tired. 'After all, he never had it easy when he was young, and he's just trying to have you follow in his footsteps. I know it must seem kind of crazy to you, sending you to the best schools, then down South to pick cotton; but to his way of thinking, you'll see both sides of life. I don't know, maybe he's right, but you know I've never agreed with him.' She hesitated, then seemed to make up her mind about something. 'I've never told you this before, Jack, and I don't know exactly why I'm telling you now, but your father expected a big family. When you were born, though, something got twisted inside, and the doctor said there couldn't be any more children. It was a bitter disappointment to him.'

"She turned her head slightly, and a tear slid down her

cheek. 'I guess that's why I haven't stood up to him more about you—I just can't bear it when he throws that up to me, I feel as though I've failed him. You're all he's got, Jack, his only son and heir, and it makes me miserable that you've grown farther and farther apart. But cheer up, my darling, it's just one or two more months of picking cotton, then you'll be off to Harvard with your whole life ahead of you.' She put her arms around my neck, and we said our goodbyes. I almost told her about my plans then, and sometimes I wish I had—but I don't think it would have made her any happier. That was the last time I saw her alive. I didn't even know she was dead until I'd been in the Navy for two weeks.

"Now, do you wonder why I hate my father?" His voice was full of bitterness. "I need a drink."

Kathy didn't answer. She felt deep sympathy for him, for the pain and hatred nurtured all these years, but anything she could say would sound like a platitude. He had shown her a piece of the puzzle that was Jack Wentworth, but she was sure there was a great deal more. There was his stepmother, for example, and Betsy, his ex-wife; probably he hated them as much as his father. And Pam—where did she fit into his life? She was equally sure that he would share no more confidences with her tonight.

It was almost nine o'clock by the time they were ready to leave for dinner; she'd fixed her slip with a safety pin Jack managed to find, but he was adamant when she wanted to stop by her place to change her clothes; for some reason or other, he actually wanted her to wear her nurses' uniform. Luckily for her, it was one of the form-fitting ones Pam's dressmaker had made.

They went to a large restaurant and cocktail lounge in Arcadia, and almost everyone seemed to know Jack by name. She glanced around as Jack introduced her, and didn't see a soul she knew. Nobody from the Club or Irene's party was there, and Jack was an entirely different person. At Irene's, he had been dour, quiet, almost stuffy. In this setting, he was grinning, back-slapping, buying drinks for everyone, the typical life of the party. They had dinner with a few cronies of his from the Rams, and the owner, when he wasn't jumping up to greet new customers, sat with them, too. She was enjoying herself immensely, and even forgot she was wearing her uniform, which Jack had explained away with a casual "She's my doctor."

After dinner, they all moved to the large circular piano bar, and drank and sang until closing time. Kathy was getting slightly smashed, but throughout the whole gay evening, there was a small nagging thought tugging at her. Just which one was the *real* Jack? She decidedly liked this one better, but how could he carry on his business and stay out until all hours, or was this just an exception?

It took him a long time to say all his goodnights, and when they finally got in his car, she gave a sigh of relief. All she could think of was crawling into bed, but evidentally he had other plans. "My place or yours?" he asked, grinning wickedly.

"Mine, of course," she answered, "you know I have to be at work in the morning."

"Yours, then. Got any booze?"

"Sure. But, Jack. . ." she said, then stopped. Oh well, it was late and she'd have a hangover anyway, so one more drink couldn't hurt too much. She gave him the address, and asked him to park halfway down the street. "The neighbors, you know."

"Plebian," he said jokingly.

They got to her bungalow quietly, and for once, Topsy didn't bark. Not that it would have mattered, really. The owners in the front had long since taken out their hearing aids, and were fast asleep. He looked around him as he loosened his tie, and picked up the table cigarette lighter.

"Sterling, huh? On your salary? Betsy got all our stuff

167

when we got the divorce; that is, except the Doberman, and he turned on me two years ago. Had to have him put to sleep. God, how I loved that dog." He started unbuttoning his shirt. "Where's that drink?"

She ignored the question. "Jack, what are you doing?"

"Getting ready for bed, what else? No sense ruining a perfectly good evening at this hour. Let's skip the drink—for once I think I've had enough. Where's the bedroom?"

She stared at him in amazement. "Jack, this isn't Hollywood. I have to go to work tomorrow, and you can't just go waltzing out of here at any old time, when my landlords live in the front. Why do you think I had you park down the street?"

"There you go, with that middle-class morality again," he laughed. "Believe me, honey, no matter what time I go to sleep, I always wake up before dawn, so I'll be out of here in plenty of time. Matter of fact, I haven't slept more than three or four hours a night in years—think that's what's wrong with me?"

She looked at him, resigned. After all, she couldn't start acting virginal at this point, even if she was tired as hell. "Okay, it's through there. I'll be in after I let Topsy out."

When she got back, his clothes were neatly folded on the chair, his jacket hung up, his socks tucked inside his shoes. Suddenly she was glad it had been a long quiet weekend, that she had cleaned the place thoroughly, and there were fresh sheets on the bed. He was already there, the pillows propped up beneath his head, grinning at her again. "Hurry up, it's cold without you—or do you have to go through all that cold creaming and stuff?"

"Not tonight, I don't. Just let me brush my teeth." She finished brushing her teeth, then put on a pair of pajamas, hoping he'd get the idea; maybe he was too tired, anyway. As she came through the door he looked at her and squinted his eyes. It was the same look she'd seen in his apartment.

"Take those damn things off."

Without a moment's hesitation, she took them off quickly, slid in beside him and turned off the lights. "That's better," he murmured, and pulled her toward him, cradling her in his arms. At first she thought he just wanted to sleep that way, but when his hands started slowly exploring her body, she realized sleep hadn't occurred to him. Quite a record, she thought. This will be the third time tonight. At Irene's he hadn't impressed her as a particularly sexy man; but then, appearances could be deceiving.

This time was different, though. The first two times had been savage and demanding, as if he really didn't care about her emotions, but she had gone without sex for so long that it didn't matter. Now he was soft and gentle, kissing her lightly as he caressed her. He was in no hurry, and although she hadn't felt like sex again tonight, almost against her will, she could feel herself becoming aroused. Finally, he rolled on top of her, and as he began to penetrate, all thought of work the next day left her mind. The deliciousness of feeling coursed throughout her body, and their rhythm was the same; slowly at first, then gathering momentum until they came together in the final explosion of passion. He stayed inside her for a long time, breathing heavily, kissing her eyelids, her nose, her cheeks, nibbling at her neck, until her quivering spasms gradually subsided. Yes, she thought, this time was definitely different. Finally, he rolled off her, still holding her in his arms.

"Thank you," she managed weakly, then realized just how ridiculous that must have sounded.

But then he answered her as though it wasn't ridiculous at all. "I should be thanking you," he said seriously. She started to get up, but he stopped her. "Don't get up now, dammit—I want you close to me." He lit them both cigarettes, then put the one ashtray on his stomach. "I gather you don't have many men spending the night with you, from the ashtray situation," he said.

"No," she said quietly, "I haven't slept with anyone since I moved here."

She felt him tense slightly, but he made no reply. They lay there in the still darkness, silently, but she felt such empathy with him at this very moment that she could feel something building up inside of him. They finished their cigarettes and he put the ashtray on the table, then turned to take her in his arms again, his cheek against hers.

"Oh Kathy, Kathy," he groaned hoarsely, "what have I done to you?"

She took his face in her hands in the darkness. "You made love to me," she said gently.

"Yes, I made love to you . . . but I never intended to. I haven't made love to anyone that way in years. All I've had was sex partners, and that's all I've wanted to have, like it was earlier tonight. All I've ever done is hurt people I've loved, and the people who loved me have been hurt—you don't know how much. I could love you so easily, Kathy, but I can't, I don't want to, because in the end I'd hurt you. Oh God, I know I'm not making any sense, you can't possibly understand, and I can't tell you, not now, not now, because I have to wait, you see, and I do't know how long I'll have to wait—"

She cradled him in her arms, not understanding, but feeling his pain, and trying to take some of it from him with her closeness. They lay there together for a long time, not talking now, just feeling each other's closeness, when suddenly Topsy started barking. Someone was walking toward the bedroom window.

"Kathy?" It was Dwight. Oh God, no, not now, not when everything had been so perfect. "Are you asleep?" She didn't answer him, and Jack abruptly reached over and lit a cigarette.

"Kathy?" he persisted, "It's me, Dwight. Are you all right?" Well, it was obvious he wasn't going to give up, so she turned on the small bedside lamp and peeked out the window.

"Of course I'm all right," she tried to sound drowsy, "what are you doing here, anyway? Don't you know it's the middle of the night?"

"Oh Kathy, I'm so sorry," his voice sounded more relieved than sorry, "I've been trying to call you all evening, but you weren't home. I thought something might have happened. Where were you?"

"It's none of your business, but I went out to dinner, and I'm very tired. Please go home, Dwight."

He didn't say anything for a few minutes, and she waited to hear his footsteps leaving. Then he asked hesitantly, "On a date?"

Kathy was beginning to explode. My God, what must Jack be thinking? "Of course, on a date. Now, go home!"

"Can't I come in for a while?

"Of course not, damn you," she snapped at him. "You woke me up, and probably all the neighbors, too. For the last time, GO HOME, you idiot." She slammed the window shut, turned off the light, peeked out the window again and saw him walk slowly towards his car. Then she got up and calmed Topsy down.

When she came back in the bedroom, Jack had lit another cigarette, and was thoughtfully blowing smoke rings towards the ceiling. "Well, what do we do now? Will he park down the street to see if someone comes out, or is there a back way out of here?" His voice was cold as ice, and all the closeness between them had disappeared.

"Oh, Jack. . ." she stood there helplessly, not knowing

what to say. "This has never happened before, I swear it. I don't know what possessed him to do this tonight. I've never had anything to do with him, but he thinks he owns me, and just because I dated him a few times. You remember, I was with him at Irene's party—" her voice trailed off, and she didn't know whether he believed her or not. Tears welled up in her eyes, and slowly started down her cheeks. Damn!, she thought, damn Dwight, damn his stepmother and his whole damned family. She looked at Jack, but his face was expressionless.

"Get back in bed, you'll freeze to death."

Gingerly, she slid in, careful not to touch him. The silence was awful. "Funny," she finally said, "how things can be one way, then change so quickly. There are so many 'ifs' in life." Her voice was choked with tears.

"Kathy, don't," he said gently, "you're just making things worse." He pulled her against him, and kissed the tears away. When she stopped crying, he cupped her face in his hands and laughed suddenly. "We did have a great time tonight, though, didn't we?" Then he made love to her again, with the same savage intensity as before.

When she finally woke up, it was after eight o'clock, and she had to be at the doctor's by nine. Jack was gone. She looked for a note, but there was none. She let Topsy out, then looked in the mirror. She had one hell of a hangover and her eyes were puffed, but thank God for the tan. She consoled herself with the thought that she'd see Jack at his two o'clock appointment; that is, if he showed up at all.

Chapter 8

The girl sat on the edge of the bed smoking a cigarette as Ted lay beside her, stroking the soft fleshy part of her plump thigh. He had been with her several times before; she was serviceable and efficient and did whatever he wanted her to do, although she talked too much and at the wrong times.

"You know anything about hysterectomies, Judy?" he asked her casually.

"Me?" She looked at him in surprise. "At my age?"

"I didn't mean had you had one, not at nineteen," he laughed, "I just meant have you ever known anyone who had one."

"Why, did your wife have one?"

"No, a friend of mine," he answered, although she'd struck a nerve. He wondered why all prostitutes were so curious about men's wives, and tried to pump them. His own two stock answers were, "my wife doesn't understand me," or "my wife understands me too well." It really didn't matter which one he used; they were always instantly concerned for his welfare and commiserated with him, especially since they knew they were going to get a fifty or a hundred dollar bill (depending on his mood and how good they were). Also, they wanted his repeat business.

"Well, let's see." She shifted her weight back on the bed, her head against the wall, and propped up her feet. "Don't stop rubbing, it feels good. My aunt had a hysterectomy and it didn't seem to change her much, but then I wasn't around her a lot. But this other working girl I know; well, she had one, and I kind of think she went back to work too soon. She had all kinds of complications, and she said it hurt her a lot. Sometimes she had to just settle for doing it French, which didn't bother the guys she was with. She said it was pretty hard to describe to someone who hadn't been through it; sort of like getting a real bad sunburn, when you get real hot then think you're gonna freeze, then you get hot again. Then she'd get real mean. She was always kind of mean at times before, but it seemed like she got worse."

"How long did it last?"

"Oh, she's still that way. If anything, she's getting worse."

"How long ago did she have this operation?"

"Two—maybe three years ago."

Ted counted swiftly, and propped himself up on an elbow. "Two or three years ago, and you said you knew her before. Judy, how long have you been in this business?" he asked her curiously.

"Since I was fourteen," she answered defiantly. "Now I suppose you want to know how I got started—all you men get around to that sooner or later."

"Not unless you want to tell me."

"Oh, I don't mind. It wasn't my fault, you know," she said bitterly. "To put it bluntly, my stepfather started messing around with me, and one day my mother caught us. She blamed it all on me and kicked me out, then I hitch-hiked to California. I got laid a few times on the way—just for eats, or a ride, or a place to sleep, can you imagine? Then

174

when I got out here I tried to get a job as a waitress, but I didn't have no experience, and the other way kept me going. Then I met a couple of other working girls and they taught me the ropes. I tried Hollywood first, but you have to look like a movie queen or do all kinds of wierdo stuff to make a decent living there, so I moved out here. We don't all have it easy, you know." She thought for a moment, then looked at him anxiously, afraid she'd said too much. "But I really dig you, Ted. It isn't just the money, I really like being with you."

He felt a twinge of compassion for the girl. He had never asked any of the others how they got started, although most of them volunteered the information while he listened with half an ear. Good God, this one was only nineteen, three years younger than April, and he still thought of his daughter as a child. He suddenly wondered just what she was doing at that school in Switzerland, and wanted her home very badly. Irene might like the idea, with the hysterectomy coming up, but then again, she might be dead set against it. He never knew what to expect from her these days.

"I like being with you, too, Judy," he stopped massaging her thigh and gave her a light slap. "Come on, let's get our clothes on and I'll drive you home." Irene might still be awake, and he wanted to talk to her about April.

"Oh Ted, I'm kind of tired," the girl said, snuggling down in the bed. "You took an awful lot out of me. I think I'll take a nap for a while, if you'll just leave a little extra for cab fare." She yawned, feigning exhaustion.

Instantly, the slight feeling of compassion he had felt for her vanished. He dressed quickly, took fifty dollars out of his wallet, hesitated, and took out another twenty. After all, he could afford it. But he knew surer than hell that as soon as he was out the door, she'd be up and dressed, back down to the bar to see if she couldn't turn another trick before two o'clock. He glanced at his watch; only ten, she might have time for two or three more, and the room was paid for the night. He went over to the bed to say goodbye, but she was pretending sleep; what the hell, that was her business. He laid the fifty and the twenty on the bedside table. As soon as he was out of the door she was out of his mind.

He opened the door to Irene's bedroom as quietly as possible. The bedside lamp was still on, and for a moment he thought she was still awake until he saw the book laying face down on her stomach. He walked over silently and stood looking down at her. He touched her forehead lightly and it felt cold and clammy, but she looked very soft and sweet and vulnerable when she was asleep. She can't help it if she's such a bitch most of the time when she's awake, he thought. He glanced down at the book she was reading—the Bible. Suddenly he felt—what, a presentiment? When she'd told him about the operation, she hadn't seemed particularly concerned. In fact, thinking about it now, she'd been almost casual, which wasn't like Irene at all. She usually blew things up all out of proportion. Why hadn't he caught it then? The feeling of foreboding deepened. He hadn't really bothered about Irene much lately. He'd call Larry Sturgess first thing in the morning. Time enough to talk about April after that, too. He switched off the lamp and went to his own room.

He undressed slowly, thinking about Irene. He couldn't even remember the last time they'd had sex together, or when they'd started drifting apart. Suddenly, the day she'd caught him masturbating when she was pregnant with April popped into his mind. He hadn't thought about that in years. No, she couldn't possibly be holding that against him, not after all this time. And he really had been trying to be faithful to her then; after that episode, though, he never did it again. Instead, when the pressure got out of hand, he went to one of the local houses. He was sure Irene didn't know.

But she hadn't loved April, of that he was sure, too, not the way most mothers loved their babies. My God, when he thought of all the wrangling, the constant bickering that went on over that child. Maybe if they'd had more children it might have been different, but Irene had flatly refused. Then again, it might have been worse, although he didn't see how it could have been.

Wearily, he got into bed, but it was a long time before he fell into a restless sleep.

Irene had stayed perfectly still while Ted was in the room, although she was wide awake. She was in no mood for conversation, and it had taken a great deal of will power to keep the tears from squeezing out between her closed lids. She heard him turn off the light and close the door, but she couldn't turn the light on again; he might come back for some reason. So she just lay there in the dark, without even the Bible for comfort. She felt hypocritical sometimes, using the Bible this way, but what else did she have?

She remembered when she talked to Dr. Sturgess on Monday, it had been almost anti-climactic. She had stared at him steadily while he talked about the hysterectomy, (yes, she'd have to have one) the hospital arrangements, papers to sign. Finally, she stopped him. "Larry, do I have cancer?"

He looked at her uneasily. "Irene, we don't know yet. You do have a tumor, yes, and it's a pretty large one, but we don't have the results of the biopsy yet. Even if it's malignant, there's every chance in the world that we'll get it all when we do the operation."

"Larry, I want to wait a while." He started to protest, but she stopped him. "Now wait, I know you're going to tell me the tumor is growing, and the sooner the better, and all that, but I have my reasons. Above all, I don't want you to tell anyone that it's anything more than a simple little hysterectomy. And I don't want to wait too long—just two months."

"Irene," he tried to reason with her, "I don't know what

your reasons are, but two months! And surely you'll want to at least tell Ted, if nobody else. You'll need his support through all this, even if you don't want anyone else to know."

She smiled slightly. "That's where you're wrong, Larry. It's especially Ted that I don't want to know. You see, I have to put my house in order."

Larry hadn't understood, but he had agreed to wait; two months, but no longer. And she really needed so much longer. She wanted April home, but that would have raised Ted's suspicions, and she couldn't have that. After all, the tumor could be benign. A little nagging voice kept saying, "What's the use of kidding yourself?"

That night, for once, Ted was on time for dinner. She waited until they were having coffee, as if it wasn't of much consequence, before she broached the subject. "By the way, I saw Larry again today."

"Oh?" he looked up from his paper, interested. "Get the results of those tests?"

"Most of them," she paused, then said jokingly, "it seems that I've reached that awful age when I'm supposed to have a hysterectomy."

"No kidding? At forty-four?" He put down his paper. "Seems kind of young to me. There's nothing seriously wrong, is there?"

She had hastened to reassure him that there was no hurry about it, and he'd gone back to his newspaper. She sat there, too, pretending to read. Is he really that easy to fool, that insensitive to her, had they grown that far apart? There was an awful lot of fence-mending to do in just two short months.

April Enwright hung up the phone, rolled over on the satin sheets, lit a cigarette and inhaled deeply. Although the long distance call to Switzerland had been fuzzy and blurred at times, she could tell enough from her father's conversation that he was deeply worried. From what she gathered, her mother had to have an operation—nothing serious, but serious enough for her to come home. *Home*! Juan would be furious. She had overstayed her homecoming for over two years, making up excuses about extra courses, invitations from friends, although in actuality she hadn't even been near the exclusive finishing school her parents had sent her to for over three years. Not since she met Juan. God, it seemed a long time ago.

She and Greta had met him on a skiing trip in St. Moritz, and the weekend wasn't over before they became lovers. It didn't matter to her then that he was older than her father, and it didn't matter now. To April, he was everything she wanted in a man; virile, powerful, exciting, and above all, he gave her everything and anything she wanted. She, in return, stayed in the background when he wanted her to, and in no way questioned him about his business. If some of his business acquaintances seemed a bit on the seamy side, that was his concern, not hers.

She had worried at first that her parents would find out she had left school, but Juan had made all the arrangements, and they were surprisingly easy. A very authentic cablegram had been supplied for the school from her parents, requesting her immediate return, and Greta had enthusiastically agreed to intercept and forward any mail. She also supplied her with bits of news and gossip at the school, which April incorporated in her replies to her parents.

She crushed out her cigarette, stretched, and sat up. It was time to do some serious thinking. She glanced at her watch, a dainty sapphire band set with diamonds that Juan had given her for her birthday. She had no idea when he'd be home, but she'd better look her best, and have some pretty good excuses for rushing off this way. She called the airport, jotted down some time schedules, and made a reservation for the eight o'clock flight. Then she went quickly and started a bubble bath in the large sunken marble tub—it always put Juan in a good mood when he came home and found her in a bubble bath.

While the water was running, she piled her long silken blonde hair on her head, got out her blue satin robe (Juan was partial to blue) and had just eased into the tub when the front door slammed. "April?" he yelled. Oh Lord, he wasn't in a good mood. This was going to be harder than she anticipated. A few minutes later he stood in the doorway, looking down at her. She tried to read his eyes, but his expression was unfathomable.

"Hi, darling," she said, trying to break his mood, and turned on more hot water, although it was hot already, but he always liked to watch her actions in the tub. "Do my back, will you?" she asked sweetly.

She handed him the large pink sponge, and he accepted it gloomily, not saying a word, as he methodically started soaping her back. Oh God, she thought, when he got like this, he was impossible to handle. Probably some business deal had fallen through, but business was not discussed between them. He had made that perfectly clear at the beginning of their relationship, when she had asked him casually about someone he was talking to in St. Moritz. "Who is that man?" They had been talking at some distance, and rapidly in Italian. She had caught no more than a few words, but the man looked vaguely familiar.

"*Querada*," he had answered her gently but firmly, "you will see me speaking with many men, but you must not ask such questions. My business life is—how to say it? Much varied, and I do not care to discuss it with you. You will have your place in my life, but it will not be in business. There will be times when I will be gone for periods of time, but you will not question, you will accept. There is no danger for you," he hastened to assure her, as she looked at him with alarm, "but what is that expression you Americans have? Ah yes, 'What you don't know can't hurt you.' When I come home," he had continued, "I do not care to discuss my business with you, I want to relax and forget my cares. Is that understood between us?"

She had agreed, although at times her curiosity almost got the better of her. Almost, but not quite. Somehow, she was a little afraid to find out what Juan really did.

But there was no time for the little subtleties now; her plane left at eight tonight, and it was almost two o'clock now. "Did you have a bad day?"

The sponge stopped massaging her back, then he threw it in the tub and walked over to the large window overlooking the city. "So so," his voice was non-committal. "And yours?"

"Juan, I have to talk to you." He didn't answer, but continued to stare out the window. She took a deep breath, and plunged in. "Darling, my father called today, and I have to go home for a little while. My mo—" she got no further, as he suddenly whirled around to face her.

"So, you have to go home? You desert me, too? Word travels quickly. This I would not have expected of you, April." His eyes were narrow black slits, and he left the room quickly, slamming the door behind him.

She stared at the closed door in amazement. She had expected a bad reaction, but nothing like this. Then she jumped out of the tub and threw a large towel around her, forgetting the blue satin robe. He was in the bar, fixing himself a stiff drink, and she stood looking at him, dripping bubble bath and water on the thick plush carpeting. "Juan, look at me."

He did, and his eyes were not kind.

"Juan, you didn't let me finish," she said steadily, feeling more in command of the situation now. "My mother is sick, and she has to have an operation. I don't know how bad it is, but it must be serious. My father got this number from Greta,

181

and he didn't even bother to ask why I wasn't in school. So you see I have to go."

His mood changed instantly, and his eyes became soft, and filled with tears. "Ah, my little April, of course you must go. And I have been so cruel to you. I thought—but of course, you could not have heard about the business with the French government. We must make the reservations for you now."

"I already have, Juan. I leave at eight tonight. But what is this with the French government? I know we have a rule about your business, but if you thought it serious enough to make me leave you . . . *querada*, you must tell me."

He took her in his arms and held her close. "It is nothing, my little one. You must worry about your mother now, and by the time you come back, it will all be straightened out. Besides, it is just a mistake, those stupid *officianados*—" he broke off. "You are coming back, aren't you?" he asked her anxiously, tilting her face up to his.

"Of course I'm coming back," she smiled up at him, "just as soon as I possibly can."

She settled back in her seat with a sigh, after waving to Juan until she could no longer see him. Saying goodbye hadn't been half as bad as she'd thought. Of course, the French government business had helped—but then she quickly thought how selfish that was to even think about. Here she was, leaving Juan, when he was in some sort of trouble. They had spent the time they had left together in bed, making love, then quietly talking of the things they'd done, the places they'd seen together. They had steered clear of any talk of the future, as neither of them really knew what it held in store. He made no further mention of the French business, nor did she ask him, although it was on both of their minds. They had been very close this afternoon, and she knew deep in her heart that although there might be other men in her life in the future, they could never measure up to

Juan. She couldn't tell him though, as he might think she was referring to the difference in their ages, and he was sensitive enough on that point. It made no difference to her now, and she as sure it never would, but who could really tell? Instead, she just told him how very much she loved him.

While he was showering, she'd made a hurried call to Greta, to find out what she'd told her father. Greta had said she was visiting friends. She also made arrangements for her to send the French and Geneva newspapers every day, and then she'd quickly hung up, saying she'd call when she returned.

She glanced at the man seated next to her; he was asleep already. Then she looked out the window again. The twinkling lights of the city were slowly fading behind her, and the darkness ahead would quickly engulf the jet. As often as she'd flown, she would never get used to it. There was always that fear, although Juan had joked about it, saying many more people fell in the bathtub and were killed than in planes, but everytime they had flown, she had gripped his hand tightly. Oh, how she longed for him next to her now. She wondered where he was, if he'd gone out to dinner, or back to their apartment, whether he was missing her as much as she was missing him. She knew he would be lonely without her. He must be lonely even with her, she thought, not being able or willing to discuss his business with her, not even when he was in trouble. And she knew that kind of loneliness only too well, having lived with it all her life.

As much as she loved Juan, she had never told him, never told anyone, about her mother. It was shame, she supposed, more than anything else, that had silenced her all these years. Children are closer to the truth than adults, she thought. They didn't have the years or experience to build up a veneer, but they could see through one. And one of the very first things she could remember was the simple fact that her mother didn't love her. When she cried out at night from a

183

nightmare, it was always Daddy who came rushing in. If she skinned her knee, it was Daddy who bandaged it, if he was there. If he wasn't, Irene would, but she wouldn't hold her in her arms and make a big fuss about it, like other little girls' mothers did. At first she told herself that Daddys liked little girls best and Mothers liked little boys best, but it wasn't long before she gave up that silly myth. Then she began to feel inadequate, as though there was something wrong with herself. She used to look at herself in the mirror for hours, wondering what it could be. Her sense of inadequacy made her shy, and consequently she made no really close friends. No one she could ask, that is, why her mother felt this way. Her Daddy loved her, she knew, and she clung to him possessively each night when he came home.

Once she had heard them arguing, when they thought she was asleep, and then she realized it was about her! She crept to the head of the stairs and tried to listen. Irene was lashing out at Daddy, saying he was spoiling the child rotten, giving her anything she wanted, that no wonder she was bringing so many notes home from the teacher. Her father was equally as angry, shouting that Irene gave her no attention at all, that if she were any kind of a mother, her daughter wouldn't be having trouble at school. April was astonished by all this. She hadn't brought any notes home from the teacher. In fact, Miss Graham was the closest friend she had. Lots of times she stayed in at recess just to talk to her. Her mother was lying! But why? How could she be so cruel? She was so angry, she was about to run down the stairs and tell her so, but her father came out of the living room just then, with a parting shot . . . "You never wanted her in the first place!" Then he slammed out the front door, and in a few minutes, she could hear his car roaring down the road.

She crept back to her room, and pulled the covers over her head. A few minutes later her mother came in, and satisfied that she was asleep, went out again. April had lain as still as she could, scarcely daring to breathe, and still not believing what she'd just heard. How old had she been then? Six? Seven? She couldn't remember. But she'd been old enough to hear the other children at school whispering about a little boy whose father had to marry his mother. And she was old enough to know where babies came from. Did her Daddy have to marry her mother—could that be it? She had lain awake all night, crying and bewildered.

After that night, she started to lose her shyness. To cover her inferiority complex, she became extroverted. She sassed her teachers, didn't do her homework, and in general, became a pain in the neck. Then the notes really did start coming home. The first note was from Miss Ellis, about six months after the argument. She didn't know what was in the note, but she knew what she was going to tell her mother. She had pulled some silly prank, she couldn't even remember, but as her mother read the note, her neck began to get red. "Do you know what this says? How dare you humiliate me this way?"

April had looked at her calmly. "I don't know why you're so upset. You said I've been bringing notes home all the time . . . Irene."

April never knew whether it was the fact that she knew her mother had lied about her, or that she called her Irene, but she did know she got a stinging blow to her cheek. The welts were still angrily red when Daddy came home, and she ran crying to him for comfort. From then on, it was open warfare between Irene and April—and she never called her anything but Irene again.

It was more or less open warfare between her father and Irene, too; her mother constantly wanting to send her to boarding school, she needed the discipline, her father arguing that she was too young. She used to hear them long into the night, feeling like she were some sort of a ping-pong ball. Finally, they compromised—she went to summer camp when she was nine, and much to her surprise found that she enjoyed it, although she missed her father tremendously, and wrote him daily.

When she came home, Irene greeted her warmly, and for a while it was good to be there. Then the hostility started up again, if anything, worse than before. She couldn't stand to see what it was doing to Daddy. She tried, for his sake, to get along with Irene, but it just didn't work.

One day, she happened to be passing her parents' bedroom, and saw her mother peering at herself intently in a magnifying mirror. She watched her for a few moments, then silently went downstairs, stupefied. At the tender age of ten, she had discovered why her mother didn't love her, and at the same time, wondered why she hadn't realized it sooner. Irene was jealous of her; imagine, a mother actually being jealous of her own daughter! She grew up a great deal in the next few hours, and actually felt sorry for her mother; and for herself, and for her lost childhood. What fun they had missed out on; but there was nothing to be done now.

From then on, she tried harder to get along with her mother, and when it came time to go to school again, she herself had asked to go to boarding school. Irene had looked at her suspiciously at first, then with gratitude. "Well," she said almost humbly, "I don't think we can get you in this year, it's too late, but we could look around for a really good school next year—or maybe in mid-term."

Her father hadn't liked the idea, but he didn't like the wrangling when April was home, either. There were tears all the way around when April left for boarding school the first time, but it established a pattern. Boarding school, home for Christmas, sometimes Easter vacation, sometimes home in the summer, sometimes summer camp, until she went to St. Moritz.

She shook her head—what a childhood! It's a wonder she hadn't needed a shrink. And here she was, all grown up and headed home to who-knows-what. She looked at her watch, noticed how late it was, and decided to take a sleeping pill, if she was to get any sleep at all before they changed planes in New York. She looked at her watch again—how would she explain that? She decided to buy another one between planes. No use asking for trouble. She'd have to take off the sapphire ring, too.

Kathy lay in bed, feigning sleep, until she heard the back door close softly. It was raining now, and she hoped Dwight wouldn't get too wet in his circuitous route from the back door, down the alley, then to his car. She waited a few minutes, then quietly got up to put the latch on the back door. She pulled back the dutch curtains and looked out, as the rain steadily pelted down on the patch of dirt that Topsy had ruined. It was late in September now, not cold, but much too early for a storm. Dawn was starting to break, and the beginnings of a pond was starting. Just a low spot filling up, dull, colorless, wet. It suited her mood. She pulled the curtains shut, turned on the water for tea, then went back to the bedroom for her robe. She looked at the bed with distaste. It was rumpled and disorderly, and on impulse, she pulled everything off and threw it in the corner, then instantly regretted it. She was tired, and now she'd have to remake it with fresh sheets before she went to work. Well, as long as she'd started, might as well make a good job of it, so she tore off the mattress protector too, and was about to turn the mattress over when the teakettle started whistling. She went back to the kitchen and turned it off, made herself a cup of instant coffee instead, and sat down at the kitchen table. Topsy followed her, curled up on her slippers and went back to sleep.

Kathy sipped her coffee slowly, thinking. She had wanted Jack—instead, she had Dwight. And every day she asked herself the same question. Just how was she going to extricate herself from this involvement without upsetting the pre-carious position she had managed for herself in this town? Maybe Dwight was what she deserved—act in haste, repent in leisure.

As for Jack, that was someone she certainly wished she could forget. After she'd spent the night with him, she'd taken extra care with her makeup and hair the next morning, half expecting, half not expecting him to keep his 2:00 appointment. As the time grew nearer, she had become more and more nervous, but she could have saved herself the trouble. He didn't show up, much less call.

Dr. Carter had expected it, of course, and had called her in to talk and have coffee, which was usual when a patient didn't show up. She had tried to act normal, but she was jumpy and nervous, and worn out from the night before. It wasn't unusual that he finally said something about it.

"What's the matter, Kathy?" Dr. Carter asked kindly. "You look bushed."

She had wanted to tell him about Jack, but she held back. He had warned her not to go out with any of the patients, along with the other three rules, and now she'd broken every one of them. My God, it had only taken her two months! And she could just hear his reaction. She had mumbled something about cramps, and hoped he believed her. He looked at her levelly, and she knew he did not believe her, so she changed the subject. But he couldn't possibly know it had anything to do with Jack Wentworth, there was just no connection. She started rambling on about other things, Irene's party, her conversation with Ted, at least part of it, then she told him about Dwight waking her up last night. When she realized she was talking too much, she shut up abruptly.

John Carter had sat and listened, watching her with half closed eyes. He was more astute than Kathy thought. She never did much talking when a patient had cancelled, but when she did, it was to mention the patient. Now she was talking about everybody, but studiously avoiding Wentworth. He had noticed her nervousness earlier, which had grown as the day progressed, but hadn't put the pieces together until now. Just how it had come about, he had no idea, but he was damn sure she'd spent the night with him, and his blood boiled at the thought. As he looked at her slightly flushed cheeks, the faint but apparent circles under her lovely eyes, he was not seeing her as she was now, but seeing the two of them together, and it was making him ill. For the first time in his life, John Carter was suffering the pangs of jealousy, and it was frightening to him. His life up to now had not been altogether what he had expected in the beginning, but it had been adequate. All sorts of thoughts came tumbling into his mind; at first, he thought of firing her, but the mere thought of not seeing her every day was unbearable, even more unbearable than thinking of her with Jack. Then, he thought of throwing her to the floor and raping her right then and there, and he gripped the edges of his chair until his knuckles turned white. He tried to think of Edith, but she just didn't matter any more. Suddenly he realized she'd stopped talking, and he tried to pull himself together. "Well, I guess I'd better get back to work," she was saying.

"Hold the three o'clock for a few minutes," he managed, and after she left, he buried his head in his hands. I've got to get a grip on myself, he thought. These things just didn't happen; to other people, he knew, but not to him. Then he got up and fixed himself a straight bourbon. He managed to get through the rest of the day, then took a long drive through the mountains before going home.

Kathy finished her coffee, then decided to have another cup before tackling the bedroom. It was still early, and the rain was coming down in buckets. She supposed there would be a lot of cancellations today. Jack Wentworth was due in, but that was nothing new, he hadn't showed up at all, and she hadn't even heard from him since that night. For two of the longest weeks in her life, she'd kept hoping. She wasn't in love with him, she knew that, but sexually she couldn't stop thinking about him. Her vanity was involved, too, and that didn't make it any easier for her. At times, she hated him, but every time the phong rang, her heart jumped. And then there was Dwight. There was always Dwight.

He had called the day after that fateful night, and she had grudgingly accepted his apology. She continued to see him, but not on as regular a basis. He was at the hospital a good deal of the time, and evidently things at the Oil Company were hectic, although she listened with half a mind. He would usually drop by after visiting hours at night for an hour or so, and occasionally take her out for a quick lunch. She felt sorry for him, but nothing else. Nor did he seem to expect anything else, at least for the time being, which made for an easy relationship. Sometimes she wished he had turned to Nancy in this time of crisis, but love was not something you could force, she knew that only too well.

Then a week ago, she was having coffee with Pam, as they usually did in the morning. Pam seemed listless, not her usual sparkling self at all, and Kathy mentioned it.

"Oh, I don't know, Kathy," she replied. "It's Jack—you know, Jack Wentworth, you met him. We go back a long way, since I was a child, and he's fun to be around. That is, when he's not drinking too much. Last night we had a fight about it, and after he took me home, he kept calling all night. Finally, I took the phone off the hook, so he came back over, and you know the apartment house I live in. It caused one hell of a ruckus." Then she added as an afterthought, "If I'd had a sleeping pill, I'd have taken it. I didn't get a wink." Actually, she'd taken two seconals, but it had been late, and she hadn't realized she was so low on uppers. Thank

God this afternoon Dr. Sturgess would be at the hospital; she could visit a few of the nurses, and slip a few out of some of the offices. Then there were always the samples the salesmen left. These were the easiest of all to get. She sighed. Dr. Carter kept his locked up now, since the narcotics scandal. Such a silly thing, really. But she'd been scared at the time.

Kathy commiserated with her about Jack, but inside she was seething. So that's what she had been—just a one-night stand. Well, at least Pam didn't know about it; she didn't think she could have stood that.

She sat there sipping her coffee, remembering. She had gone back to her office, thankful that Dr. Carter was at the jail that morning, and she wouldn't have to see him just then. The phone was ringing when she unlocked the office door, and she caught it before the answering service did. It was Dwight, and for once she was glad to hear his voice, glad to know that at least someone really cared. He told her that his father was coming along nicely now, and in a couple of weeks the doctor said he might be able to come home. She tried to put some enthusiasm in her voice, and Jack out of her mind.

"Well, then you really have something to celebrate," she said, trying to sound warm, while all the time her mind was on Jack. "Why don't you come over for dinner tonight, Dwight? There's a new recipe for pork chops I'm just dying to try." That was it, she thought, keep yourself busy. Lunchtime she could go to the market, then go home after work and occupy herself with dinner. She just couldn't cope with another long evening thinking about Jack, especially after today. Besides, by now she knew he wasn't going to call her again.

Dwight sounded delighted. "Why Kathy, I never expected this. I was going to take you out, but if you really want to go to all that trouble—you sure it's not too much bother?" He sounded anxious.

Kathy was touched; all she'd ever done was use Dwight as a stopgap, and he was acting like fixing dinner for him was the same as offering him the crown jewels of England. "Of course not," she replied, "what kind of vegetable do you want?"

"Cauliflower," he said, without a moment's hesitation. "You know, it'll have to be kind of late, though. I have to stop by and see my father, but I'll make it short. About eight o'clock? I'll bring something to drink."

"Fine," she said, and ended the conversation. She started making out her grocery list, and wrinkled her nose when she listed cauliflower. The pork chop recipe wasn't new, but was one of Bruce's favorites—Bruce. She hadn't thought about him much since the night she spent with Jack, but he came crowding in on her now. Suddenly she began to cry; all the things she'd expected of this great big "new life" of hers were nothing, nothing compared to the times she'd spent with Bruce. And what did she have now? A job with a psychiatrist who was beginning to look at her strangely, a reputation with at least one man as a "pushover," a very eligible almost-bachelor who adored her and who she had no interest in, and a few friends. That is, if you could call Pam and Irene friends. Then there was Mrs. Keith, who hated her, and a few acquaintances at the Club.

Sometimes she wished she was back in Hollywood, and this was one of those times; but she'd made up her mind, and she was stubborn. There was no future for her back there, and maybe she just hadn't given this place enough time yet. After all, it hadn't been quite three months. She was just homesick, that's all. Resolutely, she wiped her eyes, called the answering service, and went out to get her groceries.

Pam had watched Kathy at coffee this morning. For some odd reason, when she'd mentioned Jack, her face had turned pale, almost ashen. Though she was tired herself, she wondered about Kathy's reaction. Kathy wasn't one who could hide her emotions easily, she thought. She went in to see her at lunchtime, but the "Out To Lunch" sign was on the door. Without thinking, she tried the knob; it wasn't locked. Silently, she let herself in and locked the door behind her. "Kathy?" she called softly. There was no one there.

Nervously, she walked towards the inner office. If she'd been upset enough to leave the door unlocked, maybe other things were unlocked, too. She'd think about why Kathy was so upset when she didn't have so many other things on her mind. The inner door was unlocked, and she called to Dr. Carter. No answer. Quickly, she started rummaging through the drawers that were open, but could find nothing. She looked at the glass cupboards that held the prescription drugs, contemplating. No, it was too much of a risk. So she left, and started her rounds of the nurses in the medical offices she knew. All she could have gotten from Dr. Carter were tranquilizers, probably, and right now she needed uppers.

Kathy seared the thick three-inch pork chops quickly as soon as she got home, while she was putting the rest of the groceries away, then started her bath. Dinner would be late, but knowing Dwight, when he said eight, it could mean six, which she'd been prepared for since the first time they went out together. After the chops were nicely browned, she poured off the grease, set them on simmer, and covered them with apple juice and a pinch of sage. She washed the cauliflower and lettuce quickly, set the potatoes au gratin out to thaw, then went in the bathroom and sank into the tub. She lay back slowly, and the tension started to leave her body. She soaped herself slowly, and tried to concentrate on dinner. It had been an impulsive act on her part to ask Dwight over, but she couldn't see just sitting by herself tonight. She thought about getting out her silver, and decided against it. No use going overboard.

Dwight arrived early, as usual, and they had a few martinis in the living room while the dinner was cooking. She had opened the front and back doors, as it was a very sultry evening, and the smell of cauliflower was overpowering. Actually, now she wished she'd just made a little shrimp salad and rolls.

Dwight, however, seemed impervious to the heat, as he talked about his father and the business. She watched him silently, not wanting to interrupt; and it occurred to her that she was the only one he really confided in. The lines in his boyish face seemed to have become more deeply etched in the past few weeks, and for the first time since Irene's Labor Day party, something seemed to stir in her. Empathy, maybe? Certainly not love. Admiration for his courage, possibly, that this child-boy-man was pitting himself against Vivian, against the impossible odds that his father's heart attack would have on the company. On impulse, she leaned over and kissed him softly on the cheek. As he tried to pull her closer, she laughed gently and said, "Time for dinner."

Obediently, he followed her out to the kitchen, offering to help. "Everything's done," she answered him, "but you could open the wine. I never have been any good with those cork things." Obligingly, he opened the wine, while she tossed the salad and lit the candles.

Dwight kept telling her how delicious everything was, which helped her mood, but not her appetite. She merely picked at her salad, and only ate one of her pork chops. When she said she didn't want the other one, Dwight ate it, while Topsy glared at him. He never had been one of her favorite people, and taking Kathy's leftovers didn't help matters any.

They had coffee in the living room, and for once Dwight wasn't in a talkative mood. It was comfortable, though, and Kathy was glad he was there. When he pulled her over closer to him and put her head on his shoulder, she made no

194

objection. There was no one else, no Jack to look forward to again, and she began to feel a certain numbness. When he kissed her, she tried to put some feeling into it, although before she had merely tolerated him. If he noticed any difference, he didn't speak about it, and she was grateful for that. Talking wasn't what she needed right now, but just to be held and cuddled, to have someone who cared. His kisses grew deeper, and his hands started to caress her breasts, awkwardly at first, as she'd never allowed him to do this before, then with growing assurance. She made no objection—nothing really mattered right now, although she felt no response. His hands grew bolder, as they slid down her body, pulling her closer to him.

She could feel him against her now, stiff and erect, his face buried deep in her neck, murmuring words she didn't hear. She laid her head back on the couch and sighed deeply. After all, what difference would it make? If he wanted her so much, what could it matter? The strange numbness continued. There had been men before, so many men, and he would be just one more. She hardly remembered walking to the bedroom, slipping out of her clothes and getting into bed. She felt as if she were in some sort of dream, and everything was in slow motion. She watched him as he undressed with his back towards her, and noticed that he left his shorts on. The slow motion continued as he slipped in the bed beside her, and then his hands seemed to be everywhere at once.

As he started to penetrate her, she began to hurt, and the dreaminess and numbness left her abruptly. She was acutely aware of the pain, as she was completely dry inside, and her body stiffened. Dwight wasn't large, but without any lubrication it was hard for him to enter her. Frantically, he tried harder, jabbing repeatedly, and the pain increased. Finally, he managed to penetrate her, and gasped gently in her ear, "Darling, you're so small!"

Kathy was panic stricken now. Why had she let this happen? This was no fly-by-night from Hollywood, no Bruce, no Jack, certainly no one she was in love with, or even sexually attracted to. This was a pillar of the community, someone she saw every day, a friend, someone to lean on. Now, suddenly, this man was on top of her, pumping away, a total stranger. She could smell his shaving lotion, his hair, the clean scent of his body, but he was still a stranger. And then the awful thought struck her: my God, now it's happened, and he's going to expect it again—and again, and again. Suddenly she was aware that the awful pain and pumping had stopped, and she made a beeline for the bathroom and her douche bag.

When she saw traces of blood on her thighs, she felt a sense of relief; her period had started, but she douched, anyway. She stayed in the bathroom for a long time. Dwight was waiting, she knew, but she didn't know what to say to him. He must be horrified, if he'd turned on the lights—with his old fashioned morals, he'd probably think she'd had an affair with him during her period, and just didn't care. What could she say? Finally, she stuck in a tampon, put on a light robe and went back in the bedroom.

Dwight was sitting on the edge of the bed, and looked at her adoringly. "Oh honey, I'm so sorry. I know you've been married, but it must have been an awfully long time for you until now. I hope I didn't hurt you." There was blood on the sheet, and on his shorts. It was ludicrous, of course. But if he chose to think that she had been celibate since her divorce, who was she to change his mind? And it got her out of a rather sticky situation.

He helped her change the bed, but when he wanted to spend the night, she was adamant. What would people think? After a lot of protestations of love on his part, she finally got him out of there. After that, she got back into bed, and shivered, although the night was still warm. She thought of calling Maude, but it was too late, and what could she tell her, anyway? No, she had gotten herself into this situation, and it was up to her to get herself out.

At least she had a few days before a repeat performance. She'd tell him tomorrow she'd just started her period—maybe she'd tell him they lasted a week. But she knew it wouldn't end there. One fact she had to face—of all the men in her life, Dwight was the worst. He must have been a virgin when he married Nancy, she decided, and so was Nancy. He knew absolutely nothing about the subtle nuances of making love, and she, for one, certainly wasn't about to teach him. Dwight had put her on a pedestal, and that was where she'd have to stay, if she wanted to keep the image she'd created for herself when she moved out here.

She finished her third cup of coffee, then went in to tackle the bed. Dwight would be over tonight, as usual, but she decided to have him take her out to dinner. Maybe she'd get a little bit drunk. Dr. Carter wouldn't be in tomorrow, so she had the day off, although she had no intention of telling Dwight. Besides, she wanted to visit Irene before she went in the hospital. She hadn't met her daughter April yet, although from all reports, she was a raving beauty.

Chapter 9

Vivian hung up the phone, somewhat disappointed. She had intended to visit Irene after seeing Duncan today, but when she learned Kathy was going to be there, she changed her plans. She took a last look in the mirror, smoothed her pale blonde hair once more, and put on her spotless white gloves.

The torrential rains had stopped a few hours ago, and a few hints of sunshine glimmered through the dark clouds occasionally. She dreaded these daily visits with Duncan; mainly, because she wasn't supposed to discuss business with him, and after the first few minutes of small talk, they had very little to say. Secondly, she hated hospitals; the medicinal smells, the starchy officiousness of the nurses, the clinical atmosphere. Never mind the softly muted colors on the walls, the television sets in every room, the piped music—they were still hospitals.

Duncan was making a really remarkable recovery, even Dr. Sturgess was surprised at his progress. It had been a great relief to Vivian; no more frantic hurrying to get things under control with her accountant—now they had time to plan, without any mistakes, and things were coming along nicely.

Duncan had become something of an enigma to her, she never knew what he was thinking lately. Sometimes it seemed to her as though he was just willing himself to live, to get better; she had never seen, or noticed that quality in him before. She never stayed the entire visiting time, with the excuse that he needed his rest. Actually, he made her nervous, and Dr. Sturgess said he'd be coming home in a month, maybe sooner, although he'd need 'round the clock care.

She already had the nurses on standby, hand picked for their density, ones she was sure wouldn't interfere with her business. Then, she'd had the den made into a makeshift bedroom for Duncan. Actually, it was rather pretty now, with the dark panelling freshly painted pale blue and new curtains at the windows facing out on the broad terrace. She had even had the wheelchair painted the same pale blue, although it was still a wheelchair, so she'd stuck it in the closet until time for its use.

Although she was satisfied with the nurses, the children were definitely going to cause a problem. They were constantly at the hospital, and she was sure they expected to continue this practice when Duncan came home. Well, she was certainly going to have to come up with some solution to this problem—her life had been disrupted enough, and with Duncan coming home, it would be even more so. She had called Dr. Sturgess about this and he'd been no help at all; in fact, he even encouraged the children to visit as often as possible.

"After all, Vivian," he'd explained kindly, "Duncan's been through a terrible ordeal. For a man of his age to have come through this so fast and so well, is a miracle in itself. Naturally, he'll want his children around him. It can be an awfully boring process, recuperation, but I don't want him taxed unduly, of course. Jan, Scott, Dwight, Fran, Nancy—anytime, and any of his close friends. But I'd keep Ben away as much as possible," he added shortly, "you know how those two get along."

Inwardly, Vivian was seething. All she could see was a vast procession of people traipsing in and out—Duncan had a great many friends. And what was she supposed to do in the meantime? Sit and knit? She didn't know how. The solution of stopping this daily parade still eluded her, although, somewhere, somehow, in the back of her mind, she knew there had to be one.

For appearances sake, and no other reason, she had cut down on the hours she spent at Keith Oil. The Board meeting had gone exceptionally well, under the circumstances. There had been one or two alarmists, but less than she expected. She kept waiting for the question of an audit to come up, but it never did. She hadn't slept the night before, worrying about it, so it was easy for her to present the picture she wanted to present—wan, distracted, her mind more on her husband than the meeting. Actually, her mind was clear and alert as her eyes darted from one to the other, and she could detect nothing but sympathy. Except for Dwight and Scott, who had their own worries. She had purposely worn dark sunglasses, supposedly to hide the fact that she'd been crying all night, although she actually hadn't shed a tear. Scott offered to drive her home after the meeting, but she declined, saying she wanted to drive up to the lake and just sit for a while.

She was driving up to the lake, all right, but not to sit. She was meeting Alex Dunbar, to tell him about the Board meeting, and to go over business. Under her instructions, he had rented a small cabin there, as it was impossible to go to his office anymore. The end of the year wasn't too far away, and even if there wasn't a special audit now, there was always the annual one, and everything had to be letter perfect. The fact that she had enough stashed away now in various safety deposit boxes and a numbered account in Switzerland, never entered her mind.

Alex was waiting for her when she drove up. He was pleased about the Board meeting; but when she suggested that he make another trip to Bolivia, where her connections could come up with a report of another dry well, he balked.

"Vivian, don't you think that's pretty dangerous right now? After all, your husband's condition is pretty 'iffy' at the moment, and if something happened now, our whole operation could come tumbling down. And incidentally, you and me with it. You've got well over a million now, according to my figures, more than you could spend in a lifetime, and I haven't done too badly, either. Don't you think it's time to quit?"

She had taken off her dark glasses, and stared at him calmly. "Alex, if you want to quit, that's your business. When I found you, I thought you had guts. I still think you do. The company's in a state of limbo right now, and nobody's going down to Bolivia to check out one dry well. Number 27 down there is really pumping now, and we've already siphoned off $87,000 on that one well alone. The company thinks it's petering out, and if you go down there and get the reports to me that the well had dried out, we'll come out with a half a million, at least. Don't forget, Alex, a quarter of that money is yours." She continued to stare at him, and watched the look of greed slowly come into his eyes. It's that way with everyone, she thought, even herself. Once you start, you just can't stop. And that's when she made her really big mistake.

He licked his lips a little, then took a sip of his drink. "All right, Vivian, just this one last time. But this is riskier than the other times, and you know it. I want half of the profits."

"A third," she said, ready for him.

He thought for a minute, then nodded. "I'll have to get my passport renewed," he said slowly, "some of my shots have run out."

"Get started on it right away, won't you?" she smiled at

him briefly, then got up to leave, pulling on her gloves. "I'm going to the hospital—I have to make my appearance for the day. Call me at home when you know how soon you can leave. I guess it's safe enough, for the time being, at least. After Duncan comes home, we'll have to make other arrangements."

He watched her leave, driving with the same precision she did everything. He admired her in a way, the same way he admired the beautiful colorings on a snake. But he certainly wouldn't want her as an enemy. She could be a deadly adversary. Sometimes he wondered how she had managed to fool Duncan all these years, but she evidentally had. And then there were her stepchildren—had she managed to fool them, too? He shrugged, and finished his drink. Mentally, he started adding up what he'd make from this deal, along with the other money he'd made through Vivian. It added up to over half a million; it was time to quit. He had a feeling about this deal that wasn't just right, but he put it out of his head and went to check his passport.

Jan came out of Dr. Sturgess' office with mixed feelings. The fact that she was pregnant again was definitely confirmed. She had intended visiting her father this afternoon, but decided to wait until tonight. Although her father was much better now, he wasn't out of the woods by a long shot, and both Dr. Sturgess and she had agreed that it was best not to tell him about the new baby for the time being. Besides, she'd probably run into Vivian. Not that she didn't like her, exactly, but she was beginning to see her in a new light. In fact, she was beginning to see a lot of things since the night of her father's heart attack that she'd never noticed before. And now there was another baby on the way. She thought of abortion briefly, and as quickly dismissed the idea. She adored little Ben, and being an only child was such a lonely life. She had been an only child, in a way, being born so much later than her brothers, but then her father had showered her with affection.

She certainly didn't see Ben showering their baby with affection—in fact, he barely played with him at all. She had told herself that he just wasn't the type, that he was too manly, that later on they'd do lots of things together, like sports, and ball games. The night at the hospital had changed all that. Had he been any help to her, had he been there to lean on? No, he had passed out, sleeping though the whole ghastly waiting period. The drive home had been no better. Besides her father to worry about, there was the baby. She had taken him out at night with a cold, and Ben hadn't even asked how he was. After she had put the baby to bed and taken his temperature, (which was normal, thank God) she had gotten into bed, drained and exhausted. She wanted to get a few hours sleep before she went back to the hospital. She switched off the light and turned on her side, but Ben had had other ideas.

For the first time in their marriage, she not only didn't want sex with him, he was actually repulsive to her. His breath had the rancid odor of a hangover, and stale perspiration exuded from his pores. She felt like gagging, and jumped out of bed quickly.

"You dirty lousy son of a bitch," she spat at him coldly and calmly. "My father almost died, and do you care? Do you care about anything except your own stinking, miserable drunken hide? Don't you ever touch me again, do you hear? Not ever." Then she slammed out of the room and went to bed on the cot in the baby's nursery.

Ben looked at the closed door, his mouth open, scarcely believing his ears. This from Jan, who loved him so much she pounced on him the minute he came through the door? What had he done that was so awful? He'd been trying to do her a favor, a service, to take her mind off her father—he never expected a reaction like that. God, he hoped he hadn't blown it. She was her father's favorite, and if he died, they'd be sitting on easy street. He'd been thinking about it all the way home, but at least was sober enough not to mention it to Jan. Naw, she couldn't have meant what she said. She was just unglued about her father. Besides, she was too much of a sexpot. But just to be on the safe side, he better start bathing more often, and brushing his teeth before he went to bed with her. Then he rolled over, and started snoring almost immediately.

Jan lay quietly on the cot in the baby's room, listening to his even breathing, but sleep would not come. The things she had said to Ben kept resounding in her ears. She wondered what he was thinking right now. After all, she'd never spoken to him that way before, and against her will, she began to feel just a little sorry. Maybe he wasn't all the things she'd built him up to be in her mind, but after all, he was her husband, the father of her child, and maybe another one. Funny, it had never bothered her before, the liquor, the sweaty smell of him; she'd even considered it manly. Her father had been dead set against the marriage, and none of the other members of the family liked Ben, either. But he could be sweet at times, and after all, he hadn't had the advantages the rest of them had. She sighed a little, then got up and looked down at her sleeping child, and felt his forehead. Maybe all mothers thought their babies were adorable, but even her father was crazy about him, in spite of Ben. Ben. He must be miserable now, and she decided to go back to the bedroom and apologize. When she opened the door, the stench of sweat and stale liquor almost overpowered her. Ben was sleeping spread-eagled on the bed, snoring loudly. Quickly she shut the door, then went back to the baby's room and took a couple of aspirins.

When Ben finally woke up the next day, groggy and hung-over, Jan had already left. The baby sitter, Mrs. Leonard, had just put little Ben down for his nap, and was quietly reading in the living room. Since he hadn't expected her, he had walked out in his shorts, and Mrs. Leonard jumped a little, sniffed, then avoided her eyes. To hell with her, Ben thought. "Where's my wife?"

"Why, she's at the hospital, Mr. Cameron, naturally. She said she'd call if she'd be very late."

"Well, you can leave now, Mrs. Leonard. I'll take care of little Ben."

Mrs. Leonard hesitated. "Mr. Cameron, she left specific instructions that I was to stay until she came back, or called."

"Oh." Ben didn't know what else to say, so he went back to the bedroom to get a robe. He needed a drink badly, but if that old biddy was going to be stuck there all day, it wasn't going to be easy. He went back to the living room. "Did she leave a note?" he asked her.

"I don't believe so," she said calmly, and continued her reading.

So, it was going to be that way, he thought. He really felt bad now, especially after what Jan had said last night. And scared. There must be some vodka in the kitchen. At least he hoped to God there was. After that, he'd take a shower and shave, but right now he wasn't up to it. "I guess I'll get some orange juice," he said to Mrs. Leonard. This time she didn't even bother to look up from her book.

He rummaged around in the kitchen cupboards, and came up with nothing. Oh, this is gonna be one helluva day. He opened the refrigerator, and looked at the large container of orange juice with disgust. Then he squatted down, rummaged around, and finally came up with two cans of beer. Gratefully, he snapped one open and drained the can in one long gulp. God, that tasted good. He made a final inspection of the refrigerator, but that was it. So he filled a glass full of orange juice, put the other can of beer under his robe, and walked back to the bedroom. He sat on the edge of the bed, opened the other can, and glumly took a sip. Here he was, a prisoner in his own home. Then he remembered the vodka in the glove compartment, and rushed out to the living room again. "Forgot my cigarettes," he explained. Dammit, he thought, why did he feel he had to tell her everything?

"Your wife took the car," she said, again without looking up.

"Oh," he said again, then went back to the bedroom and stared at the beer. He went into the bathroom, splashed some water on his face, then decided against shaving. He downed the other beer and quickly dressed, then combed his hair with shaking hands.

"I'm going out," he told Mrs. Leonard.

This time she looked up. "Where should I tell Mrs. Cameron you are, if she calls?"

"To get some cigarettes. And then I'm going for a long walk—to think. You be sure to tell her that."

He started walking, but not at too fast a clip. It was a hot, sultry day, and the nearest bar was eight blocks away. From there, it was another two blocks to a liquor store. God, even if he got a little drunk today, by the time he walked home he'd be sober. He looked at his watch; 2:30. Jan couldn't possibly be back before six, which would give him plenty of time to take a cold shower and shave—and use some mouthwash. And sitting in a nice cool bar, without Mrs. Leonard breathing down his neck, would give him time to think. Maybe he'd even make a visit to the hospital tonight, even though he couldn't see the old man—might make Jan feel better.

Jan shook her head. She couldn't just stand outside of Dr. Sturgess' office forever, but the last thing she wanted to do was go home. She didn't know which was worse—finding Ben there drunk, waiting for her, pleading and wheedling, or waiting for him to come home, when the same scene would take place, over and over again. This had gone on since her father's heart attack, and in spite of his promises, Ben was always drunk now, and it was getting worse. She was afraid to leave little Ben with him alone, so Mrs. Leonard lived in now; she shook her head. Poor Mrs. Leonard, she didn't know what she would have done without her. And the worst of it was, there was no one she could confide in—Vivian was out of the question, and Dwight and Scott had their hands full with the company. She could just hear Fran's smug 'I told you so.' Somehow, she'd manage. Right now, the important thing was her father; she couldn't even throw Ben out of the house—there would be too many questions. And as for telling him about the new baby, that was definitely out. No, for the time being, all she could do was try to keep her sanity, and hope she could tell her father about the baby before she started to show. When the right time came, she'd know it.

Kathy spent a great deal of time and care on her hair and makeup, and deciding what to wear before going over to Irene's. She didn't want to look too dressed up, but on the other hand, being too casual might be a mistake. She settled on a plain white linen, with a hand painted green scarf at her neck. Satisfied at last, she set off for West Covina. She had gotten a good night's sleep for a change, mainly because Dwight was tired, and after dinner had dropped her off without coming in.

She had mixed feelings about seeing Irene. It had been several weeks now, except when Irene came to the office for her appointments with Dr. Carter, and those had been the briefest of conversations. She knew about the hysterectomy, of course, and that her daughter April was back, but she had a feeling something else was going on, too. Irene's attitude had changed, somehow—her arrogance was no longer apparent, her defensiveness, brittleness—not gone, exactly, but there was a certain sweetness, a serenity that Kathy had never noticed before. She had questioned Dr. Carter, but received no answer, although his eyes had deepened, and she could sense a certain sadness.

She drove up to the house about 2:30 and sat in the car for a few moments, gazing at it. Of all the houses out here she'd been in, she liked Irene's the best, she decided, in spite of those crazy pictures. She wondered about them at times—they seemed so out of place with the impeccable taste throughout the rest of the house. Even her Arabian Nights bedroom was restful and romantic, after you got over the initial shock.

Irene opened the door herself, as though she had been waiting for her impatiently—no, patiently, and there was a difference.

"Come in, Kathy. It's the maid's day off, and April's off playing tennis somewhere," she explained. "I'm so glad you called, and could come today. Let's go downstairs. I've laid a small fire, even though it is rather early in the year. I get so cold lately, although I could put on a sweater, if you think it might get too warm for you." She kept talking as they went down the winding stairway, and Kathy noticed she held onto the rail. Her steps were slow, and Kathy couldn't help but ask her if she were in some pain.

She smiled slightly, and there was a light film over her eyes. "Oh, a little, now and then, I suppose, but Larry's given me some pills. The operation will take care of all of that, though." She took a small bottle out of her pocket and popped a small white pill in her mouth, careful that Kathy didn't see the label on the prescription. "There. I should be better in a few minutes." She motioned Kathy to sit down, then hesitated, "You sure you don't mind if I light a fire?"

"Of course not, Irene." Kathy was warm already, but as long as she had gone to all that trouble, she could stand it.

Irene lit the fire, made sure it took, then sat down opposite her, and leaned her head back against the pillows with a sigh.

"I made some sandwiches and things while I was waiting for you—although, I suppose you've eaten?" She looked at her anxiously.

Kathy had, but she couldn't refuse. "Irene, you look tired. Tell me where they are and I'll get them." Irene gratefully told her.

Kathy went out to the lower kitchen where a large silver platter was filled with dainty little finger sandwiches, several fresh dips, chips, an assortment fit for a party. She brought them in, then went back for the large pitcher of iced tea in the refrigerator. "Irene, when you do something, you never go halfway. Everything looks lovely."

Irene smiled, and some color seemed to come back to her cheeks. The pill must be working, Kathy thought. "Well, I had nothing else to do, and I like to fuss. I love my house, Kathy, but it can be awfully lonely when you're by yourself. I suppose that's why I used to give so many parties." Then she hastened to add, "And I will again, when this operation is over. I suppose you're wondering about the iced tea. Don't really like it myself, but Larry says no booze for a while. But make yourself something, please do. You know where everything is."

"No, I'll have what you're having," she said quietly. Kathy studied Irene as she gazed in the fire, all the while keeping up a steady stream of light conversation, while Kathy listened with half an ear. Kathy hadn't seen the name on the bottle, but she'd seen the pill, and the affect it was having now. Unless she was dead wrong, it was demarol, and that was pretty potent stuff. There had to be something more here than just a simple hysterectomy, if she were in that much pain. The first thought that crossed her mind was cancer, but it was out of character for Irene to be taking things so calmly. But then again, Irene's entire character seemed to have changed. How horrible, if she were right, and she was trying to go through this by herself. No, she must be wrong.

"Tell me, how's Ted lately? I haven't seen him around the Club for a while."

"Ted?" A slightly pained expression crossed her face. "Oh, he's fine. Lately, he's been home for dinner on time every night. Well, almost every night. And then, April's here. Sometimes she's here. She goes out a lot." A slight spasm hit her, and she clutched her side.

Kathy was instantly concerned, and knelt on the floor beside her. "Irene, are you alright? Do you want me to call Dr. Sturgess?"

"No, Kathy, please," she waved her away faintly, and she couldn't help but notice how thin her wrists had become, how her veins stuck out on the back of her hand. "How long ago was it that I took that pill? Do you remember?" The pain in her voice was obvious.

"I got here about 2:30; it's about four now."

"Kathy, would you pour me just a little more tea?" her voice was low, as she fumbled in her pocket. Oh God, she thought, she was supposed to have one every four hours, and it had only been an hour and a half.

Kathy brought her the tea, and this time she saw the label on the bottle. It *was* demarol.

Irene took the pill, and drank the tea with Kathy's help. "Kathy, you mustn't tell. You helped me before, remember? The night in my bedroom, Labor Day weekend. You didn't tell then, and you mustn't now." Then she remembered. Oh my God, Kathy *had* told! "Kathy, promise me," she was clinging to her now, pleading like a child, "Ted mustn't know, he mustn't *ever* know! Don't you see, I just couldn't stand having him pity me!"

The pill was starting to work now, so soon on top of the other one. Kathy stood there helplessly, Irene still clinging to her hand, then she started to laugh nervously, and the sound was pitiful.

"I promise you, Irene," she said steadily, "but you can't

just keep on taking those pills one right after the other. You could easily overdose, you know."

Irene sighed, relieved. "You promised, Kathy, and I believe you. I thought I had a month at least, more maybe, before I had to go to the hospital, but I don't think I can wait any longer. There's so much you don't know, dear, so much I can't explain, don't have the time to explain. There's April and so much I wanted to make up to her, and I thought when she came home this time—" her voice trailed off. "But it's just the same. We're no closer than we ever were. It all happened so long ago." She frowned, and tried to pull herself together. "There's one thing you can do for me, Kathy; bring me the phone."

She dialed a number, and asked for Dr. Sturgess, looking at Kathy and trying to smile. He was at the hospital, so she hung up and called there. "You can't find him? Well, page him again—tell him it's Irene Enwright, and it's urgent," she said, with a trace of her old imperialism.

"Larry?" she said finally, "The time is up, I think. I had to take demarols just an hour and a half apart." She waited, listening. "Tomorrow? So soon?" she whispered. "Alright, Kathy's here, she'll help me." She looked at Kathy questioningly for confirmation. Kathy nodded. "Well, I'll think of something. You had a cancellation, I couldn't stand the waiting around. Ted's used to me doing things on the spur of the moment, he'll buy it." She listened again. "Just some finger sandwiches and some tea, nothing else. Alright, see you in about an hour. And Larry? Keep it light, okay, for Ted's sake?" Then she hung up quickly, and got to her feet.

"That's alright, the pill's doing its job now." She waved Kathy's offer of assistance away. "And my bags have been packed for over a week. Let's get out of here before April or Ted comes home. Explanations now, I just can't take."

Kathy ran up the stairs quickly for her bag, and met Irene at the front door. Irene looked around her sadly for a moment, then on impulse, hugged Kathy. "My God, what I wouldn't do for a double martini right now."

April drove home from the Club as quickly as the law would allow, but traffic was heavy this late in the afternoon, and it wouldn't do for her to be stopped with liquor on her breath. She cursed herself mentally, as she'd been looking forward to meeting Kathy, but then she'd run into Pam, and naturally, there was nothing to do but stop and talk to her for a while.

They were almost the same age, and had become quite good friends in their teens before April had gone to Switzerland. Pam had been delighted to see her again, and was off and running on the latest gossip scarcely before they sat down. April listened to her with amused detachment, as it all seemed so tacky and small-town. Pam seemed different, somehow—in the first place, she was talking continually, which she never used to do, although she supposed that was only natural, after not seeing her for such a long time. And she was drinking a lot faster than she used to. She was already on her third, while April was still sipping her first. Not that she was getting drunk; on the contrary, it didn't seem to affect her at all. Oh well, she thought, people did change. Look at her, she had certainly changed since she met Juan. More cautious, she supposed. She thought a long time about what she was going to say before she said it now. Juan had taught her that, among other things.

It seemed like no time at all before she had the complete rundown on Duncan's heart attack (which she knew about); something strange going on at Keith Oil Company (which she didn't know about); some rumors about Jan and Ben not getting along too well, his drinking, Pam supposed; Kathy and Dwight going together, and poor Nancy just beside herself, as she was sure they were going to get back together. She paused just long enough to take a long swallow of her drink, and April managed to get a word in.

"Tell me, Pam, how's your father? And is Jack Wentworth still around, you haven't mentioned him."

Pam stared at her for a moment, like she'd hit a nerve. "Strange, you're asking about them in the same breath." All her exuberance of a minute ago was gone, and she seemed suddenly drained. "My father's about the same—I really don't think he recognizes me at all anymore, although I try to go out there every week, or every other week."

She thought for a moment. "And Jack—well, he hasn't changed much, either, although he's going to a psychiatrist now—same one your mother goes to. I wonder if they run into each other?" she mused. "But I can't see that it's done him any good—he still drinks like a fish, and still blames everything on his father. And things between him and Betsy aren't any better. She still raises hell every time he's a day late with her alimony check." She ordered another round of drinks, then looked at April calmly. "You know, I think he wants to marry me."

April almost choked on her drink, and for once she lost her cool. "Marry you! Why, you two were always—"

"Like brother and sister," Pam finished for her. "Now please don't say father and daughter—after all, he's not that much older than I am, only fourteen years."

Only fourteen! April almost choked again. She wondered what Pam would say if she knew she was living with a man thirty-four years older than she was. No, she couldn't risk it. Pam wouldn't be able to understand a thing like that.

"I've thought about it," Pam continued calmly, "although he hasn't asked me, and probably doesn't know how he feels himself, yet. But there's his drinking to consider, and all that friction with his family. His temper's something else again. Do you know," she leaned over and whispered confidentially, "I had to call the police a while ago? Really!" she nodded solemnly.

April tried to look properly shocked, and immediately thought about all the trouble Juan was in. She realized this was going to be another long story, and glanced at her watch. "Pam, I wish I could stay and hear all about it, but I really must go. I promised Irene I'd be home early, and it's almost dinner time now." She rose to leave. "Maybe we can get together next week for lunch or something; oh dammit, Irene goes in the hospital next week. Well, we'll work something out."

Pam left when she did, chattering how sorry she was about her mother, and that she couldn't stay longer, there was really so much more to talk about.

As they walked to their cars, April took a good look at Pam. In the flattering light of the bar, Pam had looked the same as always, but the harsh late afternoon sun wasn't quite so kind to her. The perennial tan was there, as usual, bringing out the startling green brilliance of her eyes. But the brilliance seemed a little dimmer than it used to be, and the tan didn't quite hide the puffiness around her eyes. She had always been slim, but now she was almost painfully so, and her legs, one of her best features, had slight hollows in her thighs. Her thick mane of black hair, which she tossed about frequently, seemed to have lost some of its shiny highlights. Looking at her now, she was still a beautiful girl, but something wasn't quite right, like a snapshot you took that was slightly out of focus.

April swung off the main road, and started driving up the mountain road at a faster clip. The sun had suddenly burst out late this afternoon, conquering the dreary day that had followed the heavy rains, sparkling over the lush green countryside. A rainbow appeared, and she pulled off on a narrow dirt shoulder to admire the view. It was too bad, she thought, that life couldn't be as simple and uncomplicated as nature. She watched the rainbow colors dancing daintily for a while, then suddenly, her eyes began to mist. There were no real seasons in California, they just seemed to blend into each other gradually, easily. There was no abrupt change, like there was in Switzerland.

Switzerland—God, how she missed it, and missed Juan. It had been good to be home for a while though, but now it had been two whole weeks, and it seemed like forever. Both her parents had insisted on meeting her at the airport, and she had spotted them immediately. Neither of them seemed to have changed much, she thought. She had expected her mother to look as though she were at death's door, from her father's conversation. She looked a bit pale, perhaps, but her hair was exquisitely tossed, and she was impeccably dressed, as usual. It was a knack, she decided; either you were born with it, or you weren't. While she agonized over what to wear for a special occasion, Irene never seemed to have that problem. Ted didn't, either; he looked equally elegant in a dark blue suit, or grubbing about on his boat. They hadn't been out on the boat since she'd come home, although Irene had urged them to go. Irene never went; seasickness was an affliction she had never gotten over, much to her regret. She would have loved to give yachting parties, but in that respect, she was out of luck—the mere thought of food on that boat made her sick. Therefore, the boat remained Ted's domain.

The first few days at home had gone as they usually did—everyone was nice to everyone else, but there was one exception, of course . . . Irene was going to have a hysterectomy. She kept waiting for the bickering to start, followed by the backbiting, then the out and out insults. When it didn't, she began to be puzzled; not only about that, but Irene treated everything about the operation very lightly, and April had expected the *Camille* routine. Her father, on the other hand, seemed much more concerned than Irene. She finally decided her mother was pulling some kind of martyrism on both of them, telling Ted to go to his business meetings, asking April to look up some of her old friends.

April had shrugged, and decided to play it Irene's way—besides, it got deadly in the house after a while. Irene wasn't drinking until after the operation, and out of deference to her, Ted rarely had more than one cocktail before dinner, if any. Then, too, Irene had to take a nap every afternoon to build up her strength for the operation, even though she looked healthy as a horse to April. Well, anyway, she probably wouldn't have a long recuperative period, so maybe she could get back to Geneva sooner than she thought.

April made it a point to get to the mailbox every day before the maid did, and Greta had been faithful in sending the papers, although she could find nothing about Juan in them. Even though she and Juan had both decided it would be best not to write unless it was terribly important, and then only through Greta, she looked forward to the mail every day. When there was a letter from Greta, her heart leaped—but that's all it turned out to be, just a letter from Greta.

She started the car up again, and continued the short distance home. Irene's car was in the garage, but Ted wasn't home yet. There was no other car around, so Kathy must have left. Damn, she was sorry she missed her. She threw her car keys on the table in the foyer, then had a feeling, somehow, that something was missing.

She stood there listening, and then for no accountable reason, she shivered. The house was perfectly still, except for the sound of rustling leaves outside. She was about to call Ann, to break the strange silence, and then remembered it was her day off. She walked slowly down the hall to her mother's room, a slight sense of foreboding coming over her. Her mother always cooked up something special on Ann's day off, usually corned beef and cabbage, but she could smell nothing cooking now, just the faint scent of flowers in the air, which her mother picked daily.

Irene's door was open, which was unusual in itself, as she always kept it closed. It was also empty. She checked the bathroom, then came back out and looked around. The closet door was open, but outside of that, everything seemed in order. She remembered how she had sneered openly when Irene had the room redone, calling it silly and ridiculous, although secretly she had adored the fairytale frothiness of everything. Irene had flushed and bridled, then told her to "stay the hell away from her room if she didn't like it, and that it was none of her business, anyway." which was exactly the reaction April was looking for.

Instead of saying "Goodnight" to her, she had frequently said things like "pleasant dreams in Bagdad," or "say goodnight to the sultan for me." Once, for a birthday present, she had solemnly presented her with a tinted portrait, framed in gold leaf, of Turhan Bey, the movie's version of the hero of the harems. But she had said none of these things to her on this trip. She had even sat in this room at night before Irene went to sleep, telling her about Switzerland, some of the trips she'd taken (always careful to say she'd gone with Greta), sometimes forgetting that Irene and she were bitter enemies. But were they really, now? She could detect no animosity on Irene's part, no great jealousy of Ted. Was there really some truth in that old adage, time heals all wounds? Part of it was true. You could forgive, but you could never forget, and that made it all very sad.

She closed the door to her mother's room and walked down the hall again. Where could Irene be? She stood in the living room, looking at the large spray of gladiolas on the coffee table, the last of the season. They were in shades of pink and red, but April had never liked glads. There was something about them that reminded her of funerals. She shivered again, and walked downstairs to the other living room.

The remains of a small fire, hastily put out, still smouldered in the fireplace. A platter of finger sandwiches, barely touched, was on the coffee table, along with a pitcher half-filled with tea, and two half-filled glasses. April's sense of foreboding deepened. Her mother might have a lot of faults, but if anything, she was overly meticulous. "Irene?" she called her loudly, not really expecting any answer. She started going through every room in the house, her heart pounding. There was nothing. The house was silent, and the only sound that could be heard was her heavy breathing. She ended up downstairs as dusk slowly settled, and she tried to decide what to do.

Automatically, she put the platter of sandwiches back in the refrigerator, rinsed out the two glasses and put them in the dishwasher, then poured herself a glass of lukewarm tea. It tasted awful, but she drank it anyway. The sound of the automatic light timers going on startled her, and she started to pull the drapes, then changed her mind. "Mother?" She almost whispered it, tasting the word strangely on her tongue. Where could she be? And where was her father? She ran to the front door and looked down the road. The lights in the city below began to twinkle on, slowly and merrily. It was too late to call her father's office, so she continued to stand there, watching and waiting, and she had never felt so alone in her life.

Dr. Sturgess had caught Ted just as he was leaving the office, and he explained the change in plans. When he hung up, Ted called home, trying to think of what to say to April, to prepare her. But she wasn't home, and there was no time to call around looking for her now—Irene needed him. He felt a certain mixture of numbness and relief as he drove to the hospital—relief that Kathy had been there, relief that the play-acting was finally over, that he could tell Irene he knew, had known almost from the beginning, that at last he could help her; but could he? Would she still want to pretend this game of hers to the very end? He thought he'd been prepared for this, especially during the last few days, when he'd caught her off guard and seen the terrible expression of pain cross her face. But then she'd go in her bedroom for a few minutes, and when she came out, she seemed like her old self again. But the numbness he hadn't foreseen.

He didn't realize, of course, that nature was sometimes kind enough to provide this sense of numbness when a situation became unbearable, and it puzzled him. He had known when Irene told him about the operation that it was something serious, and he had almost questioned her about it then—but he had held back. He had lived with her too long not to know there was more to it, even though he hadn't paid much attention to her lately. She was much too lighthearted about it, and although she was a pretty good actress, she wasn't that good. It had taken all his willpower to go back to his newspaper, although he didn't read it, just turned the pages.

He hadn't bothered to make an appointment with Larry, but had just barged into his office the next morning. Taken off guard, Larry had tried to keep up the same pretense, but Ted wasn't about to be put off. When he finally knew the truth, something seemed to snap inside his head, and he slumped in the nearest chair.

"My God, Larry, she can't have cancer!" His voice sounded hoarse and cracked, not like it was coming from him at all. "There must be some mistake." He was desperately reaching for anything, grabbing at straws, "I've heard of that happening, sometimes, they get the wrong names mixed up, or the wrong diagnosis—there's got to be something." His voice was pleading now, trying to make the past few minutes go away.

Larry shook his head. "There's no mistake, Ted," he said

wearily, "I wish to God there was. I even had a second biopsy taken, just to make sure. But the tumor's malignant, and growing every day. Why she didn't want you to know is beyond me, but you've made me break my hippocratic oath, and in a way, I'm not sorry. I know Irene will probably hate me, and she's got strong shoulders, but nobody should carry this burden alone. She should have the operation as soon as possible."

Ted sat slumped in the chair for a long time, his head buried in his hands. Jesus, what she must be going through—and what he must have done to her, not to want him to know. He tried to think back, before the money had started rolling in, before the yacht, the other women—and the other men. Oh, he'd known about them, alright, but curiously enough, he didn't really mind. In a way, he blamed himself, and she was certainly discreet enough. He had no idea who they were, but he knew there had to have been a few. Irene was a very sexy woman, and their own marital life surely wasn't enough to satisfy her. Poor Irene, he started to think, then stopped himself—no, she wouldn't have wanted that. The last thing she would have wanted was pity, or she would have told him immediately about the cancer. He suddenly felt a great deal of respect for her courage. He wasn't sure he could have done what she was doing. A great weariness overcame him, thinking of the days ahead. Then he looked at the doctor, and his eyes filled with pain.

"No, Larry," he said slowly, and his voice was thick, his mouth dry. "Irene has her reasons, and I'm sure to her, at least, they must be very good ones. So we'll do it her way." Larry started to protest, but Ted shook his head, tired but firm. "She doesn't want me to know, so for her sake, I won't know. So help me God, she won't know."

So they had played the game, and it was a deadly game. He had called April, and she had come home, although she really wasn't too happy about it. He had been nicer to Irene, but not too much nicer, or she might suspect something. Sometimes he felt as though he were walking a tightrope. He had forced himself to ignore her symptoms of pain, although he longed to reach out to her, to comfort her.

He spent less time with April than he usually did when she was home, afraid that everything might become too much for him, and he'd blurt out the truth. The tension at home became thick at times, but April seemed completely unaware of what was going on. Either she had become dimwitted, or her mind was completely absorbed with other things. She seemed changed, somehow. She had gone away still his little girl, and now she was a woman. He supposed she was no longer a virgin—any other time, the thought would have horrified him, but it didn't seem to matter anymore. Nothing seemed to matter anymore except Irene, and for the first time in his life, he felt completely helpless.

The hospital loomed up in front of him suddenly, and just as suddenly, his numbness disappeared. He parked the car quickly, and started walking towards the entrance, not knowing what to expect.

Kathy stood by the entrance desk twisting her hands nervously, waiting for Ted. Dr. Sturgess had been waiting for them at the hospital when they arrived, and quickly whisked Irene away in a wheelchair. Kathy had wanted to stay with her, but Irene was adamant. Call April, wait for Ted, don't look so worried, keep it light, she had begged. She had no choice but to agree. She called April, but there was no answer.

The waiting seemed endless, but it gave her time to think. Much as she pitied Irene, she felt a certain resentment at being thrust in the middle of a situation where she had no place. She was glad that April wasn't home—she didn't particularly relish telling a perfect stranger that her mother was in the hospital. And Ted—what was she supposed to tell

221

him? There had been no time to ask Dr. Sturgess, and she felt a certain anger towards him. She had problems of her own, and now this! Dwight would be wondering where she was, but she couldn't leave the desk now to call him, she might miss Ted. Angrily, she stood there, smoking and tapping her foot, when she finally saw Ted coming up the steps, two at a time. At the sight of him, her anger and resentment vanished. She crushed out her cigarette, took a deep breath, and tried to remain calm. "Ted?" she called to him.

He looked around him, dazed, and his hair was tousled from the wind. "Kathy?" he looked at her, confused, and from the deep pain in his eyes, she knew she didn't have to tell him anything. "Where is she?"

"They took her to her room, Ted," she said quietly. "She wasn't feeling well this afternoon, and since Dr. Sturgess had a cancellation, she decided to be admitted to the hospital today," she lied, because she'd promised Irene, knowing it was unnecessary. My God, she thought, why all this pretense? Did April know, too? She didn't understand these people at all; just when they should have been closer than ever before in their lives, they were lying, and pretending—it didn't make any sense to her at all.

He looked towards the elevators, then back to Kathy again, then at the nurse at the desk. He sighed a little, and motioned her away from the desk. "You know, don't you." His voice was low, and it was a statement rather than a question.

"Yes," she answered him as steadily as possible, but her voice trembled a little. "But she only told me today." She tried to think of something to say, as he remained quiet, as though he were a million miles away. "Dr. Sturgess should be down in a little while, then you can see her. She had a lot of pain today, so she called the doctor, and asked him to move up the operation. It's tomorrow morning," she went on, "but she said you and April didn't know about the—" she was about to say cancer, but changed her mind. "Anything," she finished weakly.

"Cancer?" He said it for her. "Might as well say it now, she can't keep this up any longer. At least, I hope she won't try to. No, April doesn't know. Either I have a fool for a daughter, or she's so wrapped up in herself and so anxious to get back to Switzerland that she hasn't even bothered to notice what's going on around her. But she didn't want us to know, Kathy; why, I don't know. So I went along with it." It was a relief for him to finally be able to talk to someone, anyone, after keeping it bottled up for so long. "You don't know what hell it's been these past few weeks, wanting to help her, to reach out to her, and being completely helpless. Maybe I should have told her in the beginning I knew, but she didn't want it that way, so I respected her wishes. I've gone over it a thousand times in my mind, and I still don't understand why. Maybe she wanted to punish me for something, but I can't bring myself to believe she could hate me that much. Maybe she wanted to spare us; maybe she wanted to prove how brave she could be; I just don't know." His voice was filled with all the anguish and despair that he'd had to cover up, and tears began to fill his eyes. "But she told you, Kathy," he said chokingly. "Why?" He sat down on one of the lounges and covered his eyes.

Kathy sat down next to him and cradled his head on her shoulder, gently. "She had to, Ted," she spoke softly. "She was in pain, and she knew that I could see it. She had no choice, anymore. If you or April had been there, she would have had to tell you, too."

"But I wasn't there," his voice was muffled against her, "and neither was April. Oh My God, April," he said, not moving, "has anyone gotten hold of her yet?"

"Yes, Daddy." Kathy looked up, and a tall slim blonde

girl was standing over them. "I came just as soon as Dr. Sturgess called." Kathy and April stared at each other, and April's eyes were dark and unfathomable.

Chapter 10

Jan sat in her father's room, reading, unaware of the activity going on elsewhere in the hospital. Her father had dropped off, but he might wake up before visiting hours were over, and he always liked to find her there. She came every evening now, as Vivian only visited in the afternoons, and she preferred to be with her father alone. Vivian talked too much, and this wasn't good for her father, not at this stage of his recovery. Whether she realized it or not, Vivian always started talking about the business after the first few minutes. Jan had spoken to Dr. Sturgess about this, so he had arranged to have a nurse in constant attendance when Vivian visited. She sighed, and dropped the book on her lap. She looked at her father, sleeping so peacefully now, and looking so much better. She remembered how ghastly he had looked the night of his heart attack, and shuddered. Soon, he'd be going home, and she wondered again about Vivian.

Dwight and Scott never talked about the business when they came to see him, much as her father coaxed. Oh, they'd mention something if it was good, but never anything bad. She, herself, knew nothing about the business, but she knew what upset her father. And Vivian's mentioning that she'd had to fire so-and-so, or the sales in Bakersfield had dropped off, that was bad. She wished he could recuperate at her home, but of course, that was impossible. It was hard enough for her to stand it, let alone an invalid.

She had wracked her brains, trying to think of some way to break with Ben without the news reaching her father. Not that he wouldn't be pleased, of course; but there was no foretelling Ben's reactions. He might just get drunk enough to come over and see her father—he was completely unpredictable now. The only predictable thing about him was that he was drunk all the time. Too bad he couldn't just drive off a cliff when he was that way.

She sat very still for a moment, scarcely believing that she could have had such a thought; it was sacrilegious, wishing someone dead. She tried to put it out of her mind, and picked up her book again, but she couldn't concentrate, and her mind strayed—it would be such a perfect solution. Such a simple thing, really—just a little tampering with the brakes, she knew how to do that; and he was always going up to Rocky's, and the mountain road was long and winding. No, she shook her head firmly, it was against God's will and the Bible, and besides, something might go wrong, and God might punish her, or worse still, the baby. She mustn't have these thoughts. There had to be another way.

Duncan watched his daughter under half-closed lids; something was troubling her, of that he was sure. And he was just as sure she wouldn't tell him. These doctors and their ideas of how to treat someone! Everyone pussyfooting around, afraid to tell him this, he shouldn't know about that—a body might as well be in his grave. He hoped it was trouble with Ben that was causing his daughter so much concern—but that would be too much to expect. He sighed, inwardly—for such a bright little thing, she'd sure picked a loser! Completely blinded by him, she was. He couldn't say a word against Ben, not in front of her. Lately, though, she hadn't mentioned him—Larry probably told her not to, that it might upset him. Well, he'd be home soon, then things would be different. If they thought he'd stay away from the company indefinitely, they had another thing coming. It was his business, by God, and he wasn't in his grave yet, not by a long shot. And there was Vivian, she'd help him . . . maybe, she'd help him.

She knew as much about the company as he did, or thought she did. Sometimes he'd forgotten things the past couple of years, but they were little things, and she'd always remind him. Lately, though, before his heart attack, she'd acted kind of funny; almost as though she were running the business. It hadn't seemed to matter much then, because he'd been well, and Dwight and Scott were always there. But just to be on the safe side, he'd drawn up a new will, she didn't know a thing about it, and of course, there had always been the extra life insurance policies for Jan. His first wife, Jeanne, had known about them, but nobody, not even Jan, knew about them now. Just his attorney, and he'd trust him with his life. In all fairness to Viv, she had made certain improvements in the company, and he'd seen to it that she'd get the house, and enough to keep her comfortably, if anything happened to him. But the business belonged to his children.

He thought about Jeanne—Jan was so much like her—the same gentle manner. He had thought he'd seen that quality in Viv, at first, but he'd been wrong—she was all business. She'd been good to the children at first, and he'd thought she'd want to stay home and be a second mother to them. But no, right after the honeymoon—back to work. It had amused him at first, then annoyed him, then he got used to it. The children were grown now, and didn't need a mother. She'd been a good enough companion to him; until lately.

Something was just a bit out of kilter—he couldn't quite put his finger on it, but it was there. He comforted himself that the business was sound, and the boys and Jan had nothing to worry about.

"Something bothering you, honey?" he asked Jan.

She looked up at him, startled, and wondered how long he'd been watching her. "Of course not, Daddy. I was waiting for you to wake up before I left."

"No need to do that, punkin. You could have awakened me. All I do is sleep around here."

She smiled at him. "And that's what you're supposed to do. You need your rest." She got up and kissed him lightly on the forehead.

"No troubles at home, or anything?" he asked her, hoping there were.

She looked at him for a long moment. Was this the time to tell him? No, not yet, she'd have to wait a little longer. "Of course not, Daddy, don't be silly. Now go back to sleep and I'll see you tomorrow night."

After Dr. Sturgess called, April had driven down the road to the hospital at breakneck speed. Just like her mother, she thought, to change her plans at the last minute, not even leaving a note. It was inconsiderate, to say the least. Now she'd have to call off her golf date for tomorrow. Oh well, all the sooner she'd get back to Juan.

She walked up the steps of the hospital, and stopped just inside the entrance, shocked. This was the last sight she'd expected to see. There was her father, cuddled in the arms of a strange young girl, for all the world to see, on a couch in the hospital lobby. For a long moment she stood there, feeling a mixture of rage and jealousy, then indignation for her poor mother. She rearranged her face and walked over to them, just in time to hear her father ask if anyone had called her.

The girl looked up at her, her eyes sad and beautiful, then

suddenly aware of how the situation must have looked, moved away from her father. "You must be April," the girl managed, "your mother wanted us to meet today."

Ted stood up and held April silently for a moment. "Now April, you mustn't worry," he tried to sound natural, "Dr. Sturgess had a cancellation, so Irene decided to get the whole thing over with. We'll be able to see her just as soon as they get her settled."

"I see," April said cooly. So that's the way they were going to play it. Just two old friends, hugging each other, waiting to see dear old Mom. She turned to the girl. "You say mother wanted us to meet?" Her tone was a breath away from a sneer.

Why, you little snot, Kathy thought to herself. "I'm Kathy Foster," she said shortly, "your mother and I were having tea today, and she asked me to drive her to the hospital."

April looked bewildered. Maybe she'd been wrong—but what was all this about? Maybe her mother was sicker than she'd thought. "Yes, she did say you were coming over today. I tried to get home in time, but I ran into Pam at the Club, and—" she turned to her father abruptly. "Daddy, is Irene going to be all right? I mean, asking someone to tea, then having them drive you to the hospital is a bit unorthodox, isn't it? Is there something you're not telling me?"

Ted seemed to slump a little, not answering, and looked to Kathy for support.

Oh God help me, what do I say? It really all depended on Irene; whether she was going to try to keep up this pretense. And she, Kathy, was in the middle again. "Why don't we all just wait for the doctor?" she mumbled weakly. "In the meantime, I've got to make a call." She excused herself quickly and rushed down the hall. This was strictly father and daughter time.

She almost bumped into Jan turning the corner, and they

looked at each other in surprise. "Irene's operation is tomorrow morning," Kathy volunteered, without being asked. "I hope your father's better."

"Oh, he's coming along fine," Jan smiled, then she frowned. "I must have my dates mixed up. I didn't think Irene went in until next week."

More explanations, Kathy thought. Am I going to have to be the town crier? "No, they changed it," she said hurriedly, "now I really must go call your brother."

Irene was finally settled in the hospital bed. Later on, she thought, I'll probably smell like hospital disinfectant—but right now she smelled of Chanel No. 5, and had on the brand new beige negligee set that just matched her hair.

One nurse had taken a blood sample which she hadn't minded, and another a urine sample which she hated, as she considered it an invasion of her privacy, but she was too tired and sick to argue. They had stuck her with other needles, and then, that blessed shot in her rear, which had brought almost instant relief from the pain. It also made her drowsy, and she was thankful for that.

Ted and April were waiting to see her, she knew, and Kathy was with them, but she'd asked for a few moments alone before the nurse sent them in. She looked around the room, and then out the window. It was dark outside now, but the room was beautiful, not like a hospital room at all. Everything was beautiful. Tears came to her eyes when she thought that she might have to leave all this beauty after tomorrow morning, but the thought swam hazily away from her. Cancer. Even that didn't seem to bother her now.

It must have been the shot; yes, she was sure it was the shot—too bad you couldn't go through life feeling this way, always. She wondered how long before it would wear off—not before she saw her family, she hoped. And there was someone else—who? Oh yes, Kathy. Kathy wouldn't tell.

Kathy had brought her here. Blessed Kathy. And April—tears started again, April hadn't come home in time to meet Kathy. Maybe Kathy would look after April when she was gone. She wiped the tears away, groggily, smearing her mascara. She mustn't think this way. Everything was beautiful, everything was going to stay beautiful.

Ted and April came into the room quietly, and at first Irene didn't see them. She looked so small and helpless to Ted, almost as though she'd shrunk, and he wanted to cradle her in his arms, to tell her that everything would be alright. But he just stood there, waiting.

April waited, too, but with different thoughts. Something was terribly wrong, but her mother looked the same. She noticed the lovely new negligee, the carefully arranged hair, but something was out of place. She quickly walked over and wiped the smudged mascara from her mother's cheeks. Irene caught her hand and held it. "April darling," she tried to smile, her voice thick with sedation, and another tear trickled down her cheek, "and Ted," she held out her other hand, "I didn't hear you come in.

"You know," she whispered confidentially, "I think I'm kind of high. They gave me a shot of something. Can you imagine? And for a simple, little, hyster—" her voice trailed off, and she started crying, hard, wracking sobs.

Ted sat on the bed next to her and scooped her up in his arms, as though she were a tiny child. "Irene, baby, baby," he gently rocked her back and forth, "everything's going to be alright. Believe me, baby, there's nothing to worry about." He continued to rock her, gently smoothing her hair, kissing the tears away, talking to her, until she gradually quieted. Finally, she dozed off, but he continued rocking her for a long time, staring into space as if into a vast distance.

April stared at the two of them in amazement, her mouth slightly open. She had never seen her father act this way—except with her, of course, when she was little. Ever since she could remember, there had been more or less constant bickering between them. And she had never seen her mother break down—shout, throw things, yes; but this! She had never thought her father and mother cared about each other at all, but now? Her whole world was turning upside down before her very eyes.

Finally, every so slowly, her father lowered Irene down on the bed, and stood up just as slowly, so as not to wake her. Then he leaned down and kissed her gently on the forehead. She smiled slightly in her sleep, but did not waken. He motioned to April, and they left the room together. He called the nurse, and told her they were leaving, that she could put up the bed rails now.

April, with some sixth sense, knew better than to talk while riding down in the elevator. Kathy was waiting for them, and he seemed glad to see her.

"She's sleeping now." He gave her a warning glance, which didn't slip past April. Then he turned to April. "April, why don't you leave your car here? We'll both have to be back at the crack of dawn." He turned to Kathy again. "Will you be here? I think she'd like that." Kathy nodded.

"Well, that's settled," he said, with a pretense of briskness, "shall we all go home now?"

April was quiet on the ride home, although her thoughts were racing. When they pulled up in the driveway, lights blazing away in the house, she tried to talk to him.

"Not now, April," he said wearily. Then, as she continued to stare at him, he pulled her over and held her close. "Alright. You're her daughter, and you have a right to know, although God knows, she tried hard enough to keep it from us."

Then he held her by the shoulders, while she looked him in the eyes, half-knowing what he was going to say. "It's cancer. We may lose your mother tomorrow." His voice broke.

"Now please, no more questions tonight. You can ask Dr. Sturgess all about it in the morning."

Pam got home long before dark after leaving April. She had taken uppers this morning, and was still pepped up when she had finished work. A few drinks at the Club would relax her, she thought, and she always ran into someone she knew. But there had only been April, and then she had to leave. She hadn't even considered remaining at the Club alone, it would ruin her image. The drinks hadn't done a thing for her, and she was still restless—who could she call? Kathy was going over to Irene's today, and she was probably tied up with Dwight tonight. All her other friends had to work tomorrow; well, so did she, but they didn't like going out on week nights.

She considered calling Jack—but she was still punishing him for the ruckus he'd caused at her apartment. That was certainly cutting off her nose to spite her face. She mixed herself a stiff drink, then started to look through her phone book—nothing looked interesting. Besides, men were supposed to be calling her, not the other way around. Her restlessness grew, and she wandered around her apartment. A hot bath, maybe? No, she'd tried that before, and it never worked. It was too early to go to bed, anyway, and she wasn't hungry. Those pep pills sure ruined your appetite. Visit her father, perhaps? No, that just depressed her, and the nurses would be sure to smell the liquor on her breath. She decided to call Jack, and hang up if he answered. Maybe he'd think it was her and call back. She dialed his number and let the phone ring twenty times before she hung up. Even if he was in the shower, he would have heard it by then.

Then she dialed Kathy. Maybe Dwight hadn't picked her up yet, and maybe she'd ask her to go along. She wasn't home, either. She went out to the kitchen to fix another drink, and looked at the dirty dishes piled high in the sink. Funny, she never used to let things go like that. Half the time she didn't even make the bed in the morning anymore, unless she expected company later. Well, she certainly wasn't expecting anybody now. She took her drink back to the living room and switched on the television. She found a variety show, and settled down on the couch.

Some new comic was going through his routine, and she tried to concentrate. Then a funny thing began to happen. She felt completely sober, and her mind was crystal clear, but as she watched the comic, slowly he began to separate, until there were two of them. She shook her head quickly, and when she looked again, there was only one comic. She sipped her drink, wondering; this had never occurred before. The comic finished his routine, and the MC came on, applauding his act. Then it happened again—slowly, there were two MC's and two comics. A feeling of fear shot through her, and she automatically finished her drink in one long gulp.

It hit the pit of her stomach quickly, and she could feel the coldness as it slowly spread through her, although it was warm in the apartment. She kept shaking her head, but two of everything remained on the screen. She mustn't panic, she thought. God, what was happening to her? She started to get up, and lurched against the coffee table. The room started to spin, slowly at first, and her hands were like ice. She fell back on the couch, shaking. She knew she should call someone, but she couldn't let anyone see her in this condition. Maybe if she just talked to someone, this awful feeling would go away.

She reached for the phone, then remembered—Jack and Kathy weren't home. She certainly couldn't call Dr. Sturgess, he'd know in a minute what was wrong with her. She was afraid to lie down, she might never get up. She looked at her watch, but the hands were blurred. She looked out the windows—it was dark now, and she should pull the drapes, but she was afraid to get up. Maybe Kathy was home by now. She dialed her number slowly, and got the wrong number. She tried again, and the same thing happened. She put the receiver down, and stared at it as if it were her mortal enemy. Then she picked it up again, and called the operator.

Kathy could hear the phone ringing as she fumbled for her keys. Topsy was jumping up and down, as usual, then made a beeline for the back door, scratching to get out. She dropped her things on the couch, and opened the door. The phone was still ringing, and wearily, she considered not answering. It could only be Dwight, and she was much too tired to talk to him, let alone see him. But it kept on and on, and finally she picked it up.

"Kathy?" Pam's voice sounded blurred, but Kathy was too fatigued to wonder why. "You and Dwight just get home? I've been calling you for the longest time. Can you talk a while? I want to ask you something." She spoke slowly, but there was a certain urgency that Kathy missed.

Kathy sighed. About the last thing she wanted now was to get into a long conversation with Pam, but she didn't want to hurt her feelings. After all, she was a good friend. "Pam," she said carefully, "I didn't see Dwight tonight. There was a change of plans, and Irene's operation is tomorrow morning. She asked me to be there, so you see, I really don't feel like talking now. I've been at the hospital for hours, and all I want is a hot bath, and a little rest."

"I'm so lonely, Kathy," Pam said, as though she hadn't heard a word Kathy had said. "I haven't seen my father for the longest time, and I hate to go out there by myself. It's so depressing. Would you drive out with me tomorrow?"

Kathy listened in amazement. Had Pam gone daffy, or was she just plain stoned? "I guess you weren't listening," she repeated, 'I have to be at the hospital tomorrow morning. I've been there all afternoon, I'm worn out, and I have to be there again tomorrow. Irene's being operated on."

She finally got through to her. "Oh." There was a silence for a moment, then, "Well, could you drive out with me Sunday? It's really a beautiful drive, and I haven't seen my father in the longest time," she paused, "but I said that, didn't I?"

Kathy was getting impatient. Her feet hurt, so she kicked off her shoes, and Topsy was scratching to get in. "Pam, we'll talk about it later. Right now I have too much else on my mind. Why don't you ask Jack?" She was trying to end the conversation without being downright rude.

"Oh, I couldn't do that," she said quickly, "He knows all about the—" her voice trailed off. "The what?" she said wonderingly, "now why did I say that?"

At any other time, Kathy would have been curious, but now she was thoroughly irritated. She had told Pam twice how tired she was, and about Irene, but she didn't seem the least bit interested, and just kept rambling on. She'd have to be rude, after all. "Pam, I have to go. I'm sorry, but I just can't talk any longer, I'm bushed. Get some sleep." And then she hung up the phone.

She had no sooner hung up her coat and taken off her dress, when the phone rang again. Pam must really be stoned, and she was so furious, her adrenal glands started working overtime. After this, she'd take the phone off the hook. Oh God, she couldn't do that, either. She hadn't been able to contact Dwight, and had left a message at his exchange. If she didn't answer, he'd be sure to come over. She answered the phone, and icicles dripped from her voice.

"Kathy?" It was Dwight, and his voice was filled with concern. "I just got your message a little while ago, Scott and I were tied up. Then I called the hospital, and they said you'd already left. And your line was busy at home, so I figured you'd taken the phone off the hook. Honey, I'm so sorry, you must be bushed. I'll be right over."

"No, Dwight, really," she protested, "all I want is a good night's sleep."

"Now, I won't take no for an answer. You jump in the tub, and by the time you're through, I'll be there, and give you a good rubdown. I won't bother you tonight, I'll even sleep on the couch if you want me to," he said virtuously, and clicked up the phone before she could answer.

Viciously, she slammed down the phone, picked up a magazine and threw it across the room. Topsy jumped in surprise. She was on the verge of nervous exhaustion now, and the last thing she wanted was Dwight hanging around all night. Determinedly, she started her bath water, and purposely left out the scented bubble bath.

He got there just as she was stepping out of the tub, but she took her time about answering the door. He had asked for a key several times, and each time had been turned down flat. After all, she had to have some independence, and he didn't own her yet, even if he thought he did. The night had turned suddenly cold, and he was shivering when she finally opened the door.

He tried to put his arms around her, dripping sympathy, but she pulled away. "Dwight, if you hadn't hung up so soon, you'd have known I didn't want you over here tonight. You did it on purpose, didn't you?"

"Honey, I just had to see you." He looked guilty. "If you're that tired, though, I'll just rub your back, and I'll sleep on the couch, like I told you."

"No, you won't sleep on the couch, either. You'll go home and sleep in your own bed," she said firmly.

"Honey, I thought you'd want me here. After all, when you love someone, you want to share your problems. And I want to know about Irene."

When you love somebody, yes, she thought, but she couldn't say that to him. "Well, I don't want you here. I want to go to sleep." And then she said something she never would have said if she hadn't been so near the breaking point. "And if you slept on the couch, I wouldn't get any sleep at all. You snore."

His mouth dropped open, in surprise, shock and hurt. "Kathy, I've never seen you this way before." He tried to regain some of his shredded dignity. "Nancy never said I snored. And if it bothered you so much, why didn't you wake me up, or nudge me? And how do you know you don't snore?" he asked.

"Do I?" She was already regretting bringing up the subject. She really didn't want to hurt him.

"No," he had to admit, grudgingly. "Do you want me to rub your back, at least?"

She looked at him suspiciously. It sounded tempting—her muscles were tied in knots, and it might relax her enough to get a few hours sleep. He surely wouldn't try anything tonight. "I'm sorry, Dwight, I'm a bundle of nerves tonight. Ten minutes, and that's all," she said firmly.

They went in the bedroom, and she took off her robe, then got into bed, face down. She waited, wondering what was taking him so long, then looked around. He was taking his clothes off.

"You don't have to do that to rub my back." Instantly she was sorry she'd agreed to the backrub, but it had sounded good at the time.

"It gets hot in here," he said indignantly, "and besides, I don't want to get that lotion all over my clothes. You know, I've had one hell of a day, too. And you didn't even bother to tell me you were taking the day off."

He had her on that one, and she had no answer. "Just rub my back. Oh, before you do that, though, would you set the alarm for 5:00, and the one in the living room, too? Otherwise, I'll never get up. You better put the one in here across the room, just to be on the safe side."

"What about when you get up to put the latch on the back

door?'' he said, with a hint of sarcasm.

So, he'd noticed that, she thought, with a twinge of guilt. "Tonight you'll be leaving early enough to go out the front, and the latch is already on the back.''

He set the alarms, got out the body lotion, and straddled her buttocks. She sighed softly, and as his fingers started working on her neck, she began to relax. She loved having her back rubbed, and she had to admit, he was one of the best. She used to go to massage parlors in Hollywood once in a while, and he measured up to any one of them. Bruce used to rub her back every night, too.

There was one difference between Bruce and Dwight, though. Bruce used to rub her all over, and then they'd make love. With Dwight, she let him make love to her first and then rub her back, so she could relax and enjoy it, knowing that the sex part was over, for the night, at least.

She thought about the sexual differences between Bruce and Dwight—Bruce could bring her to feverish pitches, back off a little, then start all over again. How do you explain orgasms, anyway? Except that there was absolutely no other feeling in the world like it. She had had orgasms without love, as with Jack Wentworth, but when it was combined with love, the deliciousness of it with Bruce made her feel like she could almost die from the pleasure. Dwight, though, that was another story. After the first night, when she thought he was going to kill her with the pain, she had sense enough to buy some lubricating jelly. She always went in the bathroom, and stuck plenty of the jelly deep inside herself before they went to bed. And he did have one saving grace—after the first night, with the help of the jelly, he was like a rabbit. Four, five, six, at the most eight quick jabs, and he'd reach a climax, thank God. It didn't even leave her feeling frustrated, as she hadn't become aroused in the least to begin with, not with him.

She was becoming more and more relaxed as his thumbs

239

kneaded her spine. Then he shifted his weight lower down, in order to rub her lower back, and she felt him. His penis was stiff and erect, shoved between her legs, and he was breathing heavily. She had been so engrossed with her own thoughts, that she hadn't noticed this happening. What should she do? Pretend sleep? No, that wouldn't work, when he'd just mentioned the latch business after he'd left. She decided to play it honest. "That's enough, Dwight. I told you I was too tired."

"Kathy, please," he begged, and laid down on her back. He was actually trying to get in dog fashion, the stupid fool. Didn't he know that even men who were built big had trouble in that position? She tensed herself, and tried to push him off of her.

"I said no, Dwight, and I meant it." Her voice was like ice, and all the good the backrubbing had done was gone now. "Now, get the hell off me, get dressed and go home, and I mean right now."

His penis suddenly wilted like a limp balloon. She knew his pride was crumpled, but for the life of her, she didn't care. "You know I won't get any sleep tonight," he said like a hurt child.

"Well, that makes two of us," she said angrily, "and I don't think I want to see you anymore. If you have no more consideration for me than you've shown tonight, then I don't want you around. I told you I didn't want you over here, but you came over anyway. Then you said you'd just rub my back and go home. Now you try this, and I've told you repeatedly I'm exhausted. If you want sex so badly, go the hell to some whorehouse. I'm sure you must know of some. Or else, the bars are still open, maybe you'll get lucky at one of them."

Dwight looked at her in horror. "Kathy, you don't know what you're saying. I wouldn't think of such a thing. I love you, only you, and I'm so sorry, so ashamed of myself, but when I get around you, I just can't seem to help myself, just to touch you, to smell your perfume, just to look at you sometimes, Kathy, you can't mean it. I know you love me, too, although you've never said it. Honey, please don't say you won't see me anymore, you can't mean such a thing, you're my whole life," he was babbling now, and his voice kept droning in her ears. Anything to shut him up.

"Alright," she practically shouted at him. "I'm upset, and I'm tired. Now, please, Dwight, I'll talk to you tomorrow. Don't say another word tonight, though, please."

It was another half hour before she finally got him out of the house, and she looked at her watch. One-thirty in the morning. No sense in trying to get any sleep now. God, she wanted a drink, but she couldn't go to the hospital with liquor on her breath. Besides, in her present mood, she could easily get drunk, and not show up at all. Not show up!

With all that had happened, she'd forgotten to call Dr. Carter. Oh God, did she dare call him at this hour? They had a full day's schedule tomorrow, and she couldn't go to work. She was shaking as she called the exchange and asked them to put her through to him.

Edith answered the phone groggily, "Hello?"

"Mrs. Carter, this is Kathy. I know it's terribly late, but something happened today, and I just now remembered to call the doctor. Could you tell him for me, please, that I can't come to work tomorrow?"

"He's right here, Kathy," she said. "Maybe you better tell him yourself."

"What is it, Kathy?" his voice sounded quick, alert, concerned.

"Oh, I'm so sorry, Dr. Carter," her voice trembled, and she was on the verge of hysteria. "Irene had an attack this afternoon, and I had to take her to the hospital, and then I had to wait with Ted and April, and then when I finally got home Pam called, and I couldn't get her off the phone, and then Dwight came over, and I couldn't get him to leave, and

241

it's just been one terrible day. And Irene wants me there when they operate. It's too late to try to sleep now, and I'm so tired and nervous, I feel like I'm coming apart. Please don't be angry, but I just now remembered to call you."

"That's all right, Kathy," he said, "just try to keep calm. I'll be right over. Have you got any vodka in the house?"

"Oh, I can't put you to all that trouble, please, I'll be all right. No, I don't have any."

"Well, I do. Just sit down, and try to relax. I'll be there as soon as I can."

Edith watched him as he dressed quickly, her face impassive. She asked no questions. What good would it have done? He was going over to his receptionist's apartment in the middle of the night with a bottle of vodka. She was in some kind of trouble, but she wouldn't find out what it was tonight. He was hurrying, but he took the time to brush his teeth and splash on some shaving lotion. If it had been a patient, he might possibly have gone, or he might have made room for him on the following day—but he would have grumbled. He wasn't grumbling now. Finally, she spoke. "If you won't be back before you go to the office, don't you think it might be a good idea to take your razor?"

He looked at her quizzically for a moment. "Thanks. But I have all those things at the office." At the door, he paused. "You're a good wife, Edith," he said, and quickly left. She heard him rummaging around in the bar, then the front door slammed, and in a few minutes she heard the car start.

She stayed in bed for a few minutes, thinking. Then she got up and looked in the full length mirror on the closet door. She had on a hairnet, a light layer of coldcream, and a blue cotton nightgown. She dropped the nightgown to the floor, and really looked at herself. She had fairly large breasts, and she used to be proud of them. Her hips had really spread, and her waistline was certainly thicker. Funny, she mused, how these things happened so gradually, you barely noticed

242

them. She turned, and tried to peer at her bottom, and quickly turned around again. Blubber! She turned sideways, and sucked in her belly, but it wasn't much of an improvement.

She put her gown back on, then concentrated on her face. There was a definite beginning of a double chin, but hardly any wrinkles, probably because of the fat. She marvelled at John, and had often remarked to him that he hadn't put on a pound since their marriage. Odd, that she hadn't thought about her own appearance when she had said that. But then, she'd always taken John for granted. They had a good, solid marriage, she thought. Maybe, just maybe, she'd taken too much for granted. The idea of him ever being unfaithful to her never entered her mind; maybe it should have.

She opened her closet door and looked at her clothes— mostly dark colors, a few light blues and greys. The one bright spot was a red coat with a white fox collar John had bought her several birthdays ago. She seldom wore it. Then she opened John's closet—checked sports jackets, plaids, flowered shirts.

She went into the den and brought back the latest copy of McCalls, went back to bed and started flipping through it. Maybe she'd get her hair done tomorrow—a new style might help—then a girdle, and a couple of new dresses. Just a couple, as they wouldn't fit her after she started dieting. At least, she hoped they wouldn't. And she'd start wearing bras around the house—she hadn't for quite a few years as they weren't comfortable for housework; besides, they made her sweat. Well, maybe if she sweated, she'd lose weight faster. Not that she really thought anything was wrong; still, it might be a good idea to try to look a little better. Maybe being too placid had its drawbacks. And she'd fix something special for dinner tomorrow night—but she wouldn't eat the dessert.

Chapter 11

Dr. Carter drove to Kathy's as quickly as he could, not without a certain feeling of trepidation. There was hardly any traffic this late at night, and as he neared her house, he felt a sense of exhilaration. He had never been there before, although he had driven by several times when she was at the office—just to see where she lived, he had told himself. He had dismissed Edith from his mind before he was out of the driveway.

Kathy had sounded desperate on the phone, almost hysterical, and the analytical side of his nature tried to dissect the situation. But the dark clear night, the twinkling stars, and the smell of late blooming jasmine in the autumn air distracted him. He tried to be objective, but the thought of seeing her in her own surroundings excited him.

He parked the car, and Kathy opened the door almost immediately as he started up the walk. The little black poodle she talked about so much came running out to greet him. Almost automatically, he reached down to pet the dog, but his eyes were on Kathy.

She stood in the doorway, wearing a blue chenille bathrobe, and as he came nearer, he could see the deep circles under her eyes, the tearstreaked cheeks, the trembling lips, the disheveled hair. She had never looked lovelier to him, or more vulnerable. He scooped up the handful of dog and carried her in with him, while she licked his face.

"That's funny," Kathy said, "Topsy doesn't take to strangers. She hates Dwight." She smiled at him nervously. "I should have gotten dressed, I suppose, but I've just been sitting here, trying to calm down, and my mind's been going around in circles. I'm all cried out by now . . . Irene—," she started to say.

"Yes, I heard about her earlier tonight," he cut her off. "But I didn't know you were with her." He had to get her mind on something else, because she was just about at the breaking point. He looked briefly around the living room, the magazine thrown on the floor, and pulled the bottle of vodka out of his coat pocket. "Where's the kitchen?"

She led him there meekly, and started to get out some orange juice.

"No, I want you to drink this straight," he said firmly. "Have you eaten anything today?"

She shook her head, then remembered. "Oh, I had a few dips and things at Irene's before all this happened, but that's all." She made a wry face. "Dr. Carter, I can't possibly drink that stuff straight—it tastes like rubbing alcohol."

He considered that for a moment. "It'll hit you faster this way, on an empty stomach. You can have some orange juice as a chaser. I don't usually prescribe this," he said, opening the bottle, "but it's too late for a sleeping pill, and with a little luck a few of these will calm you down, and you might even fall asleep. Don't worry, I'll sit up with you so you'll get to the hospital on time." He filled a tumbler full of vodka and handed it to her. "Here—drink it all."

She took a small sip, and almost gagged. God, how could anyone drink that stuff? She looked at him pleadingly, but

245

his face was stern. She took a deep breath, and downed the rest of it—it hit her stomach almost immediately, then she took a long swallow of orange juice.

"Come on, let's sit down," he led her back to the couch, bringing the vodka and orange juice with him. "Just lean back, and take a few deep breaths," he said, "I'm taking it for granted you won't tell anyone I prescribed vodka for you."

She did as she was told, but she still couldn't relax. She remembered Irene's last words to her as they left the house. Irene loved vodka martinis—maybe she'd never have another one. Tears started sliding down her cheeks.

"Now what's the matter?" he sounded slightly exasperated.

"It's Irene—she loves vodka martinis—that's the last thing she mentioned when we left her house."

He leaned down and played with the dog for a few minutes, thinking. He was all doctor now, and what Kathy needed at the moment was shock therapy, not coddling. He poured some more vodka, but he didn't give it to her yet. "Now look, Kathy, you're tearing yourself apart about someone you've known a few months, and about something that might not even happen. Sure, she has cancer—are you surprised that I know? But she's got one of the best surgeons she could have, and there's every reason to believe they'll get all of it when they perform the hysterectomy. So quit knocking yourself out over her. More people kill themselves worrying about things that never even happen than you could imagine. Why do you think I'm in this business? I certainly don't want you for a patient. But if you don't stop this, that's exactly what you'll be." He handed her the glass. "Now drink this."

She looked at him, her eyes wide with shock at his callousness, but she swallowed the vodka, then coughed and spluttered. "You are just about the most unfeeling man I've ever known. Can't you feel any sympathy for poor Irene?''

"Poor Irene," he mimicked her. "Poor Irene has been a nympho for years, and she shipped her daughter off to school just as soon as she decently could. You should be saying 'poor Ted' and 'poor April.' Just why do you think she picked you to play buddy-buddy with? Everyone else around here is on to her. Nobody in this town really likes Irene—she's too demanding, too imperious. And you can bet your life on it, when this is all over, she'll be the same Irene she was before this happened."

This time Kathy reached for the vodka bottle herself. "Well, I think you're wrong. You know, it takes two to make a bad marriage. And who are you to say that April didn't want to go to Switzerland?" She tossed her long hair indignantly. "Just because you're a psychiatrist, you don't know everything in the whole goddamn world." She was getting mad now, and the vodka was doing its job. Good, the doctor thought. "You men," she said spitefully, "you're all alike. Dwight, Jack, Fred, all of you."

He was instantly alert. "Jack? You mean Jack Wentworth?"

Oh, oh, she thought—she hadn't meant to mention him. Well, so what? "Yes, Jack Wentworth. I went out with him once—just once, and he didn't take me out to hold hands, either. He tricked me into going over to his apartment, said he'd taken an overdose, and you can guess the rest. Then we went out to dinner, and came over here, and the same thing happened—all night long, until Dwight came knocking at my window. And Jack never called me again."

The doctor's relief was overwhelming, but he tried not to change his expression.

"And then Dwight, tonight," she continued, "I told him not to come over, but he did anyway. And then he wanted sex. Don't you men know that a woman has to be in the mood for that sort of thing?'' She thought for a moment. ''That's not entirely true. I'm never in the mood for sex with Dwight. He's the worst.''

''Then why do you do it?'' He was curious.

''Oh, I don't know, John.'' The name *John* instead of *doctor* just slipped out. ''It happened once when I felt sorry for him, and ever since then, he just sort of considers me his girl. And I don't know how to get out of it. I know he wants to marry me.''

''And are you going to?''

''Are you kidding?'' she shuddered. ''The thought of weeks, months, years of Dwight; no, I'm not going to marry him. But I don't know what to do—he's put me on a pedestal. Oh, he knows I've been married once, but the men since! He'd have a heart attack.''

''Why do you keep on seeing him?'' he persisted.

''Because I feel sorry for him, I guess. He's got so much on his mind now, with his father, and the business. The timing's all wrong.'' Her explanation sounded weak, even to herself. What in the world was the matter with her, telling him all this?

''Yet you feel nothing for him?''

''Nothing—except pity, maybe.''

John Carter poured himself a double shot of vodka. The therapy session was over, there was some color in Kathy's cheeks, and for the time being, she wasn't thinking about Irene. '' 'You men,' '' he said carefully, choosing his words. '' 'You're all alike,' you said. Do you lump me in that category?''

She looked at him, considering. ''No,'' she said finally, ''I don't. When I first met you, you didn't look like a doctor. I thought you were very sexy, and I wondered what it would be like to go to bed with you. Then after I started working for you, so many things were happening, that I began to think of you as a doctor, and I guess I pushed the thought of you and sex somewhere in the back of my mind. One reason, I suppose, is you're married, and I've been through all that. But tonight, I haven't thought of you as a doctor at all. And I haven't been embarrassed or ashamed to tell you about Dwight or Jack, or all the others. But I haven't told you about Bruce—he was married. Maybe I'll tell you sometime, but not now." She hesitated, waiting for him to say something, but he just poured each of them another drink. "What do you think of me?" she stammered slightly.

He took a sip of his drink before answering. "Kathy, I've never been unfaithful to my wife in our entire marriage." He spoke slowly. "You may find this hard to believe, but I was almost a virgin when I married her. I'd been to a whore house once, on a dare, and that was it. Not that there haven't been a lot of opportunities—you've seen some of them yourself, in the office." He almost told her Irene had propositioned him, but stopped himself. "But the minute I saw you, I wanted you, and I've never stopped. I knew about Wentworth, and it almost tore me apart. Dwight never bothered me, because I never considered him much of a man, really. Edith and I have a comfortable life, and I have no reason to divorce her, so I've never approached you. I really don't have anything to offer you, Kathy. We couldn't be seen together, go out, go on trips, all the things people do when they're in love. And I am in love with you, Kathy. I'm fond of my wife, we have sex every Saturday night, and that's it. So you see, you said you've been through all this before with a married man, and I can't ask you to do it again. I do want you, Kathy, but the decision must be yours."

Kathy sat quietly, thinking. Then she started talking, almost like thinking out loud. "Of course, if I say no, I'll have to quit—it would be too hard working together after tonight. And then there's the fact that you're married—I rather like Edith. But then, if I said yes, it probably wouldn't hurt her if we can keep things in the proper perspective. I'd have to continue on with Dwight for a while—you said you weren't jealous of him, and I do need some social life. I don't know if I'm in love with you or not, John, but I do know I'm sexually attracted to you. I need sex, and Dwight doesn't arouse me at all." She looked down at her watch. "It's 3:30, much too late to try to sleep, and we don't have to be at the hospital until 7:00. Do you want to make love now?"

He had been listening to her, scarcely believing his ears. She sounded so clinical about the whole thing. "Kathy, sometimes you amaze me. I don't know about you, but now I need a drink to relax."

She smiled at him uncertainly, suddenly nervous. "I'll have one with you—and then no more talk tonight, John. I don't want to think, I just want to feel." Her words echoed in her ears—she had said them once before, painfully, and she pushed the memory from her mind. Quickly, she gulped down the drink he handed her.

John and Kathy were a little late arriving at the hospital the next morning. They had stopped by the office, and while John shaved, Kathy had called the answering service and given them the list of names to call and cancel appointments. When she came to Jack Wentworth's name, she made a wry face and skipped it. Why call him? He never showed up, anyway. When John was through, he called his wife, explaining the situation, while Kathy stood by silently. In spite of no sleep, the tensions of yesterday, and what they were about to face, she was in pretty good shape.

She had been nervous last night, partly because of her hasty decision, partly his self-proclaimed lack of experience; but she needn't have worried. As he got into bed beside her, it seemed right somehow, and her tension vanished. When he took her in his arms, she could sense the controlled urgency in him, and she responded willingly. They fit together smoothly, rhythmically, with no awkwardness between them. He held back his own emotions, while his hands and mouth explored her, urging and coaxing her desire until it was equal to his own. It was not until her own passion had spent itself that he satisfied his own.

She sat close to him in the car automatically, until he reminded her of appearances' sake. A slight depression came over her, and she moved, but he reached over and tucked her hand reassuringly in his.

Irene was already in surgery when they arrived, and Ted and April were in the waiting room. John excused himself to see if he could get any information, although it was much too early. Ted looked drawn, and April appeared to be in a state of shock. Neither of them seemed to think it odd that Dr. Carter was there, they were much too deep in their own thoughts.

John came back shortly—Irene would be in surgery for several hours. "Kathy, there's really no reason for me to stay, unless you want me to. If I'm not wrong, Dwight will be along shortly, and I've got some taping to do at the office." He pulled her aside. "Call me when the operation's over. And think of some way to get rid of Dwight tonight. I'll have an early meeting, or something—" then he said in a louder tone, so Ted and April could hear, "—if Irene needs me, I'll be at the office."

The waiting was long, and thick with silence. Two hours went by, and it seemed like two days. John was right— Dwight showed up shortly after 8:00, and after asking about Irene, tried to talk to Kathy.

"Will I see you tonight?" he whispered, pleadingly.

"No," she said shortly.

"But we have so much to discuss, Kathy, after last night and all. Look, we can't talk here. Come on down to the coffee shop." He looked at Ted and April. "Would you like me to bring you some coffee?" he asked.

April looked up, and tossed her magazine aside. "I'll go

with you, Dwight. I need to stretch my legs."

Dwight mumbled something under his breath, and Kathy smiled sweetly. "Yes, you two go along. Bring some back for Ted and me."

Dwight stared at her for a moment, then they left.

Ted smiled sardonically after them, the first time his expression had changed all morning. "Trouble in paradise, it seems," he said.

Kathy smiled back, just as sardonically. "Well, at least it broke the tension. Look, Dwight thinks he owns me, and he doesn't. It's as simple as that. So let's drop it."

Instantly, he was apologetic. "I'm sorry, Kathy. I guess we're all on edge this morning. You must have gone through hell yesterday." He looked at her. "Although, I must say, you don't look it."

She blushed slightly, then tried to look prim. "Makeup, I guess. Look, Ted, I've had about enough of Dwight today. I'm going to the restroom. When they come back, tell Dwight I've left, and then send April down to get me, will you, please?"

She started walking down the hall, but unfortunately, Dwight and April were still waiting for the elevator. Dwight sent April down alone.

"Now we can talk," he said.

"Look, Dwight," she said firmly, "my patience has just about run out. Whatever happens today, I'm not seeing you tonight. I need a few days to think things out and to cool down. So please just leave me alone, and when I'm ready, I'll call you. I mean it, Dwight."

He looked at her, bewildered, not quite understanding. "Okay, if that's the way you really want it. There were some things I wanted to talk over with you—about the business, that is. You know, get your opinion. But, if you feel that strongly . . . look, I'm going to call Scott and set up a meeting tonight, so if you need me for anything, I'll be at the office. Honey, things will work out. I know you'll get over this. And I'm sorry about last night. I really do love you.''

She sighed, and watched him get in the elevator, looking like a lost puppy dog. Then she walked back to the waiting room.

Pam woke up the next morning, slowly, groggily, with an acrid taste in her mouth. She opened her eyes and blinked, then quickly shut them again, as the sun was streaming in on her. She was lying on something cold and hard, and it certainly wasn't her bed. Fear struck her, and for a few minutes, she was afraid to move. Was she on an operating table? No, she still had her clothes on, and that just wasn't sensible. Cautiously, she opened her eyes again, then looked around her. She was lying on the kitchen floor, the sunlight was flooding in through the kitchen windows. She had no idea how she got there, if she had fallen, or what. Gingerly, she reached for the kitchen table and tried to sit up, her head spinning.

After a few minutes, the spinning stopped, and she got to her feet, still holding onto the table. She made it to the sink, and poured herself a glass of water, which she drank down greedily. God, she was thirsty! She poured herself another glass, drank it, and promptly threw up. She hadn't eaten yesterday, so all that came up was water and slime, and she was shaking all over. Beads of perspiration stood out on her forehead, and her body was bathed in sweat. She got some orange juice out of the refrigerator and sat down at the kitchen table, sipping it slowly, hoping it would stay down.

She tried to think, but thoughts kept slipping away from her. She had gone to the Club after work and run into April, that much she remembered, but what then? April couldn't stay long, so she'd come home—or had she? She looked down at her clothes; yes, of course she had, she still had on her shorts, and if she'd gone out, she would have changed.

But then what? She'd heard of blackouts, but she'd never had one. Had she called anyone? Then she looked at the clock. My God, eleven! And she was due in the office at nine! She started to rush to the phone, but her head began spinning dizzily again, and she had to catch herself from falling. She couldn't call in this condition—she'd take a pep pill first. But what excuse could she give? She could hold her nose and pretend she had a cold. It was Friday, and by Monday, she'd be over it. But was it Friday? How long had she been out? Of course it was Friday, otherwise someone would have been over to see what was wrong. Someone might be on their way over now! She'd take the pep pill later. She rushed to the kitchen phone and dialed her office.

"Bonnie?" she tried to make her voice sound weaker than it really was, and held her nose.

"Pam? Is that you?" Bonnie asked. "Where in the world are you? I've been calling and calling, and nobody answered. I was about to call your neighbor."

Just in time, Pam thought with relief. "Bonnie, I have a terrible cold. I guess I must have turned the phone down low. I just woke up. I'm sorry, but I won't be in today." Mustn't talk too long, she might catch on.

"Oh dear," Bonnie sympathized. "Can I bring you anything on my lunch break? Have you got a fever?"

"No, nothing—I don't know—I'm going back to bed now. Bye, Bonnie." She hung up before she could ask any more questions. She felt rotten, but at least that was taken care of. Now she could take a pep pill, and then in a few minutes, she'd feel better. She started towards the living room, and stopped at the door in horror.

The room was in a shambles—her satsuma lamp had been knocked over and shattered in a million pieces, the drapes on the sliding glass doors leading to the patio were pulled down, snow was on the television set, liquor spilled all over her velvet sofa, completely ruining it, and there were stains on her coffee table that would never come out. Tears came to her eyes. Who would do such a thing? Another drink was spilled on the Persian rug. The lamp, the coffee table, the sofa, the rug—all of these things had been her parents prized possessions. She had always been so careful—she kept the sofa covered with a towel, except when she had company, and took her shoes off before she walked on the rug. A thief, she thought, and ran to the bedroom. She rummaged through her jewelry, but nothing had been touched. Something was strange, though. She couldn't quite put her finger on it in her confused state. Then she saw it. The picture of her father, her brother and herself that she always kept on the dresser was missing. Frantically, she searched for it. Finally she found it, in a corner under a pile of dirty clothes. The gold frame looked like it had been stomped on, and the glass was broken. The picture wasn't there at all.

She sat down on the unmade bed, dazed and shaken. Vaguely, she remembered ripping something into shreds and flushing it down the toilet. There was no thief—she had done all these things—but why? She loved her father and her brother, and she loved the memory of her mother. What, inside herself, would make her want to destroy all the treasures that were so dear to her and to those she loved? Is that what she'd done in those missing hours? What other terrible things could she have done? She got up wearily, and went into the bathroom for the pep pills. She looked in the toilet. Yes, she'd done it all right. One little scrap of the picture hadn't flushed down, and she started to reach for it. Oh, to hell with it. It was just a little scrap of scenery.

She took two pep pills—one just didn't work anymore—then she wandered back out to the living room, waiting for them to start working. She'd clean up this mess, and after that, when her stomach had settled down, she'd force herself to eat something, even if it killed her. She looked around the living room more closely. There were a couple of things she'd

255

missed. A painting by some obscure artist that her brother and father were particularly fond of had a long rip in it, and in a corner of the room an old clock of her father's was smashed. It didn't bother her so much now, so the pills must be starting to work.

The first thing to do was get the drapes up. Then she'd have to call an upholsterer—or the Good Will. She giggled, she wondered if they could come at night. Then she remembered having called Kathy. Oh God! She'd asked Kathy to go with her this Sunday to see her father. Kathy had something else to do today, but what was it?

Why had she asked Kathy? She hated to go there, but it was better if she went alone, because she was always in such a lousy mood afterward. And why did she always feel so guilty? Just as it was about to come through to her, it was swept away in a swirl of nothingness.

She got the stepladder out of the kitchen, and struggled a good hour to get the drapes back up and hanging right. Then she took a long shower, scrubbed her teeth, and automatically started putting on her makeup. Why? She wasn't going anywhere. Then she changed the sheets, made up the bed methodically, took the sheets, the dirty clothes and towels and put them in the washer. She started the machine, went in the living room, swept up the smashed glass and satsuma, and put it in the trash. She tried to scrub the Persian rug, but it was no use—it was ruined. The same with the coffee table. She got out the vacuum and went over the whole apartment, anything to keep from thinking. She put the clean laundry in the dryer, and started on the dishes in the sink. She looked at them in disgust—God, some of the glasses even had scum on them. She waxed the floor and went back to the living room. She stared at the mutilated furniture, and it seemed to stare back at her accusingly. She looked at her watch, and considered calling the Good Will.

Oh, no, you don't! The voice seemed to boom and echo

through the apartment, and it was her father's voice. *You did it, and you get it fixed!* the voice said.

That was mother's favorite rug. It was Jimmy's voice now, accusing her. *She bought it on their honeymoon.*

"I didn't know what I was doing," she whispered, and she covered her ears, trying to shut the voices out.

But it didn't help, and now they were both talking to her at once. *Oh, you knew, alright. You didn't ruin any of your own things, just Dad's and mine and Mother's. You did it for a reason, and you know why,* the voices droned, execrating her.

"But you shut me out," she cried, "I couldn't help it that my mother died when I was born. But you never forgave me, Daddy, even though you pretended you did. And you always loved Jimmy more, you know you did. And you never loved me, Jimmy, and you don't know how hard I tried to make you love me, to make you both love me. I even wished I were a boy, so I could be more like you, Jimmy, but nothing did any good. And then when you both took me on that hunting trip, I was so excited, and I thought everything finally would be alright. But then I heard you both talking, and I knew it was the same, just the same, and it would always be the same, and I wanted to die—do you hear me? I wanted to die!" She was sobbing now, and her voice was not her voice, but a little girl's voice.

The loud knocking on the door brought her to her senses, and the droning voices stopped. "Miss Sterling?" It was her next door neighbor, Mrs. Adams. "You alright in there?"

She pulled herself together with an effort, and walked to the door. "Yes, Miss Adams," she answered in a normal voice, "I'm sorry, I guess I had the radio on too loud. I hope I didn't disturb you."

Then she quickly covered the sofa with two large beach towels, put the Persian rug in the closet, and scattered the latest fashion magazines on the coffee table. She decided against taking down the painting, the bare spot would be too noticeable.

She called the sanitarium, and asked if it would be all right to come out and see her father before dinner.

Dwight went directly to the plant after he left the hospital. No sense waiting until tonight to talk to Scott—they'd let matters slide long enough. Not that it was Scott's fault, Dwight had just been too wrapped up in Kathy to take any serious action. And now she didn't want to see him. "Don't call me, I'll call you," she had said, in effect. Well, this was no time to just sit around and moon about her. Duncan was coming home soon, and there was a lot of planning and pin-pointing to do—starting quite a few years back, and it would take time. None of this could be done while the staff was there, of course, but at least they could set up some pre-liminaries. There was a helluva lot of backlogging to do, and Kathy would just have to be put on ice for a while—that's the way she wanted it, anyway. He would have liked her advice, though; besides her physical attributes, she had a damn good head on her shoulders.

He found Scott in the shipping department and set up a meeting for seven that night, hoping that no one would get ambitious and decide to work overtime. He stopped by Vivian's office in the way to his own, and her desk was as clean as a whistle. That, in itself, seemed peculiar to him. Since Duncan's heart attack, she seldom came to the office, but instead of having her mail delegated to Scott or himself, she had her secretary drive it over to the house. He and Scott made nothing of it, however. She thought she was in the clear, and they wanted to keep it that way as long as possible.

He sifted through his mail, but there was nothing very im-portant. There was a report that No 27, just outside of

Cochabamba, was slacking off a little, but that was nothing new. He paid little attention to it, then sat back in his chair, thinking. It was only ten in the morning, and it looked like he and Scott would have a long night ahead of them. They'd have to go back a good many years, but there was no way to start putting things together until everyone left. He hadn't had any sleep last night after the quarrel with Kathy; she'd seemed like a changed person, and this morning, too. He certainly couldn't help it if he'd gotten horny. Women! He'd never understand them. Well, that wasn't exactly true— Nancy was predictable enough. Maybe that had been their trouble, she'd been too predictable. But they had two beautiful children, and he loved them dearly. He thought about going over to see them, then dismissed the idea, although he'd been neglecting them lately. All he needed now was a hassle with Nancy, or worse than that, her woe-begone reproaches. Instead, he called his secretary, told her he was taking the rest of the day off, and that he couldn't be reached. Then he went straight home, pulled all the curtains closed, set the clock for five o'clock, and went to bed.

The alarm awakened him with a start, and after turning it off, he lit a cigarette and lay back for a few minutes. He had slept soundly, which was good, but now he was looking forward to tonight with a good deal of trepidation. He wasn't nearly as smart as Scott when it came to books, charts and graphs; and he knew it. Most of his work had been in the field, and he spoke and understood Spanish and most of the dialects like a native. He seriously doubted that they'd get through in one night, but they could make a stab at it. He finished his cigarette, jumped up, took a fast shower, dressed, and headed for the plant.

Scott was already there when he arrived. Besides the large blackboard in the Board Room, he had tacked up several smaller ones, and the long conference table was literally covered with ledgers and files. He had also taken the precaution of putting up black shades at the windows. Dwight felt a twinge of jealousy at his ingenuity.

"Well, it looks like you've really been working," Dwight said. He decided not to tell him he'd been sleeping all day.

"Not really. I went out this afternoon and bought some more blackboards, then brought them in after everybody left. I got all the ledgers, too. Had a hell of a time finding the old ones, they were in the storeroom. Just look at how dusty some of them are." He blew on a stack, and a cloud of dust swirled up. "And I've got to remember just where they were, we'll never work our way through all this stuff tonight, unless we get lucky. Pulled some of the files, too, on some of the wells we've been having trouble with." He gestured to a couple of large thermoses. "I figured we'd need some coffee tonight."

Dwight had an idea. "Scott, before we get started on all this, and before it's too dark, let's go through Viv's desk," he said, pulling out his keys.

Scott gasped at him. "You know she always keeps it locked. How in God's name did you get her keys?"

Dwight grinned. "Not her keys, duplicates. Remember a few months back when I was dating her secretary? And Viv thought she'd lost her keys? Well, she hadn't. The kid had dups made. Then Viv had the lock on her desk changed, and her secretary managed to get one of those, too. I took her out a few more times, then let her down easy. You remember Phyllis? She's not here anymore, but she's the one. I figured they might come in handy one of these days. So let's go, Buddy-Boy."

Scott shook his head. "Dwight, sometimes you amaze me. Let's just hope she hasn't gone and had the locks changed again."

They walked down the hall to her office and used the master key. The drapes were drawn, but there was still plenty of light, although it was slowly fading. Dwight pulled the key to the desk out of his pocket, and the two brothers silently crossed their fingers in unison. The key slid in easily, and they both gave a sigh of relief. Scott took the left side of the desk, Dwight the right, but they came up with nothing unusual. The middle drawer was practically empty, except for the usual pens and pencils, paper clips. Vivian Keith was a very neat woman. The small white business card wedged in the back of one of the lower drawers escaped their attention. They went over the rest of her office, but found nothing that could be of any help to them.

"Well, it looks like a dry run," Scott said.

Dwight nodded. "We'd better get back to the Board Room." He locked the desk, and they went out and walked down the hall. The small white business card remained where it was.

Pam arrived at the sanitarium shortly before five. She had driven irratically, nervously. The pep pills had worn off, and she felt physically drained. Mentally, she cursed herself for forgetting to put some in her purse. There were none in the glove compartment, either. Well, anyway, this would be a short visit. Dinner was served at 5:30 promptly, and even though her father was fed intravenously, for some reason, the nurses frowned at visitors during that time. She wrinkled her nose. Probably didn't want them to see the swill they fed the patients who could eat normally. She started to get out of the car, and quickly sat down again, as things started to spin again. Oh God, not now—she had to go in and see her father, she'd already called. Fear shook her, and she searched her purse again, frantically, and again came up empty handed. Somewhere she'd read that if you took deep breaths, it calmed you, so she sat for a few minutes, the car door open, breathing in the cool clean air. She looked up and around her at the trees, some of them just beginning to turn golden, others slowly losing their leaves as slight breezes blew through them. She looked at the grounds, and listened to the crackling noises of leaves, already dead. Summer was ending, and autumn was wasting no time in taking over. She had always hated autumn, ever since the accident, when Jimmy . . . she shook her head. She mustn't think about that now. She looked at her watch, and got up again, more slowly this time. There, that was better.

She moved gradually towards the entrance, and her walk was steady. She tried not to think of anything, and continued to take deep breaths. It was a mistake to take deep breaths when she opened the door to the sanitarium, though, and she almost gagged. They were having fish of some sort for dinner, and the unpleasant aroma was mingled with the inevitable stench of sickness and death that was impossible to mask. Oh God, she shouldn't have come today, and she was about to turn and leave when one of the nurses saw her.

Bracing herself, she squared her shoulders, smiled at the nurse, hurried for her father's room and quickly went inside. Her father's eyes were closed, and his face looked grayer than usual. The same old fear that she always felt when she came here coursed over her, more forcefully than ever, and her heart was pounding like a trip-hammer. Quietly, she walked over and sat in the chair beside her bed.

"Hello, father," she whispered hesitantly, but his eyes remained closed. This was not uncommon, and in a way, she preferred it. At least, with his eyes closed, she didn't have to make conversation with someone who could not answer, and who very probably didn't hear or understand. But the wrenching, unnerving part of it was that she was never really sure, one way or the other. She thought about taking his hand, and decided against it. Better to wait until just before she left. She leaned back and closed her eyes; almost immediately and against her will, the events of the day came crowding in on her. She opened her eyes again quickly, but she could still see the mutilated furniture, the ripped painting, the broken glass. She started to perspire heavily, although the room was chilly. Things began to spin, and Jimmy suddenly appeared before her, staring at her accusingly, and her father seemed to recede. Instead of the hospital bed, there were rocks and dirt all around her and Jimmy. She stayed absolutely still, frozen in time and space for what seemed like a long time.

Then she reached for Jimmy, to take his hand, and he started to disappear under the rocks, small ones at first, then bigger and bigger, and finally boulders, that kept falling, falling . . . then she couldn't see him anymore, and she was alone on the edge of the cliff, and she could hear her father's voice calling in the distance. . . .

She shook her head, and the room was back as it should be. "I killed him," she whispered. Fear shot through her, and she reached for her father's hand. "Father," she whispered again, "I killed Jimmy." She gripped his hand tighter, but his eyes didn't open. His hand felt different; it was . . . cold, stiff. She looked at his face in a daze—he'd looked gray when she came in—was it her imagination, or was he grayer now? Her whole body shook violently as realization overcame her. My God, he's dead! He was dead when she came in the room! "Nurse," she tried to scream, but it came out a whisper. She tried again, but the muscles in her throat became more rigid. She couldn't breathe, and she felt as though she was strangling.

Frantically, she rang the buzzer that dangled idly by the bed, and kept ringing for what seemed like an eternity. Finally a white blurred figure appeared, and she struggled to get up, trying to speak.

"He's dead!" she managed to choke the words out, although they screamed in her ears, roaring, rushing at her, drowning her. "And Jimmy's dead! Oh My God, and I've killed them both!'' Then she crumpled in a dead faint, hitting her head against the arm of the chair.

Kathy had overslept, and if she took the time to make herself some tea, she'd be late for work. She decided to have some tea. She had stayed at the hospital until Irene's operation was over; Dr. Sturgess had said it was a complete success—but then he didn't know she knew about the cancer. And she hadn't asked him—she didn't really want to know, not right now. He had also told her Irene would be unconscious most of the day and night, so she had gone home and called John. He had been as eager and willing and loving as the night before, but he had left early, leaving her slightly depressed. She should have been tired out, but she was still much too keyed up by the last two days and nights. Much as she hated to admit it, she would miss Dwight calling her. And she was damned if she was going to call him at the office. She kept wandering around the apartment, touching things, and staring at the phone. She called Pam, but she was out somewhere.

Finally, she had gone to bed and stared at the ceiling for a long time, thinking. She had left Hollywood because she wanted to meet some nice, simple uncomplicated people, and definitely a single man, and just where was she? Involved with another married man, and even worse; his wife was around. At least, Bruce's wife had been on the other side of the country. In the bargain, she was turning down an eligible bachelor; well, almost bachelor, just a few months before his divorce was final. She thought of Maude, and cringed at what she would have thought of the situation. It had been very late when she finally dozed off.

She looked at her watch, then rushed to finish getting ready for work. She was just going out the door when the phone rang. She hesitated for a moment—if she answered it, she'd be late for work; if she didn't, she'd wonder all day long who it was.

"Hello?"

"Kathy?" John's voice sounded concerned. "I'm glad I caught you. I won't be in until later, and I may not get a chance to call you again for a while. Now I don't want to upset you, but Pam's father died yesterday, and she's in pretty bad shape."

"Oh, my God," Kathy's voice was a monotone. "Where is she? Do you want me to come?"

"No, Kathy," he said firmly. "I don't have the details yet, but she's at the hospital. You go to work and cancel my morning appointments. If I have to cancel the afternoon out, I'll get word to you. Now please, don't worry."

Kathy hung up the phone without saying goodbye. *Don't worry* was a pretty dumb remark for a psychiatrist to make. Everything was happening at once. Duncan's heart attack, Vivian's hysterectomy, Pam's father dying, now Pam all upset—enough so she had to go to the hospital.

She drove to the doctor's office, called the answering service, then all the patients and cancelled their appointments, in a slight daze. Pam, pretty, sparkling little Pam; she couldn't imagine her in the hospital. She had seemed nervous at times lately, but surely she must have been prepared for her father's death. After all, he'd been living like a vegetable for years now, from what she'd gathered, and it would seem as though it would be a relief to Pam, in a way. Then she remembered Pam had asked her to go with her to see her father; maybe if she had, she could have helped her, been there for her to lean on.

She shook her head, and her lips curved wryly. Life was so full of twists of fate. Everything seemed to be based on "ifs." *If* she hadn't had trouble with her car; *If* Bruce hadn't been married (or John, for that matter); *If* Irene had seen the doctor for regular checkups; *If* she hadn't slept with Dwight on impulse; *If, If, If!* There was really no way to plan out or plot your life; everytime you did, and had it all arranged, neatly and precisely, something or someone always screwed it up.

Suddenly she thought of Jack—certainly he should be told about Pam. On impulse, she picked up the phone, then checked herself. The phone was no way to tell him; besides, she didn't know enough about the situation herself. Instead, she called the hospital and had Dr. Carter paged. His voice sounded weary when he finally answered.

"John?" she hesitated slightly, "I hate to bother you, but can you give me anything more definite on Pam? I really think Jack Wentworth should be told, and I almost made the mistake of calling him, then I realized I didn't have any details. Incidentally, will you be in? I'll have to call the afternoon patients pretty soon if you aren't." She waited for a moment, as he didn't answer. "John? Are you still there?"

"I'm here." His voice sounded a little brisker, more businesslike. "Let me get back to you in a few minutes. I don't want to tie up the switchboard. And no, I won't be in. Call the answering service and have them make the cancellations." He clicked off.

She sat there, staring at the phone in her hand. Then she realized he was probably in the lobby, or some doctor's office. She'd have to get used to that. She called the answering service and quickly gave them the information on the afternoon's cancellations. The other phone rang before she was quite finished, and it was John.

"Kathy, I'm calling from the pay phone in the lobby." His voice was more normal now, although very serious. "I was with Dr. Sturgess and the staff psychiatrist, and there was no way I could talk. Of course, you realize what I'm about to tell you is privileged information, but as far as I know, Pam has no other family, and you are a good friend of hers. As for telling Jack, maybe it would be better coming from you than me. But for God's sake, don't tell him anything if he's been drinking.''

"Tell him what?'' Kathy was concerned. "So far, you haven't told me a thing, except to cancel out for this afternoon. What happened to Pam?''

John was silent for a long moment, when she heard him take a deep breath. "Pam went out to see her father late yesterday afternoon, shortly before dinner. Several of the nurses saw her go in, and they were busy, so she stayed through the dinner hour. They forgot about her until they saw the red light, and when one of the nurses came in, Pam was just standing there, white as a sheet, the nurse said. Then Pam said something about killing him, the nurse couldn't quite make it out, and killing someone else, then she fainted. Of course, she didn't kill him, we got the coroner's report this morning, and my guess is he was dead long before she went in to see him. Now this is just conjecture on my part, but she probably thought he was asleep, and she just sat there, talking to him. When she realized he was dead, the shock was too much for her, especially in her condition.'' He paused for a minute. "Kathy, I want you to get a grip on yourself, because the rest of the story is even more unpleasant. She's in a catatonic state, and she has been ever since she fainted. That much you can tell Jack. Now, the rest of this is strictly confidential.''

"Oh my God, you mean there's more?'' Kathy sat there frozen, not quite believing. Pam, in a state of catatonia!

"I mentioned her condition. I don't know if you've noticed it or not, but Pam's been highly nervous lately, and I understand she's been drinking too much. So I had a blood test taken. That girl's system was full of amphetamines. That, coupled with the shock of her father's death, might have triggered her—but I've got a hunch there's something more. Now this is strictly between you and me. So for her sake, don't tell Jack.''

"I'll call him as soon as we hang up."

"Kathy, where are your brains?" he almost shouted. "You can't tell him a thing like this over the phone."

"My brains are in my head, thank you," she shouted back. "Don't you think I'm as worried as you are? But I have to locate him first. I'll try his office, then his apartment, then if I have to, I'll call all the bars."

"Kathy honey, I'm sorry," his voice was soft now. "But the hospital called me last night almost as soon as I got home from your place, and I've been here ever since. Now I'm going home and try to get some sleep."

"Should I call you after I talk to Jack?" She felt a twinge of jealousy at the thought of his going home.

"By all means. Have Edith wake me." He hesitated. "Be careful what you say, though. We've got an extension." Then he hung up.

Kathy pulled up in front of Jack's apartment about twenty minutes later. She sat in the car waiting, thinking of what she was about to face. In a way, she'd been lucky; she'd called his office first, and he hadn't shown up yet. Next, she'd called his apartment, and the phone had rung and rung. She was just about to hang up when he finally answered. His voice was thick and groggy with sleep, and in this way, she wasn't so lucky—she'd have to contend with a hangover. But at least he was home, and she wouldn't have to call all his favorite haunts. He'd been irritated at first, when she told him who she was, but the minute she mentioned Pam, he was instantly alert.

"She's not hurt, is she? Has she had an accident? Where is she?" He had bombarded her with questions.

"Jack, don't worry," she had lied to him. "I just want to

talk to you about her. I'll come over now, if it's convenient; I mean, if you're alone, we can talk about it now." She had heard his hand cover the phone, and a muffled conversation taking place.

"Sure, I'm alone." He had lied right back to her. "But give me about a half hour to take a shower, okay?"

She sat in the car a little longer, tapping her fingers on the steering wheel. This wasn't going to be easy—Jack with a hangover, and in all probability having a short drink now, to straighten himself out. A cab was waiting down the street, and she saw a tacky looking blond walking nervously towards it, her clothes rumpled, looking from one side to the other. For a moment, their eyes met, and Kathy smiled wryly. Probably a one-night stand, she thought. Well, had she been any different? The cab pulled away, and she tried to get her mind back to the business at hand. This was no time to have bitter memories. Reluctantly, she got out of the car, locked it, and walked past the swimming pool to Jack's apartment. The door was ajar, and to her surprise, she could smell fresh coffee brewing.

She knocked lightly, then walked in. The living room was immaculate, as it had been before. The smell of coffee was strong, but it couldn't quite disguise the scent of stale perfume in the air. Kathy deliberately avoided looking down the short hall to the bedroom. Jack was sitting at the table in the small dinette, neatly dressed in a dark blue suit. He was staring into space, and for a few minutes, she wasn't sure he was aware of her presence. Then he turned to her suddenly, and his eyes were full of pain, and tears.

"She's dead, isn't she?" His voice was flat, and his words weren't as much a question as a statement.

Kathy's first reaction was shock, and her mouth dropped open. She certainly hadn't been prepared for this. Then she realized suddenly that Jack was in love with Pam, probably had been for years, and her heart went out to him. Her own eyes started to well over, and she walked towards him swiftly.

"Of course not, Jack," she assured him, and cradled his head against her. She felt a sigh of relief go through him. Why couldn't it stay this way, why did she have to tell him now? The relief he felt would be so short-lived. He had already accepted her death, and it seemed too cruel to strike another blow so suddenly, and so soon. But then, life was cruel sometimes, many times, and people seemed to survive. But God Almighty, why did she have to be the one to tell him? Suddenly she thought of John; he should have been the one to tell Jack—she had the feeling she'd been manuevered into this, and she silently cursed her latest lover. Damn you, you bastard, John, you knew something like this would happen, and you probably know a helluva lot more about Pam and Jack then you've told me. She steeled herself. She was here now, and there was nothing else to do but to tell him the truth, as plainly and as kindly as she could.

"Thank God, thank God," she could hear his muffled voice saying against her breast. She pulled herself away from him slowly, and sat down at the table next to him, taking his hands in hers.

"Jack, look at me." Her voice was shaking. His eyes met hers, as though pleading for her to tell him that Pam was alright. She tried to ignore it. "I said Pam wasn't dead, and she isn't; but there's been some trouble—bad trouble."

"Just tell me she's all right." His voice was thick now, begging her.

"Jack, please, just let me tell you from the beginning. She's going to be all right, I'm sure of it, and you have to be sure of it, too. But she's going to need you now, Jack, more than she ever has. I don't pretend to know what there is between you, and it's really none of my business, but I know she always turns to you." Kathy took a deep breath, and plunged in. "She went out to see her father yesterday. Evidently, when she got there, she thought he was asleep,

270

because she was in his room for a long time before she called anyone. He was dead, Jack.''

Jack sucked in his breath suddenly, almost as if he knew the worst was yet to come. Other than that, he said nothing, and she could read nothing from the expression on his face. She had the feeling that she was intruding in a very private matter, and she started to feel uncomfortably warm. But he was waiting for her to continue.

''Nobody knows exactly what happened, Jack. Dr. Carter called me this morning from the hospital. As he said, it's all conjecture—maybe she knew he was dead when she went into his room, but Dr. Carter didn't seem to think so.''

Jack interrupted her, trying to control his voice. ''You said he called from the hospital—is Pam in the hospital?''

''I was getting to that.'' Oh God, she thought, how can I tell him? ''When the nurse finally came into the room, Pam had fainted, and she hit her head against the chair.''

''You mean she has a concussion?'' he asked, starting to get up. ''I've got to go to her.''

''No, Jack, wait.'' She tightened her grip on his hands. ''There's more, and it's worse.'' The words tumbled out. ''You've got to be prepared.''

He looked at her grimly, and slumped back down again. ''Go on.'' His voice was a monotone now, and she could only imagine what he was going through.

She searched her mind frantically for the right words, anything that would soften the blow, but there were none. ''Jack, I swear to God, I'd do anything to keep from telling you this, but there's no other way to say it. Pam's been in a catatonic state ever since she fainted.'' There, the words were out, and it was done. She was afraid to look at him, afraid of his reaction, so she looked at the floor and waited.

Gently, he loosened her grip on his hands. When she finally looked up at him, he was staring off into space, and she wasn't even sure he was aware of her presence. Then he

271

said a very strange thing. "Tell me," he asked in a kindly tone, "what did she say before she . . . fainted?"

She stared at him in surprise. How could he know she said anything? Odd. "Well, she did say something, as a matter of fact. Dr. Carter said the nurse couldn't quite make it out, but it sounded something like she'd killed her father, and someone else. Of course, it was just gibberish, she didn't know what she was saying. And the nurse could have gotten it wrong, too."

He looked at her then, really looked at her, and his eyes were dimmed with tears. Then he said another strange thing. "It finally happened, Kathy. She remembered. And now all the hurt that's been inside of her all these years, all the resentment . . . don't you realize what this means? We can start all over again."

She looked at him as though he'd suddenly gone insane. "Jack, don't you realize what I've told you? Pam's in a state of catatonia! My God, she could live that way the rest of her life!"

He shook his head. "You don't understand, it's just a stage. She'll come out of it—and I'll be there to help her. No more drinking, no more other women, like there have been while I've been waiting for her."

He doesn't even realize he's just slapped me in the face, Kathy thought. But what in the hell was he talking about? She couldn't make any sense out of it. He had mentioned Pam's remembering—remembering what? She hadn't killed anyone, it was too ridiculous. Her father was already dead when she went in his room. As for anyone else—suddenly she thought of the hunting accident, and Pam's brother. No, it was unthinkable. And what had Jack to do with all this? She couldn't ask him, and she didn't really think she wanted to know.

"Six years," he continued, "it's been six years now, since that accident." Oh my God, he was going to tell her about it,

272

and she didn't know how to shut him up. Please, please, Jack, I don't want to know.

"Did you know that?" he asked her, not waiting for an answer. "And all that time she's shut it out of her mind. She was hardly more than a child at the time, only sixteen. I found them, you know," he went on conversationally, "I was with the hunting party that was looking for them, and I found them first. The first thing I heard was the screaming, and it led me to them. There she was, pretty little Pam, screaming over and over to her father that she'd killed Jimmy, and that she was glad, and now maybe he'd love her. Her father wasn't paying any attention to her, he was digging through the rubble, trying to get to his son. But it was too late. Jimmy was dead long before they ever found his body. When I got to them, she was still screaming, so I hit her, hard, and she just crumpled up like a little doll. Her father told me later that it wasn't really her fault, she was just frozen with fear when the landslide started, and she did try to reach for Jimmy, but it was too late. And I think he felt guilty, too, at all the terrible things she was screaming at him—most of them were true. He told me all this later, when we got back to their house. He had resented Pam because her mother had died in childbirth; somehow, she had known. I guess his guilt caused the first stroke, and worrying about Pam."

Kathy was fascinated now, and made no attempt to stop him. "What happened then?"

"Oh, his worrying about Pam, you mean." He paused, remembering. "Well, when she came to, back at the house, she didn't remember a damn thing. I mean, nothing even about going hunting, or how she got all those bruises. In time, bits and pieces came back, like they went on a hunting trip and Jimmy got killed, but nothing more. And I'm not sure she remembered that, or if it was just told to her. Her father and I decided not to tell her what really happened— she seemed happy enough, although she missed Jimmy.

273

"Before the accident, she was always a shy little thing, but after that, she seemed to blossom. And she couldn't do enough for her father. As I said, at the time, it seemed like a good idea not to tell her—but then later I started to wonder. After her father's second stroke, I almost told her, but something stopped me. Pam had changed, and I didn't want to put any added strain on her. She was about eighteen then, and I was married, but that had already gone sour. Then I discovered I was in love with Pam. She was much too young for me then, but it doesn't really seem to matter now, does it? Ah hell, life's all screwed up."

Jack sat there silently now, apparently all talked out. Kathy made no attempt to break the stillness, as her mind was reeling with the information she had gleaned in the last half hour. Did John know any of this? Could she, did she have the right to break Jack's confidence if it would help John in dealing with Pam's condition? And what about Pam's drug problem? Did Jack know about that?

The pieces began to come together. Pam's guilt, hidden deep within herself all these years, had to be triggered by something. Her father's death had been the trigger—and then she just couldn't face it. But somehow, she had to be made to accept reality. The amphetamines; Kathy should have seen it sooner. Certainly she had seen enough addicts in Hollywood to recognize the pattern. A certain tiredness or boredom, a trip to the powder room, followed by a rush of vivacity. But she just hadn't been looking for it—drugs seemed so out of place in a small town.

And Jack—in a way, she felt even more sorry for him. He must have lived in agony for the whole six years, wondering whether or not he and her father had done the right thing in not telling Pam at the very beginning—and look where she was now. That's why he was skirting around Pam's catatonic state; he couldn't quite face it yet either.

She sighed, leaned back and closed her eyes. She wished

274

she were back in Hollywood with Bruce—they had had their share of problems, but nothing compared to the complexities of the people in this town. She had left Hollywood in search of a life among "simple happy people"—and what had she found? Misery, sickness, drugs, death—how could she have been so incredibly naive to think that people were any different in small towns than they were in Hollywood? In her mind, she had fancied white picket fences around rose-covered cottages, housewives in gingham dresses, husbands coming back from work to a well-cooked meal, and where were all the Saturday night barn dances? Not around here, that was for sure.

And how had she improved her life? Another married man, and worse, one she couldn't even be seen with. At least with Bruce, they had almost half of each year together—she thought of him with longing. She cared for John, but it would never be the same as it was with Bruce. She wondered where Bruce was now, this very minute, and what he was doing. Had he found someone else? In all probability, he had; she had, and why should he be any different? She thought of her apartment in Hollywood, with the terrace overlooking the city—the many times they'd sat out there at night, talking, sipping brandy and coffee. Someone else was living there now, and she couldn't bear it.

She heard something move, and startled, opened her eyes and came back to the present. Jack had poured each of them steaming cups of black coffee. "You better drink this, you look bushed." He sat down again, and lifted his cup with shaking hands. "What I really need is a good, stiff drink, but I'm not going to be any help to Pam stoned." He managed to gulp some coffee down with an effort.

Kathy stared at him, and tried to collect her thoughts. "You're also not going to be of any help to her shaking like that." She thought of the vodka routine, but vodka and coffee sounded revolting. "Jack, if you don't mind a suggestion, it's obvious you have one helluva hangover, and I don't think one stiff brandy with your coffee would hurt. I could use one, myself."

He looked at her for a moment, and hesitated. "Do you think I'm an alcoholic?"

"No," she said, very definitely. "I think you've been drowning yourself in the stuff, but I don't think you're an alcoholic. If you were, you would't have even asked me. You'd be making every excuse in the book to prove you weren't. If you look back, didn't all this heavy drinking start about the time of the accident?"

He looked at her thoughtfully. "No, you're wrong there. It started before that. But the accident didn't help matters any. You see, my marriage was all wrong from the beginning. I had to get married. Betsy was from a good family, and when she got pregnant, there was pressure from both sides, her family and my father—especially my father. I was almost thirty, it was time I got married; it seemed like the right thing to do. I really didn't love her, but she was a good sex partner, and I decided to try and make a go of it. It didn't take me long, though, to find out what she was really like."

"And what was that?" Kathy asked. "You never mentioned you had a child before."

"I don't," he said shortly. "She miscarried shortly after we were married. And the ironic part of it is, I don't even know if the child was mine. Oh, she put up a great front; still does, but to put it bluntly—she's nothing but a whore. And my father thinks she's an angel; I think that's what hurts more than anything else about my marriage. That's when I started to drink, and stopped sleeping with her, except when I was too drunk to know what I was doing." He stopped abruptly. "But that's a whole other story, and it isn't helping Pam any to get into a long conversation about Betsy now." He looked at his watch. "I guess we better have that drink." He hesitated, "Will you come to the hospital with me? I really don't think I can face this alone."

She didn't hesitate. "Of course I will, Jack." She dreaded going, but he needed her, and she had no choice. She had never seen anyone that was catatonic, and she doubted that the doctors would even let them see Pam, but she knew he had to go. He seemed calm enough now, but he could crack at any time. God, what a life he must have had—no wonder he drank. She'd like to meet this Betsy.

He went into the bedroom and came back with a brandy bottle and two glasses. He poured their drinks and sat down again, looking at her very seriously.

"You know, I don't know what made me tell you all these things—I've never told a soul before; about the accident, or Pam, or Betsy. It's all been bottled up inside of me. Even as drunk as I've gotten at times, I never told my father about Betsy. I hate his guts, but something held me back."

"Maybe you don't hate him as much as you think you do," she said, sipping her brandy.

"Maybe; although I've tried to hurt him in a lot of other ways." He downed half of his drink in a gulp. "I just don't know—but I do know one thing. I really treated you rotten. And I don't know why—I knew you weren't like all the rest of them."

"Oh come on, Jack," she had to smile slightly. "You have to admit I was pretty easy."

"I didn't think so." He sounded surprised. "Don't put yourself down that way—I plotted the whole thing. And then I felt like a heel. I'd had a fight with Pam, and I knew you were friends. I suppose I was just trying to get back at her."

Well, it was one hell of a way to do it, Kathy thought, but she wasn't about to say that now. "Let's just forget about it, Jack. It's in the past, and let's just let it stay there. And we've got Pam to think about now, so I guess we'll be thrown together pretty much." Then a horrible thought struck her. "My God, you never told her, did you?"

He shook his head, and finished his brandy. "No. I was going to, the very next day, but then Dwight came knocking at your window, and I figured I'd loused up your life enough. Besides, like I said, I felt like a heel—I just used you," he said, miserably. "And now, I feel like you're the only real friend I've got in the world."

She wished he'd just shut up. He certainly wasn't doing anything for her ego. She forced a smile. "Of course I'm your friend, Jack."

He looked at her gratefully, and picked up the brandy bottle. Then he caught her change of expression, and regretfully put it down again. "You're right. It's time we left."

They went in her car, because Jack was too nervous to drive; besides, he wanted her to stay with him, she was sure. Kathy didn't mind; she could call John from the hospital. And she had a feeling she wouldn't want to be alone herself after whatever they had to face at the hospital.

Chapter 12

It was dark when Dwight arrived at the plant, and Scott was already poring over the ledgers. Every night for two weeks now, they had met at the plant and so far, they had gotten exactly nowhere. He was discouraged and frustrated, but he'd be damned if he'd give up on this before Scott did.

Scott looked up when he came in. "Nothing," he said tersely, anticipating his question.

Dwight poured himself a cup of coffee and sat down. "I'm beginning to think Vivian is a helluva lot smarter than we ever gave her credit for."

"Did you ever doubt it? Never underestimate Viv." He started reading again, then paused. "You still have the keys to her office?"

"Sure," Dwight was surprised. "But we've already been through that routine. There's nothing there."

"Well, there's nothing here." Scott got up. "Come on, let's give it another try."

Vivian's office was unchanged. Everything looked clean and neat and . . . empty.

"Unlock the desk, Dwight." All this was a waste of time,

Dwight thought, but he did as he was asked, and they started through the drawers again. He was running his fingers around one of the lower drawers, when suddenly he stopped. "Wait a minute—I think I've found something." He pulled and tugged for a minute, then came out with a business card. "It was wedged in the back of the drawer—we must have missed it before." They looked at it together. *Alex Dunbar, Tax Consultant*, with an address and a phone number in Monrovia. They turned it over, and there were two more numbers written on it, in Vivian's hand.

Scott looked at it. "I think you've hit on something, Dwight. Why would our dear stepmother need a tax consultant? Alex Dunbar—not a very good address—never heard of him, have you?"

Dwight was excited. "No, I haven't, but I'm sure going to find out about him. Now, I think I better copy this information down, and wedge this back where I found it."

They locked the desk, looked around the room, secured her door and went back to the Board Room. Luckily, they had no night watchman to worry about. After the old one had died, they'd gotten a watch dog, over Vivian's vigorous protests.

They looked at the mess on the table, at each other, then sat down. "Let me see those numbers again," Scott said. Dwight passed the paper over.

"You better copy it, I think we'll both be needing it."

Scott looked at the numbers, then at his watch. "I wonder if he's still at his office; accountants do work late sometimes, you know."

"What would you say to him?"

"I don't know," he thought for a moment, "it's just a hunch. And I wonder what these other numbers are." He reached for the phone. "I could always say it was the wrong number—he doesn't know my voice; or yours, either, for that matter." He dialed the office number, let it ring four or five times, and was about to hang up when someone answered.

"Mr. Dunbar, please." He waited for a while, and Dwight couldn't make out what was said, although an odd expression passed over Scott's face. "Thank you, miss," he said politely, "thank you very much."

Scott got up and started pacing up and down the room, deep in thought. Dwight knew his brother well enough not to interrupt him when he was like this, although he was filled with curiosity. What in the hell did the woman say to make him react like this? Finally, Scott turned to him.

"Dwight, we've got wells in Bolivia, right?"

Dwight nodded. "You know we have."

"You know where our Mr. Alex Dunbar is right now? He left yesterday for Cochabamba. That was his answering service. Dwight, your finding that card was the most incredible piece of luck we could possibly have had. Now we have a starting point, instead of all. . ." he waved his hand vaguely at the Board table, "this."

Dwight was beginning to get excited, too. "Wait a minute! I got a letter a little while back about No. 27, but I didn't pay it much attention. Said it was slacking off, but that's nothing new—they're all slacking off." He slapped his forehead suddenly. "Oh God, I should have remembered—I was down there when it came in, and it came in a gusher."

Scott pondered this. "It would't be too hard, I suppose, to falsify reports if you had someone down there who knew the ropes and how to do it. If only we had more time, we could hire a private detective and find out just where else this Dunbar has been. But we don't have any time—one of us will have to go down there, and I guess I'm elected."

"Wait a minute, Scott," Dwight said slowly, "let's kick this around a little. It's true you know more about the business than I do. On the other hand, let's face it, I'm the one that's always made the field trips, and I know the people. They're used to me coming around once in a while, and they know me."

"You've got a point," Scott conceded ruefully. "There's another thing we've got to consider—Vivian; what in the hell is she going to think if either one of us takes off for Bolivia?"

Dwight thought hard. Obviously, Scott couldn't go now; he could never keep it from Fran, and since she had no idea what was going on, there would be no reason for her not to tell Viv. Then he hit on Kathy, and his mind clicked. "It just might work," he said.

"What?" Scott looked at him with interest.

"Kathy Foster."

Scott was exasperated. "Now what in the hell does she have to do with all this?" Then a sudden thought struck him, and he was horrified. "Oh no, Dwight—you haven't told her anything about this, have you?"

"Take it easy, big brother. Kathy has a good head on her shoulders." Scott glowered at him, but he paid no attention. "Yes, I told her—she'd half-guessed it anyway. She's no dummy, and she's given me some pretty good advice. God, I wished Viv had hired her," he said wistfully. "Do you know she didn't even let me interview her?"

Scott was getting red in the face. "Dammit, Dwight, get to the point, and quit mooning about the girl. Just how long has she known, anyway?"

"Since Labor Day. She's no blabbermouth, Scott. A lot of other things, maybe, but not that. Okay, okay," he waved Scott to silence as he started to interrupt. "I'll get to the point." He took a deep breath, and continued. "Kathy and I had a fight. Nothing that won't be straightened out in time, I'm sure. In fact, I was going to send her a dozen roses the next morning, then call, but I put it off . . . anyway, try this on for size. I send her a dozen roses alright, but instead of calling, I send her a note telling her I'm so broken up about everything, that I'm going out of town for a few days; on a fishing trip, maybe. Then I pack my car with fishing gear, go over to Nancy's and say goodbye to the kids. I stash my car someplace, you drive me to the airport, and I take off for Cochabamba.''

Scott looked at him with keen interest, and felt a new respect for his kid brother. ''It just might work. The fishing trip is good—you don't say where you're going, so you can't be reached. We'll call the airline in the morning for flight schedules.''

''There's one more detail we have to take care of. I won't be able to call you at home, and certainly not here. We could pick out a pay phone, and I could call you there, but there's no telling how long it would take for the calls to get through, and you'd look pretty suspicious hanging around a public telephone for a couple of hours.'' Dwight thought rapidly. ''I think the best thing for you to do is to tell the office you'll be calling on some of our local accounts in the afternoons. Then you go over to my apartment, and I'll place a call to you every day, 12:00 noon your time.''

Scott nodded. ''Where'd you pick up all this cloak and dagger stuff?''

Dwight grinned. ''I read a lot of mysteries when Nancy and I first split up.'' Then he stood up and stretched. ''I'm going down to my office and get that letter on No. 27. Why don't you look for the file on it while I'm gone?'' He turned to the door. ''Try not to smudge any of those ledgers more than they are.''

Scott looked at his watch, the ledgers and the stacks of files. It would be dawn before they got out of here. He felt a twinge of envy for his brother, and it wasn't the first time. Dwight could sleep on the plane, but he had to work all day. But then, he was the oldest son, the responsible one who held down the fort while Dwight made the trips. For a fleeting moment, he'd thought that this time he'd be the one to go, but Dwight had squelched that with logic and clarity. He shook his head in resignation, opened the thermos, and poured himself a cup of coffee. Then he started looking for the file on No. 27.

Scott stood by the gate at L.A. International watching the plane as it took off from the runway. He stayed there for a long time, long after the plane was out of sight. God, how he envied his kid brother. The plane ride, the pretty stewardesses, the stimulation and excitement of a new land. Cochabamba—even the sound of it conjured up all sorts of romance and mystery to him. Although, of course, all this was "old hat" to Dwight. He'd been traveling for the company for years now. Scott could count the number of plane trips he'd taken on the fingers of one hand, and still have his thumb left over. He sighed, then started making his way through the milling crowd to his car.

Neither of them had gotten any sleep last night, and he was weary. He still had to make a token appearance at a few of their accounts, and he just wasn't in the mood. Ordinarily, he enjoyed getting out in the field, but he was in no frame of mind to listen to a lot of statistics on sales, or excuses, or complaints. After that, there was Fran to face. He had called her last night, saying he was spending the night with Dwight because he was so broken up about Kathy; something in her voice didn't exactly make him think she bought it.

He headed back towards the San Gabriel Valley, stopping at two of their accounts on the way, then went back to the office. He checked his mail perfunctorily, sat back and closed his eyes. He was more tired than he thought. Dwight and he had worked hard last night; checking the figures on No. 27, then Xeroxing copies of the complete file for Dwight to take with him. The ledgers had seemed much heavier while they were lugging them back than they had when they took them out. By the time they got to Dwight's, it was almost four in the morning, much too late for any sleep. They went over the details of their plans while Dwight packed his clothes, and stashed his fishing gear in the trunk of his car. They had been practically out the door before Dwight remembered to call Western Union and order roses for Kathy.

They had drunk so much coffee, first at the plant, then at Dwight's, that the mere thought of another cup gagged him. And he realized he hadn't eaten all day. He very seldom drank, unless he was at a party, but suddenly he felt the need of one; especially before he went home to Fran. He walked down the hall to his father's office, hoping Vivian hadn't cleaned out the bar. No one was there, and when he pressed the button under the desk that rolled back the left wall, he was relieved to find the bar intact and untouched.

There was no ice, of course, but he fixed himself a gin and tonic, tepid though it was. Normally, when he did drink, it was Scotch, but gin and tonic somehow seemed more appropriate—more . . . tropical. Silently, he raised his glass. Here's to you, Dwight, halfway to your tropical paradise, while he was on his way home to meat and potatoes. He sat down at his father's desk, twirled the chair around, and gazed out at the glowing sunset filtering in and around the tropical palms. The view was practically the same from his own office, although he rarely had time to appreciate it. You could give credit for that to Viv, she certainly had gone all out in re-decorating the company, and landscaping the courtyard, although she'd cut a lot of other corners. Probably because she'd thought the whole kit and kaboodle would be hers one of these days. He finished his drink and felt a little better. He knew he should be starting home, or at least calling Fran, but he decided to have one more drink and enjoy the rest of the sunset, before he went home to another dull evening. God, he hoped she didn't give him the third degree tonight, or want all the details about Dwight and Kathy. He was in no mood for anything except some food, a hot bath, and bed. He had to be in the office early tomorrow, then over at Dwight's by noon.

Dwight waved at Scott from the plane, then settled back in his seat. God, he was tired. Scott really must be a man of iron—he had a whole day's work to get through, and all he had to do was sleep on another long, dreary plane ride. He leaned back comfortably and felt a twinge of guilt. Scott had wanted to make this trip, even though he'd tried to hide it. Dwight had never really thought about it before, but Scott sure had the dirty end of the stick as far as the business was concerned. Of course, he got to stay home with his wife, but that was no bargain, not with Fran. But Dwight used to envy him, when he and Nancy were getting along, and he had to leave her and the kids.

He had urged Nancy to come along with him many times when he started making trips for the company, but she always had some excuse. "Too many bugs," or "what if the children got sick?" Finally, she had agreed to take a short trip with him to South America, albeit, grudgingly. Dwight had looked forward to it eagerly, like a second honeymoon. Scott and Fran were going to look after the children, and he had planned the trip carefully, to get his work out of the way as quickly as possible, and then show her all the beautiful surrounding sights. He had even wired ahead to the friends he knew down there, making sure of invitations to some of the lovely haciendas he had visited on previous trips.

The trip had been utter disaster. She had absolutely no interest in the people, or the language, and made no attempt to mingle. He had been terribly embarrassed at the dinner parties he'd taken her to. She had just sat there like a bump on a log, hardly making a token attempt to hide her boredom. After two or three of those fiascos, he had gone alone, making the excuse that his wife was sick. After all, these were his friends and business associates, and he could have cheerfully kicked Nancy in the ass. The only time she showed any animation was during her daily phone call to Fran, to see how the children were doing. After that trip, he gave up in disgust, and never asked her again.

For the next six years, when he went on a trip, she was sorry to see him go, and delighted when he came home. But she showed no enthusiasm when he would try to tell her anything about it—the people he'd met, the places he'd seen, the pictures he'd taken. She would listen politely enough, sitting with her hands folded in her lap, waiting for him to finish. Then she would launch into a long and sprightly monologue about her bridge club, Angie's report card, Lonnie's fight with the little boy next door. He had realized she wasn't highly intellectual when he married her, and neither was he, but he'd expected they'd grow together—most married people did. However, she was content to stay in her little rut, playing housewife and mother, while he traveled. Not that he was any genius, by any sense of the word, but my God! It got so after a while, there was nothing they had in common except the children. He'd stayed with her as long as he had for the children's sake, but he made damn sure there weren't any more.

When he'd first suggested she get fitted for a diaphragm, she was hurt and insulted, but he'd gotten around that by saying he didn't have enough time for the two they had, and there'd be plenty of time later, when Angie and Lonnie were a little older. She'd been resentful, but mollified. And he made damn sure she had it in any time he made love to her. Even that got dull after a while, and he performed his functions almost automatically.

He smiled wryly; he was sure Scott thought he must be really living it up on these trips of his—sleeping with every dark, luscious piece of fluff he came in contact with. But the honest truth of the matter was, he'd been faithful to Nancy until they separated. Oh, not that there hadn't been opportunities, and that he hadn't been tempted, but he was just plain, old-fashioned scared. Twice, he almost had. Once, he'd been necking and petting with a girl in Mexico City in a Rent-A-Car, and had come in his pants. Luckily, it had been dark, and she hadn't known, although it had embarrassed the hell out of him. Another time, he'd gotten as far as a girl's bedroom, and was actually in bed with her. He had come before he even got the damn thing in. Both of these times, he'd been drunk, and when he sobered up, agonized beyond belief. But there was another reason why he'd been faithful to Nancy, and had been more careful about his drinking after these incidents. He had been petrified he'd pick up a venereal disease, and give it to Nancy. How could he have explained that? He shuddered at the thought.

And he didn't like rubbers. Not only did he think they were an insult to the woman, but the sensation wasn't the same. Having a woman discreetly insert a diaphragm in the bathroom was another matter. He was sure Nancy did, but how could he be sure about the others? And taking out a rubber, unrolling and inspecting it to be sure there weren't any holes, then the business of putting it on, invariably made him lose any desire. On the very few occasions when he had used them, in his youth, they had left him vaguely dissatisfied. What was the expression? *Like taking a bath with your shoes on*.

So he had his tropical trips—they were glamorous and exciting at times, and he met a great number of people that he otherwise would never have known. Latins, especially if they had money, were gracious, charming people. They were slower paced, and took time to enjoy life. And there were flowers everywhere. Even the poor, who lived in shacks, had flowers; some growing in tin cans. As a whole, he much preferred Latins to Americans, with their hustle and bustle, their *get this done yesterday*.

But there was also dirty, grimy hard work connected with these trips. There were no flowers around the oil fields. And because of the Latin's slower pace, Keith Oil had to have American overseers. Dwight sometimes felt guilty at the incongruity; forcing these poor people to work hard, when it was against their nature and the thing he admired most about them. He sighed; he forced himself, because there was the Company to think about—there was always the Company. And there were definitely no bed partners on these trips, not even since he and Nancy had separated—except mosquitoes.

He'd have to tell Scott sometime—maybe he wouldn't be quite so anxious to go. But who could tell? Scott and he were very different, really; their father had said Dwight took after his mother. He never knew whether that was meant as a compliment or not. Probably not; after all, he'd always given Scott the larger responsibility with the Company. But again, Scott was the oldest son. It was Jan he really cared for; she was the spitting image of their mother, and Dwight didn't blame him. He'd felt jealousy at times—but what the hell. Scott must have felt it, too—there was always friendly sibling rivalry.

He'd felt lonely for a while after he and Nancy had separated; especially after the first meeting in the lawyer's office. There had been something so final about it. He had gone out a few times—once he had taken Pam Sterling to dinner, but her sparkling personality and running patter of light conversation, compared to Nancy's dull pragmatism, had been too much for him.

Then he'd met Kathy—she was pure, sweet and innocent; and smart. Sometimes he had the feeling she was a lot smarter than he was, but he could talk to her, and she listened. They spent whole evenings, sometimes, dawdling over dinner, while he told her about his trips. All the things he had done, the people he had met, that Nancy had found dull and uninteresting, Kathy found fascinating. Certainly it bolstered his ego, but it was more than that. Sure, she'd been married before, but she was practically a virgin, and it wasn't long before he was so crazy about her he couldn't think straight. He wished she could have gone with him on this trip. He felt himself drifting off, and jerked himself awake. He rang for the stewardess and asked her to wake him two hours before they landed. That would give him plenty of time to go over the file on No. 27. He adjusted the seat lever and lay back, thinking of Kathy as he drifted off to sleep.

Kathy was putting on her makeup when the doorbell rang. She tipped the delivery boy, then opened the florist's box hastily. The dozen deep-red roses stared up at her accusingly. She opened the card slowly, read it, and sighed. Maybe it was for the best, Dwight going fishing for a while—it would give her a chance of decide what to do about him. She took the box to the kitchen, got down a vase, and started arranging the flowers.

She was just about through, breathing in their fragrance and thinking about Dwight, when she had a feeling that something was wrong. She picked up his note and read it again. Fishing. No hint as to where he could be reached. That wasn't like Dwight—no matter what the trouble was between the two of them, he wouldn't go off on a fishing trip with his father as sick as he was. Fishing, hell! He may have gone fishing, alright; but it certainly wasn't for fish. Somehow, she was sure this had something to do with Vivian, but if he wanted everyone to think it was because of her, she certainly wouldn't cramp his style. She looked at her watch, and rushed to finish getting ready for work.

Irene had slept badly the night before she was due to leave the hospital, and even the shot she had asked for around midnight hadn't lasted very long. It was still pitch black when she woke, and she was damp with perspiration. She was determined to be cheerful today, and since sleep was impossible, she switched on the light and picked up her Bible. She flipped the pages to the Psalms and tried to concentrate, but the words all seemed to run together. She finally put it down with a sigh—somehow, she wasn't finding the comfort from the Bible that she did before. She turned off the light again, and pulled back the curtains. For what seemed like a very long time, she lay there silently, watching the twinkling stars slowly fade into a gray mist, waiting for the nurse to come in with the inevitable morning tray.

Dr. Sturgess had assured her that the cancer had been completely removed, but a small nagging doubt in the back of her mind still remained. Ted had been equally convincing, as had April, but they all could be putting on an act. She certainly hadn't heard April making any sounds like she was going back to Switzerland right away. Resolutely, she tried to think of something else. When she got home, she'd feel better.

The first few days after the operation had been sheer agony, and when they got her up for the first time, it had been "Holy Hell." After that, little by little, she began to feel better physically, but then boredom set in. After all, you could read just so many magazines. She even had trouble remembering the passages from the Bible that she'd memorized previously. Ted and April visited her every day, and Kathy and Viv dropped by occasionally, but she spent endless hours by herself.

A week ago, she'd walked down the hall to visit Duncan. They'd never been especially good friends; she'd seldom seen him except at parties, and then Vivian did most of the talking. But loneliness and boredom are strong factors in a hospital, and she told herself it was a duty call. Irene had been pleasantly surprised. Duncan had just had his morning sponge bath, and was propped up in bed doing a crossword puzzle. He certainly didn't look like a man who'd gone through a massive coronary. He looked up at her, and a smile lit his face.

"Irene, how nice of you to drop by." He gestured to the puzzle book. "Damn boring, these things. But they won't let me read the papers yet, or the stock market reports. Think it might upset me." He motioned to the chair next to the bed. "Sit down, please. Gets mighty lonely in here, except for the few visitors they let me see."

She smiled back, and accepted the offer. In no time at all, they were chatting like old friends. Maybe it had something to do with being in the hospital together, or seeing each other in their robes and slippers. For instance, they discussed their children. He didn't mention Vivian much, although he told her all about Jeanne—rather, he was in the middle of telling her, when the nurse came in with the lunch tray. Good heavens, she'd been talking to him almost two hours, and the time had flown by.

After that, she visited him every morning, with Dr. Sturgess' permission, and they became quite close. Duncan was a very learned man, she discovered; funny, she mused, that he always let Vivian take the lead. Or maybe Vivian just thought she did. After all, as Duncan said, he didn't care much for parties. And every conversation eventually led around to Jeanne; the times they'd had, getting the company started, the surprise at having children so late in life, and then Jan . . . the spitting image of her mother. The joy of having a grandson, let alone living long enough to know him. Every time he mentioned Ben, though, his tone of voice changed. She couldn't blame him, having his adored daughter married to that slob. She thought of their closeness, then of April and herself, and couldn't help feeling a certain sadness. What the two of them must have missed. The day before she was due to leave the hospital, she went to see him as usual, and promised to continue their visits. He was much too good for Vivian, she decided.

Her thoughts turned to Pam. She had caught a glimpse of her once as she was on her way down the hall to see Duncan, and she had stopped in shock. A nurse had opened the door to her room as Irene was passing, and she only saw her for a moment, but it was enough. The sight of Pam was deeply imbedded in her brain. She was sitting in a wheelchair, staring straight ahead, and she couldn't have missed seeing Irene. But her eyes were blank, the pupils so enlarged she could barely see the thin green iris, and there was no recognition in them. Irene had stood there, frozen into immobility. Pam was scarcely recognizable, her appearance was so drastically changed. Her hair had been combed, but there was no lustre, and it hung straight and stiff around her face. Her head looked smaller somehow, as though her skull had shrunken, and her skin seemed to have been pulled tightly across her face. There were deep hollows under her eyes, and her tan had faded in splotches. The remnants of her tan seemed incongruous, a faint reminder of the glowing health that had deserted her.

She had mentioned seeing Pam to Dr. Sturgess, but he was terse and noncommittal, and she gathered that it was none of her business. She had overheard later that the nurse in question had been severely reprimanded. Since that time, Pam's door was kept carefully closed, and a "No Visitors" sign had been posted. She had seen Jack Wentworth in the corridor frequently, and was sure the sign did not apply to him. Her heart went out to the girl, and every time she thought of her, her thoughts turned to April, April, who had grown up with Pam. She had watched them as children, playing together, and the contrast between them had been striking. Pam, dark and sparkling, always the daredevil; and April, pale and ethereal looking.

She had never understood the close bond of friendship that existed between the two girls, as they were as different in temperament as they were in looks. April had been a shy child, while Pam was very outgoing, almost tomboyish. It would have appalled her to know the common bond that held them together. Pam's mother had died at birth—and subconsciously at first, April felt she had no real mother either.

She worried about April—she was almost sure her daughter was no longer a virgin. There was a maturity about her now that hadn't been apparent before she went to Switzerland, and she wondered who the boy was. She certainly hadn't confided anything, but it was obvious she was itching to get back to Switzerland, much as she tried to hide the fact.

Well, it wouldn't do to worry about it today. Today, she was going home, and she must look her best. Home . . . she longed for her own bed, her own room, and most of all, some good home-cooked meals. Funny; before she entered the hospital, she desperately wanted a dry martini, but she had no desire for alcohol now. That, too, would pass in time, she thought. She got up and took a long hot shower, with her own perfumed soap, then got back into bed and started applying her makeup. If there was time, she wanted to say a quick goodbye to Duncan before Ted and April arrived. As it turned out, there wasn't, after fussing with all the release papers, and what-not. Dr. Sturgess insisted on a wheelchair, although she'd been walking all over the hospital for days. But she didn't resist; it made her feel pampered and petted, as Ted protectively helped her into it, and carefully steered her past the waiting room towards the elevator, with April trailing behind.

Jan saw the Enwrights coming, and quickly got up and ducked behind a potted palm until the elevator doors shut. She breathed a sigh of relief; that had been a close call. She adjusted her dark glasses again, and glanced down the hall towards her father's room. It seemed as though Dr. Sturgess had been in there forever, but the clock on the wall said otherwise. She settled back down in her chair again, and tried to relax, but it wasn't easy. Last night had unnerved her to the point that she was afraid she might lose the baby. She tried to think of something else, but it was still too vivid, and she kept reliving the events in her mind.

She had driven home from the hospital the night before, and as usual, was dreading it. She always tried to be as quiet as possible when she neared the house, switching off the motor and coasting into the driveway. If Ben was home and passed out, she was safe for the evening; and if he was still out, she undressed and went to bed as quickly as possible in the baby's room. But if he was home and still awake, she never knew what to expect. Sometimes he was surly and brooding, at others wheedling and begging her forgiveness; but he was always drunk.

Last night when she had driven up, the house was ablaze with lights, and she had a sudden sense of something terribly wrong. She drove up quickly, making no effort to be quiet, and ran toward the house. The front door was ajar, and she could hear Ben banging on the bathroom door, shouting and cursing, and little Ben's screams on the other side.

She ran towards Ben, and with a surge of strength she didn't know she possessed, shoved him aside and called through the door. "Mrs. Leonard? Is the baby all right?"

Mrs. Leonard's voice was muffled and trembling. "Oh thank God, Mrs. Cameron, you're home. Do something, please. Call the police."

Jan wheeled on Ben, "What have you done, you maniac?" Her face was splotched with anger, and she picked up the nearest object that was handy. "If you've hurt my child, I'll kill you."

Something in her voice must have shocked Ben into some semblance of sobriety for a moment, and he started backing away from her. "I didn't do a thing," he mumbled sullenly. "The damn kid spilled my drink, and I gave him a little slap, that's all. Didn't hurt him none."

The screams from the bathroom told her differently, and without thinking, she threw the glass ashtray at his head. The moment she did, she knew it was a mistake. Ben reached up, dazed, and felt his forehead. Then he looked at his hand, and the blood on it. At the same time, the blood started trickling down into his left eye, and his face turned dark and menacing.

"You dirty bitch, I'm gonna kill you," he growled, and lurched towards her.

Frantically, she started looking for something else to throw at him, and started running, calling to Mrs. Leonard. "Stay in there, and don't unlock the door." In her panic and fear, she ran the wrong way, toward the bedroom. When she realized her mistake, he was almost upon her. As he started to swing, reflex action made her try to duck, and at the same time fold her arms over her stomach. The first blow caught her on the chin, but it was a glancing blow. She managed, somehow, to get away from him, and ran back toward the living room, knocking over everything she could to block his way. He caught her when she was almost at the front door, swung her around and punched her in the eye. She crumpled in a heap, and just before she passed out, her last thought was, I'm going to die, and so is my unborn child.

She couldn't have been out for very long, as the police arrived shortly afterwards, and she had heard the sirens coming up the hill. She got up groggily when she heard them and slammed the front door, then made her way to the bathroom. The house was a shambles, and Ben had fled.

She had taken the screaming child from Mrs. Leonard, and tried to calm him while she gave Mrs. Leonard instructions, her mind racing.

"Just answer the door, Mrs. Leonard, and tell them you

must have had the television on too loud, or something. I'll join you just as soon as I get the baby to bed.'' Then she had looked at Mrs. Leonard, and knew she couldn't pull it off. She was white and shaking, in worse condition than Jan was. Oh Lord, what was she going to do? She had given the child back to Mrs. Leonard and gone to the door herself.

She couldn't even remember now exactly what she'd told them—some gibberish about a family squabble, but everything was fine now. And yes, she was sorry they'd disturbed the neighbors. When they asked to see her husband, she'd been forced to tell them he'd gone. They had asked to see little Ben, and finally, after they were satisfied that he hadn't been hurt, they had left. Luckily her eye hadn't started to swell yet, or her chin. After she watched them turn the corner, she had bolted the doors and windows, then got an icepack for her face.

Little Ben had vomited up his milk, and she changed his clothes and wiped his face with trembling hands. When he finally went to sleep, exhausted, she and Mrs. Leonard went back to the living room. For once, she wished there was some brandy in the house. Mrs. Leonard kept up a steady stream of conversation, but Jan was only half-listening. She was thinking of the publicity if this got out, and of her father, and of her face; and finally, of Ben.

"I didn't know what to do, Mrs. Cameron, he was like a madman. He insisted on holding the baby, playing with him right after I'd fed him and was getting him ready for bed, and then he kept tickling him in the stomach. The baby's foot kicked out and spilled his drink, and he just went into a rage. Slapped him right in the face, he did. Then he gave him back to me, but the baby was terrified, and wouldn't stop crying. Then Mr. Cameron told me if he didn't stop crying, he'd make him stop, for good, and that's when I locked us both in the bathroom. I thought he'd break the door down. And I was afraid to try to get out the window, the baby was crying so much, he would have heard us. Mrs. Cameron, I love that baby, and I'm fond of you, but that man—we could have been killed.'' She wiped her eyes and looked at Jan. ''And you—did he hurt you very much?''

Jan shook her head—her mind was fastened on the baby now—Ben had said he'd make him stop crying for good. ''Mrs. Leonard, what happened tonight, that settles it. I'm sure you'll be discreet about this. I can't have my father duly upset, but I can't put my baby in danger, either. At first, I thought we'd be safe enough here for the night, anyway, but now, I'm not so sure. Mr. Cameron might just have been waiting out there until the police left, and he thought it was safe to come back. I think for all our sakes, we'd be better off in a motel tonight. Tomorrow, I'll have the locks changed, and iron grillwork put on the windows.'' She hesitated, ''You see, Mrs. Leonard, I've come to depend on you a great deal; and I'm going to tell you something that nobody else knows, especially my husband—I'm pregnant again.''

Mrs. Leonard had been shocked at first, then tears had come to her eyes. The only thing she said was, ''It's a sad world we live in.''

Then she went to pack some overnight things for them and the baby. Jan got up wearily, and was about to straighten the living room, when she stopped. No, she thought, if he comes back, let him see just what he did.

When they were ready, Jan had started to call a cab; if Ben were waiting, he wouldn't be as likely to try to stop them as he would if they tried to make it to the car. Then she checked herself; much as she hated to, there was something else to attend to first. She picked up the phone again, and dialed. When Dr. Sturgess answered sleepily, she told him precisely what had happened in as firm a voice as she could muster, from beginning to end, sparing no details. Then she called for a cab, and they had driven to a motel in Riverside. Neither Mrs. Leonard or herself got much sleep, but little Ben was a perfect angel, and slept through the rest of the night.

Towards dawn, Jan finally dropped off, but when she turned her head on the pillow, the pain that shot through the side of her face awakened her immediately. She rushed to the bathroom mirror, and the sight sickened her. Her eye had turned to nauseating colors of yellow, green and a faint purple; she knew from past experience with the black eyes Ben had come home with, that it would get worse before it got better. It was also swollen and puffy, and her chin had fared little better. She touched the swelling under her eye lightly, and groaned. She could learn to live with the pain, but no amount of makeup could cover the mess her face had become. Oh God, she thought, when her father saw this!

She glanced at her watch, Dr. Sturgess had said to meet him at the hospital at ten; she had plenty of time. She went back to bed, but sleep was impossible. She lay there, thinking of the scandal, and shuddered. There was no way of avoiding it now; she certainly couldn't leave town, but she couldn't be seen, either. Suddenly, she wished she was a little girl again, with none of the pressures and tensions that adults had to face.

And now here she was, waiting to see her father. When Dr. Sturgess had first seen her, he had winced, and muttered something under his breath about wife-beaters. She could just imagine her father's reaction. The doctor had checked her over, and could find no physical damage, which relieved her a little. But his concern about her father was as real and as great as her own. He had suggested she wait in his office while he talked to Duncan, to soften the blow, but she had preferred the waiting room just outside her father's room, even though she did run the risk of being seen. At least, there were no mirrors in here.

She had sent Mrs. Leonard out early this morning for some pancake makeup, powder, and large sunglasses. Painfully, she had tried to apply the pancake, but just touching the area around her eye was excruciating, and before she was half done, tears would start rolling down her cheeks, ruining any effort to hide the damage. Gingerly, she had washed the stuff off and tried again, with the same results. Finally, she had given up, dusted as much powder as possible around her eye, and concentrated on her chin. She had a little more success in that area, but the bruises were still visible. Even putting on the dark glasses had hurt. Dr. Sturgess had given her something for the pain, but it hadn't helped much.

She looked at the wall clock again, then at her watch; she couldn't believe how slowly the time was going by. Finally, she saw the door to her father's room open slowly. Dr. Sturgess stood there, his back towards her, still talking to her father, and Jan's heart started beating like a trip-hammer. She began to get panicky, and tried to take a few deep breaths to steady herself. Any moment now, he would turn around, and then she would have to face her father. Finally Dr. Sturgess shut the door, and swung around and looked at her. He started smiling broadly as he came down the hall, and Jan's mouth dropped open. She hadn't known what to expect, but certainly not this. He put both hands on her shoulders and looked down at her.

"Jan, I think you're in for a very pleasant surprise. Except for the fact that you got beaten up, your father couldn't be in a better mood. I didn't tell him about the baby, though. I thought you'd want to do that yourself."

"You mean—" her voice trailed off, dazed. "You mean, he actually feels good about all this?"

"The fact that you've left Ben, yes. He's waiting for you, my dear. There are all sorts of plans he wants to discuss with you; about the divorce, that is."

Jan still couldn't believe it. She practically ran into her father's room, then stopped just inside the door. Her father was sitting up in bed, and there was more color in his cheeks than she'd seen since his heart attack. When he saw her face, he winced, then held out his arms to her.

"Jan, baby," he shook his head sadly. "I'm sorry it had to come to this to make you open your eyes, but at least you know now just what kind of a lousy stupid bastard your husband really is. You might as well take off those glasses, and let me see the rest of it." She took them off slowly, and he groaned softly. "My God, it looks awful." Then his voice became brisk, authoritative. "Now, the first thing you have to do after you leave here is to go to a good photographer, wash that stuff off your face, and get some color photographs made. We'll need them in court. Be sure you get them dated. Did you get the names of the policemen last night?" She shook her head, dazed. "Well, never mind, they'll have a record at the station. I'm going to call my attorney in a few minutes, and make an appointment for you. Does it hurt to talk?"

She looked at him and shook her head again, afraid to speak. She thought of the unendurable torment she had gone through since her father had been ill, the intolerable presence of Ben around the house, the fear and agony of pain she had suffered last night, and against her will, tears welled up in her eyes and spilled over down her cheeks.

"Jan, honey, what are you crying about?" Her father was instantly concerned. "You don't still love him, do you?"

"Oh my God, no," she managed to choke out, and suddenly she was laughing and crying at the same time, laughing with relief that her father knew, and crying at the bitter irony of the situation. All the anguish she had endured, just to keep her father from knowing the truth, and for what? The whole thing had been pointless. She tried to collect herself, and smiled ruefully. "This isn't something that just happened last night, Daddy. He never hit me before, of course, but it's been over for us for a long time;

since the night you went in the hospital, as a matter of fact.''

"Yes, Larry told me. But I wanted to hear it from you. Your housekeeper . . . Mrs. Leonard, I believe? She knows about this?''

Jan nodded. "I had to have her move in with us. I didn't dare leave the baby alone with Ben.''

"Good. Then she can be your witness.''

She hesitated slightly, then made up her mind. "Daddy, there's something else I think you ought to know.'' She took a deep breath. "I'm three months pregnant, but Ben doesn't know. Nobody knows, except Dr. Sturgess, and now you . . . and I had to tell Mrs. Leonard, but just last night.''

She heard him suck in his breath sharply, and she looked up at him quickly. His face showed dismay, and he appeared to be in deep thought. Then slowly, he started to smile. "I'm going to be a grandfather again!'' He looked at her speculatively. "You don't show at all, but we'd better get this divorce thing over with as quickly as possible. And I'll figure out some way to get Ben out of this town, get him a job somewhere else, maybe, so he won't find out. By God, Jan, if he finds out, that's about the only thing that could throw a monkey wrench in our plans. I almost wish you'd had an affair with someone else, just so this one wouldn't be Ben's. You didn't, by any chance, did you?'' he asked, almost hopefully.

She couldn't help but laugh, even though it hurt her face. "Of course not, Daddy, you know better than that. Sorry I can't accommodate you.''

Jan left her father's room about a half hour later, feeling as though the weight of the world had been lifted from her shoulders. She had an appointment with a photographer at one o'clock, and with her father's attorney at three. After that, everything would be in her father's and the attorney's hands. Sh stopped to call Mrs. Leonard at the motel, then practically ran down the steps of the hospital to the waiting taxi. Maybe it was her imagination, but even her face didn't seem to hurt as much now.

It was late afternoon when Dwight's plane landed in Cochabamba, and a light rain had started to fall. Just as well, he thought; he'd have an early dinner at the hotel, get a good night's sleep and be out at the well before daybreak. He got through customs in record time, and took a cab directly to the Oliva. The manager was new since the last time he'd been here, but glancing in the bar on the way to the elevator, he saw that Nick was still there. He thought for a minute about stopping in to say hello, then changed his mind—plenty of time for that after he'd showered and gone down for dinner.

The rain had stopped by the time he'd unpacked and showered, and dusk was falling rapidly. He flopped down on the bed and flipped through the pages of the file on No. 27 again. Nothing on the surface looked out of order, really; just a gradual petering out of the flow. God, he wondered just how many other wells Vivian had tampered with. He thought of his father, and the Company, the work and sweat of building the business. How could Vivian have done this to his father, to all of them? He remembered when he and Scott were just kids, how good she had been to them, how they had looked up to her, how happy they had been when they found out she was going to marry their father. How could she have changed so much? Or had she changed? Had the whole stinking sweetness and light, the affection she had showered on them, all been an act, a put-on? Thinking back, she hadn't really been all that nice to Jan; but at the time he had thought the reason was that Jan was his father's favorite, if he'd thought of it at all. God, what fools she must think that Scott and he were.

And there was this other thing—Alex Dunbar; how long had he been in the picture? There had been no time to check up on him before he left; was he a business associate, or her lover, or both? He wished to God he knew what he looked like, at least; that was one thing he and Scott had overlooked. When he called Scott tomorrow, he'd have him get the information.

Then another thought struck him; he had no idea what Alex Dunbar looked like, but what if Alex Dunbar knew him? And even if he didn't, he'd been here at least two days before Dwight had arrived. Surely, he'd been out to the well by now. What if he came out tomorrow while Dwight was there?

He sat bold upright on the bed, then got up and started pacing, thinking furiously. Jesus, he and Scott had thought they had the whole thing worked out, and it just wasn't going to work out at all. There was no way to go out to the well now, Dunbar was sure to find out. And as soon as Dunbar did, Vivian would. God, how he wished Scott were here now, so they could figure out this mess together.

He started to call room service for some ice and a bottle, then stopped. What he needed was a cool head now. What would Scott have done? First, he would have tried to figure out the plusses and minusses. Okay.

First, nobody knew he was in town; the manager of the hotel was new, so that was no problem. He hadn't let any of his friends down here know he was coming, there hadn't been time, and that was a good thing. Nick hadn't seen him when he checked in; but what the hell, he'd planned on having dinner in the hotel. And his name was on the register. But Dunbar wouldn't be looking for him; there was no possible way he could even suspect he was here. So much for the plusses.

Now the minusses; how was he going to see the well? He certainly couldn't go out there in a disguise, someone was sure to recognize him, and there was no one here he could trust enough to go out for him. Besides, even if there was, the foreman wasn't going to give any information to just anyone.

And for all he knew, Dunbar might have the foreman in his pocket. God, if he only knew what Dunbar looked like.

He thought of Nick again, and stopped pacing. Nick had been with the Oliva as long as Dwight could remember, and they'd become pretty friendly over the years. But could he trust him? Nick was friendly with everybody, he had to be, he was a bartender. He stood looking at the phone, considering the situation. He'd have to take a chance on him, it was the only one he had.

He asked for the bar, and waited for Nick to answer. "Nick?" he tried to make his voice sound normal. "Remember me? It's Dwight Keith."

"Hey, old buddy, how've you been?" Nick's voice was warm and friendly as ever. "You coming in tonight? How long you been in town?"

"Nick, I'm coming down in a few minutes, that's why I called you first. I'm staying at the hotel, but nobody knows I'm in town, and I want to keep it that way. I'll tell you why when I see you, but don't call me by my name."

"Certainly, Mr. Kouri," he said, not missing a beat. Then he lowered his voice. "You want I should call you a different first name, too? After a few drinks, I might forget."

"I'm counting on you not to, Nick—this is too important. Make it Bill or Joe, whatever. Dwight's a little too unusual. There's a certain party I'm looking for, and I want to find him before he finds me."

"Of course, Mr. Kouri, I understand. You want the usual table, Mr. Kouri?"

"Hey, don't lay it on too thick," Dwight laughed in spite of himself. "I'll just sit at the bar for a while. See you in fifteen minutes."

The bar was busy when Dwight got there, but it hadn't changed much. Nobody was eating yet; they ate much later here than in the states. Nick greeted him effusively, set a scotch and soda in front of him, then busied himself with the other customers. When he got a chance, he managed to whisper to him, "It'll quiet down in a little while, then we'll talk."

Dwight smiled, and settled down, sipping his drink. There were mostly men in the bar, but there were a few women. His eyes wandered over the tables and he saw the usual class he had seen there before. There were a few exceptions, though; never had women been allowed unescorted in the Oliva bar, but he supposed it was the new management. He caught one woman's eye, seated at a table by herself, and she smiled at him beckoningly. He smiled back politely, then turned his back to her, and continued his observations through the mirror in back of the bar. Her dress was black, and cut very low in front. He noticed several other women seated at tables, and they obviously didn't look like the usual tourist trade. His view took in the rest of the room, and he caught himself smiling slightly. There were a couple of Americans; one an obvious tourist dressed in a white suit, complete with Panama. Apparently, he had been unaware that the weather in Cochabamba was much the same as it was in California, and he stuck out like a sore thumb. The other was an insignificant, wispy little man, dressed in a loud plaid shirt, and drinking heavily.

Slowly, he realized that they weren't the same class of people that used to come in here—how long had it been now? Two years? The girl in the low cut black dress had moved to another table now, and was talking to the wispy fellow in the plaid shirt. He finished his drink and they left together, and he realized the only thing that really hadn't changed about the place was Nick.

Nick Trujillo, with his curly black hair, a smile for everyone, remembering names, telling jokes, cutting down on drinks when a customer had too much; Nick, the perfect bartender. He wondered why he didn't have a place of his own by now. But then, he had always seemed to be happy; he had his wife, his four bambinos, always a girl on the side, and his gambling. He hoped someday he'd strike it rich.

Dwight had four drinks, and he was drinking them slowly, before the bar started to thin out, but Nick motioned for him to wait a little longer. Dwight sat patiently, and noticed that the girl with the black dress was back again. So was the wispy little man, but they were at different tables again. That sure must have been a quickie, he thought.

Suddenly, Nick was before him, pouring another drink, speaking softly. "You need a gun, perhaps, Mr. Kouri?"

Dwight choked on his drink, and looked quickly down the bar. There were only two men seated at the other end. "Nick, I said I wanted to find him, not kill him. Although," he mused, "maybe it wouldn't be a bad idea."

"An affair of the heart, Mr. Kouri?" Nick asked.

"No, nothing like that. It's strictly business, Nick, and the guy's been in town for at least two days."

Nick looked disappointed. "Too bad. A gun is easy to find. Or, to get someone killed, fifty, maybe seventy dollars. Clean, like that," he snapped his fingers. "There was a man in here earlier who could have done it for you."

"Well, you can forget that," Dwight said. "All I want to do is find the man; and I figured he'd come here, it used to be the best bar in town. What happened, Nick?"

"Oh, you noticed, huh?" Nick said sadly, wiping glasses. "It's the new owner—he don't know what he's doing. When he first bought the place, business fell off, because all the businessmen in town liked the old owner. So, he decides to bring in a few hookers to drum up business. Then the police come in and tell him to clean up the place, or he lose his license. So he gets rid of the hookers, and he loses business. Then the businessmen in town hear we got hookers in here, they start coming back, but no hookers. Then he bring the hookers back, but by that time, the businessmen don't come in no more. He screw everything up." Nick sighed. "But you don't want to hear about all that. What this guy look like?''

Dwight frowned. ''That's where I'm stuck; I don't know.''

''You look for a man, and you don't even know what he look like? You gotta know something; young, old, anything?''

Dwight shrugged. ''Not too old, not too young, I would imagine. He's a tax consultant, and he must have come in by plane one, two, maybe three days ago. He lives in Monrovia.''

''This man have a name, or don't you know that, either?'' Nick asked.

''Alex Dunbar; of course, he might be using an alias. You think you can find him for me?'' Dwight was doubtful; it was a pretty tall order, and Cochabamba was a pretty big place. If he were using an alias, he was sunk. ''Now tomorrow, I'll be talking to my brother back home, and I'm pretty sure he can get a description in a day or two. What are you grinning about?''

Nick finished putting the rest of the glasses away, still smiling broadly. ''How bad you need this man? You want to meet him, or just see what he looks like?''

''Well, I don't know. If he knows what I look like, I certainly don't want to meet him, but if he doesn't; then, yeah, sure I want to meet him. Why?''

''He don't know what you look like.'' Nick poured himself a straight shot, drank it down and wiped his mouth. ''He don't use no alias, either.''

''How come you know all this? Come on, Nick, don't play games with me.''

''You sure one lucky fella, you know that? You been looking at him all night—he's that guy in the corner in the plaid shirt.''

Dwight almost dropped his drink. It took all his will power to keep from turning around, but instead, he stared in the mirror again. ''That's Alex Dunbar?''

Nick nodded. "That's your man. Came in two days ago, and he's staying at the hotel."

Dwight studied him in the mirror; so that was Alex Dunbar. He was a small man, with sandy hair and a pallid complexion. His hairline was receding slightly, and from this distance, Dwight judged him to be in his early forties. But to find him at this hotel! This was a stroke of luck he couldn't have possibly imagined. Then he started analyzing; Vivian had probably told him that this was where Dwight always stayed, that it was one of the better hotels. It seemed plausible. Then he thought of the hotel register; that was the only proof he was in town.

"Nick, you're a godsend. You don't know what this means to me. There's just one more thing; my name's on the hotel register—is there any possibility of getting it changed?"

Nick shrugged. "That's nothing. The night man on the desk, he's drunk every night. I'll change it myself when I get off work. Maybe I just tear out the page."

Dwight had another inspiration. "Nick, I'm going over and introduce myself. I'll tell him you told me he was from the states, or something. Listen, if he doesn't tell me to get lost, every time we order a drink, make mine plain tonic, and load his."

"You want me to slip him a mickey?"

"I don't want him out, I just want some information." Dwight got up to leave, and left two twenties on the bar. "I owe you one, Nick, and I don't just mean this."

Nick winked and grinned. "Careful there, Mr. Kouri; I might ask you to buy me my own bar."

Scott stopped at a local hamburger stand before going over to Dwight's the next day. He'd checked Dwight's refrigerator before they left for the airport, and all he'd found was some cheese, a half-used package of stale bologna, mustard, and a sixpack of beer. Tomorrow, he'd stock up on some groceries;

this noontime waiting might take some time.

The phone started ringing precisely as Scott was putting the key in the lock, and in his haste to get to the phone, he dropped his package on the coffee table, and the root beer spilled. "Hello?" he practically shouted in the phone, as he heard the crackling noises of the overseas operator.

"Scott?" He heard his brother's voice over the incredibly bad connection, then everything got garbled. "Hello?" he kept saying, until the operator finally cut in.

"I'm sorry, sir, we seem to have a bad line. Would you please hang up and we'll call again?"

He hung up and stared at the phone; this could take hours. Meanwhile, the root beer was ruining the rug. He got a towel from the bathroom and started mopping up. What the hell did you use to take out a root beer stain, anyway? There was a big nasty brown spot on the pale beige carpeting. He sat down and took a bite of his cheeseburger. It was cold. Then he stared at the spot on the rug and waited for the phone to ring again. It took a good forty-five minutes.

"Hello?" he shouted again.

This time the line was clearer, and Dwight's voice came through to him. "Scott?"

"Thank God," Scott said; then, irrelevantly, "I spilled root beer on your rug, I'm sorry. You been out to the well yet?"

"Went out this morning early, and didn't even stop, didn't have to. I couldn't take the chance. Scott, I've had the most incredible piece of luck. I met our man last night, even got him drunk, and he gave me more information than we even dreamed of. He's paying off the foreman on No. 27 to falsify the reports we get. With our money, I might add. And I got the names of some other wells that supposedly went dry. He really spilled his guts. Vivian is up to her pointed ears in the whole mess."

"Dwight, you've gotta be kidding or drunk yourself; how could you get all that in just one day?"

"Scott, I can't take all the credit; I had a lot of help from Nick Trujillo, the bartender at the Oliva; and Mr. Dunbar thinks my name is Bill Kouri from Oklahoma City. I told him my hobby is old South American artifacts, and I take my vacation down here every year. He's staying at the same hotel, and after last night, he thinks we're old buddies. Listen, I can't take the chance of staying here, Scott. I know too many people, and we can't blow it now, although it's pretty well sewed up. I can't come home right away, either, so after I rest up today, I think I'll take a couple of side trips to some of the other wells in the vicinity, while he's busy mucking up this one. He was pretty much in his cups towards the end of the evening, but he mentioned a couple of wells just outside of Sucre that I think I should take a look at. You might look up the files on 15 and 39. Now, I gotta get some sleep; you know, I haven't been to bed since I've been here?"

"Dwight, you're a genius. You still want me to come over here every day at noon?" Scott looked at the cold cheeseburger.

"No, I can't see the point. It's Friday now, and everything's pretty much closed down over the weekend; suppose I call you next Wednesday and let you know when I'm coming home?"

"I'll be waiting."

"Uh—Scott? Anyone ask about me?"

"If you mean Kathy, yes. I don't think she quite bought the fishing trip."

"Well, I better hang up now." Dwight sounded pleased. "Talk to you Wednesday."

Vivian slept badly Thursday night; there was no reason for it, really. She hadn't heard from Alex yet, but that was no cause for worry; he hadn't been in Cochabamba very long. In fact, they'd made no definite plans for him to call her at all. And Duncan was coming along very nicely; in fact, Dr. Sturgess said he could probably come home sooner than expected. She herself could see how much he'd improved; even Jan's accident hadn't seemed to bother him too much. Imagine, slipping over a child's toy that way, and hitting the edge of the coffee table. When Vivian had first seen Jan's face, her first reaction was that Ben had hit her; that was impossible, though. Ben had been out of town on a job interview. She certainly hoped he got it; then, at least, Ben, Jan and the baby would be out of her hair.

Actually, there was no cause for her to have this feeling of anxiety; her plans were going as scheduled. Her health was fine, except when she walked upstairs too quickly. And sometimes, like now, for instance, she could feel her heart thudding in her chest when she was lying down. God, how she wished she could sleep; she'd taken two tranquilizers and gone to bed at midnight. Usually, they worked within a half hour, but last night she had laid there for hours in the dark, smoking cigarette after cigarette, and when she finally switched on the light, it was after four o'clock.

She got up and went downstairs, made herself some hot chocolate and took it back to bed with her. She lit another cigarette, sipping her chocolate, and decided on another couple of tranquilizers. She had to get some sleep, and she couldn't get rid of this feeling of uneasiness. That must be the trouble, she thought. Everything was going along too well. She took her tranquilizers, finished her drink, and crushed out her cigarette. She switched off the light and lay there in the dark, trying to make her mind a blank. Don't think about anything, don't worry, everything's going to be fine, just don't think . . . there, she could feel the pills beginning to work. . . .

Vivian woke up in a cold sweat; the sun was streaming into

the room, and her heart was pounding like a trip-hammer. She looked at her watch and blinked; one-thirty! She never slept past nine, at the very latest. Why hadn't the maid wakened her; then she remembered—she had asked for the day off. God, she'd really have to hurry to get to the hospital in time to see Duncan before he took his nap. Then, maybe if she saw Larry, she'd ask him about the trouble she had breathing sometimes. Or maybe she'd just cut down on her coffee and cigarettes for a while.

John finally rolled off Kathy, and they both fell back, spent and exhausted. She listened to his heavy breathing gradually subside into an even rhythm and smiled softly to herself. Edith had only been at the health farm for a week, after vacillating back and forth about going. And John had had more sex in that week than he'd had in a year with Edith, she was sure. Gradually, as he'd shed his inhibitions, he'd become a pretty good bed partner. Sexually, he fulfilled her completely, but there wasn't the wild passion that she'd felt with Jack. Of course, she'd only been with Jack once, and in all likelihood, they would have fallen into a pattern that precluded . . . she tried to think of a word other than ecstasy, that was too corny, but she couldn't. She supposed all, or almost all sexual relationships graduated into a routine eventually, but she felt cheated, somehow. It shouldn't have happened as soon as it had with herself and John.

It was dark in her bedroom, and Bruce's face suddenly swam before her eyes; this was happening more and more often lately, and she didn't know why. (Yes, you do, you're just lying to yourself. You had love with Bruce, and sex, and he was your best friend; why can't you admit that you had it all once and you'll never have it the same way again?) Bruce's face continued to look down on her, smiling slightly. Guiltily, as if she were cheating, she tried to pretend it was he beside her instead of John. The light timer in the living room went on, and with it, Bruce's face faded into nothingness.

She came back to reality as the light filtered into the bedroom, and turned to find John staring at her. Sometimes she got the weird feeling that he was reading her thoughts. But he never asked her about her past; she couldn't understand why, anymore than she could understand the compulsion she felt to talk about it after every time they had sex together. By now, he knew all about Fred; the turbulence of their brief marriage, the deep-seated inferiority complex he had given her that no other man had been able to assuage, until she met Bruce. He knew about all the men between Fred and Bruce, some of them whose names she didn't even remember. She had talked openly and freely about them, the sexual hangups she had run across, the weird demands of some; but she had skirted the edges when she was talking about Bruce. And she hadn't told him the dream had started again.

When the dream she'd had after Irene's Labor Day party hadn't recurred, she had been relieved. It had been a one-time nightmare, she had told herself. But it had started again a few weeks ago, and was recurring with astounding regularity. She always woke up just as she was sinking into the other building, and was never able to turn her head around to look behind her. Somehow, she had the feeling that if she did, it would be the end of her. She awakened feeling dragged out and trembling, and it took a couple of good stiff drinks before she felt calm enough to go to bed again. She had always been able to figure out what her dreams meant before, more or less; and when she did, they had stopped. But this one she didn't even try to think through. Somehow or another, she had the feeling that she didn't want to know what was behind her in the dream. And she always went to sleep after John left with a certain amount of trepidation, almost sure that she would dream.

She stared back at John, wondering if he really could get

inside her head, then smiled at him in the half-light, as a sudden warmth of affection came over her. "How long did you sleep?" she asked.

He didn't answer her right away. Instead, he reached over and turned on the bedside lamp, and lit a cigarette. "I didn't," he said, blowing out the smoke thoughtfully. "I was watching you."

"In the dark?" she teased him.

"Perhaps watching wasn't a good choice of words. I suppose I was listening to you think."

She looked at him quickly; no, he wasn't joking, he meant it. She switched on the other bedside lamp. "How can you *listen* to someone think?" she asked culpably. "And in the dark?"

"That's the only time you really can," he assured her easily, "when you aren't distracted by eyes, and faces, movements and mannerisms. You can hear a good deal in the dark."

Kathy began to feel uncomfortable; she didn't like the way this conversation was headed.

"For instance," he continued, "you sighed a good deal, which could connote a number of things. You could have been comparing me to one or more of the men you've known, and the sighs could indicate that I come up a poor loser."

"John!" she said indignantly, and sat bolt upright, "that's not true, I've never done that."

"No?" he said pleasantly. "Perhaps not. Perhaps there's some other reason you feel compelled to tell me about someone in your past immediately after we've had sex."

Kathy's mouth dropped open, her mind racing furiously. "I never compared you with anyone," she spluttered, "I thought you wanted to know about me, all about me. And the men in my life are part of me, what makes me. If it offended you, why didn't you say something before this?"

His lips curled into a slight smile. "Kathy, my dear, for

315

someone who is supposedly sophisticated, you can be incredibly naive. No man who loves a woman wants to hear about another man. He especially doesn't want to hear about another man right after he's made love to her. He may accuse her of loose morals, he may even call her a tramp or a slut, but he really doesn't want to know. And I didn't say anything before," he continued conversationally, "because I thought eventually you'd run out of men to talk about, but your supply seems unlimited. Besides, the only man you really cared about and probably still do—Bruce—you mention scarcely at all. And no, before you even ask the question, I do not care to hear all about Bruce."

Kathy turned her back to him, and lit a cigarette with shaking hands. John had practically called her a tramp and a slut, and he thought she had loose morals. Well, so much for honesty, truthfulness, no secrets between us, and all that sort of jazz. "I really didn't think you were that much of a bigot, John." Her voice was trembling, "I suppose this means we're all washed up?"

"God, no, Kathy." To make his point, he pulled her down to him, and kissed her deeply. "You know I love you," he murmured against her throat, "but Edith's coming home in a week, and I'd like this next week to be just ours, with no ghosts of the past intruding, and if they do intrude I don't want to know about it."

She pulled away, and looked in his eyes. She saw the deep love in them, the caring. "I'm sorry, John. I've hurt you terribly, haven't I?" Tears filled her eyes, and he began to kiss them away.

Then he suddenly thought of something. "You know what you called me? A bigot! If that isn't something, a psychiatrist being called a bigot!"

She couldn't help but smile. "Well, aren't you? Just a little?"

"Hell no! Every man puts the woman he loves on a pedestal, and he doesn't want to be told any differently. Especially if he's a psychiatrist, and the bulk of his patients are sexually motivated."

She snuggled in his arms, feeling warm and secure. "You know something. I wasn't thinking about another man tonight, I was thinking about a nightmare I keep having."

"Oh? About what?"

"I was going to tell you tonight, but now I think it had better wait for another time; in the morning, maybe."

They lay there together silently for a while, then Kathy sighed. "Sorry."

John laughed. "That's okay."

"John?"

"What."

"Couldn't you possibly stay here all night?"

"Honey, you know the service might call me at home. And you've told me flat out you won't spend the night there."

"I couldn't. It just wouldn't . . . seem right."

"And this is right?"

"Umm hmmm."

"Women!"

Edith got on the scales at Greenbriar at the end of the first week, and dropped her robe. She could scarcely believe her eyes; nine pounds! Her flesh felt firmer, more taut, and there was a healthy glow to her skin, a new sparkle of determination in her eyes. Another week, and she'd have to get a whole new wardrobe. Well, John could afford it; she could just imagine the look of surprise in his eyes when he saw her for the first time. Maybe she'd better stay here three weeks, instead of just two. Yes, she'd tell him when he called her this weekend that she'd decided to stay on. After all, there was no urgent need for her to go home right away. Happily, she put her robe back on, and went to get her carrot juice cocktail.

April got to the mailbox before anyone else in the household, as usual. She had no reason to think today would be any different. The mail from Switzerland was unpredictable; sometimes she would get nothing for over a week, then three or four letters from Greta and a dozen newspapers would come all at once. She could see before she got to the box that it was bulging, so this must be one of those "catch up" days. She riffled through the mail on the way back to the house; two letters from Greta marked Special Delivery, and five newspapers. The rest of the mail she put on the hall table, then went to her room.

She decided to go through the papers first, although she'd just about given up seeing anything about Juan in them. Then she'd have Anne bring her some coffee and read Greta's letters. She opened the first paper and noted it was over a week old. She opened the second, and sat there, frozen, her hand in mid-air; here it was at last, Juan's picture staring up at her, the headlines in hideous black print seeming to leap out at her: *Juan Delgado, Alias Gallardo, Escapes Police In Tax Fraud.* April's head reeled, and she thought she was going to be sick. Then she read the finer print:

Juan Delgado, aka Gallardo, Delvecchio, and numerous other pseudonyms, has evaded the French police who want him for questioning in connection with a giant tax fraud perpetrated on the French people. Senor Delgado, long a well-known member of the French and Italian underworld, is believed to have escaped just minutes before the French police raided his quarters in St. Moritz. It is believed that Senor Delgado may have left the country and headed for Cuba, where he also has numerous financial dealings. Anyone knowing the whereabouts of this man. . .''

April crumpled the rest of the paper, and threw it in a ball to the floor. Oh my God, not Juan, not when she'd been counting the days until she could be with him again. He just couldn't be all those things they said about him. She flung herself down on the bed and started to sob, muffling the sounds in her pillow.

Then a thought struck her with such violence that she shook all over; the apartment in St. Moritz! What if they connected her with Juan? Oh my God, all she needed was the French police coming to her door, or the FBI. Quickly, she opened Greta's letters in search of more information. There was none. Then she smoothed out the wrinkled paper, carefully reread it, and all the other papers, but there was no mention of a woman. That didn't mean there wasn't, of course, they might just be keeping it out of the papers. Thank God, he'd never told her anything about his business. Her fingerprints! She hoped he'd had the good sense to wipe off everything after she left, when he knew the police were closing in.

She loved Juan dearly, but right at this moment, fear had taken over, and she loved April a good deal more.

Chapter 13

The rain was coming down in torrents when Dwight's plane finally landed at Long Beach International; even in a jet, the flight had been bumpy and miserable for the last two hours. God, how was he ever going to explain being on a fishing trip in this kind of weather? And the plane was a good three hours late; he hoped Scott had checked with the airport before coming out to meet him.

His feelings had been mixed on the flight home; the other wells had proven out just as he had expected, and there was certainly enough evidence against Vivian to get rid of her, once and for all. On the other hand, he shuddered to think just how much she'd actually taken the company for, and how to break the news to Duncan. He had called Scott just before he left for home and his father seemed to be just fine; but all the same, this was going to be one helluva blow to him. Scott and he had a lot of territory to cover on how to handle this.

He attended to his luggage, then headed for the cocktail lounge; Scott was to meet him there. The bar was crowded with damp, disgruntled passengers, and it took him a while

320

to find his brother. He finally spotted him sitting in a corner, glumly sipping a drink. From the expression on his face, Dwight realized he hadn't bothered to check the schedules before coming to meet him. His face lit up, however, when he saw Dwight, and he stood up and hugged him.

"Thank God you're finally here. I've been waiting so long I've got callouses on my behind and a splitting headache." He gestured around him. "It's so noisy here, we certainly can't talk, and it takes about a half-hour to get a drink. How about finding a quieter bar before we get down to business?"

"Jesus, yes. I could stand a drink, but it can wait." They started making their way towards the exit. "I've got everything, Scott; enough to get our dear stepmother tarred and feathered and run out of town on a rail. And Dunbar! You know they could both go to prison for the deals they've pulled?" Dwight had to almost shout to be heard above the noise. "And to think we once thought Vivian was the perfect solution for Dad. How's he holding up, anyway? Any change?"

"He's fine, Dwight. Dr. Sturgess says he can come home in a few days." Scott frowned, thinking. "That doesn't give us much time. Telling Dad's going to be an awful shock; you don't suppose it might be a better idea just to confront Vivian with this, do you?"

"Scott, I can't even think in here," Dwight answered. A waitress jostled him, nearly spilling her tray of drinks. "Like you said, let's find someplace else where we can talk."

There wasn't much conversation in the car; the traffic was heavy, and the rain was still coming down in buckets, pelting and jumping off the hood like tiny stars. Scott concentrated on the driving, while Dwight looked from one side of the highway to the other for a bar. "Can't see a thing in this blasted rain," he muttered.

Finally, they found what looked like a decent enough roadside tavern, and pulled in. There were few customers, and they found a corner table. After they ordered drinks and took off their drenched raincoats, they settled back. "Well, what do you think? About talking to Viv, I mean?" Scott said.

"Bad idea," Dwight answered. "I thought about it myself, on the plane coming back. But with the deals she's pulled, we can't predict what she might do next. Scott, you can't imagine all the stuff I've got; pictures of the wells that she said had gone dry still pumping, affadavits from foremen in Sucre, everything. I've even got some pictures of Dunbar at the bar at the Oliva, and he sure wasn't conducting any business conference."

"Where'd you get the idea about the pictures?" Scott looked at his brother with new admiration.

Dwight smiled wryly. "I'm afraid I can't take credit for that. Nick came up with the idea."

"Just who is this Nick you keep talking about?"

"I told you, he's the bartender at the Oliva Hotel; and boy, has that place changed. Used to be the best hotel in town, and then it changed hands, and the bar's nothing but a pickup joint. I wondered why Nick had stayed on, until he told me he'd thought up this camera idea. Actually, he'd already taken some pictures of Dunbar the night before I got there, and wait until you see them. Dunbar drinking alone, Dunbar picking up on a hooker, them drinking together, and leaving the bar together; even a couple of Dunbar and me drinking together. I've got about a dozen; Nick said he'd send me some more, if he could get anything worth while. I told him I'd send him five hundred dollars when I got back home."

Scott choked on his drink. "You what?"

"Well, don't you think it's worth it? After all, Vivian's taken us for thousands, and five hundred didn't seem like so much. And Nick's little picture scam gave me the idea to buy a camera to take pictures of the wells."

Scott thought this over; five hundred dollars! "Why'd he take pictures of Dunbar, anyway?"

Dwight smiled. "Nick's a good buddy, Scott, but he's got a small problem; he likes to gamble, and that takes money. What better way to make a little on the side then to take pictures of tourists on the town, especially married tourists? Of course, he doesn't come right out and ask the customers for money; he just shows them the pictures and says he took them to decorate the walls. Some of them don't care, but an awful lot of them get pretty nervous, and they pay plenty. He didn't ask me for a dime, Scott, and really didn't want to take anything, but I'have come up with nothing without him. Or else, Dunbar would have spotted me first; don't forget, he's paying off the foreman on 27." Dwight purposely didn't mention Nick had also offered to get him a gun, or get the man killed for him; no reason to tell Scott the way they did things to Bolivia. Besides, they had enough to worry about.

Scott rubbed his chin thoughtfully. "Yeah, I guess you're right. Well, it looks like you've covered just about everything. Now comes the really hard part; how to tell Dad."

Really hard part? What the hell does he think I've been doing in Bolivia, Dwight thought. "Depends on how his condition is; have you talked to Dr. Sturgess today?"

"This morning, and he's fine. He's been especially fine since he found out Jan's divorcing Ben—I forgot to tell you about that."

"You're kidding! What happened?" Dwight was delighted.

"Seems he knocked the hell out of her, and the neighbors called the police. Nobody's seen Ben, I guess he thinks he'll go to jail, or something. Dwight, nobody knows about this except Dad, her lawyer, and the housekeeper; and Dr. Sturgess, of course. For some reason, Dad wants it kept quiet, and hasn't even told Viv, which I thought was kind of odd. I haven't told Fran, either."

"Was she hurt badly?" Dwight was concerned.

"No, not really; he gave her a black eye, and it was a beaut. Still looks pretty bad, but she's staying out of sight for a while. The story they're telling is that she tripped over the baby's toys, and hit the coffee table." Scott paused. "To get back to Dad—I guess we'd better tell the whole story to Dr. Sturgess first; then, of course, we'll have to go over it again with his attorney."

"That makes sense. Let's just finish this one and go over to my place. I'm bushed, but I want to show you the pictures I got. God, I hope I'm there when Vivian finally gets a look at them."

"Where are they, by the way? You got them on you?"

"Hell, no," Dwight shook his head, "they're in the lining of my suitcase."

Scott shook his head. "You read too many mystery stories."

The sun was shining brightly when Kathy finally woke up Friday morning, and automatically, sluggishly, she looked at the bedside clock. Good grief, nine o'clock! She started to get up hastily, before she remembered, then sank back into the pillows again. This was the day Edith was due home, and John had given her the day off. Big deal. She lit a cigarette and lay there, considering what to do with herself; three whole days, and she doubted she'd even hear from John, much less see him until Monday. To hell with him, she thought. Topsy was jumping up and down to be let out, so she finally got up, opened the back door, and put the water on for tea.

She could visit Irene, but she'd just done that two days ago; she could ask April to have lunch with her, but she had acted so oddly when she was over there, that she discarded that idea. She could visit Pam, but sitting in that hospital room with her was like sitting with a corpse, and she was depressed enough. Besides, Jack would probably be there, and she didn't want to intrude. One thing she could say for Jack, he'd certainly been faithful during all this; he was with Pam almost constantly, positive in his own mind that eventually she would come out of this. She wished she could be as confident; she thought of the warm, vibrant, vital Pam that she had first met, and the lifeless, empty-eyed pitiful creature she had become, and became more depressed than ever.

And she'd had that dream again last night; she sat down and pressed her knuckles against her temples. God, it was happening almost nightly now, and try as she may, she couldn't figure out what it meant. She still hadn't told John. Almost every day, she told herself firmly that today she would; but something always held her back. Maybe she really didn't want to know. But she sure wanted to get rid of it.

She got up, let Topsy in and poured the tea. She looked out the windows at the glorious day, the sun sparkling on the wet grass. There was no reason for this depression, she had known for over a week that Edith was due home today, and it hadn't bothered her. In fact, guiltily, she had even looked forward to having a little time to herself. Now she had it, and she didn't know what to do with it. She could polish the silver, she supposed, or read a book, or wash the windows. She wrinkled her nose; none of those things appealed to her. She was bored, and she was lonely. If Dwight were in town, she could call him, but then the whole thing would start up again.

Then she thought of Maude; she hadn't talked to her for quite a while. On impulse, she picked up the phone and started to dial her number, then stopped. Why not drive up and surprise her? She might have plans, though; well, if she did, she'd turn around and come back. Or, she could always stay at a motel on the Strip or Highland Avenue, there were several she knew that took dogs. Instantly, she felt better.

She finished her tea, poured another cup, then went in and started her bath water. She opened her closet doors and eyed her clothes critically. Her new black and white checked suit would do nicely, the green chiffon in case they went out somewhere. She got down her suitcase, drank her second cup of tea, then got in the tub. She hadn't felt this well in a long time; and maybe, just maybe, she wouldn't have that dream again tonight.

Then she packed quickly, applied her makeup carefully, brushed her hair until it shone, and was ready to leave in an hour. Not bad, for her. She considered calling the exchange, to let them know she'd be out of town for the weekend in case John did call, then changed her mind. Why should she? Let him worry a little. She had just finished locking up, and was going out the door, when the phone rang. She looked at it for a minute, then shut the door and carefully locked it.

Dwight let the phone ring precisely twenty times before he hung up, while Scott waited impatiently at the door. "That's funny," he said wonderingly, "the office says she has the day off, and she's not home. Kathy always likes to sleep late when she's not working. I wonder where she could be?"

"Oh, come on, Dwight, she could be anywhere," Scott said shortly, "and if we don't leave now, we'll be late for our appointment. And I really think seeing Dr. Sturgess now is more important than mooning over some redhead."

"She's not 'some redhead,'" Dwight said hotly, "and I don't want you talking about her that way." He relented a little. "But you're right, let's go. You think the attorney will make it?"

"He said he'd try; otherwise, we're to go to his office this afternoon. You've got everything?"

Dwight patted his briefcase. "Files, affadavits, notes, and the pictures. Let's go, I'll try Kathy later."

Kathy had left her apartment shortly before eleven, and it wasn't quite noon when she reached Los Angeles. She could have gone directly to Maude's, but then she remembered it was Friday, and Maude would be at work. She had no desire to see anyone from the agency; besides, she wanted to drive around for a while. Downtown L.A. was dirtier than she remembered; and this new thing, smog, hung over the area like a blanket. But the people were the same; everybody hurrying from one place to another, full of their own importance. Downtown had always been an enigma to her; expensive stores just a block or two from the slums of Main Street; the Biltmore Hotel, standing proud and impressive just across the street from Pershing Square, where the bums and winos hung out, where there were always a few "crazies" preaching about the end of the world.

She was beginning to feel nostalgic by the time she started down Wilshire Boulevard, and she was also beginning to get hungry. But the lunch crowd was just starting to come out now, and she felt funny about going in someplace alone. She drove slowly until she reached La Cienega, and turned up Restaurant Row. Nothing had changed, really; but then why should it? She'd only been gone a few months. A few months! She felt as though she'd been gone for years. The Circus hot dog stand was still there, directly across the street from *Tail 'o the Cock*, and she smiled at the absurdity of the place, flaunting itself proudly among the elegant restaurants along the Row. She and Bruce had stopped there so many times.

She drove up to the Strip, and turned left. She told herself she was just driving idly, to while away the time until Maude got home from work, but deep inside she knew differently.

Eventually, she'd drive by her old apartment. She wondered if it was rented now, and what the new tenants were like; did they have plants on the terrace like she used to have? Had they repainted, changed the drapes? Before she left, she had given all her plants to Maude, and she had hated to give them away. Funny, she didn't have even one plant in her apartment in Monrovia; probably some Freudian hang-up, John would say. Maybe she'd get some when she got back.

She drove to the end of the Strip, then turned around, went back and pulled into *Dolores' Drive-Inn*. That place, at least, had certainly changed. The last time she'd been there, they'd had beautiful looking young girls, in short costumes; now they had beautiful looking young boys, who looked suspiciously swishy. She looked around at the customers in the other cars; the clientele had changed, too. Oh well, she thought, everyone had to have their own place to congregate.

She ate half of her double cheeseburger, and carefully picked out the rest of the meat for Topsy, who wolfed it down. When she paid her check, she noticed the carhop's nails; there was no doubt he was wearing nail polish. Better polished nails than dirty nails, she thought, as she pulled out, drove down the Strip again, and turned up a winding street towards the hills. After all, she told herself, she had to find a place to let Topsy out for a minute. And it just happened to be the street she used to live on. (Oh sure it did, Kathy; who are you kidding?) She stopped the car a block away from her former apartment and got out; after all, Topsy had to stretch her little legs a bit, didn't she?

Topsy squatted immediately, and Kathy hastily jerked her leash, pulling her off the grass and into the street. Topsy obligingly squatted again, looking up at her earnestly while she did her business. Kathy tried to look nonchalant, and hoped a car wouldn't drive by, or that no one was looking out their windows. She would never get over her embarrassment at walking a dog, and thanked God for her little back yard in

Monrovia. Bruce always used to walk Topsy for her when he was in town, and always teased her unmercifully about her hangup on the subject.

It's a wonder Topsy was trained at all; Kathy would have much preferred to have her go on papers in the apartment, but the poodle would have none of it. The terrace, once in a while, yes; but only if it was raining. Otherwise, she would scratch at the door and whine unmercifully, until Kathy took her out. She had often wondered, with all the dog obedience training classes there were, why someone had never thought of toilet training for dogs? She had asked around, and been met with peals of laughter. The people she had called had either thought she was calling for Steve Allen, or in some way was connected with Candid Camera. When Topsy was finally through, she reached down, petted and praised her, then started walking slowly up the hill towards her old apartment.

Suddenly, Topsy started jerking and pulling on her leash. It was as though, once her immediate business was taken care of, she had recognized her surroundings, and was anxious to get home. Kathy looked down at her and smiled. She was anxious, too, but apprehensive at the same time. They turned the corner, and there was the apartment house, halfway up the block.

Kathy's heart started pounding a little harder, but she told herself it was the exertion of walking up the hill. Besides, Topsy was straining and tugging on her leash harder now, and would turn around every few seconds and bark at her to hurry. They had almost reached the building before Kathy could bring herself to look up, and when she did, she stopped in her tracks. She had a full view of the terrace of her apartment, and the sun was streaming down on it. She had expected some changes, but not this! It was exactly the same—the same wrought iron furniture, the large boston fern swaying in the breeze, the tall fig trees in each corner. The drapes were pulled, but they looked like the same drapes she had when she rented it. Her legs started to shake, and she turned her head away as tears dimmed her eyes; it was almost as though she had never moved away.

She stood there unsteadily for a moment, trying to get a grip on herself, then looked up again, shading her eyes with her hand, squinting. Of course they were the same drapes; they came with the apartment, the owner had just had them cleaned. White wrought iron furniture was no novelty, a lot of people liked it. But the fern, and the fig plants! Maybe the owner had told the new tenants how she had done the terrace, and they liked the idea; she stood on her toes, trying to see what sort of containers the fig trees were in, but the railing hid the view. Then she noticed that something was missing; there was no hanging philodendron. Maybe these unknown people that were living in her apartment didn't like philodendrons. She stared at the boston fern again; she stared a long time. It looked exactly like the one she'd given Maude.

A man walked out of the apartment building, and looked at Kathy; it brought her back to reality, and how foolish she must appear to him, just standing there, staring up, with a little black poodle jumping and barking at her. She blushed slightly, and knelt down to pet Topsy and cover her confusion. She waited until he got in his car and roared down the hill before she stood up again. She looked up once more, before starting down the hill to her car. It must have been the sun, she thought, and wishful thinking. Wrought iron furniture, and a few plants, indeed! Evidently, her tastes weren't as exclusive as she'd thought. But she felt sad, somehow; she shouldn't have come back, but she couldn't have not come back. Then she thought of Maude, and her spirits lifted a little; a few more hours, and she'd see her. A little common sense and down-to-earth philosophy was what she needed now, and Maude could certainly give her that. In the meantime, she had more time to kill.

She considered stopping by *Barney's Beanery* for a drink; it had always been a favorite place to go. You met just about everyone there, from women in minks and diamonds to men in denims and sweatshirts. But then she decided against it; she was bound to run into someone she knew, and right now, the only person she wanted to know she was in town was Maude. Instead, she decided to drive to Malibu, taking the long, winding road down Sunset Boulevard. She drove past *Santa Ynez Inn* slowly, remembering the first time Bruce had taken her out. It hurt, it hurt a lot, and tears came to her eyes; maybe this hadn't been such a hot idea after all. Maybe she should just turn around and go back to Monrovia . . . to what? Determinedly, she drove on, swung onto the Coast Highway and drove down through Malibu as far as Trancas. She stopped at a roadside stand for a coke and to let Topsy out, then started slowly back towards the Strip.

The traffic was heavy now, and by the time she stopped for gas, she didn't get to Maude's until almost five o'clock. She turned down the steep hill on Argyle and looked for a place to park. There never was, Maude lived just below *Bublitchski's*, and the street was always crowded. She finally found a place two blocks away, and started walking back up the hill. Suddenly she was nervous—she should have called Maude first. She decided to walk up to Turner's Drug Store on the corner and call first.

Maude answered on the second ring. "Kathy?" she sounded delighted. "Just wait a minute 'til I get my coffee, and we'll settle down for a long talk; you haven't called me for ages."

Kathy was relieved, then she had an idea. "Maude, you sure you're not busy tonight?" She could still surprise her.

"No, don't have a thing planned, except maybe catch up on my reading."

"Well, I forgot something; you mind if I call you back in about five minutes? Just stay by the phone, okay?" She hung up before Maude could reply.

She started walking back down the hill again. Maude lived in a charming old English Tudor style apartment house, as far removed from reality and Hollywood as you could find, it looked like something out of a fairy tale. The studio apartments were actually like separate houses, with deep sloping thatched roofs, criss-crossed window panes looking inward on an enchanting courtyard. There were two enormous knarled old trees shading the courtyard, and there was a feeling of peace and tranquility about the place. Maude lived in the back, and Kathy walked through the courtyard with anticipation. It wasn't until she rang the bell that she noticed something; she didn't see her philodendren anywhere, or her other plants, either—maybe Maude had taken them inside for the winter.

Dr. Larry Sturgess sat behind his large cluttered desk, tapping his pencil absentmindedly, as he listened to Duncan's two sons tell their story. He had interrupted only once, to tell his receptionist to hold all calls, but had made no comment. When they had begun the conversation, each one interrupting the other at intervals, to be sure nothing was left out, he had felt a certain skepticism, not believing that Vivian could possibly be capable of such treachery. But as the whole ugly story unfolded, he heard not only what they said, but the ring of sincerity and conviction in their voices; there could be no doubt about it. Vivian had done all this, and to his oldest and dearest friend. He barely glanced at the pictures and files they had brought with them; it really wasn't necessary. He felt a terrible sadness for his old friend, and the familiar heavy weight of responsibility on his shoulders. Duncan, at the most, wouldn't live more than five or six years; knowing what Vivian had done could shorten that time considerably.

He felt the silence in the room now, and realized the boys were waiting for him to say something. He didn't question their evidence. "You want to know what this will do to your father, I suppose?"

Dwight and Scott looked at each other uncomfortably, before answering. "Well, yes." Scott spoke first. "We were thinking of trying to handle it with Vivian ourselves, but we don't know what she'd do—and Dad would find out some way, she'd never just leave without a fight. Do you think he can take it, Dr. Sturgess?"

Dr. Sturgess didn't speak at once; Duncan was a fighter, it was true, and he had Jan's divorce and new baby going for him. It just might carry him through. "I'm going to be honest with you, boys; nothing is certain. Your father came through his heart attack, and quite frankly, for a while there, I didn't think he'd make it. This news about Vivian just might kill him. But on the other hand, the way he bounced back, and especially since he found out about Jan's getting a divorce, is a miracle." He couldn't tell them about the baby, that still had to be kept secret until the divorce got started, but he'd be as open as he could. "Your father's all wrapped up in Jan now, but quite honestly, I don't know just how dependent he is on Vivian. After all, they've been married eleven years. You boys would know more about their relationship than I would. But you're right, even if it could be handled with Vivian and an attorney, Duncan would know something was wrong if she just suddenly left." He stopped talking, while the boys waited. Jan; he'd have to talk to Jan about this.

"I think you boys had better go see Duncan's attorney, he's waiting for you. You seem to have all the facts, but I don't want you telling your father yet. I'm going to have to do that. But before I do, Jan's going to have to know every-thing; and I mean everything. Then I want her to see her father first, talk about the divorce," and the baby, he thought, but he didn't say that. "You know, get him in a good mood, then I'll tell him. And I want you boys just outside the door when I do, with his attorney, because after I tell him, he'll be roaring like a bull, if I know Duncan. I think this should be done today, if it's at all possible." He fumbled through his appointment book. "Let's see," he said, "nothing I can't cancel. If you boys leave now, I'll call Jan, and maybe we can all meet at the hospital around four o'clock. I'll call Vivian and make some excuse, that Duncan's having some tests done tonight, and she can't see him. I don't think she'll really mind," he added wryly.

After Scott and Dwight left, he sat there for a few minutes before he called Jan; this situation was going to be more delicate and intricate than any operation he'd ever performed. Silently, he prayed to God that he could pull it off. Jan was the key to the whole situation now, and there was one unknown factor—Duncan's attitude toward Vivian. He had never really liked the woman, but never in his wildest dreams could he have believed the things she had done. No time to dwell on that now, so he pulled the phone towards him, and dialed Jan's number.

Jan drove to the hospital in a state of shock; Dr. Sturgess' voice was still ringing in her ears, and she was dumbfounded. She walked through the hospital toward the elevator, unmindful of the stares she was getting, as she'd forgotten her dark glasses, and her black eye was still painfully evident. She got off at her father's floor, and the doctor was waiting for her. "I don't suppose this could all be some sort of a horrible misunderstanding, could it?" she asked him grimly.

He sighed, and shook his head. "I wish to God it was, Jan, but your brothers have found out some pretty terrible things about your stepmother," he said sadly. "They should be here any minute now, but you're the one I'm really depending on. Youre father's going to need you now, more than ever."

"Oh doctor, what can I say to him? He'll know

something's wrong; I just don't think I can pull it off."

"You can do it, Jan; I saw you after your father had his attack, remember! Once you see him, you'll find the strength. Just talk to him about the new baby, and what great times you'll have after he's born; you'll find the words, I know you can." He pushed her gently towards her father's room. "He loves you very much, Jan." He watched her as she walked slowly to her father's room. She stood there for a few moments, then squared her shoulders, lifted her head, and walked in.

The boys arrived a few minutes later, with the attorney, Lowery. They all started talking at once, until Dr. Sturgess raised his hands. "Do you want the whole hospital to hear you?" he said testily. "Let's go in the lounge; Jan's in with your father now, and there's nothing to do but wait."

It wasn't long, no more than five minutes, before Jan came out of her father's room; she looked worried. "Dr. Sturgess, he wants to see you. I told you I couldn't do it, he knows something's wrong." She started to cry.

Dr. Sturgess was on his feet with alacrity, and inside Duncan's room before anyone else could speak, leaving them to crowd around Jan.

Duncan looked up at Dr. Sturgess quizzically from under heavy brows, and smiled slightly. "What's the matter, Larry? Come on, you don't have to pull any punches with me. Aren't I going to make it, after all?" Dr. Sturgess sighed inwardly with relief, but it was short-lived; Duncan still had to be told about Vivian. "Why, you old buzzard, where'd you get an idea like that?" he said grumpily, to hide his emotions. "You'll probably outlast us all, with your hide. Hell, you'll be ready to go home in a few days—you've just got itchy feet."

Duncan stared at him steadily, and decided he was telling the truth. "Well, if it's not me, then why did Jan come in here with such a long face? She tried not to show it, but I could tell she was on the verge of tears; I know my daughter." A sudden thought hit him. "Oh my God, there's nothing wrong with the new baby, is there? Something that didn't show up at first, when Ben hit her?"

"Duncan, for heaven's sakes, relax. There's nothing wrong with Jan, or the baby, or you. For that matter, there's nothing wrong with your sons, either; Dwight's back in town." Well, he had assured him about everyone except Vivian, and now came the hard part. Always before, in a critical situation with a patient, somehow, he'd been able to find the right words when the time was actually at hand. But Duncan was his oldest and dearest friend, and the words just wouldn't come. Suddenly, he wished he were anyplace in the world except this room, at this moment.

Duncan waited for him to go on, his face expressionless. Larry had mentioned every member of his family except Vivian; something must have happened to Vivian. He waited for the pain to come, thinking of her hurt, or dead, but all he could think of was that Jan and the baby were alright, and selfish relief that he wasn't going to die. Larry looked so uncomfortable, that he finally broke the silence. "It's Vivian, then, isn't it. Is she dead, Larry?"

Dr. Sturgess looked at him in surprise. "Hell, no, Duncan, where'd you get that idea? No, she's not dead, she's not even hurt." He tried to think of some way to soften the blow, and gave up. "Oh, what the devil, there's just no way to break it to you gently, so I'm going to give it to you in plain talk. I can't tell you not to get upset, because I know you will, but think of your family, and all you have to live for. The facts are, Duncan, she's been stealing from the company."

Duncan exploded with laughter, and a sense of relief. "What is this, some sort of joke?" Then he looked at Larry, and he wasn't laughing; he was dead serious. "You really meant that, didn't you?"

Dr. Sturgess nodded. "You have to face it, friend; she's

been robbing you blind. Your sons and your attorney are just outside, and they've got all the facts. Dwight wasn't on a fishing trip, at least not that kind. He's been in South America, checking on some of your wells that supposedly dried up; they're pumping up a storm. I don't know how she did it, but it seems to have been going on for some time. The boys came to see me this morning; I don't understand all of it, I'm no businessman, they can explain it to you a lot better than I can." As Dr. Sturgess talked, he was watching Duncan closely, waiting for some reaction, some little sign that could be the beginning of another heart attack, but Duncan remained composed, except for the slight pulsing in his left temple. Otherwise, his face was implacable.

But behind the facade, he had taken it all in; he had been made a fool of. At Larry's first words, he had felt an overwhelming anger, which he managed to suppress with superhuman effort; he would deal with that later, when he was calmer, when he had all the facts. It wouldn't do to get overly excited now, there was the company to think of, and his family. He couldn't even afford the luxury of feeling bitter about Vivian now, he had to live, and the only way to live was to stay calm. And Vivian had really never been a part of his family. After the honeymoon, she had been more of a companion, a business partner; some business partner! She would have to go, of course; surprisingly, he felt a certain sense of loss. He had become used to her over the years. But he had never really thought of anyone except Jeanne as his wife; and to think he used to feel guilty at times about that!

"Duncan." Larry was talking to him. "I said, do you want to see the boys now?"

Duncan looked at him, and managed a slight smile. "In a minute, Larry, in a minute. A few more things I want to sort out in my mind first. Don't worry," he said, as Larry looked at him with concern, "I'll be just fine. Except I feel like a damn fool, being taken. Sit down, Larry, and relax for a few minutes. You look like you could use a break." Larry slumped in the bedside chair, relieved; Duncan would make it through this.

"I ought to take your blood pressure," he said.

"I think I'll need it taken more after I see my sons, and find out just how much she's taken me for." He tried to smile. "But right now, I feel all right. You know something funny, Larry? I think I'm going to miss her for a while. I'll have to change my will, of course, I'll never give her the house now, but I wouldn't think she'd want to stay in town anyway, would you? But it will seem empty, that great big house, with just me rattling around." Then he brightened, "Do you think Jan would like to move in with me? We've got that big yard, and with little Ben and the new baby, it would be like having a whole new family again."

"I'm sure she would, Duncan—the house she lived in with Ben certainly can't have anything but bad memories for her."

"You know," Duncan said slyly, "as bad as this thing may turn out, Jan's taken care of. She doesn't know it, but I've got life insurance policies and annuities that nobody knows about except my lawyer, and now you. Jeanne and I started them right after she was born—figured the boys could always look after themselves, but Jan was such a frail little thing. That's one thing I don't have to worry about."

Dr. Sturgess looked at him, his eyes slightly narrowed. He had seen this happen before, in cases where he had told a patient he was terminal. Sometimes the patient would push the truth to the back of his mind, until he could deal with it, and think of other things. He had a feeling Duncan was doing just that with Vivian's duplicity. He'd better get his sons and the attorney in here now, and get the worst over with before this state of euphoria wore off. He also decided he had better spend the night at the hospital, and ask Jan to stay close at hand.

"I'm going to have them come in now, Duncan," he said. "You rest for a few minutes, and I'll be right back."

"You don't have to tell them to take it easy with me," Duncan smiled. "I'm going to be fine, just fine." He sat up a little straighter, and punched the pillows behind his head.

Dr. Sturgess closed the door to Duncan's room behind him, and turned to find four sets of eyes looking at him anxiously. "Alright, he knows, and so far, he's taking it amazingly well. Jan, he wants you to stay with him after he gets Vivian out of the house."

Jan looked delighted. "Anything, Doctor. It's such a big, wonderful house, and it'll be marvelous for the ch . . . little Ben," she corrected herself hastily.

"Good," he nodded. "And for the rest of you, just give him the facts. Don't try to whitewash anything Vivian's done, but don't dwell on what a bitch she is, either. As for that man she has working for her, Alex something, there's no need to say you think there's something else going on between them. Anyway, you don't have any proof of that. Keep it as brief and concise as you can; I'm going to be in there with you, and if I see he's getting too excited, or too tired, that's it, and no arguments. Understood?"

They all nodded agreement, and after a few more words, trooped into their father's room.

Duncan looked at them all, then smiled at Dwight. "Well, my boy, I understand you've been on quite a fishing expedition."

"Yes, sir." Dwight looked uncomfortable.

"Lowery? Is it hard evidence?" he asked his attorney.

"Yes, Mr. Keith," Lowery said. "It's unrefutable. Mrs. Keith has bribed some of your foremen through an associate of hers, a tax consultant, and falsified records on some four wells in Bolivia that we know of for certain. We have pictures and sworn affadavits."

"Think we'll have to have a complete audit?" Duncan asked.

"To find out exactly how much she's taken from the company; yes, sir. But I don't think that it will be necessary to confront Mrs. Keith; and you know the entire Board of Directors would have to be informed."

"Don't want that, if we can avoid it." Duncan thought for a moment. "Approximately how much has she taken the company for, boys? Just an estimate."

Dwight and Scott looked at each other, then at the doctor. Scott spoke first. "About a million, give or take a little, Dad. But we can make some of it back on the wells she said were dried up; about a quarter of that, I estimate."

"That much?" Duncan's voice was low. He turned to Lowery. "I want you here first thing in the morning, so I can draw up a new will. In the meantime, everything that's been said in this room is confidential. As far as Vivian is concerned, until we have everything down pat, you just treat her normally, as though nothing has happened." He looked at Dr. Sturgess. "You think you can come up with some reason why I can't see her for a few days?"

"Sure, but why?" he asked.

"Because I have a little plan. I want everything cut and dried, nice and legal. Then the next time Vivian comes waltzing in here to visit me, I want all of you here, and we'll confront her together." He turned to Jan. "You don't have to be here, honey, it could get mighty nasty."

Dr. Sturgess objected. "Duncan, let the boys and Mr. Lowery handle this. I don't want you unnecessarily upset again."

"Larry, I'm looking forward to this, and you're not going to take it away from me." His voice was determined, and he smiled unpleasantly. "Besides, she'll be off-guard. And what can she say to me that I haven't said to myself in the last hour? That she tricked me, stole from me, lied to me? That I haven't been a husband to her in the last eight years? That she used me, used my children? No, I don't think she could say anything that would upset me more than any of those things. And you can't cheat me out of seeing the expression on her face when I tell her she not only doesn't get another cent from me, or the house, but that she has exactly twenty-four hours to get out bag and baggage, with only her personal belongings." He looked around him, at his children. "I'm not really a vengeful man. But don't you think that after eleven years of deceit, I should be allowed at least a half-hour of personal satisfaction?" He sighed, tiredly. "Then it will be done with, for once and for all, and we need never concern ourselves with that woman again." He turned to Larry. "Now, before you say it, I think I've had enough for one day, and I want to rest. Larry, can Jan stay with me for a little while, until I fall asleep?"

Dr. Sturgess nodded, and they said their goodbyes. Jan kissed him lightly on the forehead after they left, and sat down beside him.

"It'll be wonderful, Daddy, living with you again. The first thing I'm going to do is fire those horrible nurses Vivian hired, and get some nice, cheerful ones. Go to sleep, Daddy, and dream wonderful dreams. If it's another boy, I'm going to name him after you."

Duncan smiled at her, tired, but glad she was with him. She held his hand, and it wasn't long before he fell asleep, his mind at ease, knowing his daughter was close by.

Jack Wentworth arrived at the hospital promptly at five o'clock, as he did every day now. No more stopping by the local bar before he went home to change for an evening on the town, or entertaining prospective clients. All the entertaining was now done by his salesmen, to their utmost pleasure, while he attended to the paper work and office details. He wasn't really surprised that business had picked up; most potential buyers and sellers would rather do business with a fairly sober salesman than a drunken broker. Not that he'd stopped drinking entirely; there had been a few nights after he'd left Pam when he'd been so full of despair that he'd gone home and drunk himself into a stupor.

But every morning he was at his desk, and by the time the day was over, he was full of hope again. And every night, just before he entered Pam's room, he prayed there would be some difference in her. Sometimes, as he sat beside her and talked, he thought he saw a faint glimmer in her eyes, the barest change of expression; but then, it could be the changing light, or his imagination. Specialists had been called in, but there was little they could do; catatonia was an unknown quantity, and all he could do was hope, and pray, and be there.

Tonight was no different than any other night; the nurses had brushed her hair, and she was propped up in bed in a fresh nightgown. If she noticed he entered the room, she gave no sign. "Hello, Pam," he said as usual, and kissed her lightly on the forehead before sitting down beside her; there was no response, nor had he expected any.

He sighed dejectedly, slumped back in the chair and closed his eyes wearily, remembering the first time he had seen her like this. Kathy and he had gone to the hospital together, and if she hadn't been with him, he didn't know what he would have done. The first sight of Pam, looking for all the world like a living corpse, had sent him into a state of shock, and the panic he felt was like nothing he could have imagined. At first he thought she was dead, until he saw the slight but rhythmic breathing, the faint pulsing in her wrists. He barely remembered shouting at the doctors to do something, help her, anything. Vaguely, he recalled Kathy finally getting him out of there, and taking care of him while he got roaring drunk.

He opened his eyes and looked at Pam now; her expression hadn't changed. He wondered what was going on behind that deathlike mask, or was she in a void somewhere, just wandering in space, feeling nothing? No one could really be sure, the doctors said. And she might be like that for the rest of her life. But he couldn't let himself think that, he told himself firmly. She would come back to him, she had to, and then he could tell her how much he really loved her.

He thought about her father; God, how she must have hated going to see him, and he had been the one who forced her to do it. Well, God moves in mysterious ways; she had to face it with her father, and now he had to face it with her.

"Pam, I wish you knew I was here," he said to her softly, as he had so many times before. "I wish there was some way you could let me know, anything. I know this is all my fault; I should have told you from the very beginning about the hunting accident, but you forgot all about it, and your father and I thought it was for the best. You were so happy at the time, and so young. We didn't want you to suffer any more than you had to. And it wasn't your fault, Pam, really it wasn't. Oh honey, I shouldn't have made you go and see your father, either, not after he had that final stroke. But I didn't know what it was doing to you, I really didn't. Don't you see, I'm going through the same thing now that you had to go through with your father?" His voice broke, in spite of himself. "And I deserve it, honey, I deserve every bit of it; I should have told you years ago how much you meant to me, but you were so young. Oh God help me, what have I done to you, what have I done to both of us?" He started weeping, and laid his head down on the bed by her side. "So many years wasted, and for what? Because your father and I made a terrible mistake years ago, when we thought we were doing something for your own good. God, please let me reach her, let her hear me," he sobbed.

Jack was lost in his emotions, oblivious to anything except

his own pain, and the pain he had felt for Pam for a long time. Gradually, he cried himself out, but stayed in the same position, exhausted and spent. He began to feel a little ashamed; he had never lost control of himself so completely. Slowly, he had the sensation that something had changed; he started to lift his head, but there was a slight weight on it. He shifted slowly, and found Pam's slender and fragile hand had moved, and was touching him lightly. Gradually, he reached for it with his own, and looked into her eyes.

They were expressionless, but as he looked closer, he could see tiny tear drops in them; just then one rolled gently down her cheek. "Oh, my darling," his voice was humble. "I know you heard me. Pam, I love you so much—and you will get better, I know you will now." He looked up at the ceiling, feeling a peace and tranquility that he had never experienced before. "Thank you, God. Thank you."

Then he looked back at Pam. "Sleep now, my love. I'll stay with you until you do—and I'll be here when you wake up. You're on the way back to me, Pam, and we'll never be apart again." He thought he caught a glimmer of understanding before she closed her eyes, and he had never been happier in his entire life.

Maude opened the door a crack, peered out, then her mouth dropped open in surprise. "Kathy!" she swung the door open. "Well, I just. . . ." she gestured towards the phone. "You just. . ." she threw up her hands. "Well, I never! I thought you were calling from Monrovia. Where were you?"

"I was up at Turner's," Kathy chuckled, and threw her arms around her. "Oh, Maude, it's so good to see you. It was just an impulse, I had the weekend off, so I decided to drive up and surprise you. I got here early and I didn't want to call the office, so I've been driving for hours." Her expression changed. "Of course, if you have plans, Topsy and I can always stay at a motel. Do you?" she asked anxiously.

"Does it look like I do?" she answered, gesturing at her blue chenille bathrobe. "I've got a potroast in the frig, and we can sit and talk while it's cooking—or would you rather have something else?"

"Oh, Maude, I don't want you fussing; why don't we just sit and talk for a while, then later on, you can throw on something and we can go to *Barney's*; there's so much to catch up on."

Maude looked at her and raised an eyebrow. "Trouble in paradise, I gather?"

"Well . . . not exactly. John's wife was due home today—I told you about John; and Dwight's out of town; and well . . . everybody seems caught up in their own problems. It wasn't only that, exactly; to tell you the truth, I was just plain homesick."

"I thought Monrovia was home now."

"Oh, Maude," Kathy said impatiently, "I was born here, for heaven's sakes, you know this will always be my home. I drove around a lot today, all the way down Sunset to the beach; I even drove by my old apartment."

"Oh, really?" Maude's tone changed imperceptibly. "Well, come on, take off your things; do you want some coffee, or can I get you a drink? Why don't I make you a drink while you get your things out of the car? I'll get Topsy some water; did you bring her food?" She started to the kitchen, "You want bourbon or scotch?"

"Bourbon, thanks; yes, I brought her food, I'll get my things in a minute," Kathy called after her, glancing around the warm and cozy living room. "Maude, where's my philodendron?" she asked.

"Oh, that," she paused, "I'm sorry, Kitten, but it died; must have been from moving it."

"You know, I didn't see the other plants I gave you, either. But I saw some just like them on the terrace of my old apartment."

Maude was in the kitchen now, and she didn't hear anything except the clinking of ice. Kathy waited patiently until she came back.

"Okay, Kathy. To tell you the truth, I'm just no good with plants, just haven't got a green thumb, I guess." Maude was red in the face.

"So you just left them there, for some strangers?" Kathy was outraged. "If I'd known that, I'd have taken them with me."

Maude's face brightened. "Well, didn't you see them? They're doing just fine where they are. I go by there myself every once in a while to see how they're doing."

"Who has the place now?" Kathy asked curiously. "Did you give them my patio furniture and the rest of the stuff I didn't send for, too?"

"Of course not," she said indignantly, "you get a bill every month for the storage, don't you? And you should be thanking me for finding a garage to store the stuff in, it's a lot cheaper than Bekin's."

"Very cheap; in fact, I didn't think any garage was going for five dollars a month, not in Hollywood. And you still haven't answered me; who's renting my apartment?"

"Kathy, you keep calling it your apartment; you only rented it. What difference does it make?"

Kathy shrugged. "Just curiosity, I suppose; after all, they have my plants, and the patio furniture is just like mine, I wondered how much they'd changed the inside. You know how much I loved that apartment, Maude." She grimaced. "I even miss that hideous painting Bruce bought in Mexico City. My place in Monrovia is nothing like it; even the few things I sent for just don't fit, they seem out of place, somehow." She brightened, "Maybe we should go over to that garage tomorrow, and see if we can find some more things I can use out there."

"Oh, I don't think that's a very good idea, Kathy," Maude said hastily, "why would you want to dredge up the past?"

Kathy looked at her quietly for a moment. "Because I can't forget the past, Maude. I've been gone for over four months, I've slept with three different men, and two of them are in love with me. I've made a lot of new friends, and I'm moving in the best circles. But I'm having nightmares practically every night, and I'm not happy. You want to know something? Driving up here, the thought of seeing you, talking about old times, has made me happier than I've been in weeks." She sat there thinking, while Maude sipped her coffee. "You know," she said slowly, "I guess I thought when I left town, that things would be different, that I'd find some sort of . . ." she paused, groping for the right word, "Utopia, or something close to it. But people aren't all that different, really; at least, not in Monrovia. They all have their problems; one of my best new friends is in a catatonic state right now, and another just had a cancer operation. And I'm going with a married man."

"Give yourself time, Kathy; after all, four months isn't very long. And you're right, people aren't all that different, they're just more open about things in Hollywood. But this doctor you're going with certainly isn't any answer; I don't know, Kathy, you just seem to jump from one impossible situation to another. Maybe I was wrong about Bruce." (There, she'd said the unspoken word between them.) "At least, he made you happy most of the time. And I don't like the idea of these nightmares; have you told the doctor about them?"

She shook her head. "I've tried, once or twice, but something always held me back. Maybe I really don't want to know; I don't want to talk about this any more."

Maude finished her coffee and looked at Kathy's drink. "Go get your things, honey," she paused, "and take Topsy with you, I don't want her wetting on my rugs. I'll fix you another drink, let's go to *Barney's* later, when the crowd's thinned out a little."

Kathy got up and stretched. "Okay." She started putting Topsy's leash back on. "And when I get back, I want to know who's living in my apartment." She paused at the door. "You think they'd be home? Maybe we could stop by and see it, do you think?"

"Oh, I don't even have the telephone number, I don't think that would be a good idea at all," she said hurriedly. "Anyway, it's Friday night, they're probably out for the evening."

Kathy walked down to the car slowly, puzzled. Maude certainly didn't want her to go near that apartment again. And it was certainly odd that she didn't have the phone number, considering she'd let them have her plants. She had the odd suspicion that the patio furniture was her own, too. She got her suitcase out of the trunk, waited until Topsy wet, then walked back up the hill again. When she got to Maude's door, she thought she heard the phone click, but she couldn't be certain.

They sat and talked for hours, with Maude doing most of the talking. After all, Kathy had left Monrovia to get away from her problems, so what was the use of dredging them all up again? She did tell her about the nightmare, though, and Maude looked at her oddly when she finished. Her only comment, though, was, "Well, you've always been afraid of water. If you don't want to tell the guy you're going with, why not see another psychiatrist? Maybe he could help you."

Kathy shrugged. "I've thought of that—but you know something? Sometimes I think I'm afraid to find out what it means. Sounds silly, doesn't it?" Then she changed the subject. Now, tell me more about the agency, and what's been going on.''

Maude was more than glad to oblige; business was booming, Logan was the same as ever. They'd taken on several new accounts, one of them an old movie ranch location that was really on the skids. ''I don't know, though, it just may pick up, they're spending a fortune renovating the place, and they changed the name. Television western series are the 'in' thing now, so they're using the place a lot. Then on the weekends, it's open to the public, for a price; you know, guest appearances, stuff like that. Right now, it's still running in the red, what with the remodeling, upkeep and guest appearances—but you know Logan, once he sets his mind to something, nothing's going to change it. He's even put two new ad people on just to handle the ranch alone.''

''Who's got my job now?'' Kathy asked.

Maude groaned. ''I knew you'd get around to that, sooner or later. There's been a bunch of them, and each one's worse than the last. This latest one's a real pip—last week she booked two TV series on the same street on the same day. There was all hell to pay, and you know what she said? She just giggled, and said, 'Well, they'll sure have a pretty big cast, won't they?' Logan fired her on the spot.''

''Think he'd hire me back?'' Kathy asked idly, inspecting her nail polish.

''Like a shot, and you know it.'' Maude looked at her shrewdly. ''Kathy, you're not thinking of moving back here, are you? I know, I said I didn't like the idea of your sleeping with that doctor; but moving backwards isn't the answer, either. You know I like you, Kathy; hell, most of the time I think of you as my daughter.'' She smiled, ''A delinquent daughter, but a daughter, nevertheless.'' She thought for a moment, then got up. ''You know what? I'm going to have a drink.'' She put out her hand for Kathy's empty glass. ''After all, it isn't every day you come to visit me.''

349

Kathy looked surprised. "You hardly ever drink; what is this, another lecture coming on?"

"Sort of," Maude answered, and went to the kitchen. "Why not, you never listen to me anyway."

"I certainly do," Kathy said indignantly.

Maude came back with their drinks and handed Kathy hers. "Okay, you listen, but you never take my advice. You're a very pretty girl, Kathy, and you've got brains; the trouble is, you just don't use them." She took a long swallow of her drink, and continued. "The first time I told you this was what? Four years ago? You were twenty two then, and you're twenty six now, almost twenty seven. I can't see that you've changed very much. Don't get me wrong, I love you, or I wouldn't even bother talking to you like this. And when I said you've got brains, I meant it; you're intelligent, and you're quick to learn—but you're just not smart about men. When you left this town, I was real sorry to see you go, but I was happy for you. You weren't getting anywhere here, except maybe older. It took real guts for you to pick up and leave, and I was proud of you. And now here you are, just four months later, mixed up with another married man, and talking about coming back."

"I really didn't mean it; about coming back, that is," Kathy said quickly.

"Okay, so maybe you didn't; so you'll go back to Monrovia, and take up with that married doctor again—it's the same difference." Maude paused, trying to decide if she'd said enough. No, she'd started this, and she might as well finish it. "Kathy, I know you don't like what I've said, and you're going to like this even less," she said, feeling her way cautiously, "but did you ever stop to think that you've slept with an awful lot of men for your age?"

"I never slept with anyone else when I was with Bruce," she defended herself heatedly. "Or John—and I didn't cheat on Fred when I was married to him, either."

"You didn't cheat on Fred because he made you feel inadequate, you told me all about that; and you were in love with Bruce, so there was no need. And you've hardly been with the doctor long enough to have had the opportunity. But what about all the men in between? Did it ever occur to you that you just don't like being alone?"

Kathy looked at her with anger, but she didn't answer. What could she say? Everything she said was true. "I can't argue with you, Maude. Sometimes I feel like being alone, but then I start thinking about Bruce, and I just can't stand it. Oh God, Maude, do you think I'll ever get over him?"

"You will in time, Kathy. But not in four months, maybe not even in four years. But sleeping around isn't the answer. I think that's why you picked another married man, because there's no permanence in it; you sure got rid of the single one, Dwight, in a hurry."

"Well, Dwight was a mistake from the beginning; but let's not talk about him." She brushed him aside with a wave of her hand. "Maude, we've been sitting here talking about everything under the sun, except Bruce. How is he? Is he in town, is he going with another girl?"

"I was wondering how long it would take you to get around to that," there was a hint of sarcasm in her voice. "That's the real reason you drove up here, isn't it?"

"Of course not," Kathy said irritably, "but it's only natural that I'd want to know about him, isn't it? After all, we spent almost four years together; and I never asked you, not once, on the phone. But being here, seeing the old apartment . . . it's funny, how you remember all the good things that happened, and forget all the bad, isn't it? So tell me, Maude, please."

"Okay, okay, I'll tell you. As far as I know, he seems just fine, but then Bruce always was a very private person. I'm sure he goes out with other girls, you certainly didn't think he'd just be pining away all this time, did you? I don't know of anyone in particular, but then he wouldn't tell me—he never discussed you with me."

"You mean," Kathy said slowly, "he never even asked if you knew where I was, or anything?"

"Of course not," Maude said impatiently, "the man has some pride." She got up and headed for the stairs. "I guess I better throw something on so we can go eat, I'm famished."

"You didn't tell me if he was in town or not."

Maude paused on the stairs, and hesitated for a minute. "No, he's not, and for your sake, I'm glad. He's due in next week, but you'll be back in Monrovia by then, and you've got enough problems to straighten out without seeing Bruce."

"He might fly in early," Kathy said hopefully.

Maude shook her head. "I called the place he stays when he's in town when you were getting your things out of the car, and there wasn't any answer. The exchange doesn't expect him until Monday."

Kathy sipped her drink slowly, waiting for Maude. Maybe it was for the best, after all. Bruce had probably forgotten all about her by now. She could picture him in her mind, a different girl on his arm every night, each one more glamorous than the one before. She passed her hand wearily over her forehead; this had been a bad idea, she shouldn't have come. All she'd done was rake up old memories that were best forgotten. She had a headache, she wasn't the least bit hungry now, and the thought of going to *Barney*'s didn't appeal to her in the least.

The doorbell rang suddenly, bringing her out of her reverie. She called up to Maude. "I don't know who it could be at this time of night, but go ahead and answer it," she yelled down. "Can't you shut up that dog?"

Topsy was already at the door, jumping and barking insanely. She always did that when someone came to the door, but not with this intensity, not since Bruce . . . Kathy stood up nervously, and her palms began to sweat. No, it couldn't be, and she tried to put the thought out of her mind. Just the same, as she walked toward the door, her heart started to pound heavily. She stood there for a moment, then opened the door quickly, forgetting to put the chain on.

Neither one of them spoke for what seemed like a very long time; they looked in each other's eyes, each searching deeply. He was the first one to move; he put down his suitcase slowly and reached out his arms to her, and she came to him willingly. It was as though the four months in Monrovia had never been, and Bruce and Kathy had never been apart.

Chapter 14

Vivian hung up the phone gently, feeling slightly relieved, but puzzled. Dr. Sturgess had caught her just as she was about to leave for the hospital. He was running some new tests, and Duncan couldn't have any visitors today. No, not tonight either, he'd be much too tired. "No, it's nothing serious, Vivian, and I don't want you getting upset about nothing. He's just fine, but Dr. Victor and I had a consulation, and we feel these tests are necessary before he can come home. There's absolutely nothing for you to worry about, but for the time being, I want him to have complete rest. You might do with a little rest, yourself," he added, "you looked a little pale the last time I saw you."

She was about to tell him about last night, then she decided this was not the time. "You're sure there's nothing wrong? Can I call him, at least?"

Dr. Sturgess had hesitated. "Better wait until tomorrow, Viv; then I'll have Duncan tell you."

Strange, she thought. Well, there was nothing she could do about it. Too bad he hadn't called an hour earlier; she could have stayed in bed. Now she was up and dressed, with nothing to do. She wandered around the empty living room, thinking. She hadn't worried about Alex; after all, it took time to set these things up, especially in South American countries. But he'd been gone a week now, and he could have at least called. She wished that she'd set up some definite time schedule for him to contact her.

She could try calling him at the Oliva—she had mentioned the hotel to him before he left, because Dwight always stayed there. He, on the other hand, may have made other plans; and possibly used a different name. She glanced at her watch; there was a four hour time difference, so it was almost seven in the evening there now. She decided to call; after all, she always paid the phone bills, Duncan never looked at them. She waited, tapping her foot, while the operators took an interminable length of time, until she was finally told there would be a three hour delay. "Never mind, operator; I'll place the call later." No way was she going to sit there and stew for three hours. Instead, she decided to call Irene; she really should see how she was getting along.

Irene lay on the sofa in the downstairs living room, idly flipping through the pages of the latest fashion magazine. She was feeling fine now, although she still got tired in the afternoon. She put the magazine aside and smiled slightly as she gazed out at her garden, sparkling in the afternoon sun. Life really was a wonderful thing; funny, she thought, people seldom stopped to realize that until they'd almost lost it.

And Ted; they had become so much closer since her operation. It was a gradual thing, and it was still happening, but they were sharing things together again, like they had in the beginning. She sighed, and thought of all the lost years between them. She hadn't even realized just how far they'd drifted apart. There had been times when she'd almost hated him, and she was sure he had felt the same. But everything was different now; he was gentle and kind, but not too much so, not the way you'd treat an invalid. They were sleeping together again, although they couldn't have sex for at least two more weeks, the doctor said. Sometimes they slept in her room, sometimes in his, but always together.

She smiled again, thinking about last night—they had slept in her room. "Ted? Are you asleep?" she had asked him.

"Almost," he had grunted.

"Ted, you hate this room, don't you?"

"No, I don't hate it, I just think it's too . . . frilly."

She propped herself up on her elbow. "You know something? So do I." She gestured around her. "But I want to explain something to you. When I had this room redone, it was sort of. . ." she searched for the right words, "of an escape hatch. I could walk in here, and just shut out the rest of the world. You know how angry I used to get at April when she called it my Arabian Nights? Well, she was right. All my problems, the fights we used to have, just seemed to fade away. I guess that sounds pretty foolish." Then she added, "But I don't need an escape hatch anymore."

He reached over and pulled her in his arms. "No, it doesn't sound foolish at all. And you know something? I always thought you did it to get back at me for something, because you knew how much I hated all that frou-frou stuff." They both laughed together.

"Well, I'm glad that's settled," Irene said. "Tomorrow night, we'll start planning on how to redo the room, so we'll both like it."

Irene glanced at her watch; almost three-thirty. Tonight, after dinner, they'd start planning on how to do the bedroom. she didn't want a decorator; she wanted everything to be what she and Ted picked out together. She had mentioned to April that they were redecorating, and asked her if she wanted anything from her bedroom, but April hadn't seemed interested. Irene frowned.

She was worried about April; the last few days she had been wan and listless, barely picking at her food. She hadn't gone to the Club, or hardly even left her room except to go to the mailbox. Not that she ever showed Irene any of her mail; she had no idea who was writing to her, but she had seen some foreign newspapers. Maybe it was some boy she was moping over, but she certainly hadn't mentioned anyone. He must have stopped writing her, that was it. She felt guilty, somehow, that she and Ted were so happy now, and April was so miserable. If only April would confide in her; but that was asking the impossible. Their relationship was better now than it ever had been, but it had been damaged years before, and you could never undo the past. You could forgive, but you could never forget. And April had never forgotten; neither had Irene, and no matter how happy she told herself she was, the nagging guilt would always remain. Maybe she should try to talk to April—but not today. She'd wait until next week, then they could start making plans for Christmas, and maybe April would open up to her. After all, it would be the first Christmas that she'd been home for three years.

The phone rang, and she heard Anne pick it up. She came in the room a moment later. "It's Mrs. Keith, Mrs. Enwright. I told her I'd see if you were awake."

Irene made a face; she was certainly not in the mood to talk to Vivian today. "Tell her I'm asleep, Anne, and you'll give me her message. Is that corned beef and cabbage I smell?"

Anne grinned. "It sure is, Mrs. Enwright. When I heard you and the mister talking about redoing that bedroom at breakfast, I figured you'd want something special for dinner tonight."

Irene smiled after her. She must have hated the room as much as the rest of the family. Well, goodbye, Arabian Nights!

Duncan was propped up in bed, ready and waiting, when

Lowery arrived at the hospital room promptly at nine o'clock Saturday morning. He had cancelled his usual golf date, but this was one time he didn't mind in the least. He had never really liked Mrs. Keith, her superior attitude irritated him at times, but it was more than that. He had watched her at the board meetings, and there was something about her that he had never quite trusted. But he had never even dreamed of what she was doing to the company. As far as saying anything to Duncan about his feelings, that would have been way out of line.

"Right on time," Duncan greeted him with a smile. "You brought the will, of course, but did you bring Jan's policies?"

Lowery shook his head. "They're in the safety deposit box; but don't worry, I have copies of them in my safe. I went over them last night, and they can't be touched, not even if you had to go into bankruptcy. I made a rough estimate, and with the accrued interests, she'll have enough to last her for life; enough to send that son of hers to the best college, too."

"Bankruptcy! I just can't believe it's that bad."

"It won't be that bad," Lowery assured him, "but we'll know better by tonight. Dwight and Keith are over at the company now, with two of my best auditors; they can spot a phony account a mile away. After all, your sons are really only amateurs at this sort of thing, although I must say, they've done a damn good job."

Duncan nodded. "Good thinking; now, let's get down to the will. Do I have to give her anything at all? After all, the house was mine before I married her."

"I've been thinking about that; you did give it to her in your last will, but that can be easily changed. I don't think she'll fight it, under the circumstances. But the things you bought her after you were married is another matter. She's acquired quite a few furs and jewelry, and if I remember correctly, you spent quite a large amount on your honey-

moon—some antiques, and a few paintings, I believe?"
Lowery opened his briefcase, and started spreading papers on
the bedside table.

"Good grief!" Duncan groaned. "I'd forgotten the Renoir
and the Degas—they cost me a small fortune! And all those
other things she bought—do you mean to tell me she can
keep all that? I'd rather rip those paintings down the middle
and burn the furniture, before I let her have them. Do you
actually mean to tell me she can keep that stuff, after what
she's done to me?" Duncan almost yelled, his face starting to
turn red.

"For God's sakes, Duncan, lower your voice, and calm
down," Lowery almost whispered. "Otherwise, they'll throw
me out of here and we won't get a thing accomplished. Now
just listen, and don't interrupt me until I'm through; there
are a lot of angles here. If she went to court on this, yes, just
possibly she might; but she might also go to jail. You don't
want a court action any more than she will."

Lowery settled back comfortably. "What I'm about to
suggest isn't exactly ethical, but I've never liked your wife,
and I'd like to see her get what's coming to her. However, my
personal opinion of her hasn't colored my vision. You know
this Alex Dunbar, the tax consultant the boys mentioned
yesterday? Well, I saw some pictures of him that Dwight got
somehow down in Cochabamba. He's not a bad looking guy;
not good looking, but not bad, just a little sleazy. And he's
about Vivian's age. I wouldn't bring this up, but you said
yourself yesterday that you hadn't been a husband to Vivian
in eight years. So, if we accuse her of having an affair with
this guy, along with everything else, I think she'll back down
pretty fast."

"So she's done that to me, too." Duncan's voice was low.

Lowery laughed. "Hell, I don't know, and who cares? It's
just another charge to throw at her when we confront her. I'll

have all the papers ready for her to sign, and she won't know what hit her." Then he added, as an afterthought, "I'd let her keep the furs, though; not much resale value. But not the jewelry, except maybe her wedding ring."

Duncan looked at him between narrowed lids. He had never realized just how cold-blooded Lowery could be. Smart, though. "In other words, we bluff."

Lowery nodded, and started gathering up his papers. "We bluff; and believe me, it'll work. Now you better get some rest. I'm going over to the company now, and see how they're getting along. And Duncan," he paused, "you better be prepared for some hard figures when we're through with the books. Just remember, you've got a helluva lot of money tied up in those two paintings alone, if it comes down to the wire. I know what that company means to you, and you're not going to lose it."

Duncan lay there for a long time after Lowery left, thinking. He knew he had to call Vivian sooner or later, or she'd be over, regardless of what Larry had told her. He also knew if he saw her, he couldn't pull it off. He'd tell her the tests had tired him out, and would she mind not coming over until tomorrow. If she caught something funny in his voice, he'd tell her the doctor had just given him a shot. He thought about tomorrow, when she walked in his room and they'd all be waiting for her. He even began to feel a little sorry for her. Then he remembered Alex Dunbar. He reached for the phone, and dialed his home.

"Kathy?" Maude yelled down the stairs, struggling with her zipper. Lord, her clothes were getting tight; every week, faithfully, she promised herself she'd go on a diet. Like this weekend, for example. Again, she'd planned to start, and now she was going to *Barney's Beanery*, and she was famished. She'd probably eat everything in sight, and she never could resist their pies. "Who was that at the door?"

There was no answer, but the dog had stopped barking. "Kathy?" she called again.

"A very nice looking man with a suitcase," Kathy called up to her, and giggled.

"Oh, quit your kidding, who was it?" she asked again, as she put on her shoes.

"Oh Maude, as if you didn't know—no wonder you didn't want to go to *Barney's* until later."

"What in the world are you talking about?" Maude came out of her room, and stopped at the head of the stairs. "Oh My God," she said flatly, clutching the railing. "It's you. You're not supposed to be here until Monday."

Kathy looked from one to the other, puzzled. "I don't get it. Maude, didn't you arrange all this?"

"I most certainly did not," she snorted indignantly. "Bruce, what are you doing here, anyway?"

Bruce shrugged. "I don't know, really. I was going to fly in Monday, then suddenly this morning, I decided to come today. I called the exchange from the airport, and they said you'd called—so here I am." He smiled at her pleasantly. "What did you want?"

"I wanted to make sure that you weren't in town, that's what," she said bluntly. "Nothing personal, Bruce."

He laughed outright at that, then turned to Kathy. "And what about you? Are you back to stay, or what?" His eyes were twinkling, as though he was thoroughly enjoying this. "Did you want to make sure I wasn't in town, too?"

"I didn't even know she'd called you," she said irately. "No, I'm not back to stay, I just came up to see Maude for the weekend. That's funny," she said thoughtfully, "I just decided this morning, and so did you—that's like precognition, isn't it?"

"Precognition, my foot," Maude said sarcastically, "Just plain bad luck, if you ask me."

"Speaking of precognition," Bruce said, "it seems to me

361

that you two lovely ladies were about to go out—to eat, I would imagine. I'm starving myself, so could I induce you both to join me?''

Kathy looked at Maude with so much pleading in her eyes that Maude melted. So much for a large thick juicy steak, french fries and lemon chiffon pie. ''Actually, Bruce,'' she lied, ''I really was going to start on my diet tonight, but then Kathy arrived out of the blue, and the truth of the matter is, I'd rather not. We've spent all evening talking, and I'm kind of tired.''

''You sure you don't want to go with us?'' Kathy said half-heartedly.

''Yes, I'm sure.'' Kathy looked so happy, that for a moment, Maude got a little angry; she didn't have to look so doggone pleased at leaving her alone like this. Then she relented; after all, she'd been young once herself. She kissed her on the cheek. ''Take care, Kitten.''

Kathy put the leash back on Topsy, picked up her purse and coat, and they started toward the door.

''Wait a minute,'' Maude said, trying to play it straight. ''Haven't you forgotten something?''

''What?'' Kathy looked around her.

Maude gestured toward her suitcase, and Kathy blushed. Bruce laughed, and picked it up. ''Thanks, Maude. You think of everything. And thanks for calling me tonight. You know, otherwise, I might have missed Kathy altogether. We'll call you tomorrow. Lunch, maybe?'' He blew her a kiss as they went out the door.

They didn't talk until they reached the street. Kathy was full of questions, but she was suddenly shy. Did he have another girl—had he been true to her? But that would give him the right to ask her, and she certainly didn't want that.

When they reached the street, he stopped. ''Wait a minute; I've got a company car, and I assume you have yours. Do you want me to follow you, or pick it up tomorrow?''

She didn't want to let him out of her sight. "I'll pick it up tomorrow."

The minute they were in his car, he pulled her in his arms and kissed her deeply. Her shyness left her as suddenly as it had come, and everything was as it should be. The last four months were forgotten, and her love for him was greater than she had ever thought possible.

Finally, reluctantly, he released her. "Where do you want to eat?" his vice was low, husky.

"I couldn't eat a bite," she said happily, "but you must be starved."

He shook his head in the darkness. "I ate on the plane. I was wondering how I could manage to get through another dinner."

She sighed, contentedly. "That's good. Let's just go to your place. Where are you staying now?" she asked.

"You'll see," he grinned through the darkness as he started the car. "It's not too far from your old apartment."

"I drove by there today." Suddenly, she sat up straight. "Bruce, did you know that Maude gave all my plants to whoever rented my apartment? I don't think that was a very nice thing to do. And I suspect she let them have my patio furniture, too, although she says she didn't." She sighed. "I hate to think of anyone else living there; do you know who they are?"

He drove for a few minutes before answering. "I've met them." His tone was non-committal. "They seem like pretty nice people—you want to stop by for a few minutes?"

"Bruce!" Kathy was shocked. Maude had been nice enough to beg off dinner, so they could be alone, and he wanted to visit some strangers. She was not only shocked, she was hurt. Well, if he wasn't all that anxious to be alone with her, two could play at that game. And she was damned if she'd let him know how she felt. "Don't you think it's a little late?" she said, rather coldly. "It's almost eleven; they could be in bed, or out somewhere. It is Friday night, you know."

"Well, we'll stop and have a drink, and I'll call them. *Cock 'n Bull* alright with you?"

"Fine," she said shortly, settling back and folding her arms. Then she remembered her lipstick and her hair, and hastily reached for her purse; she must look a mess.

The *Cock 'n Bull* was crowded, as usual; and the bar was three deep. It took Bruce a while to get their drinks, and Kathy looked around her; there wasn't a soul she knew, and there were no empty tables. The evening certainly wasn't turning out the way she expected. Finally, he came back, took a quick sip of his drink, and handed her the glasses.

"Mind holding these while I go call? Sorry there's no place to sit—but then, we won't be here long." He looked down at her, grinning.

Kathy was beginning to get angry; surely he must realize she wasn't happy with this situation, but he seemed oblivious. Maybe Maude was right after all; maybe she hadn't given Monrovia a long enough chance. Her feet were beginning to hurt, and the noise and smoke in the bar were giving her a headache. She drank her drink quickly, then out of spite, drank half of Bruce's.

He was back sooner than she expected, and she handed him his half-filled glass. He looked at her quizzically, but made no comment. "Well, we're in luck, they're home, and said to come right over." He downed what was left in his glass in one gulp. "That is, unless you want another?"

She didn't bother to answer him, and started walking towards the door. They had to wait a while for the car, and Bruce breathed in the cold clean air appreciatively. "Beautiful weather for this time of year; you should have seen New York, it was colder than the devil when I left."

She couldn't believe all this; they hadn't seen each other for months, and he was talking about the weather! He seemed completely unaware of her attitude, although she had certainly made it plain to him that she wasn't at all happy. "Just who are these people, anyway? Do they know I have a dog with me? I'm certainly not going to leave her in the car very long."

"Oh, I told them about Topsy; they said to bring her up, too."

"They said to bring a dog up, when they don't even know if she's housebroken or not? And you still haven't told me who they are."

"Ah . . . Peterson," he hesitated slightly, "Dick and Jo Peterson. Joanne, I mean. You'll like them."

"Do we have to stay very long?"

Something in her expression must have gotten through to him, and his mood changed. He cupped her chin in his hand, and looked down at her tenderly. "Not if you don't want to, Kitten," he said softly. "But let's wait until we get there."

They didn't talk much in the car, not until they started up the hill to her old apartment. "I hope I don't cry, and make a fool out of myself. Bruce, have they changed it much?"

"You'll see, in a few minutes. I think you'll like it."

He drove around to the rear, and into the underground garage. Topsy started jumping up and down, once they were on home territory. Riding up in the elevator brought back all the old memories. Suddenly, she didn't want to see the apartment any more—she wanted to remember it the way it was. She clutched Bruce's arm as they reached the floor.

"Bruce, let's not go; I don't want to see the place after all, not with strangers living in it. It just won't be the same anymore."

Bruce looked at her intently. "Does it really mean that much to you?"

"It really does. I know it must sound silly to you, and sentimental, but I don't want to see the place all changed. I want to remember it the way it was. Couldn't I just wait here, while you go tell them I got sick, or something?" she pleaded.

He sighed, then reached in his pocket, searching for something. "I really wanted this to be more of a surprise." He brought out his key ring, and started going through it. "You would have known in a minute, anyway. There," he said, detaching a key and handing it to her, "I don't even know anybody named Peterson."

She looked at him, puzzled for a moment, then realization swept over her. "Oh, Bruce," she threw her arms around him, "you kept the apartment." She had dropped Topsy's leash, and the dog had run down the hall, scratching at the door to get in. Kathy ran after her, fumbled with the key, but there were tears in her eyes, and she couldn't get it to fit.

"Here, let me." Bruce opened the door and switched on the lights. Kathy looked around her in delight—nothing was changed, except for the few small things she'd had Maude send her. "Of course, it looks a little bare without all the pillows you took with you; then, I had to buy new dishes and flatware. Otherwise, it's pretty much the same—except it's been awfully empty without you." He closed the door and wrapped his arms around her. "There now, no more tears."

"How did you know I'd be back?" her voice was muffled against him.

"I didn't," he said drily, "But I had to have someplace to stay while I'm in town, and I didn't think you'd really mind my using your furniture." He released her gently. "Now, I'm going back down to the car for our bags. Here's some money." He handed her two fives and a ten dollar bill.

"What's this for?"

"I thought we might get hungry later. So, while I was supposed to be calling the mythical Petersons, I was calling Kosher Murphy's for some cold cuts and stuff. I told them there'd be a five dollar tip for delivering so late.'' He kissed her on the tip of her nose.

He left to get the bags, and she started wandering around the apartment. First, she pulled the drapes and looked down at the city sprawled beneath her. She couldn't quite believe she was back here again. Then she went out to the kitchen to inspect the dishes he had bought. Blue and white Spode, much like the pattern she'd taken with her. She looked in the refrigerator; it was well stocked with liquor and soft drinks, but the only food was a half-filled jar of mustard. Then a sudden thought struck her, and she hurried to the bedroom, looking for traces that another woman had been there. Not that she could blame him, she told herself, she was just curious—so why did she fell so damn guilty about snooping?

At first glance there was nothing. All her things were gone from the dresser, of course, replaced by a few of Bruce's. Then she got down on her hands and knees and felt under the bed for . . . what? A hairpin, or bobby pin, maybe? Nothing. Next, she inspected the bathroom thoroughly, and the medicine chest. Nothing incriminating there. The closet proved equally disappointing. She looked at the bed again, and decided to try the other side. She was down on her knees again, reaching as far as she could in all directions, when she suddenly heard Bruce's voice behind her.

''What are you doing?'' he asked curiously. She looked up slowly, and could feel her face getting beet red, thinking of how ridiculous she must look. Bruce was leaning against the door jamb, his arms folded nonchalantly.

''Uh. . . .'' she tried to think fast. ''I think I lost an earring.''

''Under the bed?'' his voice was teasing. ''Besides, you weren't wearing earrings.''

She struggled to her feet, brushing herself off, and feeling utterly absurd. She tried to think of something to say, but nothing sounded plausible, even to herself. "Okay, you win," she said guiltily, "I was snooping." She looked at him suspiciously. "How long have you been standing there?"

He burst out laughing. "Kathy, you are completely incorrigible. I have been watching your utterly charming behind long enough to be concerned that you'd wrench your back. And that wouldn't do at all, would it?" He tried to be serious for a moment. "Just to spare you from asking me; no, there haven't been any other women, except at parties, but never in this apartment. Your bed has been unsullied, except by me." The doorbell rang. "That must be the man from the delicatessen."

She picked up her suitcase and flung it on the bed, her feelings still rumpled. Oh my God, she thought, she didn't have a thing that was sexy to wear. Not that she ever slept in anything when she slept with Bruce, but what about the morning? All she had with her was her terry cloth robe. Well, it was too late to do anything about that now; tomorrow she'd go shopping. Bruce had said there hadn't been any other women, at least in this apartment. She paused, thinking about the way he'd phrased his remark. Then she shrugged, and put it out of her mind; she wasn't going to let anything spoil their weekend. She shivered with anticipation, and Monday morning seemed miles away.

Vivian sat at her dressing table, applying her makeup with extra care, as she sipped her third cup of coffee. Alex had finally called her last night, and assured her that everything was well in hand. He had all the necessary falsified documents that would assure the company that any further drilling would be throwing good money after bad, and they would be in her office Monday morning. Then one of her dummy companies could walk in and buy them out for a song. Everything had been taken care of, and all the loose ends were neatly tied up. She would close the deal herself on

Monday, and nobody would be the wiser. Then why was she so nervous and tense?

This apprehension had started when Dr. Sturgess called her on Friday, and hadn't stopped since. Duncan had called her twice, and had been pleasant and cheerful; she detected nothing in his voice that was out of the ordinary. Of course, he complained about the tests, and the fact that he couldn't have visitors, but that was certainly normal.

She finished her coffee, and smoothed her perfectly coiffed hair. Maybe she should take a valium before she left for the hosital; it wouldn't do for Duncan to see her so wound up. She peered at herself in the mirror, and put a little more powder under her eyes. She took the valium, picked up her things and went downstairs. After all, she hadn't seen her husband for two days, so she really should be on time for a change.

She got to the hospital with time to spare, then she hesitated. She decided to stop in the gift shop and buy him some flowers, or a plant. It would add a nice touch, even though he was coming home in a few days.

Duncan's room was a scene of bustling activity, and the tension was so thick you could cut it with a knife. Extra chairs had been brought in, but nobody felt like sitting down. Dwight and Scott stood by the window, shifting from one foot to the other, nervously. Mr. Lowery kept opening and closing his briefcase every few minutes, to be sure he hadn't forgotten anything. Jan stood by her father's bedside, fussing over him. Dr. Sturgess stood by the door, looking out occasionally for Vivian's arrival. About the only person in the room that seemed completely relaxed and at ease was Duncan, but then, Dr. Sturgess had taken the precaution of giving him a light tranquilizer this morning.

"For Heaven's sakes, will you all please just sit down?" Duncan finally spoke. "We went over everything last night, in detail, and Vivian doesn't have a leg to stand on. Now here you all are, acting like she's going to come in here and devour us all in one gulp."

Dr. Sturgess spoke first. "Duncan, I think I'm speaking for all of us; it's just that it's going to be a mighty unpleasant scene."

Duncan laughed shortly. "You bet it is." He turned to Jan, "Honey, if the going gets too rough, I want you to go on down to Larry's office."

"I'll be all right," she said quietly but firmly. She looked at the rest of them. "I think Daddy's right, let's all sit—Vivian's always late."

It wasn't two minutes later before there was a light tap on the door, and Vivian walked in, carrying a potted plant, and smiling brightly. The smile froze on her face, and she almost dropped the plant as six pairs of eyes slowly turned and riveted themselves on her. She tried to maintain her composure, and clutched the plant tightly, but a chill of fear went through her.

"Well, what is this, a family gathering?" She tried to keep her tone light, and walked over to Duncan's bed. She started to lean down to kiss his forehead, but he moved his head away.

"Knock it off, Vivian." Duncan's voice was cold. She straightened up immediately, and placed the plant carefully on the table. She could feel the eyes still staring at her, watching her every move, and the hostility in the room. She must remain calm, but her hands started shaking, so she clutched her handbag, and tried to bluff it out. Her heart started to pound heavily as she looked around her. First at Jan, whose face was white and immobile; then at Scott and Dwight, in whom she could sense a faint trace of mockery. Dr. Sturgess was watching his patient, and she finally looked at Lowery, who stared right back at her, while his lips curled slightly. Somehow they all knew, they had found out, but how? And how much did they know? She could see her whole house of cards tumbling around her, and she began to feel dizzy. Then she remembered the numbered Swiss bank account, and the safety deposit boxes, and tried to pull herself together.

"I don't know what this is all about," she said in a low, carefully modulated voice, "or why you're here, but I would like to speak to my husband alone."

Duncan looked up at her with something like respect. She might be treacherous, and an embezzler—still she'd have to be a damn fool not to know something was wrong. But by God, she had class and dignity. Of course, just how long that class and dignity would last was something else again. "Oh, I don't think that will be necessary; you see, it concerns all of us. It's about my new will."

Relief swept over her immediately, and she sat down in the only available chair. But the relief was short-lived; the tension was still in the room, and why was it necessary for the whole family to be there? They hadn't been present when the last will had been drawn up. She had to remain calm. "Well, of course, my dear. You know any changes you want to make will be just fine with me." She laughed, nervously. "You really had me concerned that something was wrong."

"You might say that." Duncan looked at her levelly. "You're out."

She stared at him, uncomprehending; then realization set in. "But Duncan, you can't do that! What about the house? And the company, what about the stocks you gave me?"

"Taking them all back." He folded his hands on his stomach and smiled at her pleasantly. "And the cars, and the jewelry, and everything else that's in the house. You can keep your mink, and the rest of the furs, though," he added as an afterthought.

Vivian jumped up, her face splotched with anger, her heart pounding furiously. "Duncan, you can't do this to me. I don't know what you've been told, or what you think you know, but after all, I've been your wife for eleven years."

"Correction, you've been married to me for eleven years—you've never really been my wife."

"There are certain laws, you know," she said menacingly.

Duncan laughed outright, and his sons snickered; she looked at them furiously, but she was too choked up to speak. "Oh, I'm well aware there are laws, Vivian; too bad you didn't think more about that before you started dipping into the company till." He turned to Lowery, "Bill, you want to read her the report?"

Vivian slumped down in her chair again while Lowery opened his briefcase and took out a thick sheaf of papers. This couldn't be happening, it was a nightmare. Her head was spinning, but she tried to concentrate on what the attorney was saying. It wasn't all there, but there was enough, starting some five years back. She kept waiting for Alex Dunbar's name to come up, but he wasn't mentioned. She listened attentively; if they didn't know about him, there was still some hope. Lowery interrupted himself after about a half an hour.

"You really don't want me to go through this whole thing, do you? My throat's getting sore."

Duncan tried to cover a smile. Lowery was really a pretty darn good actor, and right on cue.

"It's too damn bad about your throat," Vivian flared up. "There's not a thing in that report that you can prove, except maybe bad judgment on my part; and that's certainly no crime."

Lowery pretended a sigh. "Oh, very well, if you insist. Could I have some water first?"

Vivian looked at Duncan. "Certainly you can't believe all this. I knew your family didn't like me, but to cook up something like this!"

Duncan ignored her, and spoke to Dwight—now it was his turn. "By the way, Dwight, how was your fishing trip?"

Dwight inspected his fingernails nonchalantly. "Just fine, Dad, but I didn't go fishing around here. I flew down to Cochabamba." He watched Vivian between narrowed lids, and her face became pale.

"Did you, now? Anything interesting going on down there?" Duncan asked softly. They were all watching Vivian.

"Yes, very. I stopped by No. 27." He looked directly at Vivian now. "You know, Viv, the one we've been getting all those reports on that it's been petering out? Looked just fine to me."

"There . . . there must have been some mistake," she said weakly.

"Oh, I'm sure there was," he said sarcastically. "And I'm sure we'll be getting another report any day now, that the well's not worth working at all any more, and we'd better sell out."

Vivian thought of the reports that were due in the morning mail, and thought she was going to faint.

Duncan looked at her, and thought it was time to intervene. "I think we've had about enough horseplay. Vivian, Bill's got some papers for you to sign, then I want you to get out of my sight. And I want you out of the house in twenty-four hours."

"I'm not signing anything!" she said shrilly, in a last gesture of defiance.

Duncan shrugged. "Very well. You want some more, you'll get some more. Dwight, didn't you say you met a friend of Viv's down there?"

"Oh yes, I almost forgot," Dwight said innocently. "Alex Dunbar; seems he thinks you're a pretty smart operator, Vivian. He's quite a talker; told me all about how you two worked out the deal on No. 27, the one in Sucre, and a few others; before he passed out. Of course, he didn't know who I was; thought I was just a tourist. I've got some pictures of him here, and one of the two of us together." He fumbled through his pockets. "Want to see them?" He finally found what he was looking for, and thrust the packet of snapshots toward her. "Here, have a look."

She shook her head violently, then covered her face with shaking hands.

Duncan started to feel sorry for her again, and had to force himself to remember what she'd done to him, and to his family. He motioned to Lowery to take over.

Bill Lowery cleared his throat. "I have all the papers here, Mrs. Keith. All nice and easy, and then it will be all over. That is, unless you want to go to court—and Mr. Dunbar, too, of course." His voice was fraught with overtones, and she looked up at him quickly. "It's very likely you'd go to prison, you know," he added, smiling courteously.

She took the pen he offered her, and scribbled her name in the places he indicated, without bothering to read them. Then she looked at Duncan piteously. "But where will I go, Duncan? What will I do? All my friends are here."

Duncan was about to answer, but for the first time, Jan spoke. "What friends, Vivian?" Jan's voice was so full of venom that Duncan couldn't believe it was his sweet little girl talking. "What friends do you have in this town, or anywhere else, for that matter? You wouldn't know what to do with a friend if you had one—all you know is how to use people. I should think you'd be glad to get out of town, and as quickly as possible. My father is being very generous, giving you twenty-four hours. If I were in your shoes, it wouldn't take me twenty minutes."

Vivian was livid. "Don't worry, it won't take me twenty-four hours." She was thinking rapidly now. If she couldn't take anything in the house, she could do as much damage as possible. And she had to clear out her safety deposit boxes, too. "I've been left with practically nothing," she said spitefully.

As though reading her mind, Scott spoke. "Dad, I really think it would be a good idea for one of us to go with her to the house. She doesn't look too well."

Vivian glared at him.

Duncan nodded. "Fine. You go, Scott."

Bill Lowery started putting the papers back in his briefcase. "Well, I guess that just about wraps it up. Just one more thing, Mrs. Keith; do you have the keys to the safety deposit boxes with you, or are they at the house?"

She stared at him in shock. "What safety deposit boxes?"

Lowery shook his head. "You really should be more careful what you sign, Mrs. Keith. You agreed to turn over the keys to your boxes, and the contents therein, to your husband."

"Try and get them!" she spat at him.

"You're making things most difficult, Mrs. Keith; it would be so much easier if you just gave me the keys. You see, if you try to get anything out of them now, you're in contempt of court, and that automatically means a jail sentence." This was the biggest bluff of all, but in Vivian's state of mind, he was almost certain it would work. "I really wouldn't like to see that happen, now that everything's settled. And you still have all that money in Switzerland."

She stared at him dully for a moment, then her eyes glazed over. "They're in the lining of my jewelry box." She didn't bother to deny it. What was the use?

Lowery was elated, but tried not to show it. "Fine," he nodded. "You'll get them, Scott."

Scott helped her out of her chair, and she leaned unsteadily on his arm as they left the room.

Duncan looked at the closed door, and couldn't help but feeling saddened. Vivian had walked in here a half-hour ago a bright, self-assured, confident woman, and had left broken and defeated. Well, she had brought it all on herself, but he didn't feel like gloating.

"I wonder how much she has in Switzerland?" Jan said, almost to herself.

"I wonder how much she has in those safety deposit boxes," Dwight said gleefully. "Mr. Lowery, that was certainly a stroke of genius. It wasn't in the script, how'd you come up with it?"

"I had it in mind," Lowery said modestly, "but I wasn't sure just how much she could take when we started this thing. Towards the end, I was pretty sure I could swing it. At that, it was a gamble."

Duncan intervened. "Listen, everyone; it's over now, so let's drop it for a while. Lowery, you better go after them; tell Viv if she wants to go to Reno, I'll pay for the divorce. You better go with them to the house, too, she might get hysterical when the initial shock wears off. You all did a great job, and I'm grateful, but now I think I want to get some rest. Jan, I'll see you in the morning, and we'll start making some plans." He patted her hand, and they all left the room, except Dr. Sturgess.

Larry looked at him with compassion. "I think I know what you must be going through—you want a dinner tray sent in?"

Duncan shook his head wearily. "No, Larry. All I want now is to get some rest. I'd appreciate a sleeping pill."

Larry rang for a nurse, then checked Duncan's pulse. "Seems pretty stable, under the circumstances." The nurse came in and he gave her instructions. "Sally, Mr. Keith would like a sleeping pill now, and if he wakes up during the night, he can have another one. No more visitors, and no phone calls." He turned back to Duncan and smiled. "See you in the morning, old friend."

Kathy lay next to Bruce Sunday morning, listening to his even breathing, and thinking back about their weekend. Friday night it had seemed to stretch ahead of her endlessly, and now it was almost gone. After the delivery boy left, they had taken the food out to the kitchen, and half-heartedly started taking it out of the bags. Then Kathy looked at Bruce, and knew he wasn't any more interested in food than she was.

She stood there staring at him, and he had taken a package of pastrami from her hand and placed it on the counter top. "Come on," he said huskily, "let's just put all this stuff in the refrigerator for later. I'll put some champagne on ice, too."

When they were finally in bed together, and he held her in his arms at last, she felt safe and warm and content. It wasn't just the physical part of it, although God knows that was perfect between them, but it was all the other feelings that went along with it. It was hard to explain, even to herself, but it was almost like being one person, or one-half of a whole, even when he wasn't actually making love to her. The foreplay and the gentle kissing and nuzzling afterwards were all part of it, certainly, but there was more; it was as though she could feel what he was feeling, think what he was thinking. But of course that couldn't be, she told herself; there was a complete other side of Bruce that she didn't know at all, that lived all the way across the continent in New York with a wife and two children. Although that never bothered her when he was with her; in fact, she never even thought about it—it was only when he was out of town that she was tortured. Why was she thinking of it now? Determinedly, she put it out of her mind as his arms closed around her, and his mouth covered hers. She kissed him back with equal passion, as all the need and longing of the last four months surged up in her.

Later, much later, they got hungry, and decided to have something to eat. Bruce laughed when Kathy put on her bathrobe, and she flushed angrily. "Well, what did you expect? I thought I was spending the weekend with Maude. I even brought a flannel nightgown, too."

"Good Lord," he said mockingly, and tossed her his pajama tops. "Here, wear this, and I'll put on my shorts."

They sat up and talked, drank and ate until almost dawn. Both of them were careful not to talk about the future, but reminisced about the past; after all, they had the whole weekend. They made love one more time before they both fell asleep, exhausted. They slept until early afternoon Saturday, and Bruce awakened her with a glass of champagne.

Kathy stretched and yawned, then smiled at him sleepily. "I could really get used to this kind of treatment—but I suppose we should get something to eat."

Bruce sat on the edge of the bed and kissed her lightly. "Okay; you want to take a bath together first?"

Kathy laughed, and sipped her champagne. "You know what that leads to."

"Do you remember the first time I asked you to take a bath with me?"

"I certainly do; I was embarrassed, and more than a little shocked, so I said I thought it was dirty."

"And I said, how can it possibly be dirty to take a bath?"

"My vocabulary has improved since then—now I feel sybaritic."

Bruce smiled, and pulled her to her feet. "Come on—we'll finish the champagne in the tub."

By the time they were finally dressed, it was late afternoon, and Kathy was famished. She suggested they call Maude to join them; after all, they had left her in the lurch last night, and Bruce agreed.

"Breakfast!" Maude snorted, "You know what time it is? I was about to fix dinner."

"Okay, you have dinner, and Bruce and I'll have breakfast. Pick you up in half an hour."

They went to *Barney's Beanery*, and while Maude ate a huge steak, Bruce and Kathy had bacon and eggs. They sat and talked for a while, mostly about the business, while Maude polished off a large piece of pie, but when Bruce suggested they all go bar-hopping, she begged off. "Getting too old for that sort of thing; besides, I'm not dressed for it. And Kathy, you better pick up your car."

Kathy turned to Bruce. "That's right—I don't want to leave it on the street again tonight. Let's go get it now. I'll go back to the apartment and change, and you can stop at the store and pick up some things for breakfast." She was glad now that she'd brought along the green chiffon.

They had gone to several of their favorite haunts, but when Bruce suggested they drive down to Santa Ynez Inn, Kathy said she was too tired. She wasn't, really, but something so final about going there. It was the first place Bruce had ever taken her to dinner, and it might be the last place he'd take her now. She just didn't want to face that. So they had gone home, and made love again, but they still hadn't talked; not really.

And now it was Sunday morning, and the perfect weekend was almost over. She thought of Monrovia for the first time in two days, and sighed. It seemed like a whole other world, somehow.

Bruce rolled over and flung an arm across her. "What time is it?" he asked sleepily.

"It's early yet," she said softly, "go back to sleep." She didn't want to get up yet, didn't want him to wake up yet; if time could only be suspended right here and now. But she was trying to live in a dream world, and she knew it.

"Can't," he mumbled, "I have to call New York."

She froze—there went her dream world! Of course, it was

Sunday, he'd have to call his wife and children. "It's almost ten o'clock; I suppose you're right, it's not so early after all."

He opened his eyes, and really looked at her. "I guess it's time we talked, isn't it?"

She nodded. "Go make your phone call first."

"It can wait."

"No, Bruce, please get it over with first." She wanted some time to collect her thoughts. He got up and put on his pajama bottoms, then went in the living room. She had often wondered about that; he never called his wife without putting something on, it was almost as though he thought she could see him over the phone. She heard him dial the number, then his low voice, but she didn't try to listen. After a while, she could hear the change in his tone, lighter and more jovial, and knew he was talking to his children. The conversation was short, and in a few minutes he was back. He sat down on her side of the bed, and neither of them spoke for a while. "Want some coffee?" he finally asked.

She shook her head. "Later, maybe." He knew she always drank tea in the morning; he must really be distracted. She reached out and took his hand in hers, and a lump rose in her throat.

"When do you have to leave?" he asked huskily.

"Not for a while, yet. Later afternoon, or early this evening."

He looked down at her, and tried to smile. "You know I've missed you terribly, Kitten. I love you very much. And if there was anything I could do about my family situation, I would. Believe me, I've thought about it a thousand times since you left. But there's so much involved, so many people would be hurt. She's a good woman, Kathy, she really is, and the kids—"

She reached up and put her fingers gently over his mouth, and tears came to her eyes. He had never talked this way

380

before, and at the moment he was very vulnerable. For a fleeting moment, she thought of pressing her advantage, and just as quickly dismissed the idea. "Don't, Bruce. I know you love me, just as I know there's nothing you can do. And even if you did, you and I might last for a while, but in time you'd grow to hate me. So you see, my darling, this is all we can ever have."

He got up and started pacing the room, running his fingers through his black wavy hair, thinking. "I don't suppose you'd consider staying, would you?" he finally said. "You know, you haven't told me where you've been, or what you've been doing."

For a moment, she was sorely tempted. It was an agonizing decision; half a life, or maybe none at all. Finally, she shook her head slowly. "I just can't, Bruce. You know what it was like before; at the end, we were tearing each other apart. Please understand." She looked at him pleadingly.

"It really wasn't fair of me to ask. But you still haven't answered the rest of my question."

She hesitated. "Monrovia—I've been working for a psychiatrist. He had plans for this weekend, so I had three days off."

He sat down again, and tried to smile. "I just can't imagine you in Monrovia. You like it?"

"It's not bad. I've met a lot of people, made a lot of new friends. But I've never stopped thinking about you." She hoped he wouldn't ask her any more questions.

"You know," he said slowly, thinking, "Christmas is only about three weeks away. You'll have some time off then, won't you?"

She nodded. "A week, I guess."

"Christmas is on a Thursday this year. I was planning on going back East on the Tuesday or Wednesday before, but I could think of some reason to stay over until Christmas morning. We could spend Christmas Eve together, at least, and the better part of the week. We never had much time over the holidays, you know.''

None, she was about to say, but she was almost speechless with joy. ''Oh Bruce, and we'll get a tree, and a turkey, and decorate—darling, it would be marvelous!''

''You will come, then? For sure?'' He looked at her anxiously.

''I'll be here the Friday night before.''

He looked relieved. ''Now I'll go make you some tea.'' He paused at the door. ''Did I say coffee before? I must be off my rocker.''

They spent the rest of the day in the apartment, except when Bruce walked Topsy, talking and making plans for Christmas. They sat out on the terrace for a while, as they had in the past, until dusk began to fall. Kathy looked at him and tried smile when they finally came back indoors. ''This is really a switch, isn't it? For once, I'm leaving you.''

They kept their goodbyes light, as they had tried to do in the past, and it was easier this time because it wouldn't be for long. She didn't want him to walk down to the car with her, though, so he took her suitcase down earlier. ''I want to remember you here when I leave—and don't you dare go buy a tree or anything until I get back.''

Driving back the traffic was heavy, and she didn't have much time to think, but something kept nagging at the back of her mind. When she arrived at her apartment there was a note on the door from John, but she decided to wait until morning to read it. She knew when she saw him she couldn't lie to him, he could see right through her, but she was too happy to think about it tonight. It wasn't until she was in the apartment and had tossed her suitcase on the bed that it came to her. The dream! She hadn't dreamt it, or even thought about it for the past two nights; that must mean something.

She unpacked slowly and methodically, thinking about

Christmas. The phone rang, but she didn't answer it. She'd forgotten to give her number to Bruce, and she didn't want to talk to anyone else. But he could have gotten it from Maude; frantically, she ran to pick it up, but the ringing had stopped. She started to call him back, then stopped. He might think she was checking up on him, or worse, he might be out, and then all night she'd wonder where he was. Instead, she took off her clothes and went to bed. She fell asleep almost immediately.

Chapter 15

Dr. John Carter sat behind his desk, and waited. He had cancelled his usual Monday morning appointments at the County Jail, and instead had spent the time with Pam, as he had on the previous two mornings. It was really amazing how quickly she had started to recover, once the breaththrough was made. She was beginning to open up to him, now the hidden secret in her mind had been uncovered. He had a lot to thank Jack Wentworth for, in that respect. She had even hinted that she had been the one who stole the drugs from the different offices, and he was sure the whole story would come out in time. The difference in Jack was apparent, too. His hatred of his father, his venom towards his ex-wife, his drinking, were all coverups of his true feelings; his guilt about whether or not he and Pam's father had done the right thing. He shook his head; all these months of sporadic treatment, and he had never even come close to the truth of Jack's real problem.

He looked at his watch; almost twelve o'clock. He had expected Kathy to be back at her desk when he came in, but she'd called the exchange and said she wouldn't be in until noon. Normally, he wouldn't have minded; she knew he wasn't in the office Monday mornings, and he had told her she could have the exchange switch the calls to her apartment.

But he wanted some time alone with her, there was so much to talk about, and he was booked solid the entire afternoon. He wondered briefly where she'd gone for the weekend, but he didn't worry about it. She was probably upset because Edith was due home, and it pleased him to think she might be jealous. There was no basis for it, not really.

Although, he must admit, seeing Edith for the first time was quite a shock. She didn't want him to meet her, but said she preferred coming home in a cab. It's a good thing she had; he never would have recognized her.

Her hair was a lot shorter, done in an upswept fashion, and he suspected she'd had it tinted. Her body, instead of the comfortable lump he'd grown accustomed to, had definite curves in the right places, and the waist that had disappeared years ago was plainly defined. She must have lost a good twenty pounds! Her sagging chin line was firm and taut, and there was a healthy glow about her. Edith hadn't worn makeup in years, and very little at that. "Edith," he managed finally, "you look like a million dollars!" He almost made the mistake of saying, that place must have geniuses working there, but instead, "I never would have recognized you."

She twirled around for him, her eyes sparkling. "Oh John, you really like it? Of course, I still have a long way to go, I want to take off some more weight, but do you really think I've changed?"

"That's pretty obvious, isn't it?" he said, happy for her. "You're going to have to buy a whole new wardrobe. And just to celebrate, I'm taking you out to dinner."

"Oh John," she threw her arms around him, "we haven't

done that in ages. Pay the cab, will you, dear? I want to freshen up.''

He took her to the Zanzibar, and as she walked ahead of him, he noticed the admiring glances she got, and was pleased. When they were seated, he asked for the menus, but she stopped him. "John, dear, I know I don't drink very often, but I think I'd like a dry martini before we order.''

He ordered their drinks, then leaned back and looked at her. She really had changed. It wasn't only the physical aspect, but she had a new self-assurance, and he found it very attractive. "You know," he said, half-jokingly, "I don't know what it's going to be like going to bed with you tonight—it almost seems like cheating on my wife.''

She didn't answer right away, but sipped her drink slowly. "I don't know why it should—it's not Saturday night yet.'' She smiled, to take the sting out of her words.

He almost choked on his scotch; so she'd noticed the sameness of their life, too? Could she possibly know about Kathy? No, of course not, he'd always been true to her, and their sex pattern hadn't changed since he'd started having an affair with Kathy. Still, he felt uncomfortable. He wondered just how many women had been at the health farm, and what they talked about. She may have picked up some ideas. As the evening progressed, her new-found self-assurance became even more evident. She ordered for herself, which she never did on the rare occasions when they dined out—broiled halibut, lettuce with oil and vinegar dressing, and black coffee. She kept up most of the conversation, too, and he found it entertaining. Evidentally, she'd been doing some reading.

When they got home, he suddenly found himself becoming nervous. Oh, come on, he told himself, you're a psychiatrist, and this is your wife, not a new mistress, and you've been married for years. Still, he had the ridiculous idea he was cheating on Kathy. "Would you like a nightcap?" He really needed another drink badly.

"Why, yes, I'll have a brandy. Why don't you bring them in the bedroom?"

They had made love that night, and her body in the dark was like a different woman's. For the first time in years, it wasn't a chore, or a habit, and as he became more and more aroused, he momentarily forgot Kathy.

Just then, he heard the door to the outer office open, and it brought him out of his reverie. He glanced at his watch again; right on time. They'd still have an hour to talk before the patients started arriving.

Pam watched the door close behind Dr. Carter. He really was such a nice person, and so kind to her. But she dreaded his coming every morning, even though she knew everything had to be talked out before she'd be completely well. Once he arrived, and she started talking, it wasn't so bad, but after he left, she felt completely drained. She had almost told him about stealing those drugs this morning, but she couldn't quite bring herself to do that yet. She was still too ashamed, although she realized she shouldn't feel that way, she'd been sick.

She wondered how long they'd keep her in the hospital; probably until she remembered everything. Funny, she remembered all about the accident now—but she couldn't remember driving out to see her father the day he died. Probably one pill too many; she shuddered when she thought of all the driving she'd done when she'd been high on pills. It's a miracle she hadn't killed herself; or worse, someone else. Maybe she wouldn't have to remember everything, though; after all, people got drunk and had blank spots and never remembered. Like when she tore up her apartment— she didn't remember it, but she knew she'd done it.

Or maybe they wanted to be sure she'd kicked the drugs. Well, they needn't worry about that, she never wanted to take so much as an aspirin. She had trouble sleeping at night, though. Dr. Sturgess had said she could have sleeping pills, but she didn't want them. She'd get over it, in time, when she could learn to live with the memory of her brother's death, and with her own life.

She didn't like to face the fact, but she knew she'd need therapy for a long time. She had even asked Dr. Carter about it, and he seemed pleased that she'd mentioned the matter herself. Jack needed help, too. What a terrible waste; both of them carrying this guilt around for so many years, and in a way, it was much worse for him, because he was conscious of it. She lowered the bed, and snuggled down under the covers. If it hadn't been for Jack, she'd probably still be out there in no-man's land.

The doctors had asked her questions, but she couldn't tell them a thing. She remembered nothing from the time she got in her car the day her father died, until she heard Jack's voice, telling her he loved her, and heard him crying. It was almost as though he was calling her back from some dark, lonely, weightless place, but it was all foggy and vague. It was too bad the doctors knew so little about catatonia. She'd have to ask Dr. Carter if there was someplace that was doing some research on it; Jack had a lot of money, maybe they could both contribute to it.

She was getting drowsy; Jack was coming over for lunch, but there was plenty of time for a nap now. Funny, she could sleep in the daytime, but it was so hard at night. . . .

Pam was still sleeping soundly when Jack arrived. He tiptoed over to the bed and stood looking down at her. She looked for all the world like a helpless child huddled under the covers. Except for the fact that her tan was gone and she looked very pale, it was difficult to imagine the hell she'd gone through. He had met Dr. Carter in the lobby, and was anxious to tell her the good news, but God knows she needed all the rest she could get.

He sat down next to the bed and waited. It was enough to know that when she did wake up, she'd recognize him. He had asked Dr. Carter when he thought she could come home, expecting two or three months anyway, and was astounded when the doctor said a couple of weeks.

"I'm rather worried about where she'll stay, though; I don't think it's a good idea for her to go back to her apartment, and I don't want her to be alone."

"She could stay at my place," Jack said, without thinking. Dr. Carter had raised an eyebrow. "I hardly think so."

"How about Kathy's, then?" For some reason, Dr. Carter's face reddened. "They're good friends, and I'd be glad to buy twin beds, instead of the one Kathy has now."

"I don't think that's a good idea, either. After all, Kathy's at work all day, and Pam will have to have a nurse with her for a time. Just a precaution, she's all right physically, but I don't want to take any chances." Good God, that would really mess things up for him.

"Look, Dr. Carter, I intend to ask Pam to marry me. I haven't asked her yet, I want to get the engagement ring first, and surprise her. But I'm sure she'll say yes. So you see, she wouldn't be at Kathy's very long."

Dr. Carter looked at him speculatively. He had expected this, but not so soon. Pam was just recovering from an extremely traumatic experience, and marriage to a man as emotionally unstable as Jack would certainly not be his recommendation. But that was an area he wanted to steer clear of for the time being. Of course, staying with Kathy would be the ideal situation, under normal circumstances; but the situation was not normal, and he was not going to give up his arrangement with Kathy. "I still don't think it's a good idea," he repeated. "After all, Kathy works for me, and I'll be seeing Pam as a patient. Too many conflicts could occur," he said vaguely, trying to think. "And her apartment is too small. Perhaps she could move into your place, after all, and you could move into hers, for the time being."

Doctors! Jack still didn't see the sense to it, but he'd agreed. He leaned back and closed his eyes. Tomorrow morning, he'd buy her an engagement ring, or maybe he'd get half a dozen or so, on consignment, and she could pick out her own. He wondered if Pam would want a big wedding; maybe they could be married by Christmas. There were so many things to discuss.

"Jack," Pam was sitting up in bed, her hair tousled, "why didn't you wake me up when you got here?"

His eyes flew open, and he sat down on the bed and swooped her up in his arms, kissing her passionately, until finally she squirmed free.

"Jack, what is the matter with you? Someone might come in any time."

He grinned at her adoringly. "Let 'em." Oh hell, he couldn't wait until he got the ring. "Dr. Carter says you can come home in a couple of weeks, and you're going to stay at my place and I'll stay at yours."

"Two weeks!" Her mouth fell open. "Two weeks," she repeated, as if she couldn't believe it. "But why am I supposed to switch apartments with you?" she sounded bewildered.

"He doesn't think it's such a hot idea for you to go to your place. And anyway, it's just temporary, just until we can make plans for the wedding—what's your ring size?"

"Five-and-a-half," she answered, then it struck her what he had just said. "Jack—are you proposing to me?"

He nodded, happily. "I was going to wait until tomorrow, and surprise you with some rings to choose from, but I couldn't wait. Do you want a big wedding?"

"I don't care," her eyes were bright and sparkling now.

"You know, somewhere in the back of my mind, I always knew you'd ask me. I even told April."

"This wasn't a very romantic proposal," he said, suddenly concerned. "I should have waited."

She put her finger to his lips as the nurse came in with the lunch tray. "Later."

"Off the bed, young man," Nurse Murphy said grumpily. "This is still a hospital, not lovers' lane, you know."

Jack got off the bed hastily, and sat back down on the chair, red faced.

Pam grinned at him, and waited until the nurse left the room. Then she looked at the tray, and wrinkled her nose. "Ugh."

He looked at it and agreed. "I'll go down to Sam's and bring us back some cheeseburgers and malts." He got up. "Meanwhile, you can flush most of this stuff down the john." He kissed her goodbye and left.

She looked after him happily. Then she started thinking; did she want a big wedding? It would probably please his father. She certainly wanted at least one shower, maybe more. Kathy would give her one; and April, maybe. She started planning, waiting for Jack to come back; suddenly she was starving.

Then her smile slowly faded; his enthusiasm had been engagingly infectious, and she had been swept along with him. She realized much more than he did, that although she was *back in the world*, again, she was far from well. Weeks, probably months of therapy stretched ahead of her, and in spite of her youth, suddenly she felt far older and wiser than Jack.

There were his psychological hangups to contend with, too. Sure, he had stopped drinking, but it had been for such a short time. His senseless uncontrollable rages, his hatred of his father and Betsy—all these things had to be worked out some way, and certainly before they took on the responsibility of marriage. The first thing she had to do was to convince him to resume his therapy with Dr. Carter.

Suddenly, she wanted to keep their engagement a secret for a while. It would take some doing, but if she convinced him that it was mainly because of her hangups and not his, he could be persuaded. There was a lot of fence-mending in Jack's life to be taken care of, and she didn't want it hanging over their heads on their wedding day.

Kathy awakened early Monday morning, but she was in no hurry to get to the office. John's note said he had a big surprise for her, but it couldn't be anything all that earth-shattering. Besides, he wouldn't be in this morning, so there was no great rush. She turned on the water for tea, then wandered around her apartment; there wasn't very far to wander. It seemed so much smaller than it had on Friday. She felt cramped for space, and wondered why on earth she'd rented it in the first place. She heard the tea kettle whistling and went back to the kitchen.

She dawdled over tea, vacillating back and forth. Of course, she could just say she went up to spend the weekend with Maude—that certainly wasn't lying. If he didn't ask her any questions, and they were busy, maybe she could get by with it. On the other hand, if he wanted details, she'd have to tell him the truth. She could have told Dwight that black was white, and he would have believed her; but John was another matter. Besides, their relationship had always been open and above board, so why should she try lying to him now?

She felt angry with herself for feeling guilty; after all, John slept with his wife. So why should she feel at fault for sleeping with another man, especially the only man she'd ever really been in love with? She also felt juvenile and slightly foolish that she was so nervous about facing John.

Firmly, several times, she got up to start getting ready; then she decided to have another cup of tea and think some more. Finally, after five cups, she began to feel slightly nauseated, so she quickly dressed and headed for the office.

Driving down the boulevard, she noticed they'd put up the Christmas decorations over the weekend, and everything looked very festive. There were even a few Christmas trees up in some of the offices along the street. Then she thought of Christmas with Bruce, and it put a little starch in her backbone.

The door to the office was unlocked, which meant that John was already there. That was unusual in itself. "John?" she called.

He came out of his office beaming, grabbed her in a bear hug, and whirled her around.

"Wait a minute," she couldn't help laughing nervously, "you never get through at the County this early. What are you doing here?"

"I didn't go this morning; Kathy, the most wonderful thing has happened. Pam's almost back to normal."

"No!" She couldn't believe it. "John, how did it happen? Oh John, let's put the Closed sign on the door, I want to hear all about it."

He opened the door, flipped the sign around, and they went into his office, John talking all the way. He told her in the minutest detail, and Kathy listened intently, for the time being forgetting her weekend. "Jack said he was going to ask Pam to marry him when he gets her a ring tomorrow, but judging from the state he was in this morning, he's probably already asked her. She asked me to tell you she'd like you to come by. Oh, another thing, Jack suggested that Pam move in with you while she was recuperating. I had to think fast to get around that."

"Well, it would have been pretty crowded," she tried to smile, but his remark reminded her of Bruce, and also why

John didn't want anyone else occupying her apartment. "You want some coffee?" she asked.

"Not right now." He leaned back in his chair, and looked at her. "You look nice and rested. How was your weekend?"

"Just fine," she smiled at him. "How was yours?"

"Well, you wouldn't believe the change in Edith," he started, then paused, "oh no, you're doing it again."

"Doing what?"

"Answering a question with another question. You know I meant where'd you go, who'd you see? Did you leave because Edith was coming home? Seems like you made up your mind pretty fast; at least, you didn't tell me you were going anywhere."

"Well, it was a spur of the moment thing; and yes, it was partly because of Edith. It looked like a long, boring weekend stretching ahead," she said carefully, "so I decided to drive in and spend some time with Maude."

"Oh?" he was watching her. "You two have a nice time?"

"Well, yes, for a while." She fumbled in her purse for a cigarette. "We talked a lot about old times, and the company—they've taken on a lot of new clients, and . . . but you wouldn't be interested in that. Just shop talk."

He nodded. "Brought back a lot of old memories, I'll bet. See anyone else you know?"

Oh, what the hell, she thought. "Yes, I saw Bruce," she said evenly. "It was completely by accident, he wasn't due in until next week. Maude called his service to make certain of that, but he returned to town early, got the message, and stopped by to see what she wanted. It never would have happened if she hadn't called to make sure we didn't see each other."

"I gather she doesn't approve of him."

"No, she doesn't, not for me," Kathy replied. "As a matter of fact, she doesn't approve of you, either."

"She doesn't even know me!"

"What I meant was, she doesn't approve of my going out with any married man, she thinks I'm just throwing my life away."

"I see," he said thoughtfully. "Well, you do seem to follow some sort of a pattern. So, you spent the weekend with Bruce." He didn't ask her, it was a statement.

His remark stung her, but she was determined not to show it. "Yes, as a matter of fact, I did. Just like you spent the weekend with Edith."

"That's hardly the same thing, and you know it." He tried to control his voice.

"Well, two in a bed is two in a bed, as far as I'm concerned." She got up and started pacing the room. "Look, John, I don't want to argue with you. What happened, happened. I left Hollywood to get away from a married man situation, and I'm right back in the same situation with you. You said it yourself, I follow a pattern. And right now, I'm very upset. I don't want either of us to say anything we might regret later on."

He didn't answer for a long time, trying to sort out his feelings. He'd been sick with jealousy when he found out about Jack Wentworth, and the pain had been intense. Dwight Keith hadn't bothered him at all. And now there was another man to contend with. The fact that he'd had sex with Edith more than once this weekend and enjoyed it thoroughly had left his mind completely. "Are you going to see him again, or was this just for old times sake?"

She could feel her cheeks flush. "John, I don't go to bed with a man for old times sake. Yes, I told him I'd spend Christmas Eve with him—he took over the lease of my old apartment."

"I see." He was seething inside. "I'd planned on talking to you later about decorating the office; that's rather ironic, isn't it?"

"Well, we can still do that—I noticed on the way to work

that a lot of the offices have decorations and Christmas is still a month away."

He changed the subject suddenly. "Kathy, can you get pregnant?"

"Well, of course," she answered, surprised. "What brought that on? You know Fred got me pregnant, and the hell he put me through just to lose the baby. I told you all that. I thought we were talking about Christmas."

"I was just wondering," he said deliberately, "if you got pregnant now, how would you know who the father was?"

Her face turned white, as though he had slapped her. Slowly, she picked up her purse and coat, and stood up. "That wasn't worthy of you, John," she said coldly. "You were without a receptionist when I first came here, I think you can get along without one again for a few days until you can find someone else. Under the circumstances, I hardly think any notice is necessary." She looked at him briefly, but his expression hadn't changed. He seemed to be lost in his own thoughts, and she wasn't sure he had heard her.

She was halfway down the hall before he came running after her and grabbed her from behind. "Kathy, don't go." He held her in a vise-like grip, while she struggled to free herself. "That was a rotten thing to say, I didn't mean it, but you drive me crazy sometimes."

She managed to pull away from him, and stood with her back against the wall. "Oh, you meant it, alright," she said, her eyes blazing now, "I tried to be honest with you, I thought we had that kind of relationship. And I warned you not to say anything you might regret."

"Kathy, please," he was pleading with her now, "can't you understand? You came at me from left field, I thought you were jealous of Edith, and you can't possibly know what that meant to me. I wanted to make it up to you, then to find out you'd been with another man—it was just such a shock. You know I haven't had the experience with other women the way you have with other men. Can't you see what this does to me?"

She relented slightly. "Yes, I guess I can," she said wearily, "but I still think it's better that I leave. We need a cooling off period."

"Kathy, don't, I'm begging you. If you want time to think things over, I won't press you. You know what I mean, I won't try to make love to you. But my God, you can't leave, you practically run this office." He sounded desperate. "And we will decorate the office; I'll call Edith, and tonight we'll go out and get a tree, and—"

She interrupted him, "John, I'll stay," she said quietly. "But we won't go out and get a tree tonight. We'll go out tomorrow at noon."

He almost groaned with relief. "Thank God!" He started towards her, then backed off. "I think I need a drink—please, have one with me?"

She thought it over, then nodded slightly. She had never seen him take a drink this early in the day, but it might ease the tension for both of them. They went back to his office and sat quietly until the first patient knocked on the door. He polished off three straight shots while she sipped just one.

Irene tapped lightly on her daughter's door before coming in. April lay on the bed, idly turning the pages of a fashion magazine, and barely glanced at her mother. "April, I want to talk to you," she said briskly.

April sighed; how well she knew that tone in her mother's voice. "I'm tired, mother," she said wanly, "can't we talk later?"

Irene sat down on the edge of the bed and looked at her daughter. "Honey, you've been moping around in this room for days. You pick at your food, you don't want to talk to your friends, you haven't been to the Club in ages. Now, April, I know something's wrong, and I want to help." Her tone softened, "Can't you tell me what's the matter?"

April looked at her mother; God, how she wished she could. But she just shook her head, hopelessly.

Irene lowered her voice. "April, are you pregnant? If you are, honey, I'll understand."

April almost laughed for the first time in weeks. "No, mother, of course not; whatever gave you an idea like that?"

Irene looked bewildered. "Well, I just thought . . . I couldn't think of anything else; you're not eating, and it all happened so suddenly. What is it then? Is it because your father and I are getting along, at last? Have we been neglecting you?"

Irene looked so worried that April felt sorry for her. "No, Mother; I'm glad that you and Dad are getting along, I really am. And I don't feel neglected; I've just wanted to be alone, that's all."

"I notice you still go out to the mailbox every morning; you never have told me much about Switzerland. Is that it, is there some boy there that you miss? Has he stopped writing you?"

"You just won't give up, will you? Okay, it's someone in Switzerland." Some boy, she thought; she wondered what her mother would say if she knew the whole truth. (Yes, Irene; I miss someone in Switzerland very much. You see, I was his mistress for three years, and he's older than Daddy. But it turns out he's wanted by the French government for tax fraud and he's involved in all sorts of underground activities, all over Europe. And I didn't get my fancy education from that girl's school you sent me to, I got it from him.)

Irene looked relieved. "Well, honey, is it serious? If it is, these things can be straightened out. Why don't you try writing him?"

April shook her head. "You don't understand; I can't write him. I don't know where he is, and I really don't want to talk about it any more."

"April, I know you think of me as the older generation, but I was young once, too, you know. Believe me, dear, you'll get over it in time," she said gently, feeling very motherly. "If you ever feel as though you want to talk about him, I'm always here." She kissed her daughter tenderly.

April rolled over and got off the bed; her mother would never, in her wildest dreams, understand about Juan. "Irene, I don't think of you as the older generation at all. And you're right, I'll get over it in time." She changed the subject. "Come on, I want to see how your new bedroom is coming along. When are we going to start decorating for Christmas?"

Irene looked at her shrewdly; she had changed the subject too quickly. Well, anything to get her out of her room. "The bedroom's almost done. I'm glad you're showing an interest. As for Christmas, I thought we'd get a tree this weekend, or do you think it's too early?"

"Mother, it's three weeks away, it'll be dead by then. That is, unless you're planning a big party a week or so before."

"No, I don't think so," she frowned slightly. "You know, I started planning one, almost automatically, because I have one every year." They started walking down the hall towards her bedroom. "Then your father asked me when I planned to have it, and I suddenly realized I didn't want to give one after all."

"I know, you only did it before because you knew Daddy hated big parties," April said.

"You knew that?"

April laughed. "Certainly; you think I'm dumb?"

"Of course not; well, anyway, I decided to skip it. Maybe, one day between Christmas and New Year's, we'll have a small open house, and then I thought we'd have Duncan and Jan over for dinner one night, if he's well enough. He's coming home tomorrow, you know." They stopped at the door of her bedroom, and Irene threw open the door. "Voila!" she said.

The bedroom looked lovely; all soft muted tones of warm brown, bronze and gold. "Oh Mother, it's lovely!" April exclaimed.

"It is, isn't it?" Irene said with pride. "And the best part is, Ted and I picked out everything together. He loves it." She turned to her daughter. "Now you can't kid me about Turhan Bey anymore."

The front door slammed. "I'm home!" Ted yelled.

Irene hugged her daughter quickly. "Don't worry, darling, I won't say anything to your father about . . . you know, our talk, and that boy."

April looked at her mother in gratitude, and her throat choked up. "Thank you, Mother," she said. They really were becoming a family again. Arm in arm, they walked down the hall to greet Ted.

Duncan's hospital room was alive with activity the morning he was due to come home. He had awakened early, showered and insisted on shaving himself in the bathroom instead of in bed, over his nurse's strenuous objections. After all, he intended doing just that when he got home, and he wanted a good close shave when he left the hospital. He had to admit, though, that it was an ordeal, and it felt good to get back into bed again when they brought his breakfast tray.

He wasn't due to be released until noon, but Jan arrived shortly after ten, bubbling with enthusiasm and full of conversation. It wasn't much later that the nurses started coming in, one by one, to say goodbye. He thanked each one of them in turn, saying he'd see them all again before he left, but dammit, it was getting embarrassing. Where the hell were Scott and Dwight? He had specifically told them to get here early with the five-pound boxes of candy and crisp new ten dollar bills from the bank. He had counted on fifteen nurses, but had told them to get twenty, just to be on the safe side.

It's a good thing he had; some nurses he had never seen before were coming in. But where were the boys?

Jan was chatting away gayly. "Daddy, little Ben just loves the big house. I thought in the spring, or when the weather gets a little warmer, we'd put a swing just outside the den under the big oak; maybe a sandpile, too. And he's going to have to take swimming lessons; it's too dangerous, with the pool and all. I've already started doing some Christmas decorating, but I thought we'd wait and get a tree later. Do you know they have artificial ones in the stores now? Can you imagine? They'll never catch on. One of the best thing about Christmas is the smell of fresh pine. I want a real old fashioned tree, not the way Vivian used to decorate them, they were so formal. And I changed the den, she had it so cold and clinical-looking. I thought—"

Duncan interrupted her, "Jan, will you simmer down for a while? Have you any idea what's keeping your brothers? Don't you realize I'm downright uncomfortable, having all these nurses coming in here, and I don't have presents for them?" He reached for the phone.

Jan looked bewildered. "I'm sorry, Daddy—I didn't think. Are you going to call them?"

"No, I'm going to call Larry and tell him to stall," he said.

Just then Scott and Dwight walked in the door, their faces beaming. And, empty handed.

Duncan looked at them, exasperated. "Just where in God's name have you been? And where's the candy and the money?" he said. "The nurses have been walking in and out of here like it was a bus depot."

Their smiles faded, and Dwight groaned, "We forgot."

"Forgot!" Duncan roared. "Do you want me to have another heart attack? Get a move on, while I call Larry."

Dwight and Scott looked at each other. "I guess our news will have to wait," Scott said. "Dwight, you go to the bank, and I'll get the candy. Sorry, Dad." They left the room quickly.

"Jan, you call Dr. Sturgess and explain; tell him not to come over until I call. I'm going in the bathroom, I just can't face any more nurses for a while."

Duncan sat on the toilet and tried to concentrate on the *Reader's Digest*, but it was no use. How could two such intelligent young men forget such a simple thing? He felt ridiculous, hiding from the nurses this way. He heard Jan's light tap on the door.

"Daddy? I didn't get a chance to call; Dr. Sturgess is already here."

Duncan opened the door. "Larry? Keep the nurses out of here. Those fool boys of mine forgot to bring the presents."

Dr. Sturgess grinned. "Simmer down, Duncan; that's no problem. And quit fussing. I passed the boys in the hall, and they were in such a hurry, they barely said 'hello.' Now come on out and start getting ready. The wheelchair will be here pretty soon."

"But I've got to sign all those cards first!" he fumed.

"Okay, get back into bed and I'll examine you again." He called the desk. "Nurse, we don't want to be disturbed for a while—not until Mr. Keith's sons come back. There," he said, and sat down. He looked around the room. "My, you've got a lot of plants and flowers to take home."

"Just the ones by the door, doctor," Jan said quickly, "the nurses can have the rest." She had separated the ones Vivian had brought.

Scott arrived first, flushed and out of breath, and handed the envelopes to his father.

"Good, I can start signing these. Jan, honey, give me that list in the side table." He started writing furiously, checking to make sure the money was in each envelope. He was almost finished when Dwight came in, and there was a quick assembly line of attaching the cards to the boxes of candy.

"There," he sighed. "Larry, do you think we can just leave these at the desk? There's five extra ones, I never even saw some of the nurses who came in here. Think you can take care of it?" He got out of bed again. "Jan, honey, you wait out in the hall, I want to get dressed and out of here."

At the hospital exit, there was another fuss about leaving; all three of his children had their cars, and all three wanted to drive him home. While they were arguing, he motioned the attendant to get him out of his wheelchair and into the nearest available car, which happened to be Jan's. Dwight and Scott followed.

Turning into the long curving driveway of his house, he felt the first real peace he'd felt all morning. My, it was good to be coming home again. The outdoor Christmas tree lights had already been strung up, and there was a huge green wreath adorned with red and gold balls and ribbons on the front door. Jan honked the horn, and almost at once Mrs. Leonard opened the door, and little Ben came rushing out to greet his grandfather, all dressed up in a red jumper suit. Fleetingly, he wondered where Vivian was now, what she was doing, but he put it out of his mind. Jan and little Ben would fill any void in the house from now on.

Dwight and Scott were right behind them, and after he kissed his grandson, they helped him up the stairs into the house. Duncan was tired, and really wanted to go to bed, but there was a fire going in the living room, and the mantle was decorated with greenery. Over the fireplace was a large banner that said "Welcome home, Daddy," and he smiled. Jan really had gone to a lot of trouble. A little visit with his family wouldn't hurt; then he'd go to bed.

He settled on the couch before the fire; Mrs. Leonard had hot chocolate and sandwiches waiting on the coffee table. Jan fussed over him and brought him a blanket, but he protested. "Honey, I'll roast to death; don't you think the fire's enough?" He looked at his two sons; they stood there, first looking at him and then Jan, and they were grinning. "Well, what's the matter with you two? You both look like the cat that swallowed the canary." He leaned back against the cushions. "Well, I'm waiting. I want to know why you forgot to bring the presents today."

Dwight looked at Scott. "You tell him."

Scott looked at his father. "It's about Ben."

Duncan sat up, instantly alert. "What about Ben? Mrs. Leonard, take the child out to play."

"Now, don't get all upset." Scott watched Mrs. Leonard leave the room.

Dwight looked at Jan—she had turned pale. "Nice going, Scott. Sometimes I think your diplomacy stops at the office door." He turned to his father. "It's good news, not bad. We don't have to worry about him any more."

Scott interrupted, "I'm sorry, Dad—Jan. I certainly didn't want to worry you but when I heard the news this morning, I was so relieved, I completely forgot about the presents. Then when I told Dwight, I guess he did, too."

"Will you get on with it?" Duncan was completely exasperated. "Honestly, Scott, sometimes you can take forever." He turned to Dwight. "What happened?"

"Well," Dwight said, "you know we haven't heard a thing about Ben since he beat up on Jan; and I know you've had people out looking for him. It seems he's been holed up in a cheap motel in El Monte, hiding, I suppose, and he's been on a bender ever since. I guess he's been doing most of his drinking in his room, that's why he hasn't been spotted. At least, that's what Lowery thinks."

"Lowery! What does he have to do with all this?"

"The police called him early this morning. I guess Ben got sick of sitting in that room all the time, and he went to a bar in El Monte. He got into a brawl, and the bartender called the cops. When Ben heard the siren, he panicked and ducked out the back way. He stole a car, and they chased him all the way to Baldwin Park before they caught him. He wrapped the car around a telephone pole—he wasn't even scratched, but the car was totalled. He tried to give a false name, but somebody recognized him, and they knew Lowery was your attorney, so they called him. Scott has more of the details, he's the one who talked to Lowery." He turned to his brother. "Why don't you take it from there?"

"Well, Lowery got down to the station around four this morning. By that time, Ben was pretty well sobered up, and scared to death. After all, he'd stolen a car, and it seems he took a swing at a cop. Then when Lowery told him you were going to throw a wife-beating charge at him; you know, with the pictures and all, he completely fell apart. Naturally, he couldn't get any waivers or anything signed at that time in the morning, but it's a cinch there won't be any trouble with the divorce. After the papers are signed, the charges can be dropped. Then you can just give him a few hundred to get out of town, and Jan can get her divorce here; nice and easy. How's that for a Christmas present?" Scott beamed at them.

Duncan was elated. "Boys, I forgive you about the candy." He turned to Jan. "Aren't you relieved, honey?"

"Oh Daddy, I was so afraid he'd come back and try to make trouble. You can't believe what a load this is off my mind."

Duncan was suddenly quiet. "Boys," he said slowly, "this has been a big day, and I'm really tired. Do you mind . . . that is . . . would it be all right if I asked you to go home now? I really think I should get some rest."

Dwight and Scott were concerned, and left almost immediately, assuring him they'd take care of the details with Lowery. The moment they left, he turned to Jan. "Honey, it's marvelous news, but you can't get your divorce here; it's too risky. It takes a year in California, and I notice you're starting to get a little thick around the middle. Right after Christmas, I think you better leave for Reno and get it done there.''

"But Daddy, I don't want to leave you, not so soon after you've come home," she protested.

"Believe me, Jan, it's for the best. Mrs. Leonard and little Ben can stay with me, and six weeks will be gone before you know it. That husband of yours is crazy, and I want your divorce final before the new baby comes," he said firmly.

She agreed, reluctantly, then helped him to the den. He looked around him with approval, then sat down on the bed gratefully.

"Before you go to sleep, Daddy, look out the window."

He looked, but saw nothing out of the ordinary. "What?"

"Wait." She pushed the sliding glass window, and switched on the outside light. The oak tree outside his window lit up with Christmas lights. "I know it doesn't show from the street, but I thought it would be a nice view for you when you're resting at night." She kissed him lightly on the forehead. "You want me to send the nurse in to help you get undressed?"

"Jan, it's beautiful," he said. Vivian never would have thought of doing that. "No, dear, I think I'll just loosen my tie and take off my shoes. Just throw a blanket over me." She switched off the lights on the tree. "You just wake me up when it starts getting dark, and we'll have dinner in here, and look at the tree together."

She pulled the drapes and went out, closing the door gently behind her. He lay there quietly for a while, thinking. He would miss her while she was gone, but it was for the best. And at least, they wouldn't have to worry about Ben any more. Slowly, he drifted off to sleep.

Jan picked up the phone on the second ring, hoping that it hadn't disturbed her father. Who in the world would be calling at this time of night? "Hello?" she almost whispered.

"Mrs. Keith, please," a man's voice said pleasantly.

Jan stiffened. "Mrs. Keith no longer lives here. I'm sorry, but I have no phone number or forwarding address for her." She hung up the phone abruptly; then she picked it up and left it off the hook.

Alex Dunbar stared at the phone in his hand, dumbfounded. He listened to the steady hum and finally hung up himself. Something told him this town wasn't very healthy for him anymore.

Chapter 16

The next week crawled by at a snail's pace for Kathy, and she heaved a sigh of relief when it neared noon on Saturday. John was with his last patient, and as soon as he finished, she could lock up and go. The strain on both of them at the office had been tremendous; it was almost impossible to remain completely professional with someone you'd slept with, but they both tried. She still brought him his coffee at a quarter-to-three, but she had hers in the coffee shop. They no longer had lunch together; instead, she used the time to make a dent in her Christmas shopping. This afternoon, she wanted to finish it, then get her gifts wrapped and delivered tomorrow, if she could.

She still hadn't told him she was leaving next Friday night. She remembered telling him she was spending Christmas with Bruce, but not the whole week. It was just as well she put it off until the last minute; any added stress could be the breaking point in their relationship. And she wasn't sure she wanted that, not now. She realized she was being selfish, keeping him dangling this way, but she had left Bruce before. When she could think logically, which hadn't been too often, she realized it might happen again. One way or the other, she would have to make up her mind before Christmas was over.

She had dinner with Dwight twice during the week. She hadn't intended seeing him again, but when he called, she accepted at once. She had heard Vivian had left; word gets around fast in a small town, and rumors were flying. Even with all her own problems, she couldn't help being curious.

She had listened avidly during their first dinner, while he told her everything, down to the smallest detail. Well, at least that problem was solved. She hadn't let him come in, though.

When she closed the door, the first thought that crossed her mind was that she could hardly wait to tell John about Vivian. Then she remembered. She and John just weren't on that basis any more, and discussing anything outside of simple office routine could lead to other things. Instead, she kept it to herself, although she was almost bursting.

The second time she had dinner with Dwight because he said he had something important to discuss with her, and he didn't want to talk about it over the phone. He had seemed embarrassed all through dinner, and she kept wondering when he'd get around to it. When he finally did, she had to bite her tongue to keep from smiling, it seemed to trivial. He couldn't spend Christmas with her; Jan was planning a family gathering, and wanted his kids there, which naturally meant Nancy. He could spend Christmas Eve with her, though. His relief when she told him she was going out of town for Christmas was obvious, although he tried to hide it.

She slept badly that night; but then, she'd been sleeping badly all week. Christmas Eve, she'd be with Bruce, but Christmas Day she'd be alone. If her life had gone differently, she'd be spending Christmas with a family of her own, maybe a couple of kids by now. It took her hours to get to sleep, and when she finally did, it was fitful—and she had that dream again. But she never even considered sleeping pills, not after what pills had done to Pam.

Pam was looking marvelous these days. She was still in the hospital, but she'd be home for Christmas. She'd confided in Kathy that she and Jack were going to be married, but it was a secret for the time being. John knew, but she didn't discuss that with him, either.

She heard John's door open, and saw him standing in the doorway with his patient. Well, maybe she'd sleep tonight. The stores were jammed with shoppers now, and with the list of things she still had to buy, she should be worn out by the time she got home.

It was seven o'clock before Kathy reached the men's department at Altman's. She hadn't stopped to eat, her feet hurt, she was loaded down with packages, she had spent far too much money already, and she still had to buy Dwight something. On impulse, she had bought herself a pale green chiffon negligee set that was outrageously expensive, but she didn't regret it. She had decided on a cashmere sweater for Dwight, and started looking around the department. She had debated about getting John something, but under the present circumstances, decided it wouldn't be in good taste. There was a tie-silk paisley robe that would have been perfect for him under different circumstances—he could have left it at her place to wear. A woman who looked vaguely familiar was fingering the robe, but Kathy couldn't place her. Suddenly, the woman looked up, smiled, and motioned her over. Kathy smiled back, and hesitated. Had she met her at the Club?

"Kathy," the woman said, and instantly, she recognized the voice. "I'm so glad I ran into you; do you think John would like this? She ran her hands over the material. "It's just his size, but I was wondering about the colors."

"I think it's lovely, Mrs. Carter," Kathy managed. "My, you look just wonderful." She was at a loss for words; Edith had lost pounds, and looked years younger. "You've lost so much weight, and your hairdo! It's just fabulous."

"Why, thank you, Kathy—you mean John didn't tell you? He hardly recognized me when I got home."

"Oh yes," Kathy stuttered, "yes, of course he did, the very first thing Monday morning. But, you know, telling someone something, and then seeing them, are two different things. You know men, you think they tend to exaggerate, but he certainly didn't in your case." She forced a wide smile. That son of a bitch, she thought. He hadn't said one word about the change in Edith. She'd bet her bottom dollar he wasn't suffering nearly as much as she'd thought he was, and Edith's next words confirmed it.

"You know," she said in a confidential voice, "it's really something how a person can let themself go. You go along for years, looking in the mirror every day, and not noticing a thing. That is, until you stop and really take a good look. You think you're just the same, and then all of a sudden, good heavens! You realize you're a mess. But I just never thought about it before. And in a way, I have you to thank."

"Me!" Kathy didn't understand; at least, she hoped she didn't. "What did I have to do with all this?"

"Well, you remember that time a month or so ago, when you called John late at night?" She interrupted herself as she caught the eye of a saleslady. "Miss, I'll take this—and could I have a gift box, please?" She rummaged in her purse. "Here's my charge plate." She looked at Kathy and continued. "You know, that night you were so upset, when you had to take a patient of John's to the hospital?"

"I remember," Kathy said uneasily.

"After he left, I started thinking how pretty you are. Oh, not that I was jealous or anything like that," she hastened to reassure her, "but I had a picture of you in my mind, and then I got up and looked in the mirror and realized how much I'd changed, and it really wasn't fair to John. I don't mean he ever complained, you understand, but he always kept himself so fit, and I hadn't. I tried dieting at home, but it wasn't easy. That's when I decided to go to the health farm. Not that we didn't always have a good marriage, but you can't imagine what a difference it's made. Why, it's almost like a second honeymoon. And taking all of Christmas week off—he's never done that before."

"He's taking the whole week off?" Kathy blurted out.

Edith looked dismayed. "Oh dear, he hasn't told you? He must have been saving it for a surprise—and now I've spoiled it for you. Some of our relatives are coming in from out of town, and he's closing the office for the week. Oh, he's going to be so angry with me for tellingyou before he did; but I was sure he would have told you by now." She looked so worried, Kathy couldn't help but feel sorry for her—she was such a gentle woman.

"Mrs. Carter, don't worry, please." Kathy smiled at her. "He probably did want to surprise me." (Like hell he did; he wanted to see me squirm until the very last minute.) "I'll tell you what; let's just keep this our little secret—we won't tell him we saw each other. Then, when he tells me, which I'm sure will be soon, I'll act very surprised." (And she would, too; otherwise, he'd know she'd seen Edith, and she wanted to save that little bombshell for some future date.)

"Oh wonderful," Edith was delighted, but then she frowned. "Really, he should have told you before this—it was very inconsiderate of him. He should have known you'd want to make plans."

"Well, there's really no harm done," Kathy forced another smile. "Now, I really have to run, I've still got some shopping to do." They said their goodbyes, and Kathy went to pick out a sweater for Dwight. Inwardly, she was seething. Second honeymoon, indeed! And making her feel so guilty about Bruce, when all the time he was playing footsy with Edith. Men! He was just as bad as the rest of them. She picked out a greyish blue cashmere without giving it much thought, not bothering to check the price. On the way out of the store, she saw an expensive Sasha ashtray and on impulse, bought that, too.

She finally got all the things in the trunk, then remembered she'd forgotten to buy any Christmas wrappings, and marched back into the store again. The jostling customers irriated her more than ever, and by the time she was finally through, she was really in a state.

Driving home, she opened all the windows and tried to cool down. Why should she be so upset? Actually, she should be glad she didn't have to feel guilty any more. She should feel relieved; instead, she had to admit, she felt jealous. Oh, this was ridiculous, she was acting like a schoolgirl. You can't have your cake and eat it, too. Here she was, getting ready to spend almost an entire week with Bruce, and up until an hour ago, she had felt smug and selfishly secure in the knowledge that John would be miserable while she was gone. It was a dog-in-the-manger attitude, worthy of a sixteen-year old, perhaps, but not of her. Where was her sophistication, her worldly outlook? Suddenly, she felt pretty damn dumb.

She parked the car in the driveway, let Topsy out, then opened the trunk and struggled with the packages. She made several trips, dumping everything on the couch. She stood there, looking at them. Usually, this was a happy time of year for her, wrapping presents. She always did it after the tree was up, sitting cross-legged on the floor, with the lights twinkling on the tree. But there was no tree here, and wrapping the gifts loomed ahead of her as a huge chore rather than a pleasure.

She let Topsy in, fixed herself a stiff drink, and decided to call Maude and chat for a while. As she was about to pick up the phone, it rang, and Dwight was on the other end asking her to go out to dinner. She looked at the gift-laden couch; well why not? She could wrap them in the morning. She told him to come right over, then she hid the cashmere sweater. She hesitated, then she hid the Sasha ashtray, too. She had bought it for John, although for the life of her, she couldn't imagine why. She certainly had no intention of giving it to him. Then she fixed herself another drink and went into the bathroom to fix her makeup.

Jack walked Kathy to the hospital parking lot after she visited with Pam. Pam had been sparkling and bubbly, anxious to leave the hospital, and devastated when Kathy told her she'd be away for Christmas.

"But you just can't! You're the only one who knows we're engaged, and there's so much I want to talk to you about."

Pam had shown her the ring. She couldn't even wear it around her neck, because of the nurses. Instead, the ring stayed concealed in her purse. It was a large square cut diamond. She was bursting to tell the world, but stubborn enough to think Jack's father should be the first to know officially.

"I'll be back soon; probably the day after Christmas, and I'll see you then. We'll have plenty of time to talk," Kathy had assured her.

Jack was quiet in the elevator, and much more solemn than he had been around Pam. When they started walking to her car, he began talking. "Kathy, I'll be keeping regular appointments with the Doc right after the first of the year. Pam thinks it's a good idea, and I'm inclined to agree with her. I've still got a lot of guilt feelings to work out before we get married. I want this to be right for us." They stopped at her car. "That's one reason I wanted to talk to you alone. If I'm going to be completely honest with him, I'll have to tell him about you and me."

She looked at him, and nodded quietly. "He already knows, Jack. I told him."

He looked a little surprised, and then relieved. "Well,

that's one thing out of the way. But there's something else; you and Pam are good friends, in fact, I think you're about the best friend she has. April used to be, but she's been gone so long, they've grown apart. And I want you to keep on being good friends—that's why I don't ever want her to know about you and me."

She flushed slightly. "She'll never hear it from me, Jack. I know confession is good for the soul, and all that, but there's another saying—discretion is the better part of valor." She reached up and kissed him on the cheek, then got in her car and drove off.

At three o'clock the following Friday, John Carter sat alone in his office, pulled open the bottom drawer of his desk, got out a bottle of Scotch and poured himself a drink. Mr. Dudley had just left, and he had a free hour before his last patient for the day. He'd have to quit this, he thought, as he downed the drink and poured himself another one. He'd been drinking far too much the past two weeks, but he'd been going through hell, and the liquor eased the pain a little. This armed truce between himself and Kathy couldn't go on much longer. Every time he got near her, he longed to take her in his arms, and sometimes he had to clench his fists to resist.

And the there was Edith. He felt so damn guilty after all the trouble she'd gone to, to make herself attractive for him. Sure, the first night she was home, he'd become sexually aroused, it was like making love to a completely different body. But the second night, he'd become used to that body, and the stimulation hadn't been there. Edith only knew one way to make love; after a few kisses, she lay on her back, spread her legs slightly, and waited. But after being with Kathy, and knowing just how marvelous sex could be, the delicate nuances, the different positions . . . he became panicky. Sex with Edith two nights in a row was something he simply couldn't cope with. And there she was, just laying there, waiting for him. He reached down and felt himself, and he was completely limp. He certainly couldn't teach her anything; she'd wonder where he'd learned. He didn't know what to do, so he pulled her over against him and kissed her. "I guess I've had too much to drink."

He felt her stiffen slightly, and he knew he had hurt her. Then he had an idea; he switched off the night light, and started kissing her again in the darkness, thinking of Kathy, conjuring up mental images of the two of them together in his mind. He knew it was a rotten thing to do, and he tried not to think of that. Instead, he thought of the first bath they'd taken together, soaping each other, laughing and making love talk, then rinsing each other off. He thought of other times they'd made love, like the first time in the shower, and on the loveseat in her living room—while he kept on kissing Edith. Slowly, it began to work, and he felt his passion rising. He swung himself on top of her, his mouth still glued to hers. He knew if she spoke, the illusion would be shattered.

It hadn't taken him long to reach a climax, and after he did, he felt just about as low and rotten as a man could feel. But Edith was satisfied, and that was the important thing. Since that time he'd had to do the same thing whenever they made love. And each time, he felt even viler.

He knew the situation was affecting his work; some of his patients' problems seemed so trivial compared to his own, and he had to control himself at times to hide his irritation. And Kathy wasn't there to fill the void, to talk things over with. He finished his drink and poured himself another one, then looked at his watch. Twenty minutes to four. He considered asking Kathy to come in and join him, but he hesitated. Frankly, he was puzzled. She must have noticed he hadn't booked any appointments for tomorrow or next week, but she hadn't said a word about it. He hadn't told her they'd be closed Christmas week, he kept waiting for her to ask—but she didn't. It was childish, of course, and he realized that; but somehow, he felt it would give him the upper hand.

He also had a Christmas present for her that he'd ordered made over a month ago, and he kept changing his mind about whether or not to give it to her. It was a black onyx pin in the shape of a French poodle, with emerald eyes for her birthstone, and the collar was tiny seed pearls for the day of the month. It looked a great deal like Topsy, and had cost more than he'd spent on Edith for Christmas.

"Oh, what the hell, it's Christmas," he muttered out loud, and buzzed her on the intercom. She answered almost immediately. "Kathy? You want to come in and have a Christmas drink with me?"

She hesitated for a minute. "Sure, be right in." She opened her middle drawer and started to take out the Sasha ashtray she had wrapped with such care. Then she changed her mind, shut the drawer again, and walked down the hall to John's office.

"Merry Christmas," he said as she walked in. His face was a little flushed, and she knew immediately he'd been drinking.

"Merry Christmas to you," she smiled, and sat down.

"Brandy, scotch, or bourbon?"

"Brandy, I guess, since we don't have any ice. And make it a double, so I can catch up," she kept smiling, and waited.

"Does it show that much?" he asked, thinking of his next patient.

"John, practically everybody that's come in here today has had liquor on their breath. I really wouldn't worry about it. Anyway it's Mr. Robertson, I doubt he'll even show." He handed her the brandy, and she took a deep swallow.

"I guess you've noticed I haven't booked anyone for next week."

(Here it comes.) "I wondered about it, a little," she lied, "but then, I just thought people were too busy to come in, with Christmas and all."

Somehow, he felt deflated, and as though he'd been outmaneuvered. "No, we're going to be closed all next week. I was saving it for a surprise." The explanation sounded flat, even to himself. Damn her, anyway; he felt like locking the door, and taking her right there in the office.

"Oh John, how wonderful." She tried to sound sincere. (You bastard. If you only knew my bags are all packed, and all I have to do is go home, take a bath, change my clothes, and pick up Topsy.)

"You really don't have to come in tomorrow, either, if you don't want to," he added magnanimously, as though it was an afterthought. "You must have lots of shopping to do."

"Oh, I do, I do," she tried to sound delighted. "This is very generous of you, John."

"When do you plan to leave town?" he asked flatly.

She was prepared for this. "Oh, I don't know," she said vaguely, "early next week, I guess. I still have so many presents to buy and deliver here; I'm really not sure." There was no possible way he could know it was all done, except through Pam, maybe. But then she'd warned Pam not to say anything. Anyway, Pam didn't know exactly when she was leaving, just that she wouldn't be here for Christmas. "I hope you have a nice week off, John." She would have loved to say something like—and continue your second honeymoon with Edith—but she bit her tongue, and finished her drink instead. He stopped her when she started to get up.

"Please, have another drink with me." She sat down again, he poured her drink, then started fumbling in his lower drawer. "I have a little something for you," he sounded a little embarrassed, and finally found a small package. "I ordered it for you before . . . well, you know. I hope you like it."

It was Kathy's turn to feel disconcerted. "I have something for you, too. It's in my desk, but I didn't know whether or not to give it to you . . . under the circumstances." Suddenly, they both looked at each other and laughed, and the tension was temporarily broken.

"I guess we've both been acting pretty childish," he said.

"I guess we have," she answered, and started opening her present, but he stopped her.

"No, don't open it now. Open it before you leave town, but don't open it now."

She looked at him quizzically. "All right, John, if you wish. And thank you."

"Kathy," he was looking at her seriously now, and he sounded completely sober. "I want to say something to you before you leave, and I want you to believe me. I'm truly sorry about the past two weeks; I'm sure it's been hell for you. I know it has for me. Some of the things I said to you; well, they were completely unforgivable. I love you very much. You've got to remember, when you love someone, hate is the other side of the coin. There have been times these past two weeks when I've hated you, Kathy. Where there's no strong feeling one way, there can't be any strong feeling the other; can you understand that? God, I hope so. I know I've put it badly, but it's so hard to find the right words. My patients are one thing—with them I can be completely objective, clinical and analytical. But I can't be any of those things with you. God knows, I want you back, Kathy, but even more than that, I want your happiness. I hope you find what you're looking for, I really do. But I'd be a liar if I said I hoped you found it with Bruce. I'll be here waiting, when you come back; you will come back, won't you?" He looked at her longingly, and there were tears in his eyes.

"I'll be back, John," she said gently. Kathy was confused; she knew John's words were sincere, he meant what he said. But then what had Edith been talking about? Was she living in a fool's paradise? She had hated John sometimes these last two weeks, too; did that mean she loved him, as well?

"Will you kiss me goodbye, Kathy?"

Suddenly, she was in his arms, and he kissed her for the first time in almost three weeks, gently at first, then with more and more urgency. She felt her lips parting as she started to respond, and slow warmth spread through her body. His hands slipped down, pressing her closer to him, and her fingers gripped his back. Suddenly, she realized what was happening, and abruptly pulled away from him.

"Not now, John," she whispered hoarsely.

There was silence in the room except for their heavy breathing, as they stared at each other. Finally, he spoke. "I don't think Robertson's going to show up—you might as well leave now, if you want to."

"I'll help you lock up," she offered, still staring at him.

He shook his head. "No, you better go now, if you're going. I'll stay here for a while." He tried to smile, but it was a sad attempt. "Then I've got to meet Edith and pick out a Christmas tree."

She hesitated. "I may be back before next weekend."

"God, I hope so, Kathy," he said. A ray of hope lit up his eyes momentairly, and quickly dimmed. He wanted to say more, but the time had passed. Instead, he helped her on with her coat, and walked her to the door. "I'll call the exchange every day. Just leave a message and I'll be there."

She drove home through the heavy traffic, wondering whether she was immoral, amoral, or just simple minded. As soon as she got in the door, she tore open the present he had given her. Tears came to her eyes; it was such a thoughtful gift. She tried to remind herself he had ordered it before Bruce had come back into her life, but it did no good. The fact remained that John had almost made love to her in the office, when she knew she was going to sleep with Bruce tonight, and she wasn't really sure which of them had stopped in time.

It was later than she expected when she finally swung in to the underground garage. She had bathed and dressed hurriedly, but then she had a few phone calls to make. She called Dwight first, then Irene, and told them she was leaving tonight. Neither of them were particularly anxious to end the conversations; she had to promise to call Dwight the minute she got back to town, and accepted a dinner invitation from Irene the Sunday after Christmas. Then she called Pam and asked her, please, not to tell Dr. Carter she was leaving tonight.

She put her bags in the car, went back to check all the doors and windows, and took a final look in the mirror. She was wearing the pale green cashmere sweater set with white mink collar and cuffs that Dwight had given her for Christmas, with a matching skirt. She looked just fine, she thought; her cheeks were flushed and her eyes were sparkling. She scooped up Topsy, put her in the car, and headed for Bruce.

She parked the car carefully, then leaned her head back against the headrest and closed her eyes, savoring the moment; she was finally here! Topsy started barking and jumped on her stomach, anxious to get out. She walked her up the ramp to the street, where she squatted immediately. Then she went directly to the elevator—Bruce could get the bags later.

She used her key instead of the bell, and threw the door open. "Bruce, I'm here!" she called out happily—but she was talking to an empty apartment. Oh no, this wasn't possible; where could he be? A light was on near the terrace doors, and she was reassured momentarily. Then she remembered she'd always left a light on, too, when she'd gone away for the weekend. She switched on the light by the door and ran out to the kitchen; the refrigerator was fully stocked. She went into the bedroom and flung open the closet; his clothes were there, and the scent of his aftershave lotion still lingered in the room. She looked at her watch, almost eight-thirty.

She walked back to the living room and stood there, her legs apart, her hands on her hips; this was one hell of a greeting. Sure, she had told him she'd be late, but she certainly had expected him there waiting for her. The office party was never until two days before Christmas, so he couldn't be there; anyway, he could have made his excuses. She called the office number just to make sure; there was no answer. Then she called Maude, and let the phone ring and ring. She wasn't home; probably out Christmas shopping. She debated about fixing herself a drink or going down and getting her bags; she felt foolish just standing there. She decided on the bags first, and took the phone off the hook in case he called before she got back.

When she got back upstairs, she threw her bags on the bed, put the phone back on the hook, and mixed herself a drink. She pulled open the drapes and wandered out on the terrace, trying to enjoy the view. The city beneath her was alive with lights, and it was really breathtaking; it was also very chilly, so she came back in and closed the doors. She sat down by the phone and sipped her drink; where in the hell was he? She hesitated using the phone to make inquiries; he might be trying to call her. By nine-thirty, she began to get worried—she was about to pick up the phone and call Maude when it finally rang.

"Kathy?" Bruce's voice sounded apologetic. "Honey, I'm so sorry I wasn't there when you got in. You just get there?"

She could hear a lot of noise in the background. "Yes, just a few minutes ago," she lied, "Where are you?"

He lowered his voice. "Kitten, I'm with a new client, and

he's talking my head off. I just can't get away from him—do you think you could catch a cab and join us? We're at the Beverly Hills Hotel."

"Bruce, you know it's Friday night, and it may take a while. I've got a better idea; why don't you go outside now, there's a cabstand at the corner. Give him an extra five and send him over."

"Good idea," Bruce agreed, "And Kathy . . . I'm really sorry about tonight."

"Oh, forget it, Bruce. See you in a little while." She took her drink and her purse, and went in to freshen her makeup. She felt deflated, somehow. Funny, she'd forgotten how often this had happened in the past, once word had gotten around town that she was Bruce's "private stock." Instead, she'd remembered all the funny little out-of-the-way places he had taken her to in the beginning, when there were never any clients along, and the agency business was seldom even part of their conversation. And she'd forgotten all the clients who either didn't know or didn't care that she was Bruce's "private stock," and made passes at her anyway when Bruce wasn't around, or tried to touch her under the table when he was. Or the arguments they'd had, when she preferred to stay home rather than spend what she called, "a client evening." It reminded her too much of when she first worked for the agency, before she met Bruce. If there was another girl along, it wasn't much better; the girl was also a reminder. Had she really acted as coy and giggly as some of those girls? She doubted it, but she wasn't sure. Resignedly, she touched up her lipstick, patted a little powder on her face, brushed her hair, and went to wait for the cab.

When the cab arrived at the Beverly Hills Hotel, both Bruce and the client were waiting for her. She'd expected at least a few minutes with Bruce alone, and now she wasn't even going to have that.

"Hello, darling," Bruce said jovially, "you look wonderful. Kathy, this is Phil. Phil, Kathy. Honey, we're all going to Dave's Blue Room. Phil, you wait outside for a minute while I kiss my girl." He got in the cab and kissed her thoroughly, then muttered in her ear, "I couldn't explain over the phone, he was standing right beside me. Kathy, I'm at my wits end; he wants a girl, but he didn't tell me until about two hours ago. I've made at least a dozen phone calls, and I can't find anyone available. If we don't run into something at Dave's, I don't know what to do."

"Oh, dammit," she said angrily, "this is going to be some evening. Why didn't you think of it before, and have someone in reserve?"

"Well, look at him; he hardly looks the type." They both looked. Then he grabbed her again, and pretended to be kissing her ear, so Phil wouldn't think anything was wrong. "Can you think of anything?" he whispered.

"I'm not going to pimp for you, if that's what you mean," she whispered back, furiously. "But I'll excuse myself when we get there, if there's nothing around. There's a phone in the ladies' room at Dave's, and I'll call the bartender at Player's. I certainly don't want to be stuck with him all evening—what there is left of it."

Bruce motioned Phil to come around the other side and get in the cab. He seemed innocuous enough; he was mild-mannered and polite. She shrugged; you never could tell.

It was after two in the morning when Kathy and Bruce finally got back to the apartment. Dave's Blue Room and Player's had proved equally fruitless; it appeared as though all of a sudden, the town was bereft of available girls. Kathy and Bruce were getting hungry, and they both drank slowly, but Phil was feeling no pain. He began looking at Kathy strangely, and she started getting nervous. Then suddenly, she remembered Ron, a photographer friend of hers. He knew plenty of models, all of them gorgeous. She excused herself quickly, and went to the phone, praying he was in. He was, he was having a party, and there were plenty of pretty girls; why didn't Kathy and her friends join them? Kathy explained the situation to Ron, listened to his reply, and hung up. She scribbled something on a piece of paper and handed it under the table to Bruce when she rejoined them, motioning her head slightly in the direction of the phone.

Then it was Bruce's turn; he went to the phone in the men's room and read the note: "Call Ron, tell him who you are. There are three extra girls at his place—Sue, Cheryl and Nancy. The financial arrangements are up to you. Here's the number."

It hadn't taken Bruce long, and he was grinning when he came back to the table. But by this time, it was almost eleven o'clock, and they had to wait for the girl (it turned out to be Sue) and then there was dinner to get through.

She heaved a sigh of relief when the door of the apartment was finally shut, and they were alone. She kicked off her shoes, slumped down in the nearest chair, and Topsy jumped in her lap.

Bruce stood there, looking at her uncertainly. "Honey, I really am sorry. I had no idea it would turn out this way. Phil was in the office today, and I just asked him to have a drink with me; but then, he wanted to make an evening of it. Things just got out of hand."

She looked at him, but she didn't say what she wanted to. Why couldn't he have just said he had other plans. But no, the possibility of a new client, the chance of landing a big new account, a fat commission for himself, and new business for the agency; that always seemed to come first. Any ordinary evening would be bad enough; but tonight, of all nights. Why, Bruce, why? But she didn't say any of these things—she was tired, and they'd gotten off to a bad enough start already. Instead, she just said, "Well, these things happen sometimes; I guess you just have to roll with the punches. I just thought . . . well, I thought we'd be alone tonight, that's all. But we still have five more days."

He looked relieved. "I'm glad you're taking it this way—I really feel rotten about it, though. Does your leg hurt you?"

She looked at him, surprised. "No, why?"

"You've been rubbing it on and off all evening; you're doing it now."

She looked down, and her hand was massaging her left leg. "I didn't even realize it," she frowned. Abruptly, she pulled her hand away. "It must be a nervous habit I've acquired; several people have mentioned it lately. You know, like some people tug at their ear lobes. Sorry." She changed the subject. "Would you mind taking Topsy out? I've got to unpack."

"Sounds like old times," he grinned at her, and picked up Topsy's leash. The dog jumped off Kathy's lap immediately and started jumping up and down. "Tell me, who walks her for you in Monrovia?"

She made a small face at him. "Nobody, I have a back yard."

She sat there for a few minutes after he left, thinking. She hoped he hadn't made any more plans for the time she'd be here; all she wanted to do was be alone with him. Except for Maude, of course. She realized she was rubbing her leg again, and got up quickly to go unpack.

She was almost through by the time he came back. He came up behind her and put his arms around her, nuzzling her neck. "Have I told you lately that I love you very much?" His words made her feel warm all over. "And that I had different plans for tonight, too?"

"Like what?" she asked, turning around in his arms.

"Like, for instance, there are two big thick steaks thawing out in the refrigerator, and there's some champagne on ice. And I rummaged around in the basement and brought up all

426

the ornaments and lights you had. There aren't very many, you know; unless I didn't find them all."

"You probably did; I never had a very big tree."

"Well, we will this year, to celebrate our first Christmas Eve together." He started kissing her again, until she finally broke away.

"Honey, I hate to mention this, but if you don't go shave, you're going to have to look at me for the next few days with a raw face."

He grinned, "Well, we can't have that—we don't want Maude or Logan making cracks."

"Oh Bruce, you mean you told them at the agency that I was coming here?" She was dismayed.

"Of course," he looked puzzled. "Didn't you want me to? I thought after we got the place decorated and all, you'd want to see Maude and Pete, and some of your old friends. You know, maybe even have an open house Monday night; nothing big." He looked a little uncomfortable now. "After all, it's just one night."

"Just one night," she wailed, "and two days before getting ready for it, and two days after cleaning up. You know you don't mean maybe, you've already asked them. Oh Bruce, how could you?"

"Well, don't worry about the work, I'll have it catered—or I can call it off."

She shook her head. "No, you've already committed yourself, I guess. Now I'll have to see them, so we might as well get it over with in one fell swoop. No buffet, though, just canapes and hors d'oeuvres. Damn it though, Bruce, I wish you'd asked me first."

"I'm sorry, Kitten; but you always loved to give parties, and I really thought you'd be pleased."

"Normally, yes, if we were going to be together for months; but we only have five days!"

427

"It doesn't have to be just five days." He looked at her closely. When she didn't answer, he waited. "I take it by your silence that it does. I'm not going to be in New York long this time, you know; I have to be back here by the middle of next month."

"I have obligations, Bruce," she said evenly, "just the same as you do."

"Obligations! You've only been there four months; just what are they? Sorry; I wasn't going to ask."

"No, it's all right. I have a job, and I'm expected back. And I'm supposed to give a shower for a friend of mine who's just been through a very serious illness. There are other things, too," she said vaguely, "but they wouldn't interest you."

He rubbed the stubble on his chin, and she knew him well enough to know he was thinking of the possibility of another man. All he said though, was, "I better go shave."

She finished her unpacking, then undressed quickly and got into bed. The sheets were cold, and she shivered. In a few minutes, Bruce would be beside her, and they would make love, and the events of the evening and the open house coming up would be completely blotted out of her mind—for the time being, at least.

Kathy moved among the guests in her smoke-filled living room, a fixed smile on her face, the picture of a perfect hostess. From a "nothing big" party, it had certainly grown; there were some people here she didn't even know. They had hired a couple to cater the party, and a bartender. The two caterers took turns moving among the guests with hot and cold hors d'oeuvres, and the bartender was kept busy. Reluctantly, she had finally agreed to a simple buffet as the guest list had grown. The Christmas tree stood directly in front of the sliding glass doors to the terrace, and she opened the doors on either side to let the smoke out, but it didn't help much. The tree kept getting jostled, and now she wished she'd put it in a corner somewhere, at least until the party was over.

She looked at the tree, and thought about the weekend; it had been idyllic, and after tonight, they'd have two more nights alone together. They had gone out Saturday to get a tree, and Bruce had taken forever until he found one that was perfect from every angle, an enormous blue spruce. With the tree strapped on top of his car, they had shopped for more ornaments and lights, and some outdoor ones for the terrace. When they finally finished, she was fairly well bushed and would have settled for a hamburger and bed—but he reminded her of the steaks in the refrigerator. While she fixed those, some baked potatoes and a tossed salad, he had put the lights on the tree. Eating revived her, and they decorated the tree together.

It was midnight when they finished. Bruce stepped back and looked at their handiwork critically. "Well, I guess that just about does it. I'll have to put the outside lights up tomorrow; it's too late to start hammering tonight."

They had sat on the couch in front of the fireplace, holding hands and sipping brandy while they admired the tree, the first one they'd ever had together. Sunday had been perfect, too; they had stayed in bed late, then asked Maude over for brunch. Sunday night, they'd taken a long drive around town, looking at the decorated homes in Beverly Hills and Westwood. Then when they got home, they'd . . . .

"What?" she said, startled. Someone was asking her something. It was Dick Spencer from the agency, with a drink in his hand and a leer on his face.

"Where you been?" he asked. "You look like you were a million miles away. I asked you how you liked that podunk town you've been living in; what's its name again?"

"Monrovia," she smiled, determined to be pleasant. "And it's not a podunk town."

"You mean you actually like it there?" He was deliberately baiting her. "Come on, Kathy, tell me the truth; don't you wish sometimes you were back with the agency, instead of in that one-horse town?"

People were listening now, expecting trouble; she looked around for Bruce, and saw him making his way towards her through the crowd. "Dick, have you ever been there?"

"Me?" he pretended shock. "I wouldn't be caught dead in the sticks with a bunch of hicks."

"Dick," she was still trying to be pleasant, but she could feel her face starting to get warm. "In the first place, Monrovia is neither podunk, one-horse, or the sticks. The people there are not hicks; they all eat, sleep, work, play, and believe it or not, they all have indoor plumbing. They also fornicate, get drunk, get thrown in jail sometimes, cheat, steal, and play around on their wives . . . or husbands, as the case may be. They go to church, contribute to charities, raise families, and vote. There are some good people, and some that are not so nice." She paused, "In other words, Dick, they're just like the people in this room, and this town. They're just not quite so open about what they do as we are." Then she turned her back on him, and Bruce was at her elbow. "Let's go out on the terrace, I need some fresh air," she said.

"Bravo," Bruce said quietly when they were alone. "I'm glad you told that punk off, he had it coming. I never did like the guy, and I've told Pete. I think we should get rid of him." He looked at her, trying to make out her expression. "You want me to get you a drink?"

"Yes, would you, please?" She didn't really want one that badly, but she wanted to be alone for a minute, to think. While she had been talking to Dick, she realized everything she said was true; she'd just never put it into words before. The people *were* the same; actually, what was Hollywood? The majority of the people here at this party were from small towns—how often did you meet a native? She was the odd-ball, because she'd been born here. Funny that she'd never thought of that before. The people in this town put on a big act most of the time—but then, didn't Irene, and Pam? Good Lord, Vivian's act had been a masterpiece! She felt cheated, somehow. She had thought a small town would be the answer; but the people were the same. And somehow, she knew it would be the same no matter where she went. Where were all the simple, happy people? Maybe there weren't any, except in storybooks and movies. She'd been looking for something that didn't even exist, and she felt very foolish and very sad.

Pete Logan stuck his head outside, spotted her and rushed to her side. "Kathy!" His face was splotched with anger. "I just heard what that jerk did. I know it's your party, but I sent him home in a cab, and I told him I wanted him in my office, first thing in the morning. Can I get you a drink? Are you terribly upset?"

In spite of the way she felt, she couldn't help laughing. "Pete, forget it—he was just drunk, and trying to bait me. It's forgotten already. And no, Bruce is getting me a drink."

"Thank God; I thought he'd ruined the party for you." He looked relieved. "By the way, it is one hell of a party; we've all missed you. Kathy, why don't you come back to the agency? We need you."

The question caught her unaware. "Oh, I don't know, Pete—can you ever really go back?"

"Go back!" he exploded, "Good God, Kathy, you've only been gone a few months—it's only been a hiatus. Look, if you come back, honest to God, I'll quit swearing. I'll even fire that son-of-a-bitch Spencer."

She couldn't help but smile; Pete Logan couldn't quit swearing if his life depended on it—it was as much a part of him as breathing. "I'll think about it."

Bruce returned with drinks for both of them. "Pete, I

didn't know you were here; trying to steal my thunder?" He handed Kathy her drink and draped his arm around her shoulder casually.

"I've been trying to talk her into coming back to the agency."

"Good; I hope you got farther with her than I did." Both men looked at her and waited.

"I said I'd think about it," she protested, "just don't rush me." She took a sip of her drink; she had other things on her mind than the agency, and changed the subject. "Don't you think we better get back inside now? After all, we are the host and hostess," she turned to Pete and laughed, "and you're the official bouncer."

They went back into the living room, and Kathy took a quick, practiced look around her. Good; some of them had already started eating from the buffet, and nobody looked too drunk. She looked around for Maude, and finally spotted her, gorging herself on crab casserole. Poor Maude; she tried so hard to diet, but she just never could resist food. She remembered she hadn't eaten anything herself today. "Bruce, Pete; let's go get some of that food before it's all gone—I'm starved."

When they closed the front door on the last of the guests, Kathy and Bruce looked at each other with relief. "I don't know about you, but I'm exhausted," she said, as she started emptying ashtrays.

Bruce stopped her, "No you don't. I said you wouldn't have to do any work on this party, and I meant it. The caterers are waiting in the kitchen, and they'll do all the cleaning up."

"Well, that's nice," she said, walking around the room, inspecting the furniture. "What do we do in the meantime?"

"I hadn't thought of that; have a nightcap and watch them, I suppose. What in the world are you doing?"

"I'm looking for cigarette burns, or any other damage; you know I always do that after a party, or have your forgotten?" She stopped behind one of the couches. "Oh hell, somebody spilled a drink; it must have happened when we were outside."

"Well, let's not worry about it tonight." He called to the caterers, "Everybody's gone home."

"I'll just put some soda water on it; maybe it'll take it out." She passed the caterers on her way to the kitchen. She got the soda and a cloth and started back, wondering why she should be so concerned. After all, this was Bruce's apartment now—not hers.

She stayed awake long after Bruce had fallen into a heavy sleep, thinking. There was the office party that they'd have to make a brief appearance at tomorrow; sometime during the day, she wanted to go to Rodeo Drive and pick up the present she'd ordered for Bruce. And she was thinking of the discovery she'd made tonight. Then she realized she was rubbing her leg again, and eased herself gently out of bed. Bruce always kept some tranquilizers in the bathroom cabinet, and she knew she'd never get to sleep without one.

April sorted through the thick pile of mail hurriedly. It had been almost three weeks since she'd had any mail from Switzerland, not even a newspaper. Of course, she realized the mail from Europe was always sporadic, and Christmas mail didn't help matters any. Still, three weeks was a long time. She picked out the large, bulky envelope from the center of the pile, and recognized Greta's firm, heavy scrawl. Finally! Maybe it was some good news for a change, she could certainly use some. It was the day before Christmas, and it had taken every ounce of her self-control to hide her feelings from her parents. After all, there was no sense in ruining their holiday, too.

She locked her door as soon as she was back in her room, and ripped open the envelope. There was a letter from Greta, and another sealed envelope inside, with these words on it: "April; please read my letter before you open this envelope."

An icy feeling of foreboding started creeping over her, and her hands began to shake. She unfolded the letter slowly and started to read: "Dear April: My good and dear friend, there is really no easy way to tell you this. Of course, you know as well as I that you cannot believe everything you read in the newspapers, and I think you should. . . ."

She looked at Greta's envelope—it was dated two weeks ago. Oh God, why did it have to come now, today? Why not a week ago, or a few days later? It seemed so cruel somehow, to arrive the day before Christmas. She got up to get a cigarette, and the envelope fell off her lap. She stood in front of the window, looking out at the peace and quiet of the bright, sunny day, wondering how she'd get through Christmas.

Juan was dead, she thought dully; she didn't have to open the envelope to know that, she felt it in her bones. Once she'd faced that fact, she somehow felt calmer. Wearily, she picked up the envelope and tore it open. She pulled out the sheaf of newspaper clippings, and saw Juan's face staring up at her, and the bold black-faced type that confirmed her suspicions. Bits and pieces of the clippings went through her mind. "Body found in Lake Neuchatel. . . .badly mutilated. . . .positive identification made, although body in advanced state of decay. . . .search finally ends. . . ." Then something caught her eye. Greta had circled part of one article in red.

"Juan Delgado's apartment, it can now be told, was searched thoroughly at the beginning of the investigation. This information was withheld from the press, as search at the time was also going on for Mr. Delgado's female companion.

However, the apartment was wiped clean of fingerprints, and no feminine articles of wearing apparel or other evidence was found. It is believed that Mr. Delgado disposed of all evidence before he disappeared. All that is known of her is that she is young, blonde, and certain of Mr. Delgado's acquaintances believed her name was April, and she was an American. It is also believed that she has returned to America, and search for her has been abandoned. Mr. Delgado's death is listed as 'at the hands of person or persons unknown. . . .' "

Quickly, she picked up Greta's letter and finished reading it. There was no further information, just platitudes to soften her up for the final blow. She sat there on the edge of the bed, the letter dangling from her hand. It was all over, and she should be feeling something now. She should be yelling, screaming, crying, something . . . but all she felt was numbness, and a sense of loss, almost as though she were wrapped in cotton batting. The real pain would come later, she knew, when she could handle it. She shoved the clippings and the letter under her mattress. Maybe, in a few days, she could bring herself to go through them again, but right now, she was thankful for the numbness. For the moment, Christmas had priority; friends would be dropping in, and there were her parents to think of. The luxury of tears would have to wait.

Quickly, she dressed, ran a comb through her hair, straightened her room. Then she closed the door carefully and started toward the kitchen to see if she could help her mother and Ann with anything.

Christmas Eve was unusually quiet at the Enwright's. There were only the three of them, and Irene was content. They had a light supper, then sat around the roaring fire in the lower living room, drinking eggnog.

"I don't think we've had a nicer Christmas Eve in years,"

Ted announced. "We have a lot to be thankful for this year; Irene, you came through your operation with flying colors, and April, to have you home again. . . .well, you can't possibly know what it means to us." He raised his eggnog cup, "A toast to the three of us, and many more years to come. Until of course, you get married, April, and make us grandparents."

The only light in the room was from the fire and the twinkling lights on the tree, but Irene thought she saw April's expression change, and the glint of tears in her eyes. It could have been the firelight, possibly; or maybe she was thinking about that boy in Switzerland. She nestled closer in Ted's arms, and thought about the present she'd bought April. It was a lovely, very feminine wristwatch, with a thin gold band. That cheap one she'd worn home—really! Of course, she had no way of knowing about the one Juan had given her—the emerald and diamond watch that was carefully hidden in the lining of her jewelry box, along with the emerald and diamond ring.

Jan and Mrs. Leonard had a devil of a time getting little Ben to bed Christmas Eve; usually he was very good about bedtime, but now he was old enough to know about Santa Claus, and his excitement led to all sorts of excuses. One more bedtime story from grampa, one more cookie, one more glass of water, one more trip to the bathroom. Finally, Jan had resorted to threatening, "If you don't go to bed like a good little boy, Santa Claus isn't going to fill your stocking or bring you any presents."

That had done the trick, and little Ben had toddled off as fast as he could and jumped into bed. "I be good little boy, Mommy, see? I'm 'sleep now." He pulled the covers over his head and pretended to be snoring noisily. Jan and Mrs. Leonard had retreated hastily, before they burst into laughter.

436

Now Scott and Fran were here, and they were all involved in trimming the tree, although Jan kept looking at her father anxiously. She didn't want him overly tired; Dwight was bringing Nancy and his children over tomorrow, but Jan had thought two days in a row would be too much for her father, and had asked him not to come tonight. Mrs. Leonard and Scott were laughing and chatting, but Fran was always so solemn. In a crowd, it wasn't so noticeable, but with so few of them there, she stood out as such a sour note.

She sat down next to her father, announcing she had to rest for a while, explaining that the baby had kept her jumping all day. Quietly, she asked her father if he wanted her to call Dwight and ask him over.

"Jan honey, will you stop fussing over me? I'm sure Dwight has other plans for the evening. Anyway, as soon as the tree's finished, I'm going to bed."

She patted his hand. "I understand." She looked at her father. "Where's Mrs. Applegate? I haven't seen her around for a while." Mrs. Applegate was the night nurse, a jolly woman who looked very much like her name.

"She isn't; I gave her a few hours off to finish up some last minute shopping," Duncan said. "Now, don't start," he added sternly, as Jan frowned. "She'll be back by ten o'clock." Honestly, he loved his daughter, but ever since he'd come home from the hospital, Jan had fussed over him just like a mother hen. She acted like she was the parent and he was the child. "Why don't you go help them with the tree? I'll tell you from here where there's a bare spot. Scott, you have too many red balls together; no, not there, over farther to the left. And some of those blue lights should be changed up towards the top."

Jan got up. "Here, I'll show you." She worked quickly and efficiently, stepping back occasionally to look at the effect. She made light conversation with her brother—after a few attempts, she made little effort to draw Fan into the conversation. Honestly, sometimes she wondered why her brother had ever married her. She was so plain, and dull; tonight, she was downright sullen. She hadn't smiled once this evening; come to think of it, Jan had very rarely seen her really smile. When she did, it came out more of a sneer. And Scott was so good-looking; suddenly, she wondered what their sex life was like, and paused. She hadn't thought of sex for a long time now, not since her father's attack. Well, this was certainly no time to think about it, she thought, and concentrated on the tree again. Maybe Fran was that way because she didn't have any children; somehow, she just couldn't see Fran as a mother.

She stepped back again and looked at the tree; it was just about perfect. She looked at her watch—another twenty minutes, maybe, to put on the tinsel, and they'd be finished. Then she'd tell them that father had to go to bed, and the two of them could have a quiet cup of hot chocolate before he went to sleep.

Fran started putting the tinsel on the right side of the tree, slowly and methodically. She was not unaware that Jan had been watching her, but if she'd known what Jan was thinking, her face would have been red with anger. And she was angry enough already, and feeling utterly defeated. To think that only this morning, she had been almost happy, daring to hope again, and after such a long time. She had been five days overdue starting her period, and was almost sure that this time she really was pregnant. They had tried so hard in the beginning, but then after six years of false hopes, had slowly adjusted to the idea that there would be no children. At least, Scott had; she had never stopped hoping. But every month, she was as regular as clockwork. Now, after ten years of marriage, she was late again. She hadn't said anything to Scott, it was too early to be sure, but her breasts felt swollen; and secretly, she believed.

She was even making plans to see Dr. Sturgess next week, but just before they left the house to come over here, she had gone to the bathroom, and seen the blood. There was no time even to cry, because Scott was waiting, so she suffered in silence.

She had watched the family fuss over little Ben tonight in stoic silence, and tomorrow she would have to endure the presence of Dwight and Nancy's two children, as well. Seeing Jan tonight had only increased her suffering; were they all blind to the fact that Jan was pregnant again, and not just a little bit? Her small breasts were rounded out and sharply defined, her tiny waist had thickened and spread, and her loose dress couldn't quite hide the fact that her stomach was no longer flat. But Jan said nothing of her condition, so Fran made no mention of it. She would wait until she was told, and try to express surprise. And she, Fran, would still be the barren one, the outsider, and she would continue to endure and suffer the indignity of sex, still continuing to hope, until that hope would gradually fade, and there would be nothing left.

Pam and Jack spent Christmas Eve quietly in his apartment. She had been home from the hospital for three days, and they were alone now, but the nurse was due back at midnight. They discussed the pros and cons of buying a house against building one, what type of architecture they wanted, what neighborhood. But their conversation had been sporadic; both of them were really thinking of the more immediate future, although they avoided the subject. Tomorrow morning they were going over to Jack's father's house to tell him they were engaged.

At ten o'clock, Jack opened the bottle of champagne he had brought with him, and poured them both a glass. "You still think I was wrong, don't you?" he asked, watching her.

She took a sip before answering him. "No," she said

cheerfully, "not if you feel that strongly about your step-mother. But I think you should at least consider the possibility of being civil to her, in time."

"Oh God," he said wearily, "I suppose I'll have to, in time. It won't be honest, though. Still, you just can't get along in this world and be completely honest; but not yet, not tomorrow."

No, you couldn't be completely honest, she thought. She certainly wasn't being completely honest with him; she didn't dare tell him that she'd never reached a climax in her life with the few men she'd been with, and that she was terrified she was frigid. God, she wished Kathy was here—it just wasn't the same talking to Dr. Carter about this as it would be with another woman. But Jack was looking at her, waiting for some sort of response. "No, of course, everything can't be done all at once; tomorrow, we'll see your father alone. It's a start, Jack." She smiled at him and sipped some more champagne.

He picked up the bottle and squinted at it. "You know," he said ruefully, "if anybody told me I'd be spending Christmas Eve with one lousy bottle of champagne, I'd say he was nuts. I don't even like the stuff."

"I do," she said, and held out her glass.

He poured her another glass, and one for himself. Pam's nurse would be back soon, and he'd have to leave. He considered going out and getting drunk, and quickly discarded the idea. That was no answer. Besides, he had to be in good shape tomorrow. But it hadn't been easy for him these last few days. Sexual abstinence with Pam in the hospital was one thing, but to have her here beside him, alone, was another. Yet, he knew he had to go easy with her. He wanted her so badly, but he sensed she wasn't ready for him yet. He knew she wasn't a virgin, but she wasn't very far removed from one. Still, there really wasn't any reason why they shouldn't go to bed together; he didn't know anyone in this day and age that waited until they were married.

In the past, he knew his deepseated guilt had held him back; but that guilt was out in the open now. Why did he still feel this hesitation? There were no easy answers for him these days; Pam was right, they both had a long way to go with analysis. He pulled her to him, and just held her for a while. She lay quietly in his arms, sensing his need.

Finally, he heard footsteps coming up the walk, and turned her face up to him to kiss her before the nurse came in.

Lights twinkled all over the valley Christmas Eve; there were lots of parties going on. But a few lights went off early. The Enwrights went upstairs at midnight; Duncan's household was already asleep; and Pam was in bed with a glass of hot milk at one in the morning. The lights may have been off, but not everyone was sleeping. Jack tossed and turned all night in a fitful sleep; Dwight lay quietly in bed, thinking of Kathy, and of spending Christmas with Nancy; and April went silently downstairs to pour herself a tall glass of eggnog which she took back up to her room. She sat by the window, looking out at the lights, watching them go out, one by one, until dawn, sipping her eggnog and chainsmoking. She got no sleep at all.

Chapter 17

Kathy got ready for bed slowly Christmas Eve; actually, it was Christmas morning now, and there were only a handful of hours left before Bruce had to leave. The six long days that had stretched ahead of her on Friday had sped by with astonishing rapidity, and now they were almost gone. The tacit understanding between them was still standing; she had made no mention of her future plans, nor had he pressed her. Still, the subject, heavy and impregnable, was never very far from their thoughts, waiting patiently to be answered. And she had no answer; she needed time to think, and time was running out. She realized suddenly that Bruce had been watching her in the mirror, and finished brushing her hair.

He flipped back the covers on her side of the bed and she got in quickly beside him. He turned towards her, holding her face with both hands, and kissed her forehead and cheeks, then he looked in her eyes.

Oh God, he was going to ask her now, oh please, Bruce, don't, I don't know, I have to step back from this, get some perspective. She shut her eyes tight, and tears squeezed out between the corners.

He kissed them gently away, then tipped her head up and kissed her mouth softly. "Kathy, don't, please. I know a lot of this holiday has been spoiled for you, and it's been my fault. But let's not spoil tonight." He caressed her gently, "Kitten, I don't want you staying here alone tomorrow, not on Christmas. Call Maude—I know she's going to be alone, too. That is," he hesitated, "unless you've made plans to be back in Monrovia tomorrow."

She opened her eyes slowly, wondering. She knew that wasn't what he intended to say; but he had changed his mind, and she was grateful. "No, I'm not going back, not until Friday or Saturday. I really want some time alone here, Bruce; I need some time to think, to sort things out. But you're right, of course; I really hadn't thought about Maude, and that was selfish. I'll call her tomorrow; there's plenty to eat here, or I'll go over to her place. But tomorrow night, I just want to be here alone. Then before I leave, the tree has to be taken down." She tried to smile. "It would be a pretty sorry sight if it stayed up until you got back."

He looked at her gravely. "I haven't given you a very happy life, have I, Kathy? If it weren't for me, you probably would have married again by now—maybe had a couple of kids."

"Bruce, don't ever say that," she stopped him. "You've given me all that you could; and more than any man ever has or ever will. I'll always love you, no matter what happens. Nothing can change that."

"Thank you for that," he said, and kissed her again. "Oh hell, Kitten, if it's any comfort to you at all, you must know I feel more married to you than I do to my wife. Going back to her has become the trip out of town now, and coming back to you is coming home," he sighed, "but I'm not being fair, am I?"

She put her fingers to his lips. "Bruce, you're the one who said let's not spoil tonight. Do you remember what I said to you the first time we made love?'' she asked, snuggling closer to him.

"I sure do,'' he said, and a slight twinkle came into his eyes. "Let's see,'' he pondered, "I seem to recall that you used some language that I usually hear at smokers or in a locker room. If I remember correctly, you said—''

She stopped him hastily, blushing slightly, "No, I don't mean that. I said, 'we have so little time.' ''

He was silent for a while. "Yes, I remember that, Kitten. Just don't make it final—I don't think I could stand that. I remember something else you said. You said, 'I don't want to talk any more, I just want to feel.' '' He silenced her reply with his mouth covering hers, and they clung together a little desperately, trying to forget that time was running out.

Kathy sat on the edge of the tub watching Bruce shave, as she always did when they were together. The time for talking was over, and there would be no tearful farewells. The guidelines and rules they had laid down long ago still applied, and everything would be kept light and casual this morning as usual, just as though he would be home for dinner. She bit down hard on her lip, and tried to think of something else.

"Damn,'' Bruce cursed, as the blood spurted out of his cheek, "why is it you always cut yourself when you're in a hurry, and never when you have all the time in the world?'' he asked, looking for the styptic pencil.

"I don't know, but it's the same with me, when I shave my legs.''

He wiped the shaving cream off and held the pencil to the cut. "Speaking of legs, if you don't leave your leg alone, you're going to rub all the skin off.'' He looked at himself critically, and splashed aftershave lotion on himself, wincing when it touched the cut.

She looked down at her leg, and snatched her hand away; this habit was getting to be ridiculous. She stared at her leg, barely noticing the faint white scar. "I don't know why I do that," she said, shaking her head, "people are going to think I have fleas, or something."

He laughed. "No, it doesn't look like that, it looks like it hurts you." He turned and looked at her suddenly, then knelt down and picked up her leg. "Good Lord; the scar's still there. You don't suppose there's a chipped bone in there, do you?"

She looked at him, bewildered. "No, of course not. Why should there be?"

"From the time I slammed the car door on your leg; Kathy, for Heaven's sake, don't look at me like you don't know what I'm talking about. You didn't speak to me for three days, you thought I did it on purpose, and then you swore you were going to sue me. God, your leg was a bloody awful mess, but you wouldn't even let me take you to a doctor."

She stared at him, suddenly remembering, but that had been so long ago. They had a silly argument, she could hardly remember what it was about, except they had been out with some clients, and she wanted to get out of the car. Bruce didn't want her to; when she'd put her foot out of the door, he had accidentally slammed it on her leg. The gash in her leg had been deep, and the sight of all that blood had made her almost faint. "The dreams," she said, "my leg always hurts me in the dream, just like it did then. But what does it mean?"

"Kathy, I haven't the slightest idea what you're talking about," Bruce said, looking at her oddly. It was the same expression he had when she had told him about some of her other dreams.

"It's nothing, honey, just a dream." He couldn't help her with it, and this was no time to talk or think about it. He was still kneeling before her, and she put her arms around his neck, changing the subject. "Do you want some breakfast?"

Bruce wasn't about to be put off. "You really had forgotten, hadn't you? I just don't see how it's possible; unless of course, you deliberately put it out of your mind. Did you?"

"No, and quit playing psychiatrist," she kissed him lightly, and blew in his ear. "Now let's drop it. Do you want some breakfast or not?"

"No, I'll have some on the—" He stopped himself before he said *plane* and instead said, "I'll have some later." He stood up, lifting her along with him. "But I don't have to leave for another two hours." He was looking down at her now, "I haven't the faintest idea why we got up so early, do you?"

She shook her head, and buried her face against his chest. Now they'd go back to bed and try to forget the minutes were slipping away, and lose themselves in making love. Last night, he had said he felt more married to her than he did to his real wife—but married people didn't solve their problems this way.

Kathy stayed in bed long after she heard the front door close, and knew that Bruce had finally gone. She sat propped up against the pillows, smoking one cigarette after the other. Nothing had been settled, really. Bruce would continue to give her as much of himself as he ever could, but would that be enough? It hadn't been before; certainly, she never would have left him if it had. Still, there was one important difference now; when she had left him in July, she had been a silly fool, full of hopes and dreams of finding some sort of Shangra-La, where plastic people did plastic things and life was simple and uncomplicated. Almost all of her remaining innocence had deserted her when that dream had been shattered, and she had felt the beginning of a new feeling creeping in, and she didn't much like it. She had always accused others of being cynical, and now she was starting to find out what it was like.

Staying in Monrovia would be next to impossible. She couldn't go back to the arrangement she had with John, and the only other alternative the valley offered her was marriage to Dwight. What else could she do? Pack up and try another town, and if that didn't work, move on to another one, and then. . . .restlessly, she pulled the covers back and stared at her leg. She had thought the dream was just connected to Monrovia, but it must have some other meaning; something tied in with Bruce. Quickly, she pulled the covers back up over her. It was late, and she had to call Maude.

She looked over at the mink coat Bruce had given her for Christmas. Maude might snipe at Bruce, but she certainly couldn't call him cheap. She lit the last cigarette in the pack, and dialed Maude's number.

Kathy and Maude settled down after dinner in the living room, with coffee for Maude and brandy for Kathy. Maude had picked up the phone almost immediately when Kathy called her earlier, and promptly accepted her invitation; it was almost as though she expected it. Kathy suspected Bruce had called Maude, but she didn't mind; it had been a nice day, all things considered, and she was glad Maude was here.

"Did Bruce tell you I might call?" Kathy asked her now, swirling the brandy in her glass.

"From the airport, the second time," Maude said without hesitation. "Said he didn't want either one of us to be alone on Christmas, and if you didn't call me, to be sure and call you. I can't say I remember him being so considerate of me in the past."

Kathy smiled, and sipped her brandy. "Maude, can't you even admit that Bruce just might possibly have a few redeeming qualities?''

"Oh dear, here we go again—when are you moving back?"

Kathy's smile froze slightly. "I didn't say that, Maude; and this is nothing to joke about. I've created an impossible situation for myself in the valley, but I haven't decided to move back here.''

She looked so unhappy that Maude's tone immediately changed. "Sorry, Kathy; I didn't realize that everything wasn't settled between you and Bruce. You didn't say anything all through dinner, so I just naturally assumed. . . . sorry, I should have been more observant.''

"No, it's all right; and we were happy, most of the time I've been here. Maude, it's just that I don't know if I can settle for half of Bruce any more. And I certainly can't just drop in for the weekend from time to time.'' She got up and started pacing the room. "Dammit, I used to make decisions quickly, confidently, but now. . . .I can't seem to make up my mind about anything.'' She stopped and looked at Maude. "And Bruce—he's been so sweet about everything, and he hasn't pressed me for an answer. Not even when he left, Maude, and for all he knows, he might never see me again.''

"Maybe he didn't press you because he was afraid he'd get the wrong answer,'' Maude said slowly.

"You might be right; probably you are.'' She picked up her drink and sat down again. "Maude, I know you think it's just an affair between Bruce and me, and that it's mostly. . . .sex,'' she hesitated, "but it's more than that. Why do you think it's lasted so long? Or that the minute I saw him I was right back with him again?''

"Well, you certainly didn't have any trouble making a quick decision about that,'' Maude said caustically. "But ask yourself this; where will it all get you, if you come back to Bruce?''

"God, I don't know," Kathy sighed wearily. "I know he loves me now, Maude; he's even mentioned the possibility of a divorce, and I'm sure that if I had pressed the point. . . .but I didn't. Oh, not that I'm all that decent or noble, but even I know you can't build a marriage on someone else's unhappiness."

"Kathy, he thinks he's lost you and he wants you back. I'm sure he does love you, in his way, and if he's desperate enough, I wouldn't put it past him to say anything to get you back," she said bluntly.

Kathy stared at her; that had been a cheap shot at Bruce, but she let it pass. "Okay, I won't argue, because that's not the point. He loves me now, but what about a few years from now? I'm almost twenty seven, and in a few years I'll be thirty—don't smile like that, you know as well as I do what I mean. And men don't get older, they just get better. I'm damned if I ever want to be known as Bruce Kennedy's cast-off."

"What you're saying is, you want security, I think. Kathy, you're beginning to confuse me; right now, I don't know whether you're arguing for Bruce or against him."

"I wasn't aware I was doing either one." Kathy picked up the brandy bottle and hesitated. "Maude, I do wish you'd have at least one drink with me; after all, it is Christmas."

Maude complied amiably. "All right, but just a little. Remember, it's Christmas, not New Year's." She really hated brandy, but if it made Kathy happy, she'd drink it even if it gagged her. "Why don't you turn on the Christmas lights outside? With the mob you had here Monday, I couldn't really appreciate them. You haven't turned on the lights on the tree, either."

"No," Kathy said quickly. "That is, someone might see them from the street, and decide to drop in—I don't want to see anybody else right now."

Maude looked at her quizzically. "Good Lord, Kathy,

nobody's out on Christmas night; even if someone rang the bell, you wouldn't have to answer the door."

She picked up her brandy glass, then put it down again. "It's not just that—if I turn on the tree and the lights outside, I'll start thinking about when we bought the tree and did all the decorating. Right now, I don't want to think about those things, or I'll start wallowing in self-pity; that comes later tonight, when you've gone home."

"Well, if you're going to be morbid," Maude kicked off her shoes and picked up her brandy, "maybe I better spend the night."

"Oh Maude, you know what I meant." Kathy got up again, and started pacing restlessly. "You said before you didn't know whether I was arguing for or against Bruce—maybe I was doing both. And maybe I've just been talking out loud, using you as a sounding board." She stopped pacing. "That's not a very nice thing to do, is it?"

"It's not a bad thing to do; it's certainly better than keeping it all bottled up inside yourself. I don't know if I can be of any help, but I can listen."

Kathy picked up the poker and jabbed the logs in the fireplace. "It's ironic, in a way. You're the only woman I know that I can talk about Bruce with, and you're also the only woman I know that has never put him down; at least, in front of me. Everyone else thinks I'm the luckiest girl in the world to have landed him, even the girls at the office, in spite of the fact that he's married. You know as well as I do the way heads turn the minute he walks into a room. And then they size me up, wondering just what it is I've got that they haven't. Sometimes I even wonder myself—especially lately. But in spite of everything he's got going for him; his looks, his charm, his charisma—he's completely lacking in conceit. Still, with all that, life has never been a bed of roses between us." Kathy poked the dwindling fire again, then picked up another log and carefully knelt down to add it to the fire. Her face was half-turned from Maude, and she looked very sad and tired in the flickering flames.

Maude watched her for a while without speaking. Her heart went out to her in her suffering, but she knew she really couldn't help. For years now, she had felt like a mother to Kathy, and she yearned to take her in her arms and comfort her, telling her everything would be all right, that it would all work out—but she couldn't bring herself to say something she didn't really believe. She shivered suddenly, and took a large swallow of brandy, forgetting momentarily she hated the stuff. The warmth spread through her quickly.

"Kathy," Maude spoke slowly, choosing her words with care, "you said that everyone thinks you're the luckiest girl in the world. Did you ever stop to think that maybe Bruce is really the lucky one? You're a very beautiful girl; do you realize how much you've been putting yourself down? You've given up four years of your life for him, in exchange for no marriage, no real home, and no children." (God, it was hard to find the right words, without hurting her even more.) "You know one side of him, honey; but the other side, the side that lives in New York, with a wife and a family—what do you really know about what goes on there? I don't doubt for a minute he mentioned divorce to you, but he was scared, really scared, and he still is, that you're going to leave him for good. Now that I think of it, I don't think he thought you had left him for good in July, even though you thought so. He was a little quieter around the office, that's all; but it didn't last long. I think he was just waiting; otherwise, why would he have kept the apartment?"

She waited for Kathy to say something, but she just sat there, listening. "Okay, you say he's not conceited, and you're right. There's no reason for him to be. Honey, he's one of the golden people, and everything's come his way with little or no effort. Conceited people are always striving for something, hiding something, and Bruce just doesn't have

451

to. He's got everything you said he has, and more; so why show off?'' She broke off. "Could I have a little more brandy?''

Kathy got up and poured her another drink, still without speaking.

Maude drank half of it quickly. Good Lord, maybe she should stop now, but somehow she felt obligated to continue, even though it would hurt Kathy, and possibly alienate her. "To get back to this divorce thing—''

"Maude, I told you I didn't encourage it,'' Kathy interrupted quietly.

"I know, I know,'' Maude quickly, "but the mere fact that you mentioned it at all. . . .Kathy, maybe Bruce is different, maybe he would go through with it; but I honestly don't think so. Honey, men are different than women in that respect. Even Pete Logan, who can't stand his wife, is still married to her after twenty-some-odd years. They get in a comfortable little rut, and they stay there. I'm not saying that they like it, but it's easier than going through the mess of a divorce, especially if children are involved. The wrangling over who gets them for the holidays, visitation rights, all those things, not to mention the expense. Women are different; if they want out, they get out. And Bruce. . . . well, he had two comfortable little ruts. There's the rut in New York, and the one in Hollywood with you. Maybe that's a bad choice of words, but you know what I mean. And I sincerely don't think he ever cheated on you when you were together, nor do I think he would if you went back to him. Why should he? After all, he's had all that, and we both know he can get anyone he wants. Personally, I think he's sated with a succession of women, and I really think he loves you. You're worried about being almost thirty; well, Bruce is almost forty, and with the pace he keeps at work, it's about time he started slowing down. Besides that, he's scared, Kathy. I don't think he's ever been turned down before, and

I don't think he can stand it. But even with that on your side, if it came down to the wire, and he had to choose between you and his family. . . .I really think you'd lose." She tried to smile a little, nervously. "Well, I guess I've said too much, as usual. And you were going to use me as a sounding board." She finished her drink in one noisy gulp.

Kathy sat very still, staring at the crackling fire. "Everything you've said, Maude, I've said to myself—and more. But you know something?" She turned and stared at Maude suddenly. "Whenever I think that I might never see Bruce again. . . .I don't know how to explain it exactly. . . .but it seems like my whole insides turn over, and I feel as though there would be nothing left. I said I'd never see him again once, when I left in July. But I felt differently then—we'd been through a particularly bad time, and I was determined to make a new life for myself. I was also naive enough to think that people were different outside of Hollywood, and that those people would help make that new life for me. The thought never entered my mind that the change would have to come from within me. ME, not other people, they're just window dressing. And I haven't changed, Maude, not really; maybe a little sadder now, a little disillusioned—and not nearly as smart as I thought I was. Do people ever change, really?"

Maude leaned back and smiled at her gently. She had said it all, and Kathy had taken it well, and they were still friends. "I don't have the answer to that, Kathy—some people do, maybe. But people grow up. And they start growing up when they realize they're not as smart as they thought they were."

Kathy stared at her for a minute, then leaned over and kissed her on the cheek. "Thanks, Maude."

"For what?" Maude asked, a little flustered.

"Oh, I don't know." Kathy smiled. "Just for being you, I guess. For being here, and listening. For giving me some good advice, without getting on a soapbox. For saying things

I've said to myself, and just talking things through together. It helps, you know; although nothing's really settled. I wonder if anything ever is; you try to plan your life, to project, but something always happens. Sometimes I wish I could be one of those people that just drift with the tide." She stood up. "Come on out in the kitchen with me while I wrap up the rest of the turkey and stuffing for you; there should be enough to last you for a couple of days. And then I want you to go home; it's late, and I have a lot of thinking to do."

Maude lifted her heavy bulk off the couch and followed Kathy to the kitchen. "In front of the tree, with the lights on, I suppose?"

"You guessed it. And I'll probably put on a pair of Bruce's pajamas and the mink coat he gave me."

"I wouldn't exactly call that a completely unbiased way to think, would you?"

"Of course not," she said, as she finished putting most of the leftovers in a large sack. "I told you earlier I intended to wallow in self pity tonight. Don't you think I'm entitled to a good old-fashioned crying jag? After all, it's Christmas." She put her arms around Maude at the door and they hugged each other tightly. "Oh Maude, why aren't there ever any cut and dried answers?"

Kathy put the latch on the door and leaned against it wearily until she heard the elevator doors clang shut. She picked up the brandy glasses and coffee cups, took them out to the kitchen, washed and put them away. She went in the bedroom and stopped in the doorway. When she had shown Maude the mink, she had carelessly left it spread out on the bed, and now Topsy was fast asleep on top of it. She picked her up gently and hung up the coat, rubbing her cheek against the softness of the fur. She undressed quickly, and put on the pajamas Bruce had worn the night before. She went back to the kitchen, got out a chilled bottle of champagne and two glasses, and brought them into the living room. The fire had dwindled, so she added another log. Then she pulled back the drapes and switched on the outside Christmas lights, remembering the time and care Bruce had taken with them. She plugged in the tree and looked around her.

Everything was as she wanted it. The breathtaking view from the terrace, the glowing fire, the Christmas lights. She curled up on the couch, and Topsy came in from the bedroom and jumped up beside her. She uncorked the champagne slowly, the way Bruce had taught her to, and poured herself a glass. She hesitated a minute—it was silly, of course, and a little childish, but she filled the other glass.

She sat quietly, listening to the crackling fire, the soft fizzing of the champagne, the dim traffic noises of the city, Topsy's even breathing; all familiar sounds, and she felt almost peaceful. She sipped her champagne slowly, and for a while she was lost in time and space. This was no time for problems or decisions, not when she was more tranquil and relaxed than she'd been for weeks. She sat there suspended for a long time, then she realized her glass was empty. She reached for the bottle, and looked at the other glass—Bruce's glass. He was miles away from her now, probably asleep. She wondered if he'd made love to his wife tonight. Probably he had. Of course he had.

She felt a tear trickling down her cheek, and filled her glass quickly. "Merry Christmas, Bruce," she whispered, and downed her drink. "And Merry Christmas, Kathy," she said, pouring herself more champagne, "here's to you, and your loused up life." The fire was getting low again, but she made no effort to put another log on. "And here's to all the other lives you've loused up along your merry way." The tears were coming faster now, and she realized she was getting drunk and should go to bed. "Oh, what the hell, I'm entitled," she said aloud, and decided to finish the bottle. "After all, isn't this the best Christmas I ever had? I got to spend Christmas Eve with Bruce—I even got a mink coat." She started getting chilly, so she reached over for the afghan on the end of the couch. She poured herself another drink, took one gulp, then put the glass down carefully.

She was getting very sleepy now, but there were things she had to do. The lights had to be turned off, the drapes pulled, the fire put out. Methodically, she did all these things, but the thought of sleeping in that big bed tonight without Bruce was more than she could bear. Instead, she curled up on the couch, hoping she wouldn't dream again tonight. She was all cried out by now, and very tired. She drifted off slowly, not even aware that she was rubbing her leg again.

Kathy woke up with a start. The nightmare, if possible, had been even more clear and vivid than ever, and she was drenched with perspiration. She sat up slowly, trembling, and tried to clear her head. This has got to stop, she told herself firmly. Always before, after the nightmare, she had tried to push it as far away from her thoughts as possible; now she decided to face it and try to figure it out. If she only knew what it meant, then maybe it would go away. Okay; there was water, and there was death. All her bad nightmares had been about water and death, but none as bad as this one. And now she knew about her leg, so it must have something to do with Bruce. It had started after she left Bruce, but not right away, not until the night of Vivian's barbeque. Shakily, she lit a cigarette, got up and started pacing up and down the living room, thinking. All that day, at the Club and at the party, she had been mentally comparing every man she met or talked with to Bruce, and they had all come off a poor second.

All right; but why had she forgotten about the time he slammed the car door on her leg? Or had she deliberately

456

forgotten? Looking back, they had argued because she wanted to go home, and he was entertaining a particularly important client who had gotten fresh with her. She stopped pacing; that's what all their arguments had been about, really. . . .clients. Come to think of it, a lot of those people in the loft in the nightmare had looked like some of those clients, and the beautiful young girls could have been in a foursome with them. It was beginning to make some crazy sort of sense.

Topsy was scratching at the front door, so Kathy picked her up firmly and put her out on the terrace. It looked like rain, anyway, and she didn't want to stop her train of thought long enough to get dressed and take her downstairs.

The next thing that happened in the nightmare was the buzzer ringing, and everybody running around hitting large glowing balls, something like a merry-go-round. Well, sometimes she felt like she was on a merry-go-round, grabbing for the brass ring. Had she begun to feel that way in Monrovia, too? It hardly seemed likely; at that time she hadn't yet slept with Jack, or John, or Dwight. God, what a mess! Her head was throbbing, but she felt as though she was getting somewhere, and didn't want to stop now.

She could never find a place to sit after the running stopped; she was always the outsider. Was that because she felt insecure about being the other woman in Bruce's life? Consciously she didn't, but what about the subconscious? The rest of it was fairly easy; being pushed outside and upstairs on the other building could be an analogy to her leaving Hollywood and moving to Monrovia. Was she even then, beginning to think that it wasn't the answer for her? It was all beginning to come together now, and she began to feel relieved.

She let Topsy back in, and by the time she had made breakfast for both of them, she was almost happy. The nightmare didn't seem nearly as frightening, now that she had tried to analyze it. Then another thought struck her; if her correlations were correct, then her life certainly held some unhappy options for her. Grabbing for the brass ring on the merry-go-round with Bruce, or life in Monrovia.

But life in Monrovia would be impossible now; she couldn't go back to John, and the only other alternative was marriage to Dwight, both equally out of the question. Well, at least, that was decided. Now there were a lot of things to be taken care of here. First, the dishes, then take down the Christmas tree and decorations. She looked at her watch; if she was lucky, she could leave by three o'clock, and be back in Monrovia before dark. There were a lot of things to take care of there, too.

It was close to four by the time Kathy left her apartment. The decorations had taken longer than she'd anticipated to take down, then she'd had to pack, and Maude had called.

"Well, did you get a lot of soul-searching done last night?"

"As a matter of fact, no; but I did wallow in self-pity, just like I said I would. But this morning, I realized that was pretty childish, so I did some serious thinking. Maude, I think I figured out what my nightmare means."

"Oh, really? And that helped?"

"It helped a great deal. I've come to some decisions, and I've pretty well made up my mind what I'm going to do, but I don't have time to go into it right now. It's getting late, and it looks like rain. I've been debating all day whether or not to wait until tomorrow morning to drive back, but there's a lot to do, and the sooner I get started, the better."

"Well, you know I'm dying to know what you've decided, but I guess you better get a move on, if you're going. It's already started sprinkling. Will you call me tonight, and let me know you got home all right?"

"The minute I get in the door. There are a few things I've

458

still got to work out in my mind, and how to handle them, but I'll call you."

"Just tell me one thing; are you moving back?"

Kathy hesitated. "That's the one decision I haven't worked out yet, Maude."

Kathy hated driving in rain; she particularly hated driving in the rain on the freeway. But it was only a light rain when she started out, and there were still patches of blue in the sky. Maybe she should have waited until morning, but now that she had decided to leave Monrovia, she was anxious to get things in motion. Telling Irene would be the easiest; she'd do that Sunday when she went over for dinner. Tomorrow was Saturday, and she'd see Pam then. That left Dwight and John, and she didn't know which one she dreaded telling most. If she called Dwight tonight, she'd probably have him on her doorstep all weekend, begging her to reconsider. Still, she had to get it over with sometime. She'd leave John until Monday morning; if she called the exchange, he'd come over to her place, and she felt it would be more easily handled in the office. Although, when she left his office the last time. . . .well, she wouldn't think about that now. There was all the packing to do; her mind kept running around in circles, skipping from one thing to another, and always coming back to Bruce.

The rain was coming down harder now, and the sky had turned dark and threatening. She shivered, and rolled up her window.

In a way, she had no choice; what else could she do other than go back to Bruce? Moving on to another town was no answer; she'd found that out the hard way. Besides, Hollywood was her home, and why shouldn't she go back? She didn't necessarily have to go back to Bruce, and she could always get another job, Pete Logan didn't have the only agency in town. Or, she could go back with Bruce, and still get a job somewhere else. That would eliminate the client controversies. Maybe she'd just tell Bruce flat out that there would be no more client dinners, not for her. But she couldn't imagine life without Bruce now; she had tried it, and it had been impossible. So what if he was married? Half a loaf was better than none. She knew she was rationalizing, but she didn't care.

A sudden bolt of lightning split the darkness, and she jumped in alarm. Oh God, why hadn't she waited until morning? This was the worst storm she had ever seen, and there was still at least another ten or fifteen minutes of freeway driving before she could turn off and wait until it let up. The rain was coming down in buckets now, and she started looking for the next cut off. She was in the middle lane, and tried to edge over; it was impossible, she could barely see the lights of the cars in front of her or behind her. Cars went racing by, and Kathy drove slower and slower, shaking uncontrollably.

The flash flood hit suddenly, without warning, and the big truck crashed into her rear end violently, sending her car spinning into the inside lane and over the divider right into the oncoming traffic.

In that one split second, Kathy screamed. She knew she was going to die, and her entire life flashed before her eyes. She wasn't terrified, there wasn't time, but she felt bitter, cheated, now that she had finally made up her mind and was going to set her life in order. It wasn't fair, and Bruce would never know how much she loved him, would never know that she was coming back to him, that she never should have left him. Oh God, why hadn't she waited until morning to drive back; why hadn't she told Maude; why hadn't she left a note? Oh dear God, I can't die yet, I can't leave things like this, there's too much to make up for. Oh God, please let Topsy be thrown clear, my sweet little dog. Oh God, please. . . .

The car crashed into something with such intensity that the car door flew open, and Kathy was flung spinning out into the turbulent, drenching blackness, and she knew no more.

Chapter 18

Maude hung up the phone in a state of shock and disbelief. No, it was all a ghastly mistake, it just had to be. Kathy couldn't be dead, she had just talked to her a few hours ago. She looked down at the turkey leg she was still clutching, and slowly put it on her plate.

A broken neck, the man had said, and something about the car being in a flash flood, and then she didn't remember what he said, because she didn't want to hear any more. She had told him very politely that he must be mistaken, that it couldn't be Katherine Foster, but the cool impersonal voice at the other end of the line kept insisting that it was, and could she come down and identify the body, the morning would be soon enough. Years of training had made her automatically write down the address, and she looked at it now, living proof that the last few minutes hadn't been a hideous nightmare.

She picked up the phone and dialed Kathy's apartment in town, in the vain hope that she'd changed her mind and decided to wait until tomorrow to drive back, but there was no answer. Then she called Monrovia and let the phone ring for a very long time before she finally put it down. She sat by the phone dully, thinking there must be things she should do, but not knowing exactly what. She half-expecting that Kathy would call any minute, saying she had turned off the road until the rain let up, and she just got in. She must have sat there for an hour, while hope gradually faded, and reality finally set in. A lump rose in her throat, and it was hard for her to swallow.

Shakily, but resolutely, she got up, and walked to the window; the rain was still coming down in torrents. She went back to the phone and looked at the clock; it was almost eleven, but she couldn't wait until morning. She dialed Pete Logan.

"Pete?" her voice sounded harsh, tinny, "I know it's late, but I got a call from the Highway Patrol. I don't know any easy way to tell you, but there was an accident on the freeway, and they want me to identify the body. They think it's Kathy." She heard his sharp intake of breath, and plunged on before he could interrupt. "I'm just not up to driving down there by myself, could you come over now and go with me?"

"Oh my God," he groaned, "are you sure? Of course I'll be there, just as soon as I can get dressed. Was she alone, was Bruce with her?"

"No, she was alone, just Topsy. Oh Lord, I forgot about Topsy. They didn't mention anything about a dog. Pete, please get here as soon as you can."

It was after four in the morning when Pete and Maude arrived at Kathy's apartment in Monrovia. Maude carried the mud and grime-caked Topsy in a towel, who was shivering and howling at the top of her lungs. Pete unlocked the door and switched on the lights, and Maude dropped in the nearest chair, still holding the filthy dog. She'd have to give her a bath before she went to bed, she thought wearily. The dog squirmed free, and ran to the bedroom, looking frantically for Kathy.

Maude stared at the muddy tracks she was making on the carpet. "I suppose we'll have to pay to have the rugs cleaned," she said dully. Miraculously, Topsy had been thrown clear of the car, and landed in a pile of mud on the side of the freeway. She had been brought to the police station just as Pete and Maude were going to the morgue, and Maude's heart sank. It was true, she thought, and steeled herself to look at Kathy, dead and lifeless. Pete had held Topsy when they went in, but Maude hadn't been prepared for what she saw.

When they pulled the sheet down, Kathy's head hung at an odd angle, her jaw was slack and her mouth open. Someone had mercifully closed her eyes, but the deep cuts and gashes in her face had left her almost unrecognizable, and the bruises had darkened and discolored her face. The deepest slash was over her right eye, and had torn away most of her eyebrow and the upper lid, leaving a portion of her green eye staring up at them.

Maude turned away, and swallowed the vomit she felt rising in her throat. "Yes, that's her," she whispered, and turned to Pete for support. But Pete was leaning against the wall, and his face was ashen, Topsy squirming and whining in his arms. She realized she would have to be the strong one, and took him by the arm and led him out.

She thought about it now, and what lay ahead. She pulled herself out of the chair, and looked for somewhere to wash the dog. Kathy would never forgive her if she didn't. She finally decided on the kitchen sink. And Pete would need a drink; she could use one herself. She turned on the heater, then looked for the liquor cabinet; vodka, scotch, bourbon, and brandy. She settled on brandy, and fixed both of them drinks.

"Pete," she said, handing him his, as he sat staring into

space, "you realize, of course, that you have to call Bruce."
He finished his drink in one swallow; she hesitated, then
continued. "I have to give the dog a bath before I do anything else, so you might as well call your wife and tell her
what's happened, then try to get a little sleep before you
drive back. When I'm through, I'll sleep on the couch. Pete,
did you hear me?"

He looked at her through dull, glazed eyes. "What about
you, Maude? Will you be alright?"

She looked at him, and pushed Kathy's dear, mutilated
face to the back of her mind. "I'll be fine, Pete. Now you get
your wife on the phone, while I make you another drink,
then I'll get busy with Topsy."

She handed him his drink while he was talking on the
phone, and went to get Topsy, who was sitting upright on
Kathy's white bedspread, not white any longer, trembling
and whimpering. "Come on, girl," she said kindly, "let's
get some of this muck off of you so we can all get some
sleep."

She woke Pete at seven in the morning, just as it was
getting light, and he was gone by eight. It was hot in the
apartment, as she had left the heat on for Topsy, even after
towel drying her. It had taken a good hour-and-a-half to get
all the dirt off of her, while the downpour slowed into a dull,
steady rain. She decided to stay up; she couldn't sleep,
anyhow, there was too much to do. She put some food down
for Topsy, who wouldn't even look at it, just kept wandering
around the apartment, sniffing and searching for Kathy. Pete
was snoring in the bedroom, so she looked through Kathy's
address book, and tried to think of who she should call. She
had already decided to take Kathy's body back to Hollywood
to be buried, as soon as they would let her, but some people
here should be notified. She wracked her brain for the names
of people Kathy had mentioned.

After Pete left, she sat down in the chair by the phone, and went through the address book again. John Carter, for sure. Pam and Dwight, but who else? Oh yes, Irene something. At first, she decided to wait until nine to start calling; she had forgotten about Topsy momentarily, but then she felt something on her feet. The little dog, tired out at last, had settled down, staring up at her, her eyes abject with grief. Her own grief was setting in, so why should she be polite and wait until nine o'clock? Let some other people suffer with her. She picked up Topsy and put her in her lap, then dialed the first number.

Dr. Carter hung up the phone with a shaking hand, as Edith watched him curiously. The fact that Kathy was dead, shocked and appalled him, leaving him with a feeling of acute emptiness. The woman who had called had been blunt, rude almost, as though it was his fault, forcing him to stammer in self-consciousness.

"Kathy's dead," he said, with a dazed expression. "She was killed last night, coming back to me."

Edith's eyes narrowed, and she looked at him shrewdly. Coming back to *me*? What a curious thing to say. "Oh my," she said with concern, "how did it happen?"

"What?" He looked at her for the first time, and seemed to realize what he had said. "On the freeway last night, in the rain," he said hastily. "We were going to meet today, to discuss redecorating the office, that's why she cut her holiday short."

"Oh, how awful," she said evenly, "you didn't mention anything to me about redecorating the office."

"It was to be a surprise," he said quickly, knowing he had to get out of there before he broke down completely, before the full realization hit him, before he made any more blunders. "I have to get over to Pam's," he said suddenly, "before that woman calls her." He finished his coffee quickly, and kissed her on the forehead. "I won't be long."

Edith sat there, stirring her coffee, and thinking. Coming back to *me*. Absentmindedly, she reached for the sugar and put two teaspoons in before she drank it.

The short memorial service in Monrovia was arranged hastily, over Maude's half-hearted objections. After all, Kathy's home was in Hollywood, and the main funeral services would be held at Forest Lawn tomorrow. But Dwight and Pam had insisted, so she had given in. She sat quietly, half-listening as the minister's voice droned on. She had been surprised so many people were there; Kathy had only lived in Monrovia a few short months, but she seemed to have made a great many friends. Pete and Mary Logan had driven down for the service, and she'd go home with them when this was over—with Topsy. Pamela Sterling had wanted to take her, but Maude had hesitated; she hadn't talked to Bruce herself, but Pete had, and she didn't think the decision was up to her.

Her mind began to wonder—the last two days had been hectic, and she was very tired. Getting Kathy's things packed, taking care of the funeral arrangements, the utilities, and all those people coming over with their endless questions.

Dwight Keith was the one she felt the sorriest for. She knew that he genuinely loved Kathy, and she tried to answer his anxious questions about her, but they had made Maude squirm. Had she talked much about him? Had she told her how she felt about him? Did she think she really cared about him? She almost never lied, but how could she tell this eager puppy dog half-boy, half-man that Kathy had mentioned him in the most off-handed way? Instead, she had started making up half-truths; that they had talked mostly about the past, things going on at the agency, the places they had gone, things they had done together. But he began to look so miserable that she started telling him deliberate lies; Kathy had told her she was genuinely fond of him, that their relationship was steadily growing closer. She avoided mentioning Bruce altogether.

When Irene Enwright appeared at the door, at first she couldn't understand at all how they could have been friends. Then Irene sat down and talked almost non-stop for two solid hours (only interrupting herself occasionally to ask for another drink) while she told her the whole story of how she and Kathy had become friends; that she had told Ted she was sick; had driven her to the hospital; had, in fact, practically saved her life. Maude almost began to like her. Of course, she realized the drinks were making her build up Kathy's image, but she didn't mind. She had been relieved, though, when she left, and she could get back to work.

Pamela Sterling and Jack Wentworth had showed up next. Pam was very nervous, and had asked all sorts of questions that Maude hadn't been able to answer, but even as she asked the questions, her mind seemed to be on something else. Jack Wentworth had spoken hardly at all, but he was also nervous. It was a different kind of nervousness, though; she had seen enough hangovers in her life to recognize one, and he had it bad. Poor Pam—Kathy had told her all she had been through, and now she was about to marry an alcoholic. This was a pair she didn't understand at all.

She was prepared to dislike Dr. Carter on sight, and she did. Sure, he was tall and good looking, just the type that Kathy would go for, but he had taken advantage of her when she was very vulnerable, and nothing he could say or do would make her think differently. He had been the first to arrive, shortly after she called him about Kathy. He had bombarded her with questions; questions about Bruce, why she had come home so early, had she told her what her plans were, was she going to stay in Monrovia, anything?

She had answered him as truthfully as she could. "She told me she had made up her mind about what she was going to do, but she didn't tell me what it was. She said there were a few details she had to work out, and she'd call me when she got home. But she never got home. I'll tell you one thing, though; I seriously doubt she was going back to work for you, and I'm almost positive she was leaving Monrovia."

"What makes you say that? Did she tell you that?"

"Not in so many words," Maude had replied evenly, "but she did say she had created an impossible situation for herself. You're a married man, and there was certainly no future in that for her."

"Bruce is a married man," he answered defensively.

She had looked at him with scornful pity. "You just don't understand, do you? Bruce was the one great love of Kathy's life, and she met you at a time when she was troubled and upset. There are a lot of other differences, too; Monrovia is a small town, and it must have been terribly degrading for Kathy not to be able to be seen with you openly, to have to sneak around." She was gratified to see his face redden. "Bruce's wife lives in New York, and Kathy was with him openly at least six months of the year. Everyone knew it, and no one thought the less of her for it. Bruce is Catholic, with three children, so divorce for him was out of the question. You're not Catholic, and you have no children—did you even think of divorce?"

His face had reddened further, and he didn't answer her directly. "You're the one that doesn't understand. We had something very special between us. I know she wouldn't have left me, I'm sure of it."

"Well, if that's what you want to believe, I'm certainly not going to try to change your mind." She stood up, abruptly ending the conversation. "Now, if you don't mind, I have a lot of things to do." He had left, shuffling down the walk dejectedly. Some psychiatrist, she had thought.

She felt Pete Logan squeeze her hand reassuringly, and tried to concentrate on the minister, but it was impossible;

she looked around her surreptitiously. They were all there, and she wondered what they were thinking at this moment.

Dr. John Carter sat by himself, stiff and silent. Edith had stayed home; it was still raining, she had a cold, and in all probability was stuffing herself with chocolates again. Her old eating habits had appeared overnight, but it didn't bother him. It really didn't matter at all. What mattered was that Maude woman was wrong—dead wrong—he was sure of that, and Kathy had been coming back to him. He had to believe that. He had to believe, to hold on, until his life took on some sense of order and sanity again.

Jack and Pam sat together quietly, neither one of them listening to the minister, each of them thinking their own thoughts. Jack wished the whole thing was over and done with, he hated funerals, and he needed a drink badly. God, why had he started drinking again? He had Pam at last, or almost had her, so why? Something had gone wrong between them since Kathy's death, but he didn't know what it was. He was sure she didn't know he was drinking again. Well, almost sure.

Pam shifted in her seat slightly away from Jack. He had used a breath deodorant, but the smell of liquor was quite detectable. Why had he started again? But then, was she any better? She thought about Kathy, and missed her desperately. Why did she have to die so soon? She had waited for her to get back eagerly, to talk to her about her sexual hangups, and how to handle them. She had gone over it again and again in her mind; how to approach her, to ask her, Kathy would know about such things, she was from Hollywood, she was experienced. She would probably know how to fake it, if necessary. But she was dead, she thought bitterly, and there was no one she could talk to. And the minute she heard she was dead, all she could think about was the pills again. She had gone through every inch of her old apartment while Jack was out, and found nothing. If she could just get a few, just to get herself through this, just to feel better for a little while. Then she brightened. Tomorrow, she thought. Tomorrow, she'd get rid of the nurse somehow, and then tell Jack she just wanted to go for a drive by herself, just to be alone for a while. She'd find a doctor somewhere, somehow, to give her just a few. She had to find a connection.

Dwight listened to the minister's every word, talking about his sweet Kathy. Dear Kathy, in a few months, they would have been married, he was sure of that. Oh God, how could he live without her? A lump rose in his throat, and he could feel the beginning of tears behind his eyes. He tried to blink them back, but then he didn't care. He knew she didn't love him as much as he did her, but that would have come in time. Maude had said she was very fond of him, and that fondness was growing. He tried to wrap the warmth of those words around him, to keep out the misery of losing her.

Irene Enwright and her husband sat a few feet away from Dwight, and she watched him narrowly. Her mind drifted from the sermon, and concentrated on him. April hadn't come to the ceremony, but she was at home now, and had just been moping around lately. She hadn't even been to the Club. It was still that boy in Switzerland, she was sure. Maybe after the service, she should ask Dwight over to the house for tea, or a drink, he would be very vulnerable now. And she couldn't think of a better match for April.

The service was almost over when the door to the small chapel opened, letting in a blast of cold air. Maude turned her head slightly, and breathed a sigh of relief. Bruce was standing there, drenched with rain, his face grim, but he was there, and he could take over now.

Bruce and Maude drove back to Kathy's bungalow, and the silence was broken only when Maude had to give Bruce directions. Pete Logan and his wife were already on their way back to Hollywood. They had spoken briefly after the service, and Pete had wanted to go somewhere to have a drink, but Bruce had declined—politely but firmly—saying there were some things he wanted to discuss with Maude.

The rain was coming down hard again when they drove into Kathy's driveway, and they could hear Topsy barking when they got out of the car. She never did that when I went out and came back, Maude thought. The little dog was ecstatic with joy when she saw Bruce, and he scooped her up in his arms, holding her close while she covered his face with kisses. He talked to her the same way Kathy used to, while Maude watched him with amazement. "That's all right, little girl, I'm here now, I'll take care of you," he crooned to her. Then he turned to Maude. "My God, Topsy's skin and bone, I can feel all her ribs."

"She won't eat, Bruce. I put the food down, I even try to hand-feed her, but she hasn't touched anything since—the accident."

"Well, we'll fix that first thing." He carried her to the kitchen, and set her down while he opened a can of dog food. When he gave it to her, she started eating ravenously, only pausing to look up at him occasionally, to be sure he was still there. When she finished, she wanted more. "Not now, girl; you're liable to get sick." She looked up at him and seemed to understand. "Now drink your water." Obediently, she did as she was told.

Maude and Bruce went back to the living room, Topsy at his heels, and he looked around him. "It doesn't look very much like Kathy, does it? There isn't even one plant here."

"I don't think she bothered much about it. Whether she realized it or not, I don't think she thought this would be a permanent move."

Bruce sat down on the couch, and rubbed his eyes wearily. He looked very tired and pale, and she wondered if he'd had any sleep at all. Topsy jumped up and nestled beside him comfortably, content at last. She asked him if he wanted a drink.

"No, not now; later, maybe. Maude, sit down, please; I still can't quite take all this in." His voice broke. "How in God's name did this happen, especially now?"

"Bruce, I honestly don't know; the police said it was a flash flood, and you know how Kathy hated driving in the rain. She almost didn't go; I talked to her just before she left, and she said she'd been wondering all day whether or not to go back then, or wait until morning. Lord, if I'd only told her to wait. . . ."

"Why didn't you, then?" he lashed out at her viciously, and immediately was sorry. "Oh Maude, forgive me, I didn't mean it, I know you loved her in your own way just as much as I did in mine. Please, try to forget I said that."

"It's forgotten, Bruce." She leaned back in her chair and closed her eyes. It wasn't forgotten, because the same thought had been tearing at her, if only. . . .and she was seeing Bruce in an entirely different light. In all the years she had known him, she had never heard him apologize for anything. And she realized something else; Bruce was really in love with Kathy, deeply in love, and his casual and cavalier attitude had merely been a coverup for his true feelings. She opened her eyes, and he was staring at her.

"You spent Christmas Day with her." It wasn't a question, but a flat statement. "What were her plans?"

Maude sighed, and settled back. "We had a long conversation, Bruce. I'll try to tell you as much as I can remember of it. And then, like I said, I called her just before she left."

The better part of the next hour was spent in recalling their conversation. Bruce listened quietly, with few interruptions. When she finished, he only asked one thing.

"Was she coming back to me, Maude?"

"I honestly don't know for sure, Bruce; but I know she

wasn't going to stay here, and where else would she go? She loved you, and I think she'd decided that half a loaf was better than none. I'm almost sure of it."

Bruce laughed suddenly, a bitter laugh, then stood up and stretched his legs. "I've got to take Topsy for a walk. Her stomach's been growling for the last twenty minutes, and this is the first food she's had."

"But it's raining," she protested.

"This isn't the first time I've walked her in the rain," he said, "and it won't be the last."

She watched them go down the walk; the tall, handsome man with the little poodle, thinking of the incongruity, and that no one could get away with it except Bruce. Something else kept nagging at her, something out of context, and finally it came to her. He had said, *especially now*? There had to be more in back of this than Kathy's—she still couldn't bring herself to say . . . death.

They came back in about fifteen minutes, Bruce looking more tired than before, but somehow at peace. "I think I could use a drink now, Maude, and please have one with me. I'm going to dry Topsy off. Then there's something I have to tell you."

She fixed the drinks while Bruce dried off Topsy, and they sat down as before.

He drank half of his in one gulp, and laughed again, the same bitter laugh. "I think I'll get the bottle, Maude. This is going to be a long story, and I don't want to be getting up and down, I'm too tired." He returned with the bottle, and a bucket of ice. "On second thought, I'll try to make it as short as possible, because I'm exhausted, and I have to get this off my chest. It's all so ironic, really. I did a lot of thinking on the plane to New York. I've never talked about my children much, or my wife either, but the children are growing up, and Elizabeth and I have been growing steadily apart, ever since I met Kathy. But I had never even thought about divorce until I mentioned it to Kathy, then I started thinking about it seriously. In a few years, the children will be off and on their own, and Elizabeth has her own interests. Who would I be hurting the most? I did an awful lot of thinking; who, really, would I be hurting the most? Christ, my youngest son, he's thirteen, is going steady already, and the two oldest will be starting college next year.

"Christmas night, after the kids had gone to bed, I told Elizabeth that after the holidays, I wanted to have a serious talk with her. She had already anticipated this.

" 'You want a divorce, don't you?' She had been very calm about the whole matter.

"Then she told me it was out of the question. A Catholic just does not get divorced, so I might as well forget it. However, she would agree to a legal separation, and she gave me a lot of conditions; a long list of things that she had obviously been thinking about for months. Then I realized she had known there had been another woman all along. Me, the great Bruce Kennedy, juggling two separate worlds, confident that it could go on forever, and had finally decided he couldn't. But I hadn't been fooling her at all."

He poured himself another drink, neat. "It rocked me back on my heels. I agreed to everything she said, although I was only half-listening. It was all so cut and dried . . . so . . . civilized. A marriage of twenty years, and she was taking it so . . . as though it was matter of fact.

"I went to bed in the den that night, but I didn't sleep. I was in sort of a daze. Before the talk with Elizabeth, I was confident that Kathy would come back to me, but I began to have doubts. If Elizabeth could take this so lightly after twenty years, why couldn't Kathy actually leave me after only four?

"When the call came from Pete, I guess I went a little crazy. I started crying and laughing at the same time, and it was Elizabeth who made the plane reservations, and drove me to the airport. I don't remember very much about that, except that Elizabeth was supportive and kind, but she told me she was going ahead with the legal separation."

"She didn't mean it, Bruce; she was just hurt," Maude said.

"No, she meant it; and on the plane, I tried to think. I really couldn't live with her anymore. Not now, anyway. I really loved Kathy, you know." His voice broke. "Maude, I'm so tired, do you think we could stay here for a while before we start back? And there's something I have to ask you. After the funeral, the real one, I mean, do you think you could take care of Topsy for a little while, so I can go back and straighten up my affairs in New York?"

"Of course, Bruce," she replied quickly, "you didn't even have to ask." She thought about her oriental rugs, and sighed inwardly.

He looked relieved. "Thank you, Maude. Now, do you mind if I take a little nap before we go back? I really am very tired."

"I'll get you a blanket, Bruce—or would you prefer the bed?" She realized she had said the wrong thing, as tears came to his eyes. "A blanket will be fine. Thank you." He poured himself another drink, and then laid down. Topsy snuggled up next to him. He looked up at her when she came back with the blanket. "Isn't it funny, Maude? Isn't life just about the Goddamn funniest and saddest thing you can think of?"

She had no answer for him, but he was asleep almost at once, the tears still wet on his cheeks.

She tucked the blanket around him, and Topsy licked her hand. Then she walked to the window, looking out at the rain, thinking. She felt completely drained. Maybe I'll ask Pete for some time off. Yes, that's it, I'll stay home with Topsy, get some meat back on her bones, Kathy would like that. Then she stopped herself. Kathy wasn't there any longer, and life must go on.

She looked at Bruce, fast asleep on the couch, Topsy snuggled close beside him, then looked at her watch. Maybe she'd just let him sleep until he woke up, and they'd drive back in the morning. She sat down in the most comfortable chair, leaned her head back, and tried to rest.

UNDER CRIMSON SAILS

Lynna Lawton

Beautiful, spirited Janielle Patterson had heard of the reckless way pirate Ryan Deverel treated his women. He seduced them with the same abandon with which he plundered ships. To the handsome pirate, women were prizes to be won, used, and tossed away.

Ryan intrigued and repelled Janielle—and when they finally met, she was shocked to discover that her own nature was as passionate as the pirate's!

But while he was driven by desire, she was driven by a fierce hatred. Yet she knew neither of them would rest until she had surrendered to him fully.

LEISURE BOOKS   **2002-5/$3.50**